Windows

into

Zimbabwe

WINDOWS

into

ZIMBABWE

*Compiled and introduced by
Franziska Kramer
and Jürgen Kramer*

Published by
Weaver Press, Box A1922, Avondale, Harare, 2019
<www.weaverpresszimbabwe.com>

© This compilation Franziska Kramer and Jürgen Kramer
© Each individual story, the author.
(See appendix for story provenance.)

Typeset by Weaver Press
Cover illustration 'Untitled' courtesy of Edsor Colaco
and photograph by kind permission of David Brazier
Cover Design: Myrtle Mallis, Harare.
Printed by: Bidvest, South Africa.
Distributed in South Africa by Jacana Media

All rights reserved. No part of the publication may be reproduced, stored in a retrieval system or transmitted in any form by any means – electronic, mechanical, photocopying, recording, or otherwise – without the express written permission of the publisher.

ISBN: 978-1-77922-348-7 (p/b)
ISBN: 978-1-77922-349-4 (ePub)

Contents

Notes on Compilers

Notes on Contributors

Introduction by Franziska Kramer and Jürgen Kramer

1. *Queues* – Shimmer Chinodya

(i) Independence – Before, After and What Came in Between

2. *Fancy Dress* – Alexandra Fuller
3. *That Special Place* – Freedom Nyamubaya

(ii) Gukurahundi

4. *Torn Posters* – Gugu Ndlovu
5. *When the Moon Stares* – Christopher Mlalazi

(iii) Whose Land is it?

6. *The Trek* – Lawrence Hoba
7. *Sins of the Fathers* – Charles Mungoshi
8. *Trespassers* – Chiedza Musengezi

(iv) Gender Relations

9. *Mainini Grace's Promise* – Valerie Tagwira
10. *Message in a Bottle* – Isabella Matambanadzo
11. *Gold Digger* – Albert Gumbo

(v) Money Matters

12. *A Land of Starving Millionaires*
    – Erasmus R. Chinyani

13. *The Donor's Visit* – Sekai Nzenza

14. *The Rainbow Cardigan* – John Eppel

(vi) Social Relations

15. *The Mupandawana Dancing Champion* – Petina Gappah

16. *Maria's Interview* – Julius Chingono

17. *Dinner Time* – Bongani Sibanda

(vii) Exile

18. *The Letter* – Farai Mpofu

19. *Shamisos* – NoViolet Bulawayo

20. *A Secret Sin* – Daniel Mandishona

(viii) Resilience

21. *Seventh Street Alchemy* – Brian Chikwava

22. *The General's Gun* – Jonathan Brakarsh

*

23. *The Grim Reaper's Car* – Nevanji Madanhire

Annotations, Comments and Study Tasks

Notes on Compilers

Franziska Kramer was born and raised in Germany. In 2006 she went to Berlin to study African Literatures and Social Science at Humboldt University. While still a student, she worked as a research assistant and also did an internship with Weaver Press publishers in Harare, Zimbabwe. Here, her real interest in and deep feeling for southern African literatures developed, and in 2010, she obtained an MA in Postcolonial Literatures and Cultures at Leeds University, UK. Since then she has returned many times to Zimbabwe for various projects with the Harare International Festival of the Arts, the Culture Fund or when doing academic research. In 2011-12 she worked in the culture department of the German Zimbabwe Society in Harare. Since 2014 she has taught English and Political Science at the Evangelische Schule Berlin Zentrum and lives with her partner in Berlin Schöneberg.

Jürgen Kramer is Professor Emeritus of British Cultural Studies at the University of Dortmund. His main research areas have been the history of the British Isles and the British Empire, the sea as a cultural space, transatlantic slavery, literatures of sub-Saharan Africa and the Pacific, cultural memory, anti-colonial resistance, Joseph Conrad and Robert Louis Stevenson. Among his publications are *Cultural and Intercultural Studies* (1990), *British Cultural Studies* (1997), *Britain and Ireland. A Concise History* (2007), *Taking Stock* (2011) and (together with Werner Hennings and Uwe Horst) *Die Stadt als Bühne: Macht und Herrschaft im öffentlichen Raum von Rom, Paris und London im 17. Jahrhundert* [The City as a

Stage: Power and Hegemony in the Public Spheres of Rome, Paris and London in the Seventeenth Century] (2016). From 1994 to 2006 he co-edited the *Journal for the Study of British Cultures*.

The idea for this compilation arose during a joint trip to Zimbabwe in 2016. We, father and daughter, both delight in reading literary texts of all kinds, discovering new and unheard voices, discussing their potential and hidden meanings, and debating their possible interpretations. We have thoroughly enjoyed our work on this collection with all its many turns, its wonderful moments of mutual understanding, its demanding processes of negotiation and their eventually happy compromises.

Notes on Contributors

Jonathan Brakarsh is an author, teacher, and health professional. He has written four professional books. His most recent book is *Singing to the Lions – A guide to overcoming fear and violence in our lives* (Catholic Relief Services, Harare, 2017) which has been translated into several languages including Arabic and Hindi. He is proud to be published for a third time in a Weaver anthology of Zimbabwean writers. He is currently working on a children's book, a play, and a collection of short stories.

NoViolet Bulawayo was born, raised and schooled in Zimbabwe. She attended university in the USA, completing a Master of Fine Arts in Creative Writing at Cornell University in 2010 where her work was recognised with a Truman Capote Fellowship. In 2011 she won the Caine Prize with her story 'Hitting Budapest', which became the opening chapter of her novel *We Need New Names* (Chatto and Windus, 2013) which was selected for the 2013 Man Booker Prize shortlist, making Bulawayo the first black African woman and the first Zimbabwean to be shortlisted for the prize. Among other awards, she also won the Etisalat Prize for Literature and the Hemingway Foundation/PEN Award. She is currently Writer in Residence at Stellenbosch University in South Africa.

Brian Chikwava is a London-based Zimbabwean writer. His short story, 'Seventh Street Alchemy', included in this collection, won the Caine Prize for African Writing in 2004. He is an associate editor of *Wasafiri* magazine and a fellow of the Stellenbosch Institute of Advanced Studies.

Julius Chingono (1946-2011) was born on a commercial farm in Zimbabwe. Leaving school at fourteen, he worked for most of his life on the mines as a blaster. He wrote one novel, *Chipo Changu* (1978), an award-winning play, *Ruvimbo* (1980), and a collection of poetry and short stories, *Not Another Day* (Weaver Press, 2006). His poetry in Shona and English was published extensively in anthologies, and on the Poetry International website.

Shimmer Chinodya (1957) was born in Gweru, the second child in a large, happy family. He studied English Literature and Education at the University of Zimbabwe. After a spell teaching and with curriculum development, he earned an MA in Creative Writing from the Iowa Writers' Workshop.

His first novel, *Dew in the Morning* (Mambo Press, 1982) was followed by *Farai's Girls* (College Press, 1984), *Child of War* (under the pen name B. Chirasha, (College Press, 1986), *Harvest of Thorns* (Baobab Books, 1989), *Can We Talk and other stories* (Baobab Books, 1998), *Tale of Tamari* (Weaver Press, 2004), *Chairman of Fools* (Weaver Press, 2005), *Strife* (Weaver Press, 2006), *Tindo's Quest* (Longman, 2011), *Chioniso and other stories* (Weaver Press, 2012) and *Harvest of Thorns Classic: A Play* (Longman, 2016). His work appears in numerous anthologies. Chinodya has also written educational texts and manuals, and radio and film scripts, including one for the feature film, *Everyone's Child* (1996). He has won many awards, including the Commonwealth Writers Prize (Africa Region) for *Harvest of Thorns*, the Caine Prize shortlist for *Can We Talk* and the NOMA Award for Publishing in Africa for *Strife*. He has also won awards from ZIWU, ZBPA and NAMA, and has received many fellowships abroad. From 1995-97, he was Distinguished Dana Professor in Creative Writing and African Literature at the University of St Lawrence in upstate New York.

Erasmus Chinyani was born in Goromonzi, the last born in a family of eleven. He attended St Peter Claver primary and secondary schools. On leaving school, he worked for a printing company and studied in the evening, passing both his O- and A- levels in this way. He then took an electric engineering course at the Harare Polytechnic and worked with the Ministry of Construction from 1990-1996. During this time, he took a part-time correspondence courses in Freelance Journalism and Short Story Writing. He has had his short stories published in *Prize Africa, Horizon* and *Parade* magazines.

John Eppel (1947) was born in South Africa and raised in Zimbabwe, where he still lives, now retired, in Bulawayo. His first novel, *D G G Berry's The Great North Road* (The Carrefour Press, 1992), won the M-Net prize and was listed in the *Weekly Mail & Guardian* as one of the best 20 South African books in English published between 1948 and 1994. His second novel, *Hatchings* (The Carrefour Press,1993) was short-listed for the M-Net prize and was chosen for the series in the *Times Literary Supplement* of the most significant books to have come out of Africa. His other novels are *The Giraffe Man* (Queillerie, 1994), *The Curse of the Ripe Tomato* (amabooks 2001), *The Holy Innocents* (amabooks, 2002), *Absent: The English Teacher* (Weaver Press, 2009) *Traffickings* (The InkSword, 2014), and (awaiting publication) *The Boy*

Who Loved Camping (Pigeon Press, 2019).

Eppel's poetry collections include *Spoils of War* (The Carrefour Press, 1989), which won the Ingrid Jonker prize, *Sonata for Matabeleland, Selected Poems: 1965 – 1995* (Snail Press/Baobab Books 1995), *Songs My Country Taught Me* (Weaver Press, 2005), *O Suburbia* (Weaver Press, 2019), and *Landlocked: New and Selected Poems from Zimbabwe* (Smith/Doorstop, 2016), which was a winner in the international Poetry Workshop Prize, judged by Billy Collins. He has collaborated with Philani Amadeus Nyoni in a collection called *Hewn From Rock,* (self-published, 2014) and with Togara Muzanenhamo in a collection called *Textures* (amabooks, 2014), which won the 2015 NAMA Award. He has published three collections of poetry and short stories: *The Caruso of Colleen Bawn* (amabooks, 2004), *White Man Crawling* (amaBooks, 2007) and, in collaboration with the late Julius Chingono, *Together* (amabooks, 2011) . His single collection of short stories is entitled *White Man Walking* (Mwanika Publishers 2018).

Alexandra Fuller (1969) was born in England. In 1972, she moved with her family to a farm in southern Africa. She lived in Africa until her mid-twenties. In 1994, she moved to Wyoming.

She is the author of *Don't Let's Go to the Dogs Tonight* (Random House, 2001), *The Legend of Coltart H. Bryant* (Penguin Books, 2008), *Leaving Before the Rains Come* (Harvill Secker, 2015)*, and Quiet Until the Thaw* (Penguin Books, 2017).

Petina Gappah is an award-winning and widely translated Zimbabwean writer. She is the author of the novels *Out of Darkness, Shining Light* (Scribner, 2019) and *The Book of Memory* (Faber and Faber, 2015); and two short story collections, *Rotten Row* (Faber and Faber, 2016) and *An Elegy for Easterly* (Faber and Faber, 2010). Petina's work has been shortlisted for the Orwell Prize, the *Sunday Times* EFG Short Story Award, the *Los Angeles Times* Book Award, the PEN America Open Book Award, the Frank O'Connor International Short Story Award, the Women's Prize for Fiction, and the Prix Femina (Étrangers). She is the recipient of the Guardian First Book Award and the McKitterick Prize from the Society of Authors. A lawyer specialising in international trade and investment as well as a writer, after living and working in Geneva for many years, and in Berlin as a fellow of the DAAD, Petina now lives in Harare.

Albert Gumbo is a keen observer of global society, passionate about social justice and writes for the pleasure of sharing. He believes that citizens can change their society if they, believing in themselves, consciously set out to do so. He speaks on various subjects of topical interest.

Lawrence Hoba (1983) who was born in Masvingo, Zimbabwe is an author and entrepreneur. His collection of short stories, *The Trek and Other Stories* (Weaver Press, 2009) was nominated for the NAMA, 2010 and won the ZBPA awards for Best Literature in English category. Hoba's work has also appeared in The Caine Prize's *Gonjon Pin and Other Stories* (amabooks, 2014), *The Warwick Review* (2010) and Weaver Press's *Writing Mystery and Mayhem* (2015), *Writing Lives* (2014), *Laughing Now* (2007) and *Writing Now* (2005).

Nevanji Madanhire has written two novels: *Goatsmell* (Anvil Press, 1993) and *If the Wind Blew* (College Press, 1996) and several short stories published in various anthologies. He has worked as a journalist almost all his adult life, serving as editor on four of Zimbabwe's leading independent national newspapers, *The Financial Gazette, Business Tribune, The Standard,* and *NewsDay*. In journalism he developed a keen eye as an observer and chronicler of events and issues that affect Zimbabweans and keep them awake every day, which include religion and superstition, and of course politics. A third novel, *The Rhythm of the Dormitory Town*, his first in more than 25 years, will be published this year (amabooks, 2019).

He is a fellow of the Carey Institute for Global Good and is an alumnus of the Institute's Non-fiction Programme. Nevanji is now experimenting with non-fiction writing.

Daniel Mandishona (1959) is an architect. He was born in Harare and brought up by his maternal grandparents in Mbare (then known as Harari township). In 1976 he was expelled from Goromonzi High School and lived in London from 1977-92. He first studied Graphic Design then Architecture at the Bartlett School, University College London. He now has his own practice in Harare. His first short story, 'A Wasted Land', was published in *Contemporary African Short Stories* (Heinemann, 1992). He has since been published by Weaver Press in *Writing Now* (2005), *Laughing Now* (2007) *Writing Free* (2011) and *Writing Lives* (2014). He also published a collection of short stories, *White Gods Black Demons* (Weaver Press, 2009).

Bella Matambanadzo is a Zimbabwean feminist activist. She has a contribution in *Township Girls: The Cross Over Generation* (2018) and to *African Sexualities: a Reader* (Pambazuka Press, 2012), and *Beyond Beijing: Strategies and Visions Towards Women's Equality* (SADC Press Trust, 1996) amongst other works. She was coeditor with Professor Rudo Gaidzanwa of *A Beautiful Strength – A Journal of 80 years of Women's Rights Movements and Activism in Zimbabwe since 1936* (Women's Coalition of Zimbabwe, 2017). She contributed a story to the anthologies *Writing Free* (Weaver Press, 2011) and *Writing Mystery and Mayhem* (Weaver Press, 2015), and most recently 'A Very Recent Tale' in *New Daughters of Africa* (Harper Collins, 2019).

In 2006-07, Bella was named one of eleven women on the frontline of defending human rights by the global human rights watchdog Amnesty International for her work with Zimbabwe's Radio Voice of the People. She has worked in 36 countries on the African continent in print media, radio journalism and television news production.

Bella is a Dean's list Summa cum Laude Graduate of the Humanities Faculty of Rhodes University.

Christopher Mlalazi is the author of the three novels: *Many Rivers* (The Lion Press, 2009), *Running With Mother* (Weaver Press, 2012) which has been translated into German and Italian, and *They Are Coming* (Weaver Press, 2014), and the short story collection *Dancing With Life: Tales From the Township* (amabooks, 2008), which won the Best First Book award at the National Arts Merit Awards (NAMA). To date Mlalazi has written eight plays, which have been staged in Zimbabwe, including the co-written *The Crocodile of Zambezi* which won the Oxfam/Novib PEN Freedom of Expression Award winner (2008) and *Election Day*, the NAMA winner for Outstanding Theatrical Production in 2010. He is a former alumni of the Caine Prize Workshop, the University of Iowa International Writers Program, Nordik-Africa Institute, and the Hannah-Arendt Scholarship. He is currently writing a new novel, *Blade Maker*, and studying for a degree in Computer Science in Mexico. He also dreams of being a programmer one day and writing code for applications that can promote literature in this digital era

Farai Mpofu (1980) was born in Bulawayo in the dusty township of Luveve. He attended high school at Cyrene Mission and proceeded to the University of Zimbabwe where he graduated with a BA Honours in 2002. Farai is currently studying for a post-graduate Diploma in Education.

Charles Mungoshi (1947-2019) was born in the Chivhu area of Zimbabwe. He has written novels and short stories in both Shona and English, as well as two collections of children's stories: *Stories from a Shona Childhood* and *One Day Long Ago* (Baobab Books, 1989 and 1991). The former won him the Noma Award for Publishing in Africa. He has also continued to write poetry and has one published collection: *The Milkman doesn't only deliver Milk* (Baobab Books, 1998). He won the Commonwealth Writers Prize (Africa region) twice, in 1988 and 1998, for two collections of short stories: *The Setting Sun and the Rolling World* (Heinemann, 1987) and *Walking Still* (Baobab Books, 1997). His last novel, *Branching Streams Flow in the Dark,* was published in 2017. Two of his novels: *Waiting for the Rain* (Heinemann, 1975) and *Ndiko kupindana kwa mazuva* (Mambo Press, 1975) received International PEN awards. The latter was also translated into French as *Et ainsi passant les jours*.

In 1985-87 he was Writer in Residence at the University of Zimbabwe, and worked for some time as a freelance writer, script writer and editor. He was awarded an honorary doctorate by the University of Zimbabwe in 2003.

Chiedza Musengezi was born and raised in Zimbabwe. She now lives and works in Northern Ireland. She has co-edited compilations of women's voices in: *Women of Resilience* (Zimbabwe Women Writers, 2000), *Women Writing Africa: The Southern Region* (The Feminist Press, 2003) and *A Tragedy of Lives: Women in Prison in Zimbabwe* (Weaver Press, 2003). Chiedza was published in *Writing Still* (Weaver Press, 2003), *Writing Now* (Weaver Press, 2005) *Women Writing Zimbabwe* (Weaver Press, 2008) and *Writing Lives* (Weaver Press, 2013).

Gugu Ndlovu has written several short stories on the Zimbabwean experience. She was born in Lusaka, Zambia to a Zimbabwean father, a political activist and Canadian mother, an educator, and spent her formative years in both Zimbabwe and Canada. She currently lives in Canada where she spends most of her time attending to her three children and appreciating her new cultural landscape.

Sekai Nzenza is a writer and international development consultant specialising in NGO accountability, health, microenterprise and human rights. She was born in rural Zimbabwe and trained as a nurse at Great Ormond Street in London. She holds a PhD in International Relations from the University of Melbourne, Australia. Her essays, fiction and short stories have been published in a number of journals, including the *Guardian Weekly*. She had written a memoir, *Zimbabwean Woman: My Own Story* (Karia Press, 1988) and a novel, *Songs to an African Sunset, a Zimbabwean Story* (Lonely Planet Publications, 1997). After 25 years working in humanitarian aid in Australia, Africa and the United States, Sekai returned to Zimbabwe in 2010. Confronted with the consequences of HIV/AIDS and increasing deaths and poverty in her village, Sekai and the Village Women's Burial Society formed The Simukai Development Project whose aim is to seek practical sustainable solutions to solving rural poverty. At the same time, the project reclaims the voices of marginalised village communities through song, dance, writing and drama. She was elected MP for Chikomba East district in 2018 and subsequently appointed as Zimbabwe's Minister of Public Service, Labour and Social Welfare.

Freedom Nyamubaya (1960-2015) was a rural development, gender, and peace activist, farmer, dancer and writer who was born in Uzumba. Cutting short her secondary school education in 1975, she left to join the Zimbabwe National Liberation Army in Mozambique, where she achieved the rank of Female Field Operation Commander, later being elected Secretary for Education in the first ZANU Women's League conference in 1979.

After Independence, she founded MOTSRUD, an NGO that provided agro-services to rural farmers, and she worked on attachment with the United Nations in Mozambique. A founding member of the Zimbabwe Peace and Security Trust, she spent much of the last five years of her life promoting peace throughout Zimbabwe. Her home was a game farm in Mhangura where she sought to work with villagers in the area promoting agricultural and development activities, and defend her own game against poachers and predators.

Her first volume of poetry, *On the Road Again* (Zimbabwe Publishing House, 1985) was followed by *Dusk of Dawn* (College Press, 1995), both being attempts to grapple with a brutal world using powerful images and disconcerting rhythms. A selection of her poetry is available on the Poetry International website http://www.poetryinternationalweb.net/pi/site/poet/item/5756/25/Freedom-TV-Nyamubaya

Bongani Sibanda is a Zimbabwean writer based in Johannesburg, South Africa. His short fiction has appeared in the *Kalahari Review*, the *Munyori Literary Journal*, and in *Writing Lives* (Weaver Press, 2014) and *Writing Mystery and Mayhem* (Weaver Press, 2015). His short story, 'Musoke', a fictionalised account of Uganda's former LRA leader, Dominic Ongwen, was longlisted for the ABR Elizabeth Jolley Short Story Award. He has one published collection, *Grace and Other Stories* (Weaver Press, 2016)

He attended the Caine Prize Workshop in Rwanda in 2018, and his short story 'Ngozi', written at the workshop, was published in *Redemption Song and Other Stories* (New Internationalist Publications Ltd, 2018).

Valerie Tagwira is a specialist obstetrician and gynaecologist. She practices in Harare. *The Uncertainty of Hope* (Weaver Press, 2006), her first novel, won the National Arts Merit Award for Outstanding Fiction in 2008. Her short story 'The Journey' was published in the Caine Prize Anthology 2010, and 'Mainini Grace's Promise' was published in *Women Writing Zimbabwe* (Weaver Press, 2009). It was translated into Shona for the anthology *Mazambuko* (Weaver Press, 2011). She is currently working on her second novel.

Introduction

Franziska Kramer and Jürgen Kramer

Courses on African Literature(s) in European and American universities and schools have proliferated over the past few decades. Slowly but distinctly, the relevance of the African continent, its peoples and cultures is being recognised and paid heed to in many spheres of education. Unfortunately, discussions of sub-Saharan literature(s) in English have mainly focused on texts from South Africa, Nigeria and Kenya because of the economic and political importance of these countries, but also because of the great diversity as to content and the unquestionable literary merit of their writers' products. Other countries, however, have also produced texts of literary and cultural relevance which deserve to be read closely, analysed meticulously and enjoyed for their literary brilliance. The present collection of short stories is intended to open windows on the history, politics and culture of Zimbabwe over the past half century. In this period, momentous social and political changes took place which resulted from developments that can be traced back as far as the nineteenth century. Understanding today's Zimbabwe requires a brief look at the history of the British Empire.

1. History

> *Rushing does not always ensure arrival.*
> Chenjerai Hove (1991: 14)

'There was not a single year in Queen Victoria's long reign [1837-1901] in which somewhere in the world her soldiers were not fighting for her and for her empire.' (Farwell, 1999: 1) This is how one of a number of surveys begins describing the so-called 'small' or 'little' wars which, although strikingly at odds with the British self-perception of 'Pax Britannica', determined the history of Britain and the British Empire in the nineteenth century and beyond. These wars aimed at the annexation (and subsequent exploitation) of foreign territories and the subjection of their populations, the suppression of rebellions and other forms of resistance, and the implementation of punitive expeditions that were intended to prevent or to exact revenge for real or assumed aggressions. While the colonial armies were clearly superior in force of arms, technology and training, and, moreover, succeeded in splitting the forces of the colonised (true to the motto 'divide and rule'), the latter benefited from the colonisers' ignorance of the territories and their proneness to tropical diseases. The colonisers did not always meet resistance. In some cases they were accepted as a continuation of, or even as an improvement on, indigenous rule. But if they met with resistance they had to fight not just a military enemy but a whole population. For the colonised, it was a 'people's war' (Wesseling, 1989: 4). Moreover, as these wars were 'small', the transition from a state of not-yet war to a state of war (i.e. from a lesser to a greater use of violence) was fluid and, very often, without clear markers. This suggests that in fact the colonies were in a permanent state of war.

The region of today's Zimbabwe was colonised in the early 1890s by the British South Africa Company (BSAC) with the intention of gaining control of the country, mining its minerals and taking away the best land from the Shona and Ndebele peoples for the production of export crops (mainly grain, tobacco and cotton). In 1896/97, in separate actions, the Ndebele and the Shona peoples staged armed uprisings against the colonisers; both were brutally suppressed. The BSAC remained in charge of the region until after WW1; in 1923 the country became the self-governing Colony of Southern Rhodesia. After both world wars, in which Rhodesian soldiers fought with the Allied Forces,[1] the colony attracted a great number of (white) settlers

---

1   Black soldiers were recruited as well. Their expectation when they returned from the front, be it in Europe, Burma or East Africa, was that they would be treated as equals. They were not, of course.

from Britain and elsewhere so that their number grew to roughly 200,000 by the mid-1960s (Raftopoulos & Mlambo 2009: 122).

In November 1965, Southern Rhodesia, led by Ian Douglas Smith, unilaterally declared its independence from Britain because the British government favoured the introduction of black majority rule. Rhodesia's rulers, however, defying the 'wind of change',[2] were determined to maintain their white minority rule and to 'crush any form of African nationalism' (Raftopoulos & Mlambo 2009: 117). The country's first black nationalist party, the Zimbabwe African People's Union (ZAPU), was founded in 1961 and headed by Joshua Nkomo. Nkomo came from the Ndebele people, who made up 20% of the Zimbabwean population; the Shona made up 75 per cent. In 1963 ZAPU split, and the Zimbabwe African National Union (ZANU) was founded. Neither the white settlers nor the black nationalists were unified with regard to their political aims and objectives, but the latter at least achieved the forging of an uneasy alliance between ZAPU and ZANU as the 'Patriotic Front' (PF) in 1976.

The first major action in the war of liberation took place in April 1966, with Rhodesian security forces engaging ZANLA militia, killing seven of them. The conflict continued at a low level until the end of 1972, when ZANLA attacked a farm in the north-east of the country and the Rhodesian government began authorising an increasing number of external operations. Following the revolution in Portugal, Mozambique gained independence in June 1975, events which proved beneficial to ZANLA but disastrous for the Rhodesians; the indefinite postponement of majority rule was no longer viable.

At political independence in 1980, a black majority government was established under Robert Mugabe, head of ZANU-PF since 1977, incorporating Joshua Nkomo and ZAPU. Its relatively peaceful, if decidedly authoritarian, operation – concerning nation-building,

---

2   In 1960 the then Prime Minister of Great Britain, Harold Macmillan, toured the British colonies in Africa. On 10 January (in Accra) and on 3 February (in Cape Town) he gave a speech in which he said that '[t]he wind of change is blowing through this continent. Whether we like it or not, this growth of national consciousness is a political fact.' (http:// www.sahistory.org.za/archive/wind-change-speech-made-south-africa-parliament-3-february-1960-harold-macmillan; accessed 27 June 2017)

economic development, restructuring of civil society and, particularly, health care and education – was initially not without success, but two years later the ZANU-ZAPU co-operation fell apart when Mugabe, without consulting Nkomo, announced that he was planning to establish a one-party state. When Nkomo resisted – not because he was in principle against a one-party state, but in order to improve ZAPU's position vis-à-vis ZANU – Mugabe ousted him and his ZAPU colleagues from the government on the pretext that ZIPRA (the military arm of ZAPU) had collected and hidden arms because they planned to overthrow the government (Meldrum 2004: 46-48). Later in 1982, low-level resistance developed in Matabeleland and was met by the brutal oppression of Operation *Gukurahundi*, in which, in the course of five years, governmental troops killed some 20,000 civilians (Raftopoulos & Mlambo 2009: 179). Many Ndebele fled to neighbouring Botswana, their politicians were harassed and persecuted, and Nkomo fled to Britain, only to reappear for the first post-independence elections in 1985, which were won by ZANU-PF.[3] Two years later, Mugabe and Nkomo signed the Unity Accord that merged the two parties. While it ended the atrocities in Matabeleland, this political merger effectively emasculated the opposition.

Despite this internal crisis, by the end of the first decade of independence, agricultural output had reached more than satisfactory levels, substantial progress had been made in expanding the provision of health care and education, water and sanitation were provided to rural households and a minimum wage was introduced. But the boom did not last. From the late 1980s, economic decline – bad harvests caused by droughts, drastically falling exports and rising prices – was compounded by growing corruption in the country's government and administration. Both caused general frustration and popular resistance, which the government sought to appease with accelerated land distribution measures. But the latter alienated political sympathisers, failed to produce positive results for the economy, and led to a drying up of foreign investments. When, as

---

3   Whenever we write that elections were won by ZANU-PF, the reader should keep in mind that the winning, from the beginning, was ensured by intimidation, coercion, bribery and rigging.

a consequence, outstanding international debts could not be paid, Zimbabwe was subjected to sanctions and, unsurprisingly, soaring inflation threatened the economy. Instead of working to remove the sanctions (for example, by clamping down on corruption and using the money obtained by fraud to pay the loans), the government tightened its grip on the population, strangled the oppositional Movement for Democratic Change (MDC) and, by means of intimidation, violence and fraud, prolonged its hold on power. By the mid-1990s, Zimbabwe's white people (whose number had more than halved since independence) were increasingly blamed for the country's problems. The government had failed to build a just and equitable society, to establish a truly democratic order and to bring about peace and reconciliation. Instead, it continued the 'authoritarian governance' it had inherited from its colonial predecessors: 'The main characteristics of the post-independence state were lack of tolerance for political diversity and dissent, heavy reliance on force for mobilisation, and a narrow, monolithic interpretation of citizenship, nationalism and national unity.' (Raftopoulos & Mlambo 2009: 179)[4]

In June 1996, falling wages and rising prices led to a public-sector strike that almost paralysed the country. The general strike a year and a half later was the result of a broad alliance of social forces that wanted immediate and drastic change. But increasing protest produced intensified repression by the state. In 1997 the government turned to the war veterans to help consolidate its power. When the war of liberation ended, many of its veterans did not profit from the fact that they were on the winning side, but slipped into obscurity, very often ending in dead-end jobs or unemployment. When the crisis in the mid-1990s began to bite, the Zimbabwe National Liberation War Veterans' Association, led by Chenjerai Hunzvi, flexed its muscles, and in November 1997 Mugabe awarded each of the estimated 50,000 ex-combatants a one-off gratuity of approximately US$5,000 (Z$50,000), and a monthly pension of approximately US$200 (Z$2,000). These payments had not been budgeted for, and the government had to

---

4 Wole Soyinka spotted and castigated this 'crisis of leadership alienation', which inaugurated 'a new era and axis of differentiation with the same mentality of domination and/or exploitation' (Soyinka 2012: 48).

borrow the money to meet its obligations. The result was a massive depreciation of the Zimbabwe dollar which on a day referred to later as the 'Black Friday' lost 75 per cent of its value. In January 1998, food riots erupted in Harare and towns across the country because of the steep rise of the cost of basic foodstuffs. Although the reaction of the state was brutal repression, labour militancy, led by the Zimbabwe Congress of Trade Unions (ZCTU), intensified. In August 1998, the general crisis acquired an additional aspect. Robert Mugabe sent 10-13,000 troops to the Democratic Republic of Congo (Moore 2003: 44), ostensibly to prop up Laurent Kabila (who, a year earlier, had toppled Mobutu Sese Seko), but as a matter of fact to reclaim the regional dominance he had lost to Nelson Mandela and to secure a share of the profit from the Congo's mineral resources. This engagement was estimated to have cost Zimbabwe US$3m per month (Tarisayi 2009: 15).

The dire results of these economic and political developments were 'high levels of poverty; high levels of structural unemployment; a critical shortage of basic commodities; the collapse of the utilities sectors [...]; conditions of insecurity at all levels [...]; a critical exodus of professionals [...]; low disposable income; high levels of malnutrition, and rising inequalities of wealth and incomes' (Tarisayi 2009: 17). However, the determination and resilience demonstrated by Zimbabwe's civil society vis-à-vis this crisis were admirable. When the ZANU-PF government planned to introduce a new constitution which would strengthen its hand, the ZCTU, the Zimbabwe Council of Churches and numerous NGOs and civil society organisations joined forces and formed the National Constitutional Assembly (NCA) in January 1998 in order to initiate 'a process of enlightening the general public on the current constitution in Zimbabwe; to identify shortcomings of the current constitution and to organise debate on possible constitutional reform; to organise the constitutional debate in a way which allows a broad-based participation; to subject the constitution-making process to popular scrutiny with a view to entrenching the principles that constitutions are made by, and for, the people; generally to encourage a culture of popular participation in decision making' (Raftopoulos & Mlambo 2009: 206-207). The government derided and seriously obstructed the work of the NCA and launched its own alternative Constitutional Commission in March 1999. Half a year later, the oppositional Movement for Democratic Change (MDC) was formed, a move which raised the stakes around the constitutional reform process. The referendum for the new constitution was scheduled for February 2000. It was to be the first part of the 'long election' (Moore 2003: 46), to be followed by the parliamentary election in June 2000 and the presidential election in March 2002. The referendum was lost by ZANU-PF: 54 per cent voted 'no'. In response to this defeat, Mugabe strengthened his ties with the war veterans and began 'a series of land occupations that radically transformed the political and economic landscape of the country' (Raftopoulos & Mlambo 2009: 211).[5] This Fast Track land reform and the government's reorganisation of the state structures along authoritarian-nationalist lines running in parallel to it were ideologically presented as the third Chimurenga.[6] The introduction of repressive legislation – the Public Order and Security Act, the Access to Information and Protection of Privacy Act – which massively restricted the activities of the opposition, was officially justified by the opposition's alleged collaboration with the remaining white farmers

---

5 'The occupations decisively broke the back of white land ownership in the country [...]. While in 2000 there were some 4,500 white commercial farmers occupying 11 million hectares of land and producing over 70 per cent of agricultural output, by 2008 this number had been reduced to approximately 500. [...] Other major losers in the land reallocation were opposition supporters and farmworkers. [...] the occupations led to a huge drop in employment levels, estimated at 70 per cent in the Midlands and 65 per cent in the two Matabeleland provinces; by mid-2000 an estimated 900,000 people had been affected by the evictions; less than 5 per cent of the farmworkers were granted land [...]. Their exclusion as beneficiaries of the land occupations was the result of ZANU (PF) branding them either as "belonging to the farmer" and under the "domestic government" of commercial farmers, or as foreigners in the politics of "the nation". Categorised as "enemies of the state" along with white farmers and the MDC, these workers were subjected to some of the worst election violence of the period 2000-2002.' (Raftopoulos & Mlambo 2009: 216-217; see also Moore 2003: 36-40)
6 In Zimbabwean popular consciousness, the word chimurenga (Shona for 'uprising) refers to the Shona/Ndebele risings of the 1890s and the war of independence in the 1960s/70s.

and imperial powers abroad.

The parliamentary election in June 2000 was obstructed by much intimidation, violence and manipulation – huge numbers of voters were denied their voting rights in Harare and as many added in the country to a secret voters' role (Moore 2003: 46). The election was narrowly won by the ruling party which, however, lost its two-thirds majority (ZANU-PF: 49 per cent; MDC: 47 per cent). The presidential election in March 2002 was preceded and determined not only by excessive fraud, but also by unprecedented widespread violence: immediately before the election, the record stood at '70,000 displaced, 107 killed, 397 abducted, 83 MDC rallies banned, and 5,308 opposition supporters tortured' (Booysen 2003: 11). Still, Mugabe received 56 per cent, Tsvangirai 42 per cent (Raftopoulos & Mlambo 2009: 215).

No wonder that in this context the budget deficit increased, GDP fell, domestic and external debts rose and inflation galloped (Tarisayi 2009: 15). The agricultural sector above all was crippled because skilled farmers were dispossessed, large amounts of the occupied land were underutilised and a rapidly deteriorating infrastructure impeded production and trade. As a result, production decreased by more than 50 per cent and the former breadbasket of southern Africa needed food assistance for about five million people (Raftopoulos & Mlambo 2009: 217). When the government could not meet its international obligations, credits were withheld, investments shrank and aid flows were reduced (Tarisayi 2009: 15). In 2002, Zimbabwe was suspended from the Commonwealth, from which it formally withdrew in 2003. The government announced several reform programmes to initiate economic recovery, but all failed. In 2006, some 85 per cent of Zimbabweans were living below the Poverty Datum Line, trying to scrape a living in a context of hyperinflation, rapidly decreasing real wages and rising unemployment (Raftopoulos & Mlambo 2009: 220).

While the informalisation of the economy grew – people took any kind of work they were paid for – the government abused the relatively vulnerable position of these labouring poor with its Operation *Murambatsvina* in May 2005. Disrespectfully termed 'clearing out the filth', this operation involved the forcible relocation of some 700,000 people from the urban to the rural areas. In this way the government wanted to get rid of as many poor as possible in the urban centres because it could not 'provide food and fuel for them' and, more importantly, to punish the people of these areas for 'their consistent support of the MDC after 2000' (Raftopoulos & Mlambo 2009: 221). And while a small politically privileged group still reaped their profits from these developments, a great number of Zimbabweans were forced to find and make their living abroad. It has been estimated that 'over three million Zimbabweans are living in the diaspora with 37 per cent in the United Kingdom, 35 per cent in Botswana, 5 per cent in South Africa and 3.4 per cent […] in Canada' (Tarisayi 2009: 17).

The two elections of 2008[7] were conducted at a time when basic commodities were unavailable in the shops, the health and education sectors had virtually collapsed and, to add insult to injury, the government banned 'humanitarian NGOs from distributing food aid' (Tarisayi 2009: 18). Unexpectedly, but only after the then South African president Thabo Mbeki had mediated between the contesting parties ZANU-PF, MDC-T and MDC-M,[8] the pre-election environment, according to most witnesses, was 'relatively peaceful and sufficiently conducive to the free expression of the people's will in the ballot box' (Masunungure 2009a: 73). When the results became known, however, the climate changed. For the first time since independence ZANU-PF

---

7 'The 29 March elections are commonly referred to as the 'harmonized elections', a reference to their consolidating all national and local government elections [the office of executive president; the 210 House of Assembly seats; the 60 elective seats in the 93-member Senate; and the 1,958 local council seats]; the second election, held on 27 June, was consequent upon the inconclusive 29 March presidential election and is commonly referred to as the 'run-off' election. The March elections were the most peaceful (and even enjoyable) since the genesis of Zimbabwe's mega-crisis in 2000 while the June elections will go down in history as the bloodiest since independence.' (Masunungure 2009a: 61)

8 'The Movement for Democratic Change was formed in September 1999 but split into two factions in October 2005 [...]. The larger body of the opposition party remained with founding President Morgan Tsvangirai while the splinter faction was led by Professor Arthur Mutambara. For avoidance of voter confusion, the former faction became known as MDC-T while Mutambara's formation contested as the MDC though it is now commonly referred to as 'MDC-M'.' (Masunungure 2009a: 63, note 4)

had become a minority party.[9]

The results of the presidential election were unlawfully withheld for 32 days. When they were released, 43.2 per cent had voted for Mugabe and 47.9 per cent for Tsvangirai. From very early on it was argued that the Zimbabwe Electoral Commission had withheld the result with the intention of participating 'in the manipulation of the results – probably by reducing Tsvangirai's winning margin to a level below 50 per cent of the valid votes, in order to justify a second round of voting' (Makumbe 2009: 131; cf. Matyszak 2009: 142-145 and Moore 2014: 104, note 7). It is very probable that ZANU-PF had advance knowledge of the result because its campaign for the 'run-off' election started in early April. The party's conception of itself was that of a party at war with the opposition: 'legitimacy and power flowed from the barrel of a gun [...] and not from the ballot' (Masunungure 2009b: 86). Tsvangirai went into exile for six weeks for fear of being assassinated. There was neither a working parliament, nor anything like a functioning civil society. Intimidation, kidnapping, torture, arson and murder of oppositional forces were the order of the day. Exact figures are difficult to come by, but when, five days before the actual election day, Morgan Tsvangirai withdrew from the contest because he could not ask people to vote for him when that vote could cost them their lives, he gave the following figures: '86 deaths, 10,000 homes destroyed, 200,000 displaced, and 10,000 injured' (Masunungure 2009b: 93). Zimbabwe Peace Project reports showed '4,375 incidents of violence in April, 6,288 in May and 3,653 in June. By July the cumulative total had risen to 17,605 which included verified cases of 171 murders, 9,148 assaults and sixteen rapes' (Matyszak 2009: 147). Mugabe received 85.5 per cent of the vote; Tsvangirai 9.3 per cent (Masunungure 2009b: 96).

Although most observers condemned the flawed presidential 'run-off', Mugabe began his fourth term in office on 29 June. Another SADC-

---

9 While in the March 2005 elections ZANU-PF had 'won 78 (65 per cent) of the 120 contested seats and 59.6 per cent of the vote, compared to the MDC's 41 seats (34 per cent) and 39.5 per cent of the vote', in March 2008 ZANU-PF's share of the House of Assembly vote 'dropped to 46 per cent and its 99 seats translated to 47 per cent of the 210 seats', and 'the combined MDC formations captured 51 per cent of the House of Assembly vote and 52 per cent of the seats' (Masunungure 2009a: 76-77).

facilitated mediation process, again led by Thabo Mbeki, resulted in a Government of National Unity being formed in February 2009, with Morgan Tsvangirai as Prime Minister. One of the first problems this government had to deal with was the suspension of the Zimbabwe dollar on 12 April 2009 (which had become inevitable through the runaway inflation of the past two years) and its replacement by foreign currencies (primarily the US dollar). In the course of the next few years, ZANU-PF was able to consolidate its structures and strengthen its networks; the MDC, by contrast, was less well organised, disregarding opinion polls and succumbing to the lure of collaboration with ZANU-PF. Not surprisingly, in the July 2013 elections Mugabe won 61 per cent of the presidential vote and ZANU-PF won 197 seats in the national assembly.

While this book was being put together, Zimbabwean history changed dramatically. On 15 November 2017, after 37 years in office, Robert Mugabe was placed under house arrest by the army by what was in all but name a coup d'état. Four days later, ZANU-PF sacked him as party leader and appointed former Vice President Emmerson Mnangagwa in his place. When impeachment proceedings were being initiated, Mugabe tendered his resignation on 21 November 2017. Three days later, Mnangagwa was sworn in as president. At the beginning of 2018, he promised 'free, credible, fair and indisputable' elections within 'four to five months' (Burke 2018). On 30 July 2018, the Zimbabwean people went to the polls electing president, parliament and local councils. Most observers were content that the pre-election environment had been largely peaceful, political freedoms during the campaign had been respected and inducements, intimidation and coercion by state and/or ruling party had played a much smaller role than in previous elections. Regrettably though, the largely state-owned media failed to abide by their legal obligation 'to ensure equitable and fair treatment to all political parties and candidates' (EU EOM 2018: 3) and the Zimbabwe Electoral Commission (ZEC) failed to demonstrate transparency and inclusivity in its procedures. 'On 3 August the ZEC chairperson declared the presidential results with the incumbent, Emmerson D. Mnangagwa, receiving 2,460,463 votes (50.8%), while the opposition candidate Nelson Chamisa received 2,147,436 (44.3%).

With a margin of victory of 313,027 votes (around 38,000 votes over the 50% threshold) Mnangagwa was declared President-elect.' (EU EOM 2018: 35) Already before the election results were known, members of the opposition had rejected them as rigged. In the days after the elections tension was high, particularly in Harare, and public protests were brutally suppressed by the army. At least six people were killed and 14 injured (cf. EU EOM 2018: 38). Legal challenges against the outcome of the presidential election were transparently and timeously handled, but eventually rejected by the courts (cf. EU EOM 2018: 40-42).

Although Emmerson Mnangagwa had promised social improvement, in the autumn of 2018, Zimbabwe was hit by another economic crisis (with inflation officially reaching 42%, but estimated by others around 200% or more) which the government met by more than doubling fuel prices. When thousands took to the streets and rioting occurred, the state savagely struck back. Human rights groups reported massive and indiscriminate incidents of killing, torture, rape and displacement. Some felt reminded of Operations *Gukurahundi* and *Murambatsvina* (cf. National Transitional Justice Working Group Zimbabwe 2019). At the time of writing (mid-February 2019) violence against the opposition and the poor continues; the country's future is as dark as its prospects of democratic change and development.

2. Literature

> *A glance at Zimbabwe tells me that this is a bad story that needs more than thorough editing; it needs a complete rewrite.*
> **Brian Chikwava (2007a: 1)**

To begin with, looking at fictional texts involves the twofold analysis of how they apprehend, work on and reflect the world they draw on, and how they attract, appeal to and affect the readership they address. Accordingly, the first thing to find out is if and to what extent the assembled texts provide a variety of 'windows' on Zimbabwean history, culture and society, what kind of viewpoints they offer for an appreciation of the country's development over the past half century and if and how the wider context is established. Secondly, as a reader one's immediate points of interest, of approval or rejection can be found in the various protagonists (be they perpetrators or victims), their characters, motives and ideologies. The latter usually form a part of the 'messages' and 'morals' of the texts. Potentially, they are amplified or mitigated by the texts' structures and the various kinds of language employed.

More specifically, literary texts act as 'windows' on the history and culture of a particular society and form a significant part of this society's cultural memory. The latter can be understood to have three dimensions serving three different functions (cf. Assmann 1999: 138-139). Firstly, it can be used by the ruling political, social or cultural strata as a means of legitimating their rule. Moreover, whoever rules, be it by force or hegemony, may want to retrospectively legitimate their coming to power as well as to fix it firmly in the eyes of posterity. But secondly, as all exercises of power tend to generate resistance, those who do not belong to the ruling strata and/or do not believe in their ways of legitimating their rule tend to critically and subversively question the cultural 'work' supporting them. Moreover, they construct alternative memories, by which they tend to de-legitimate whatever the ruling strata want to legitimate and, of course, also to legitimate their own perspective. Thirdly, there is the dimension of distinction which is used by both parties. It comprises all cultural forms which help to enhance the collective identity of a group or society.

These ideas are applicable to more or less all kinds of societies; they can also be applied to coloniser-colonised relationships as well as to the post-colonial relationships between rulers and their subjects. In the case of Zimbabwe, it could be argued that, on the one hand, since independence, the ruling strata have not preoccupied themselves with literary matters: with one exception[10] books have not been banned, and hardly any writers been silenced. On the other hand, the censorship laws (a residue from the colonial government) were not abolished, fear

---

10 *Mindblast* (Heinemann, 1984), by Dambudzo Marechera, was banned after it was published. Marechera was arrested and held in the police cells for six days. However, after strong protests led by the poet Musaemura Zimunya and the Writers' Union, the ban was lifted.

has possibly led to self-censorship and self-imposed exile,[11] there is a constant awareness that narratives, whether literary or pedagogic, which are not sufficiently 'patriotic' may be dismissed, and their authors or teachers marginalised. All governments since 1980 have been anything but neutral in cultural matters and all texts which conveyed critical images of the country were potentially subversive, implicitly or explicitly de-legitimising the views of the ruling strata.

While literary texts can (and do) contribute to all of the three dimensions sketched above, in our collection we have focused on the second and the third, because what is represented (i.e. remembered) in literary texts is inextricably combined with ethical considerations. The latter, we think, should recall Aristotle's sentiment that 'the weaker are always anxious for equality and justice, while the strong pay no heed to either' (quoted in Leyden 1985: 63) and should, therefore, privilege the perspective of those 'who paid the bill',[12] who suffered from neglect, torture, trauma. Certainly, literature can inform and please us, but it comes into its own when moves us, enrages us and inspires us to act. It is in this context that a particular choice we made should be regarded and appreciated: roughly a third of the texts in this collection either focuses on or is narrated from the perspective of children or young teenagers. While these protagonists certainly labour the most under their conditions of survival, they also inspire the reader best through their capacity for suffering, their courage and their resilience.

The history of Zimbabwean literature is not very long; it compasses but four generations. The first generation were born and raised before the Second World War, and became part of 'the first elite of educated Africans in Rhodesia, a formative group in the rise of nationalism' (Veit-Wild 1992: 17). The second generation comprised those writers mostly born after the Second World War, whose adolescence was strongly influenced by the political climate in UDI Rhodesia and who began writing in the 1970s: 'Political and cultural isolation from the outside, fierce oppression inside and the general feeling of

---

11 The writer Chenjerai Hove chose to go into exile in 2001, convinced that following his critical articles published in the press his life was in danger.
12 Bertolt Brecht, 'Questions from A Worker Who Reads', https://msu.edu/~sullivan/TransBrechtWorker.html; accessed 3 May 2017.

hopelessness made this period what later became known as "those years of drought and hunger" [Musaemura Zimunya]' (Veit-Wild 1992: 153). With independence, the third generation of writers emerged who could enjoy dramatically improved conditions for black writing (new publishing houses, expanded education, writers' association and unions etc.).[13] However, 'while political power changed hands, political restrictions remained': the censorship laws, introduced by the UDI government in 1965, were neither abolished nor changed (Veit-Wild 1992: 303).[14] The fourth generation of writers, the so-called 'born-frees', began writing and publishing in the second half of the 1990s, when the Zimbabwean 'crisis' began to bite.[15]

While for the first generation (with writers like Lawrence Vambe, Stanlake Samkange and Solomon Mutswairo), a writer was a kind of 'moral guide' (Veit-Wild 1992: 78 et seq.) who would do well to

---

[13] Most importantly, black Zimbabwean writers could now also publish in English within the country. The colonial regime had strictly discouraged black writers from writing fiction in English and encouraged their writing in the vernacular. Veit-Wild found out that in the early 1990s 'more than three-quarters of Zimbabwe's published authors [wrote] mainly in the vernacular; the other quarter use[d] English as the or one major language of writing; ten per cent [wrote] exclusively in English [...]. – This [was], however, a paradoxical situation because the vernacular discourse had been appropriated by the hegemonic colonial power and so was not suitable for authentic expression of thought – or only in a limited way. On the other hand the colonial language, English, served as a counter-discursive tool to break away from the restrictive "native policies" of the Rhodesian government and hence became an emancipatory force.' (Veit-Wild 1992: 229)

[14] Nobody interested in the history of Zimbabwean literature until the early 1990s should fail to consult Flora Veit-Wildt's pioneering study *Teachers, Preachers, Non-Believers. A Social History of Zimbabwean Literature* (Hans Zell, 1992, whose comprehensiveness and vision laid the ground for many more studies to come.

[15] 'The crisis [of 1998-2008] became manifest in multiple ways: confrontations over the land and property rights; contestations over the history and meanings of nationalism and citizenship; the emergence of critical civil society groupings campaigning around trade union, human rights and constitutional questions; the restructuring of the state in more authoritarian forms; the broader pan-African and anti-imperialist meanings of the struggles in Zimbabwe; the cultural representations of the crisis in Zimbabwean literature; and central role of Robert Mugabe.' (Raftopoulos & Mlambo 2009: 202)

reconstruct the people's pre-colonial past and play a part in developing and spreading civilised behaviour across the country, the second generation (including amongst others, Charles Mungoshi, Stanley Nyamfukudza and Dambudzo Marechera) rather focused on the concerns of the present and the artistic nature, i.e. the literariness, of the texts they wrote. The third generation (including Chenjerai Hove, Shimmer Chinodya and Tsitsi Dangarembga) dispensed with such self-imposed demands with regard to form and content – and the next generation even more so: they simply want to write as and about what they like (cf. Kramer 2010: passim).

The members of this fourth generation – amongst them Petina Gappah, Christopher Mlalazi and Brian Chikwava – knowingly set out to tread new ground. They neither overly lament the horrors of the colonial past, nor excessively bewail the atrocities of the liberation war and its aftermath; they do not feel sorry for themselves as latecomers to a great (but largely illusive) struggle or as disadvantaged or alienated protagonists who had deserved something better. Theirs is a particular mixture of cool clear-sightedness, tough resilience and wry humour which enables them to register, record, react to, reconstruct and, most importantly, rewrite the Zimbabweans' struggle for individual freedom, social justice and human dignity. Whether they have stayed in the country or are living in the diaspora, their motto is 'we write what we like' (Christopher Mlalazi). And, although it seems hardly likely under the current economic and social conditions, they find small local publishers (cf. Staunton 2016) who invest their scant resources in the publication of poetry, novels and short story collections. Avowedly, these publishers want to provide a platform for young writers who might not otherwise be heard or read because they believe that 'fiction is a form of truth-telling, offering a perspective on life in particular periods that once told cannot be erased'.[16] Referring to the Weaver Press series (edited by Irene Staunton) which began with *Writing Still* (2003),[17] Brian Chikwawa suggested in 2007 that,

---

16 Irene Staunton, personal communication.
17 To date the following volumes (from which the stories of the present collection were selected) have appeared: *Writing Still* (2003), *Writing Now* (2005), *Laughing Now* (2007), *Women Writing Zimbabwe* (2008), *Writing Free* (2011), *Writing Lives* (2014), *Writing Mystery & Mayhem* (2015).

> *a natural progression ought to be Writing Nervous, for it is a nervous pulse that beats beneath the face of any Zimbabwean, be it a writer or a crack lipped mother in the rural areas who knows first-hand the kind of tricky relationship a child can have with its empty stomach, or a nurse in the diaspora who dreads the text message from her family asking her to wire more money back to their family who find themselves increasingly unable to look after themselves in an economy ravaged by inflation, the unemployed citizen who braves the aquatic predators of the Limpopo to become an illegal immigrant in South Africa, or the firebrand intellectual who dabbled in utilitarianism of a Stalinist variety – advocating the tearing down of the social fabric and national institutions in the name of the final revolution, the third chimurenga – and now finds him/herself sitting at his/her desk; pondering the question of again cutting off whatever is left of our national nose to show what we are capable of when push comes to shove. All are in a nervous condition; all are hostages. That includes the president himself, who is held hostage by his own will, is nervous about the future. Nervous because although he may have seen the moral shallowness of imperialism, colonialism, global capitalism and mutations of such, far from raising himself above such moral conventions, he continues to live in a moral depravity that he makes up for by exercising brutal power over ordinary citizens. His would be a fascinating contribution to Writing Nervous.* (Chikwawa 2007b)

The publisher did not follow this suggestion, but Chikwawa's diagnosis of 'an urgent pulse' in Zimbabwean writing may suitably give the reader perspective and direction for the impending reading process. Sadly, in Zimbabwe hardly anybody buys books. Except for the small local publishers already mentioned, the national book business is dead; international books are costly and hard to come by. Even if books (other than school textbooks and how-to manuals) could be had, most people would not be able to afford them.

3. How to use this collection

Our selection of twenty-three texts is 'introduced' by Shimmer Chinodya's story 'Queues', in which two narratives are interwoven: a 'personalised' version of the history of Rhodesia and Zimbabwe from the mid-seventies to the end of the millennium, and a story of two people falling in and, subsequently, out of love with each other. While this text cleverly delineates the specific properties of the individual and the collective, the personal and the political as well as their inevitable interdependence, its meaning forms the sometimes implicit, sometimes explicit common thread which runs through all the stories. We thought it worthwhile, however, to differentiate several themes or foci: (1) Independence – Before and After and What Came in Between; (2) *Gukurahundi*; (3) Whose Land is it? (4) Gender Relations; (5) Money Matters; (6) Social Relations; (7) Exile and (8) Resilience. We allotted two or three stories to each category to provide as complex an understanding of the problems involved as possible. The final story, Nevanji Madanhire's 'The Grim Reaper's Car' was already published in 2003. Strangely enough, it represents not only a kind of bottom line of the collection as a whole but could in itself not be more topical. Each author is briefly introduced, indispensable bits and pieces of information are provided and a short 'opening-up' of the text is suggested. We hope to make it clear that different readings are possible, nay desirable.

4. References

Assmann, Aleida (1999), *Erinnerungsräume. Formen und Wandlungen des kulturellen Gedächtnisses*, Munich: Beck.

'Bailing out Bandits', *The Economist*, 9 July 2016, 43-44.

Booysen, Susan (2003), 'The Dualities of Contemporary Zimbabwean Politics: Constitutionalism versus the Law of Power and the Land, 1999-2002', *African Studies Quarterly*, 7, 2 & 3, 1-31.

Burke, Jason (2018), 'Zimbabwean president promises "free and fair" elections in five months', *The Guardian*, 18 January.

Chikwawa, Brian (2007a), 'Writing the Story of Zimbabwe', *African Writing Online*, June-August (http://www.african-writing.com/aug/brian.htm; accessed 24 May 2017).

Chikwava, Brian (2007b), 'Zimbabwean Literature: A Nervous Condition', *Pambazuka News*, January 11 (https://www.pambazuka.org/governance/zimbabwean-literature-nervous-condition; accessed 24 May 2017).

Davidson, A.B. (1968), 'African Resistance and Rebellion Against the

Imposition of Colonial Rule', in T.O. Ranger, ed., *Emerging Themes in African History*, Nairobi: East African Publishing House, 177- 188.

European Union Election Observation Mission (EU EOM) (2018), *Final Report: Republic of Zimbabwe, Harmonised Elections 2018*. http://veritaszim.net/sites/veritas_d/files/EU%20Election%20Observers%20Final%20Report%20Zimbabwe%202018-.pdf; accessed 10 February 2019.

Farwell, Byron (1999), *Queen Victoria's Little Wars*, Ware: Wordsworth.

Hove, Chenjerai (1991), *Shadows*, Harare: Baobab Books.

Kramer, Franziska (2010), 'We are writing about what it means to be us' – Stimmen der jüngsten simbabwischen Schriftstellergeneration, B.A. thesis, Humboldt University, Berlin.

Leyden, Wolfgang von (1985), *Aristotle on Equality and Justice: His Political Argument*, London: Macmillan.

Makumbe, John (2009), 'Theft by Numbers: ZEC's Role in the 2008 Elections', in Masunungure 2009c, 119-132.

Masunungure, Eldred V. (2009a), 'Voting for Change: The 29 March Harmonized Elections', in Masunungure 2009c, 61-78.

Masunungure, Eldred V. (2009b), 'A Militarized Election: The 27 June Presidential Run-off', in Masunungure 2009c, 79-97.

Masunungure, Eldred V., ed. (2009c), *Defying the Winds of Change: Zimbabwe's 2009 Elections*, Harare: Weaver Press.

Matyszak, Derek (2009), 'Civil Society & the Long Election', in Masunungure 2009c, 133-148.

Mazrui, Ali A. (1970), 'Postlude: Toward a Theory of Protest', in Robert I. Rotberg and A.A. Mazrui, eds, *Protest and Power in Black Africa*, New York: Oxford University Press, 1185-1196.

Meldrum, Andrew (2004), *Where We Have Hope: A Memoir of Zimbabwe*, London: John Murray.

Moore, David (2003), 'Zimbabwe's Triple Crisis: Primitive Accumulation, Nation-State Formation and Democratisation in the Age of Neo-liberal Globalisation', *African Studies Quarterly*, 7, 2 & 3, 33-51.

Moore, David (2014), 'Death or Dearth of Democracy in Zimbabwe?', *Africa Spectrum*, 1, 101-114.

National Transitional Justice Working Group Zimbabwe (2019),

'Zimbabwe on the Brink as Violations Intensify', http://www.ntjwg.org.zw/downloads/NTJWG%20-%20CRIMES%20AGAINST%20HUMANITY%20ALERT!%20FULL%20PAGE.pdf , accessed 10 February 2019.

Raftopoulos, Brian & Alois Mlambo, eds (2009), *Becoming Zimbabwe: A History from the Pre-Colonial Period to 2008*, Harare: Weaver Press.

Ranger, Terence (1967), *Revolt in Southern Rhodesia 1896-7: A Study in African Resistance*, London: Heinemann.

Soyinka, Wole (2012), *Of Africa*, New Haven – London: Yale University Press.

Staunton, Irene (2016), 'Publishing for Pleasure in Zimbabwe: The Experience of Weaver Press', *Wasafiri*, 31/4, 49-54.

Tarisayi, Eustinah (2009), 'Voting in Despair: The Economic & Social Context', in Masunungure 2009c, 11-24.

Veit-Wild, Flora (1992), *Teachers, Preachers, Non-Believers. A Social History of Zimbabwean Literature*, London: Hans Zell.

Wesseling, H.L. (1989), 'Colonial Wars. An Introduction', in J.A. de Moor and H.L.W. Wesseling, eds, *Imperialism and War. Essays on Colonial Wars in Asia and Africa*, Leiden: Brill, 1-11.

1

QUEUES

Shimmer Chinodya

Some time in the early prime of my life I lost faith in myself.

In the mid-seventies Sisi Elizabeth earned twenty-two dollars a month working for white people. I hauled my trunk, black like a coffin and heavy with books, into her little wooden cabin at the back of that hideously large yard. I arrived bruised and sore, expelled from school, utterly desperate, banished for raising my tender adolescent fists against Rhodesia. Sisi Elizabeth returned every now and then from the white mansion and wiped her creased brow with her apron and adjusted her nanny's cap and said, 'But cousin, you must be starving. What will you have to eat? Don't be afraid, they are not here. They are away on holiday in Cape Town. Monkey Valley or something.' I shoved my modesty into my shorts and she took me to the house and showed me a 'dick freeze' loaded to the neck with steaks. I reclined in a resplendent lounge, timidly sampling Dolly Parton records and *Illustrated Life* and *Personality* magazines in that strange superior house. Later I gorged myself on the spaghetti and mince and cheese she had prepared. For a week while I waited for the news of this latest disaster to get through to my parents, I lived in that white house, eating rich strangers' food, listening to rich strangers' records and writing angry stories on a strange typewriter.

Rudo said I had to believe in myself. Expulsion sometimes felt like a bad start.

I was on the plane fleeing from I know not what going to I know not where and I know not why. I saw her profile and black-stockinged legs and short hair and the rings on her fingers and I recognised her at once. University. A quarter of a century ago. Sociology or Law. Probably now some NGO chef. She was dozing, her face turned up to the ceiling of the plane, perhaps meditating in the peaceful way people do when they are flying among the clouds, miles above the world. I mastered the courage to accost her. She spoke to me with the quick shallow warmth and precocious airs of women who become widows too early in life, of women who clutch at the tattered shreds of perceived bliss, of single mothers who cling to files and reports and Bibles to bolster their waning sanity in a vicious world. She baffled me with her newly acquired strength. I tried to be level with her, to hide the horns of my chauvinism. I tried to be honest and serious with her, with myself; not to flirt; not to patronise or to be frivolous; to avoid shocking her with the depth of my depression. She said earnestly, 'Call me any time and we can talk. But don't you have a wife to love?'

Once upon a time in the days of Sisi Elizabeth a loaf of bread cost twelve cents and you could buy a kilogram of meat for a dollar. Twice upon a moon your father sent you, by registered mail, two dollars pocket money to last half a term. Thrice upon a star you ate chicken and chips for twenty-five cents, and with Sidney at the end of the term you patrolled the train at night, munching five-penny mints and Choice Assorted biscuits. Four times upon a sun your father sent three siblings to boarding school on a milkman's pay. Five times upon a galaxy you had rice and chicken for Christmas. Six times upon the universe you were poor, but you survived.

The rains came. Rivers gurgled and dams burst, but not all the time. Hippos waded out of the rich mud. The spirits of the land smiled, and sometimes frowned. Without fertilisers you could reap thirty bags of maize and thirty-five bags of groundnuts from ten acres and the GMB sent you back with your unwanted produce, or with peanuts in your pockets. If you reaped nothing you pawned a beast for a bag of grain.

You were dirt poor, but you seldom starved.

I told Rudo that I wanted to believe in myself.

I told her I wanted a good woman to help me do that, that the best thing for a man was a good woman. A good, funny, honest woman. A woman to enjoy, to like, to love, to talk to, to laugh with, to devour, to feast on. A soul- and brain-mate. A woman who does not take herself too seriously and does not do too much of the church stuff. An intelligent woman who knows what she's about and has many layers to her that I can slowly peel off. A woman who is dependable, yet will allow me the foolishest of my fantasies. A woman who will help me organise myself. A woman who will let me talk to Hazvina or Memory or Nontokozo, and will not imprison my imagination.

'You must be an aspiring polygamist, then,' laughed Rudo.

'I suspect so,' I replied. 'My grandfather had two.'

'And what became of him and his wives? Did he become another statistic in a classic case of poisoning?'

'OK, things did not work out well. They never do, but polygamy could be beautiful. If I had two wives we would live and love and laugh together, dress to kill and go out as a threesome.'

'Where would you find women like that?'

'They must be there somewhere in this universe.'

'You, an educated man, saying such things. The feminists will immolate you.'

'I hope not.'

'Do you see a woman merely as an object?'

'God, please no.'

'OK – but why do you want to be mothered so much? Why do you want to define yourself in terms of another person?' *Why why why?*

In '67 and '73 there was drought, but that was before independence. Our mothers served us yellow sadza on the tables – the infamous 'Kenya' – so called because some of that brand of maize was imported from East Africa. In 1980, the year of our independence, Chaminuka and Nehanda smiled and released a deluge of rain to wash away all the blood and pain of the war. Crops flourished. Livestock lowed and baa-ed and bleated joyously in the plains, munching luscious grass. Even the backyards of township houses and the scrap land between factories and townships boasted greenly of abundant harvests. Silos filled fatly, trains thundered thankfully away to foreign lands, laden with exports. We were given sweet reprieve. We were declared the bread-basket of the region.

I met Rudo for lunch a few weeks after we got back home. She had on a black see-through blouse and an ankle-length denim skirt with a long slit on the side. She wore lipstick and a dark eye-shadow; her short hair had a special glow. I could tell she had done something to make herself look OK. She possessed a quiet simplicity that made me ache longingly within, that made me gasp at the degree of my despair, at the extent of my famine. She drank mineral water and ordered a cheese and tomato sandwich, which she carefully nibbled. She staunchly refused to take wine or spirits or beer, saying that she drank only on very special occasions and when she didn't have to go to work, saying that her late husband had only persuaded her to take the occasional glass. I somberly sipped my beer and fingered the bank notes in my pocket and tried to be engaging. Her answers were short. She seemed to be hovering on the borders of her own dilemma, waiting for some decided declaration from me. She laughed briefly and politely at my jokes, judging me, trying to fathom the reasons and nature of my interest in her. I wondered if she was worth the effort, if she was not chained too much to propriety; why I needed to be with her, why she readily let me pay the bill, what it would take to make her unshackle herself from herself.

We declared independence, after that long bitter war, in 1980. In the late 80s we tried to unshackle ourselves from the past. Out went the chains of the old constitution and in came the new. Out went the premiership and in came the presidency. We ploughed forward with a show of fisted arms, with calls for reconciliation, a brave new unity and work. Of course, there weren't enough funds. It wasn't easy. We massacred each other. We manufactured enemies. We squandered resources. There was mistrust, gangrene setting in. There were die-hards who chose to shit in the face of forgiveness. We fumbled with propriety, with new challenges. The world was watching, avariciously. We invited the world out for dinner and she coyly agreed. The world came with a wig and sweet-smelling musk, large round earrings, a black T-shirt, a short denim skirt and black gogo shoes. She was bra-less and pant-less and we leapt to her, our mouths drooling. The world ordered a rock shandy and a tuna-fish sandwich and watched us while we knocked back lager after lager and gorged ourselves on sadza and cows' hooves. The world watched as we paid the bill, then she gave the waiter a little tip.

Rudo wanted me. She wanted to win me over bit by bit. She called me day in day out. She left innumerable messages with my maid and my children asking me to call her. I think my estranged wife saw the messages. I feared for myself. I suspected that like me, Rudo wanted to believe in somebody else so that she could believe in herself, and redefine herself. I suspected she did the church stuff, however mildly, in order to belong to something. She declared she was Catholic, that she had a rabid mistrust of the new born-again churches. I didn't believe in myself and I didn't belong to anything. But I knew I could not leave her; that I had started something that I could not stop. Rudo wanted me but she really did not want me. Her sudden change of heart bothered me. She wanted me to respect myself, to help me salvage myself from what she thought was self-imposed gloom, but she wanted to own me like a toy. She even called me Teddy Bear. Teddy Bear! I felt a kind of pity for her. She lived with her eight-year-old daughter, her only child, in a two-bedroomed flat in a well-to-do block in the Avenues. The flat was cosy and tastefully furnished. I played CDs of the Beatles, Fleetwood Mac, Elton John, Joan Armatrading, Thomas Mapfumo, Miriam Makeba and Chiwoniso Maraire. She also had several gospel CDs by Mechanic Manyaruke and Shuvai Wutawunashe, and when I ignored the latter I told her that God had eluded me, had been too hard on me and my family.

People are defined by the music they keep and play but she confused me because of the ambiguity of her choices. I suspected some of the older music had been merely left by her husband and now she was using it to bait men. She drove an old-model Mazda which, perhaps, like her, was rust-eaten but efficient. I asked if some of her property had been left to her by her late husband, but she would not be drawn to tell me. Her daughter was beautiful and intelligent and liked me at once. Her name was Tariro. Tariro saw me like a father figure, a friend. I could tell she needed a father to cling to, somebody to love her, somebody who did not, like her mother, just order her to wash her feet or eat all her vegetables or switch off the TV and go to bed. Tariro loved books and I brought her some of the ones I had written. She curled up on the floor, between my legs, with her head in my lap and asked me to read to her. She told me the stories that she liked. She and her friends in the block decided to act out one of my children's plays. She wanted them to stage the play for me but two members of the group were away and they could not do it. When she went to bed she hugged me and kissed me on the lips and her little tongue touched mine.

Rudo smiled at me and said, 'But did you ever do this to your own children?'

I stood up guiltily and went to change the CD.

We bit off more than we could chew. We started starving bit by bit. Our teeth ached from raw meat and bone and there were not enough carcasses, not even enough dentists, so we went for the soft stuff. The national cake was getting smaller, but suddenly everyone wanted a piece. The bakeries hiccupped and coughed and sent out frantically for more wheat. The teachers wanted the cake, before it was even baked. The nurses wanted it. The doctors wanted it. The soldiers wanted it so badly that they sent in battalions in brand new Bedfords to bring it back in truckloads. The ex-combatants wanted it. The farmers wanted it. The peasants wanted it. The workers wanted it. Little children in the schools cried for milk and soup, for buns, for books. Pastors and priests in the pulpits of poverty pined for Lazarus's pitiful morsel. We squandered the national cake then turned to ordinary bread, but even that was not enough. We put up impressive schools, clinics, roads and dams. We gazetted new minimum wages, instituted quotas in workplaces, demarcated growth-points. But the new classrooms pleaded for desks; clinics squabbled for food and medicines; sun-baked roads yawned for bridges and asphalt. We printed more money. We imported doctors and teachers from other lands. We sent out planeloads of our own school-leavers to train in foreign languages, on foreign islands, so that they could come back to teach their own. We thirsted for education.

I had begun to thirst for her. She was slyly putting me through some kind of probation, as if to test me. She wanted to see whether I would behave myself and prove to be worthy of her. She deliberately called it a probation and it lasted weeks. She was clicking me off in the computer-brained folders of her psyche. I was sure she wanted me too. Perhaps it was true she had lain fallow for years, that she had survived the droughts and famines of her life, that she was now waiting dangerously to be ploughed up and seeded and fertilised. But she was holding on. Hanging in there. I felt we were both too old to pretend, that we did not need to follow any cardinal rules, that we could pass the litmus test of morality as long as we did not rob or envy or steal or maim, or do or wish anybody ill; that we could commit the lesser offences with reasonable impunity.

Our probation with the world was interminable. Night after night we took the world out for dinner and she ordered a shandy and a tuna sandwich while we knocked back lager after lager and wolfed down platefuls of cows' hooves. We would pay the bill and she would give the waiter a tip. At weekends we would order whiskies, then after several glasses we became incomprehensible and had to order a taxi home. We paid the fare and the world gave the driver a tip. Later on the world would agree to go upstairs for a cup of coffee. She took off her earrings and slipped out of her *gogo* shoes and wiped off her lipstick and eye-shadow and let down her hair and perched on the edge of the bed and chirped, 'Not quite yet, not quite yet.' She counted off on her fingers our crimes and shortcomings and reproached us but we did not listen. She said, 'Stop giving ex-combatants grants,' but we did not listen. She said, 'Stop subsidising commodities,' but we did not listen. She said, 'Stop controlling prices,' but we did not listen. She said, 'Devalue your currency,' but we did not listen. She said, 'Stop tampering with the land,' but we did not listen. She said, 'Stop grabbing farms,' but we did not listen. She said, 'OK, reimburse the white farmers you kicked out,' and we said, 'No, you do that. They are your offspring; your kind. Great-grandchildren of red-necked boys who called themselves policemen and armed themselves with rifles and rode shamelessly into our villages at dawn and planted the Union Jack and each earned themselves miles of savanna from some dainty little woman called Queen Victoria. You give us money to buy them out.' She said, 'But we've already given you the money for that,' and we said, 'Peanuts!' She said, 'You squandered that money. And there already is lots of government land lying unused,' and we said, 'Nonsense.' She said, 'But you've got to look at things differently. This is not the twentieth century any more. You can't go on flogging the colonial horse. The colonial horse is dead. You've got to find yourselves new horses, new mules. You've got to survive. You've got to change your ideas. You can't go on excusing your corruption and inexperience forever, and persecuting each other. You've got to have the rule of law.'

We were confused. We did not speak with one voice. Some of us said, 'Leave the white farmers alone,' and others said 'No way!' Some of us said, 'Don't destroy the soul of this land, the farming industry, the economy – don't turn this gem of a country into a land of peasants,' and others replied, 'Better be poor on your own land than be slaves forever.' In the towns sleek residents clicked their tongues in disapproval. In the country tottering grandmothers and grandfathers and newly reformed rustics rejoiced at the pieces of their ancestral land that were restored to them, at the little seed packs, thrifty bags of fertilisers and itinerant tractors that were availed to them. In disbelief they partitioned pastureland, dairy fields and miles of tobacco. They put up little pole and dagga huts and tilled the land with cattle and donkeys and iron ploughs. Other new farmers came purely out of greed – veritable new settlers, with not an iota of the farming instinct in their veins. Some ex-combatants and chefs were among that lot. They bullied peasants out of furnished farmhouses and barns and eyed rich valleys and well developed properties the way pot-bellied, cigar-smoking, inebriated businessmen eye virgins selling snacks outside beerhalls. Aggrieved white farmers packed up and abandoned their houses and lands to seek refuge in city flats or hotels or neighbouring countries. Highways and country roads were littered with tractors, harvesters and irrigation equipment, abandoned, pillaged or lined up for sale. The borders of chiefdoms were expanded and redefined – unwary chiefs suddenly found themselves in a quandary as their chiefdoms suddenly shrank or expanded, some of their subjects dispersed and some became victims of new ever-changing laws. The world did not speak with one voice either. It quarreled with itself. Some voices pleaded, 'Leave this little country alone,' and the most strident among the other lot shrilled, 'No, this precedent is bad for the world, a prescription for chaos and disrespect for the rule of law. This country must be stopped at all costs – punished, humiliated, isolated, starved and squeezed until it goes down on its knees and accepts defeat.'

Rudo lies on her back on top of the sheets, spent, nursing her new dilemma. Her hair is damp, her forehead laced with sweat, her eyes blank and her mouth half open. She is half facing me, with one arm thrown in wild abandonment over my chest. My heart is slowing and stilling; I am almost numb, pervaded by a deep sense of emptiness and loss. Our clothes are strewn all over the red-carpeted floor; her elegant clock clucks three on the wall. In the adjacent bedroom little Tariro coughs and moans in her sleep.

There is something ambivalent about conquests and defeats. Something innately sad.

'You never talk about your wife,' Rudo smiles, weakly.

I don't answer. Some pain is beyond words. I am stripped of all my defences. Rudo continues, 'Why don't you just divorce her if she doesn't make you happy? It's bad for you both and it's bad for your children. Many people like you suffer because they don't opt out, because they live their lives for other people, for their parents or children or neighbours and the like. Why don't you go and get yourself a hot-blooded young lass from the high-density areas – the kind with O-levels who work as typists and will serve you fried lizard tails to soften up your brain?'

'Suppose I've already had one?'

'Have you? What was her name?'

'Nontokozo.'

'What was she like? What does she do?'

'Never mind. Just don't talk badly about other women. Don't look down on other women because of their class or education or whatever. Never ever ever''

'Does it bother you so much?'

'What about you?' I croak back. 'Who are you living for?'

'Myself.'

'Are you using me?'

'No.'

'Do you want me to marry you?'

'Of course not.'

'Is it friendship you want, then?'

'Maybe.'

'Are you a feminist?'

'Maybe. Maybe not. I was never a textbook person. I never blindly believed in any "isms". And besides, who says a feminist doesn't need a good lay?'

We never truly believed in any 'isms'. We were born capitalists, raised capitalists; we lived with racism; we flirted with Marxism; we heard about humanism and *hunhuism*, we briefly espoused socialism, in lecture theatres we even dabbled with feminism and classism and ageism and now we are squashed again with the capitalists. Full circle. Perhaps the only 'isms' we truly knew were chauvinism and sexism. Maybe one day the good old world will agree to knock back several lagers and scuds and wolf down a few cows' hooves for an aphrodisiac and agree to go home with us and she will take off her earrings and rip off her wig and slip out of her *gogo* shoes and wipe off her lipstick and eye-shadow and, lo and behold, slip out of her bra-less, pant-less dress and tuck herself into bed with us and she will dream us up a brand new 'ism'. For *bitter* or worse, till death do us part, as Clopas Wandai J. Tichafa wrote.

Rudo and I did not part easily. Oh no, she didn't die. Not yet anyway. On the contrary, she started showing me off to her friends. She started saying, 'Let's go and see so and so.' Or, 'Let's go out with so and so.' Or she would say, 'Tariro is lonely. Why don't we take her out to meet her cousins?' She introduced me to people as her friend, which was fair enough, but there was always a question hovering over our relationship. People knew I was attached, that what I had going on with her could at best be described as an affair. But sooner or later we would have to come to terms with ourselves, with each other. She had a special friend that she liked, a beautiful nurse called Jean. Jean was pregnant, expecting a baby – her second – anytime. Jean was our age, perhaps a bit younger, and I thought she was taking a big gamble having a baby. Perhaps the baby was an accident, or she had done it willingly. She said the man had run off somewhere or other. I didn't ask. I couldn't ask. There are things you don't ask. We went out together, Rudo and Jean and I, and had drinks and she made us a delicious pot of oxtail, tripe and intestines. We listened to rumba and jazz and talked. I asked Jean if it was OK for the baby if she drank wine and she said, 'No problem. You can't live by the book all the time. After all, rules are meant to be broken.' I wanted to believe her. After all, she was a nurse. The wanted, hunted kind who were fleeing our ramshackle clinics and flocking out to the world to work in lavish, well-lit hospitals. I liked Jean. She was a survivor. She laughed a lot, a tinkling little laugh. She and I created a wicked camaraderie and we fenced Rudo in with it, into our circle. She wanted Rudo to be happy. She nursed Rudo out of her loneliness. She had small features, a kind of quick precariousness. I knew what she would be like once she delivered the baby. She was going to have a Caesar. I did not ask why she was going to have one when she looked so healthy. I couldn't ask. There are things you don't ask. Rudo glowed with pride. She was happy to have me, to have Jean. To have friends.

After the thorny land business, we quickly lost our friends. One by one they packed their bags and left, most without saying goodbye. We woke up in the morning and found their houses and offices empty and their doors and windows wide open. There was rubbish on the unswept floors, cracked windows in the bathrooms and some of the toilets did not flush. We wrenched out their drawers and found condoms. We flung open their cupboards and found only paper clips and pins. We raided their kitchenettes and found remnants of mouldering meals. We rummaged through their trashcans for valuables and found useless coins. The world phoned back long-distance with a crackling voice and said, 'Look, you little truant, just say you are sorry and we will come back,' and we sulked. The world said, 'Look, we want to come back and play with you. We'll give you back your marbles and bring you many more. We'll give you liquorice and candy and cake and teddy bears,' and we sulked some more. The world said, 'Now you are going to be really sorry.'

Now we were really sorry. The banks ran dry. We queued helplessly for cash that wasn't there. The industrialists went off to visit our neighbours. We ran out of foreign exchange. Our friends said, 'Enough is enough. You are a bad friend. You don't pay your debts. Now we can't give you any more fuel. Now we can't give you any more food,' and we cried, 'We'll give you half our estates – we'll mortgage them to you,' and they said, 'OK, but that's not enough.' We ran around borrowing. Borrowing and borrowing. Borrowing from other friends. Borrowing from ourselves. We borrowed and borrowed until we borrowed the word borrow. Now we were really, really, sorry. We had no power. We had no electricity; aeons of coal lay unmined beneath our trees and rocks and mountains. Our own spirits, Chaminuka and Nehanda, sulked and turned against us. They said, 'No more rain, kids.' For years in a row we had no rain. It was the worst drought in memory. Crops wilted in the fields. Rivers ran dry. Cattle tore down the thatch off roofs and chased women carrying empty buckets. Baboons invaded households and grabbed live chickens. Animals died in the plains. We had no food to eat. Our shops were bare. Our granaries sneezed dust. We turned to Chaminuka and Nehanda and said, 'But what have we done? How can we have a drought now, when we have other problems?' Chaminuka and Nehanda sulked. Chaminuka caressed the knob of his staff and looked away from us, towards the distant hills. Nehanda picked the threads off her cloth and said, 'You know what you did.' We said, 'We don't understand. Please explain,' and she said, 'You are too young to know. One day you will know.' Now we had no water to drink. Our dams filled with sand. Our taps ran dry. We stood in queues in the scorching sun, taking turns to suck the greenish water trickling from rusty taps. We dug wells in our backyards. Our toilets leaked into our wells. We got sick. We went to empty hospitals. There were no beds. There were no medicines. There were no nurses. The nurses had run off to lavish, well-lit hospitals in foreign lands. There were a few doctors who spoke a funny language. Prices doubled every month. There were massive retrenchments. We turned to strikes, stayaways and go-slows. We printed more and more money.

Rudo did not have much money. She had only seemed to have much money. She did not worship money, really. She was a civil servant, a poor struggling servant, a widow in her early forties, but she was content with what she had. She wanted something more than money, something she could not define, or was not prepared to define. She wanted to share her time, her miseries, herself with somebody else. She did not want my money, really. She wanted something else from me. Or so I thought. But we sometimes talked about money. Money, money, money. Like when I couldn't buy Tariro a jumbo-size pizza because the price had doubled overnight. Like when she showed me her latest salary slip with nothing on it but deductions. Like when she showed me her monthly medical-aid bills. Like when she told me she had to see three specialists every month. Like when she told me, out of the blue, out of the very, very blue, out of the bluest of blues, that she was a chronic manic-depressive. Like when she told me she had taken herself off medication because it was too expensive, and addictive. Like when she told me she had turned to yoga and meditation to get to sleep. Like when she told me she had a brain tumour for which she would have to be operated on outside the country. Like when she told me her Mazda needed a complete overhaul. Like when she showed me papers from the Salary Service Bureau detailing the paltry amounts she would get if she took an early retirement package for health reasons. Like her plans to buy a stand, or rent a stall at a flea market, or even purchase a hammer mill to grind maize if she got that precious package. Like when she asked me if we could take Jean out to comfort her after her miscarriage.

I did not know how to help her. I was impotent before her wishes. If she had asked to borrow money I could have considered helping her, very much against my better instincts, I suppose, but she never asked. Not directly anyway. Perhaps the word 'borrow' did not exist in her vocabulary, or had once existed, and long ago expired. Perhaps she had already borrowed the word borrow.

Last Wednesday I was in the petrol queue all day. I phoned the garage and they told me they might have something that day and when I rushed out there I found a kilometre-long stretch of cars waiting. It was six in the morning. I was hungry and unwashed and hastily dressed. The queue snaked round three street corners and at the mouth of the garage it split into four columns of cars. The diesel queue, the trucks and kombis and buses and lorries, wound in from the opposite direction. They had camped for two days in the queue, waiting. There was pandemonium at the garage. The road was blocked. The garage attendant and security men were battling with a rush of blaring cars. A policeman was negotiating with a ring of enraged drivers. This garage usually received petrol every day but for the past few days it had had nothing. Petrol, no diesel; diesel, no petrol. It was always like that. Alternating. If you had one then you didn't have the other. I made a U-turn and parked behind the last car in the queue. The queue was not moving. I did not go to work. It was no use going to work when you did not know if you could get there and how you would come back. Somebody in our lift club had taken my children to school and I just had to find the fuel to go and pick them up and bring them back. I got out of the car and talked to other men under the trees. We talked about garages that sold petrol to selected customers at night. We talked about backstreet boys who sold the stuff at ten times the official price. We talked about cars or households that had gone up in flames when unwary hoarders lit cigarettes or candles in makeshift store rooms. We talked about ailing wives; about children who go to fancy schools and talk with funny accents and refuse to cook for their daddies; about newly elevated company directors who stashed away billions. We talked about mushrooming churches that made fortunes from unsuspecting millions. We talked about the drought. We talked about new farmers who won prizes growing wheat and winter maize.

We talked about others who stole irrigation pipes and fencing wire and tried to sell them off. We talked about price freezes. We talked about hoarding. We talked about houses in the townships where one could buy, at five or six times the normal price, unlimited supplies of bread, sugar, maize, mealie-meal, salt and cooking oil without having to join the queue. We talked about queues at the banks, in the supermarkets, in the pubs, at the bus stops, at the mortuaries, at the cemeteries. We talked about people stumbling like zombies, waking up at three in the morning to get to work and getting home at midnight. People turning into alcoholics to survive each and every day. We talked about catastrophes on the highways, of smashed up designer cars, of busloads of students burnt to ashes on the roads, of overturned trucks and mangled trains; the foul breath of unappeased departed souls prowling the air. We talked about men who now deserted their wives for days and slept with their girlfriends on the pretext that they were in the petrol queue. We talked about crime and divorce. We talked about AIDS.

We argued about elections.

'Our case is beyond politics,' said one resident drunk. 'We need some kind of supernatural intervention.'

The woman in the twin-cab behind me heard us and smiled and vaguely nodded us on. She threw her head back over the seat and tried to sleep. It was hot. I bought two pink freezits from a vendor and offered her one and she said 'Thank you' and sucked on it and tried to go back to sleep. I wanted to talk to her, but I don't think she had had breakfast. There were cases of cosmetics in the cab. I wondered if she was a shop owner or a sales lady. Or a border jumper.

At four o'clock Rudo phoned me on my cellphone to ask me where I was. She said she had tried to get me all day but as usual the network was jammed. She said she had not phoned me at home because I had told her not to. The other day when my phone was dead she had decided to burn up precious juice and driven right up to my gate and hooted me out to give me a brand new shirt for a Valentine present. I had reluctantly accepted it and thanked her but told her not come to my house again. The gardener and the maid could see her. My children could see her. Besides, I didn't care a hoot for Valentine's

Day and Christmas and New Year's Day and Independence Day and the like. I was too old for that. Holidays depressed me. I told her she must stop leaving messages for me at home, or else. And now she was saying the doctor's results had come and she would have to be operated on in three weeks. She was saying her psychiatrist had said she must go back on anti-depressants. She was asking – what was I doing in the queue? How long was it? Was I bored? Who was that young girl at the bakery I had said could keep bread for her? Did I want two litres of cooking oil? How long was this petrol queue? Was it moving? Had there been any delivery yet or were we just waiting? Could she come and keep me company in the queue? Talk to me? Bring me some beers? Tell me about her retirement package? About her operation? About the anti-depressants that bloated up her body and made her numb? About Tariro? Did I think she should send Tariro to boarding school? Would she then be lonely? Could we talk about Jean's recent miscarriage? About myself?

I told Rudo not to come. I did not want her to come. She was wearing me down with her miseries. The last thing I wanted was somebody wearing me down. I didn't like the way she went on about Nontokozo and the hot-blooded, high-density lasses with five borderline O-levels and typing certificates who were supposedly dying to serve me fried lizards' tails to soften my brain. Rudo offered me new possibilities, but I didn't like the way she was crowding me into the little corner of her snobbishness and prejudice. By the time the tanker arrived, at seven in the evening it was too late anyway, and she would be preparing dinner for Tariro.

When the tanker arrived, people banged out of their cars and scrambled up from the kerbs to gather along the fence of the garage. A young man rode down past the fence and nonchalantly shouted, 'Diesel only! Diesel only!' A hubbub went up. Was it diesel? Was it petrol? Was it both? Surely it must be diesel because the last delivery had been petrol! No, but this green tanker had two compartments, one for diesel and one for petrol! But was it big enough for that? No, it wasn't. Yes, it was! But how was that possible? Didn't the two fuels mix? Oh, but didn't you know the tanker had two divisions inside? Didn't you know the green tankers had divisions inside? All right, but how much were they delivering? Four thousand, five thousand litres?

And look at the queue! Two hundred cars at the very least. Would the delivery be enough for all the cars? Would they give full tanks or half, or only twenty litres perhaps? Would they serve until the fuel ran out or would they send the customers away at closing time and tell them to come again tomorrow? Were garages governed by closing times anymore? And this garage was lucky, wasn't it? Getting deliveries when others went for weeks without anything. Look, the attendant is dipping his stick into the two tanks and they should be serving within an hour or two. Come, guys. Get into your cars and close off all the gaps. Order, patience, people. We'll all get served. Patience please. Gosh, I wish they would issue us tickets so we know who gets served and who doesn't, so those who won't get served don't have to waste their time in the queue. Now look, those stupid kombi drivers are jumping the queue and jamming the entrance and mobbing the policeman! God please no …

I got served at ten to eight – the day's ration of twenty litres, which would last me three days, but it was better than nothing. I threw money at the attendant, swerved away from the pump, thrust my car in front of a blaring bus, waved back the incredulous driver and inched out past the wall of kombis, into the fresh air. When I got to the school, at eight, the kids were waiting, sitting patiently in the dark, clutching their bags under the trees in the deserted yard. No one said a word as we drove home.

Now I know, Rudo.
I have been queuing up all my life.
I have been sleeping in endless queues, yawning in the tired mornings of my dreams; unwashed and hastily dressed, and naked to abuse; hungry for friendship and tolerance and thirsty for intelligence and respect. I have U-turned into lots of queues, many a wrong queue, only to be told at the crammed garages of my fantasies that I am in the wrong lane, or to be turned away. I have idled in snail-paced queues, burning up my precious juice, only to be sent away with a quarter of my fill. I have waved away kindness and trapped myself among the kombis of my own selfishness …
I'm sorry, Rudo …

(i)

Independence – Before and Between

2

Fancy Dress

Alexandra Fuller

My mother dressed me up as 'I Never Promised You a Rose Garden' for a Fancy Dress party at the de Wet's farm. Being a closet-lover of Barbie dolls, fairy princesses and high-heel shoes, I had been lobbying hard to attend the fancy dress attired in something pink and frilly.

'But, you don't even like dresses,' my mother told me.

'Yes, but how can I dress up as a Rose Garden?' I argued. 'Nobody can be a Rose Garden.'

'No, no. That's just the point, Alison. You're *not* a Rose Garden. "I *Never* Promised You A Rose Garden."'

'But why?' I wailed.

'It's your song. It's what was playing on the radio when you were born.'

'That's even *worser*. How can I dress up as a song?'

'*Worse*,' said my mother, 'that's even *worse*.'

Tears pricked the back of my eyelids but I could not let them spill. My mother resented tearful children whom she usually treated with a sharp smack, 'To give you something *real* to cry about.'

'How come Veronica gets to be a princess?'

'Because the tutu that the Viljoens gave us fits her and it doesn't fit you *and* she has long hair.'

Veronica smirked. My hair had recently been chopped to within an inch of its life. Now it stood in uneven bristles.

Mum stripped me down to my brookies. 'Now stand still,' she warned me. She wired a cardboard rose (depicted as wilting and clearly on its way to death) onto my head and then lowered a drum, which had until moments earlier contained pesticide, onto my shoulders. The drum smelt stinging and deadly. 'Hold onto the drum while I find a way to attach it to you,' Mum said.

I clutched the drum. Veronica ducked behind my mother and mouthed, 'Ha! Ha!'

'Veronica's teasing me!' I wailed.

'Stop that both of you, or I'll give you both a jolly good hiding.'

'No one's going to know what I am,' I protested.

'Yes they will. Look. It's written all over the drum.'

'But I am not supposed to be *Pesticide*,' I said, peering over the edge of my imprisoning outfit at the skull and cross-bones with which it was decorated. 'Nobody will *understand*. How will anyone guess that I am supposed to be *not* a Rose Garden?'

'The clever ones might guess,' said Mum. 'I think it's really very witty.'

I sagged inside my poisonous box. We lived in the Burma Valley, in the far eastern crease of a hollow on the very edge of Rhodesia in 1977. Nobody clever lived here. The clever people lived in cities and towns far away from terrorists and landmines. Clever people did not scrape together a living on remote farms in the middle of a War. They lived in real houses that had running water and electricity and some of them even had television.

The horse boy, the cook-a-boy and the nanny had to wrestle me into the back of the Land Rover. Only the front half of the vehicle was mine-proofed, and I was in the back half. I pointed this out to Mum. 'If we go over a landmine, you and Veronica will live and I will get blown to pieces.'

'Oh, stop making a fuss, Alison,' said Mum, and after that we couldn't talk until we got to the de Wets because the Land Rover shrieked and roared and rattled and, in a general way, contributed to the future loss of hearing of all who rode in her for any length of time.

Strapped into the cardboard pesticide container, I was forced to stand up, knees bent, all the way to the party while Veronica blocked my view out of the front window with her gold-painted crown made of Pronutro cereal boxes and her frothing pink tutu. I seethed and sweated and itched and glared at the back of my mother's head. I even hoped, in a self-pitying way, for a landmine. That would show them. When I was hung up like biltong drying in the sun from all the bushes and trees on the side of the road, then they'd be sorry.

But nothing happened to release me from my mother's overactive imagination. We trundled on without mishap and I was still Alison encased in a pesticide container and Veronica was still smug in her princess outfit.

I had some difficulty getting out of the car at the de Wet's house. Their dogs growled at me and had to be locked away before I could be retrieved from the back of the Land Rover by their cook-a-boy, Tickie. I tottered unhappily toward the front lawn where the mothers were sipping tea and the other children were parading in a circle waiting for the winner of the best costume to be announced. The sweat, which had begun to steam up from my armpits and belly, seemed to be having a chemical reaction with the pesticide residue and I was emitting a powerfully polluting odour.

The other children were adorable, as elves and pixies and cowboys and soldiers.

'What are you?' they hissed at me.

'Stupid,' I replied. 'Can't you tell? I'm *not* a Rose Garden.'

'What?'

'If you were clever,' I said, fighting back the urge to collapse in a heap of tears, 'you would understand what I was.'

Natalie de Wet won the Fancy Dress competition (dressed as an angel) and Fiona Johns was second (dressed as an actual, blooming, healthy sunflower) and Marc Hyde (as a Red Indian) came third. Prizes were awarded: South African pens and pencils, South African chocolates and South African erasers in the shape of strawberries or oranges that smelt as if they should be eaten. I shrank with disappointment. My sister and I were, of all the children present, least likely to have access to anything from South Africa because my father had said, 'The problem with South Africa is that it's full of bloody Afrikaners,' and had refused to take my sister and me on holiday to Durban-by-the-sea; instead we had to go fishing in Inyanga where there was no chance of running into a bunch of bloody Afrikaners but a reasonably good chance of running into a terrorist ambush.

Sally de Wet, who was the bloody Afrikaner responsible for the fabulous Fancy Dress prizes, emerged from the shadows of the veranda. Her first gin and tonic had given her mouth a wet, lopsided look that I knew (even without *really* knowing it) was sad-sexy and lonely and was a prelude to tears-before-bed. She was a beautiful woman shoved down here among the insects and the heat and with a dearth of attractive men. Which didn't mean she had given up – not like the other women who had resigned themselves to post-baby bulges below the tightening bands of their homemade skirts.

Sally wore a false bun on the top of her head; an arrangement of clip-on brown balls of fake hair that reminded me of a pile of fresh, shiny horseshit. She wore clingy nylon skirts with slits up the thigh and slick-on-skin shirts that gaped showing flat, brown breasts and large purple nipples. She walked in a way that suggested that she could always unhinge her hips, if she liked. It was a walk that repulsed children ('These hips are too busy,' they seemed to say, 'go away and play!') but I saw the husbands watching her slyly from behind blue threads of cigarette smoke. Now she clapped her hand against her thigh and tossed her head so that the horseshit bun threatened to dislodge, 'Okay, children, you can all swim now. Come on, come on. Last one in is a cowardy custard!'

The other children stripped down to their brookies or under-rods and flung themselves into the swimming pool – small, muscled, sun-smoothed bodies as lithe as fish in the pale, haze-filtered afternoon sun. When I, on the other hand, was eventually freed from my fancy dress, my very white skin had erupted in an unattractive pattern of pink welts.

'Alison has leprosy. Ha! Ha!' the other children shrieked. They told me I could not get into the swimming pool with them, 'Because you'll give it to all of us.'

I glanced back at the mothers for help. They were shaded on the veranda into indistinct lumps of indifferent maternity. They had abandoned the tea tray for the cocktail trolley some time ago and their voices were starting to rise with the kind of excitement that meant the kids could bleed to death before we would get their attention again.

'Alison has lep-ro-sy,' the children sang, splashing me.

I slouched away from the pool quickly, past the old frangipani tree where Natalie and I (one victorious afternoon a long time ago) had found a boomslang and past the veranda with its distracted mothers, to the back of the house where the de Wet's nanny was doing the washing. As I approached her, I covered my bare, splotched belly with my hands, so that she would not see my leprosy and send me further into exile (although where could be further into exile than this, I could not imagine).

'Hello, Picannin Madam,' said the nanny when she saw me. She was swishing the de Wet's clothes around in a milky mixture of steaming water and soap in a large bath of peeled enamel overlooking the massive storm drain that separated the house from the tobacco barns. The clothes twisted and spun under her hands as she pounded them against the edge of the bath. She rocked with every thrust, as I had seen the women do when they pounded mealies or stirred their sadza porridge and the sound was always like a drum, thunka-thunk. Then she stood up on tiptoe and clipped the clothes to the line that stretched past the kitchen to the top of the security fence. The de Wet's old, scabby ridgeback was lying under the dripping clothes with his eyes half-closed, feeling the plip, plip, plip of the warm water on his sore-crusted back.

Mum had said, 'Bloody Afrikaners never take care of their dogs. They're worse than the *munts* half the time.'

'White *munts*,' said Dad. 'That's all they are. Bloody Afrikaners – white *munts*.' Once Dad had got us all thrown out of a hotel in Salisbury for calling the Greek manager a Mediterranean *munt*. So I guessed, although I couldn't be sure, that the only way to escape being a *munt* was to be like our family. Pukka British with inherited silver for the servants to steal and with old prints of horses chasing foxes on the walls (even though the prints had long ago lost the glass from their frames and had been stained by rain-through-the-roof and rat pee).

'Where's Tickie? Where's the garden boy?' I asked.

The nanny straightened up and arched her back against the ache of her labour (when she wiped the sweat from her nose, she left a crooked mustache of bubbles across her lip). 'Tickie is inside,' she said, 'the garden boy has knocked off for the day.'

'Good.' I slunk down on my haunches and wrapped my arms around my knees.

'Do you want for something from them, picannin Madam?'

I scowled up at the nanny and shook my head. I had been afraid that, without my pesticide-container cover, Tickie or the garden boy would see my small, flat breasts. Mosquito bites, we called them, when they were flat like this with hard, aching centers. I had been told by Natalie de Wet that even the slightest glance of a girl's breasts, however flat, might incite the 'Affies' to dreadful, barbaric acts too gruesome to detail. I wondered how the Affies managed to contain themselves with Sally de Wet around since she was always on the verge of slithering out of her clothes altogether, let alone revealing a passing glimpse of bare boobies. It must take up all their energy, I thought. No wonder they were so lazy and had to be shouted at all the time, 'Stop loafing, you boys!'

The nanny smiled at me, 'What is your name?'

Instead of answering, I stared carelessly off toward the barns and hummed to myself until she went back to her laundry. Immediately, I regretted the loss of her attention although I tried to distance myself from my need for her. I watched ants scuttle across the patted-damp red earth with tiny morsels of white soap in their mandibles, their antennae waving in gestures of panic as if there had been a dreadful ant emergency somewhere nearby. I could hear the other children shouting and splashing in the pool from the front of the house. When I thought that *they* were not having to entertain themselves watching ants, the end of my nose grew heavy and tickling with threatening tears and a sob bubbled up from the bottom of my throat and burped out of me before I could stop it.

'Ah Madam.' The maid shook the spare water off her hands and arms and came to me. She crouched down in front of me and her arms went over my legs, slithering with wet and soap. 'What is the matter?' she asked. Her breath was fresh and green with the stalks of grass she chewed and her hair smelt of Vaseline.

I longed, in my anger and resentment, to shove her away from me. To slap her or kick her or to say, 'Don't touch me.' Instead I said, 'Look,' and I uncurled myself to show her my welts.

'Ah, *ndine tsitsi*, picannin Madam,' said the maid.

'Speak English!' I shouted.

The maid said, without losing her soft sing-songing voice, 'Sorry, sorry. I am sorry for you, Madam.' She picked me up from the armpits and dangled me out in front inspecting my belly. 'What has happened to you?'

'Some poisonous *muti*,' I said, feeling in her powerful hands like a rag doll, 'it got onto my skin.'

'Ah, ah, ah. Why?'

I was crying hard now, in the face of this sympathetic ear. The maid dropped me back on the earth and she gave my stomach an experimental pat.

'Owie,' I shrieked, although the touch had been soothing to my itchy skin.

'Why did they put some *muti* on you to do this? Who would do this?'

'My mother did it.'

The maid laughed to show her disbelief.

'She did, I promise.'

'Then we must wash it off,' said the maid, although she still looked at me in a crooked way to show that she knew I was lying. 'Step up in the bath. Look, nice warm water for you.' Before I could argue, the maid had plunged me into the bath, empty now of de Wet laundry, but scummy and thick with soap. She sloshed water up my back and neck. 'Washing back,' she sang, 'washing belly, washing feet – they not be smelly. Washing face, and washing nose, washing bottom, washing toes. Wash all over, make a wish,' and giving me a friendly spank on the stomach, 'like a slap on the belly with a big, wet fish.' I looked up at the wide, blue sky above the maid's head and laughed and squirmed in her hands so that she might be tempted to slap my belly again.

At that moment Sally de Wet appeared from the kitchen with her horse-*kaka* hair and her wide-swinging hips and her gin-wet lips and she said, in her bloody Afrikaans voice, 'What the hell do you think you're doing in my washing?'

And I said, 'The nanny put me in here.'

The nanny let go of me, as if I had unexpectedly bitten her, and backed away from the bath where I floated, bobbing up in the soapy white water like a massive slithering cork. For a dreadful few seconds Sally de Wet glared from the maid to me and back again to the maid, as if deciding upon whom to unleash the full force of her fury. She settled on the maid.

'What the hell do you think you're doing?' she screamed. 'I could fire you! I could fire you! Why did you put that child in with my washing? *Sis*, man! *Sis*! Don't you have any sense? Hey? Where's your sense? Now the clothes will be dirty again.'

The maid's mouth grew sullen.

I said, 'But Mrs. De Wet, the washing is all done. Look, it's hanging up.'

'My God, child,' said Mrs. De Wet, snatching at my greasy arm, 'you come with me and put some clothes on. I don't know what your mother will say. My God. What if Tickie had seen you? Hey, hey? Or the boys at the tobacco barns. Think of it? What would they think?' Then she lowered her voice and clutched both my shoulders and turned me towards her. Now her mouth, warm and sour with gin, was very close to my nose, 'They're not like us, you understand? You understand? You don't just bath out here in the open where any Affie can see you.' She shook her head, 'You Poms have no idea, do you?'

I could see over Sally de Wet's shoulder to the maid. I tried to smile an apology to her, but my mouth was too confused to make any shape.

Besides, the maid had closed her face to me. Sally de Wet tugged me harshly by the hand. 'Come with me,' she said, and although she did not say where we were going, I knew it was to the place of far, *far* exile. From now on, I would be beyond the reach of the other children who were sure to find out about my unorthodox bath, and beyond the reach of my mother who would never forgive me for humiliating her, and beyond the reach of my sister who would say, 'Why can't you just be normal?' and beyond the reach of the de Wet's nanny who would never risk helping me again. Now I was on my own and when I knew this I stuck out my worm-swollen belly with its welted skin and I tugged disobediently against Sally de Wet's hand.

I said, 'My Dad says you're a bloody Afrikaner,' and then I waited for the sting of the slap that I knew was going to come.

Years later, I recognised that moment as the first truly African thing I ever did. It was the thing that made me change from a Pom to a *munt*. It was the moment when they started to say about me, 'What a waste of white skin.'

3

That Special Place

Freedom Nyamubaya

The light arrived like a sharp nail striking my left eye, after three days of not having seen the African sun or felt its mother warmth. I had just woken from a short sleep, after spending the whole night awake and singing to my soul. I remembered how I had arrived where I was, but not why I was there. I heard groans, coughs, sneezes, yawns – what felt like competing huffing and puffing from all directions. But nobody spoke except for the two people who were sitting outside guarding us.

I had only realised that we were being guarded some six hours earlier when I had wanted to go to the toilet. It felt like days since I had had this relief, but fortunately we'd been given nothing to eat or drink. Getting up and crossing the floor, even in the darkness, I did not want to be seen by the other comrades. My Afro hair had turned white, my face felt like a monkey's in a dusty field. My eyes were swollen. I had to struggle to force one open so that I could see where I was going. My java-print dress, which I had once been proud of, my face, arms and legs, were also covered in dust and grime. However, I rose and picked my way through the bodies. Why should I worry what people thought of me, they were asleep. But I did mind and only moved because it would have been worse to sit in my own urine in a hut.

'You are supposed to seek permission before you go anywhere!'

shouted one of the guards. 'This way,' said another whose name, Muchapera, literally means 'you will be finished off'. He took his wooden imitation AK rifle and escorted me to the toilet.

There were always people hanging around the toilet, even in the darkness, sometimes for reasons other than relieving themselves. Free discussion was not tolerated in public, and one of the few places that provided some privacy was the toilet. On other occasions, it provided a mildly safe haven from work or training if you wanted a break. So the toilet was actually an area where the only semi-liberated discussion took place. Nobody could stop you from going there, but sometimes this would only be permitted with the caution, 'Do your thing fast, I want you out in two minutes.'

I didn't know any of this then. However, the guard was hovering outside, and in that moment of comparative freedom, he told me that I was in prison. He said he felt badly about this as he came from my district, and pleaded with me to tell them that I was an enemy agent, or else they would make mince-meat of my buttocks. 'Nobody leaves this place without confessing,' he said. 'But whatever you do, don't say anything to anyone! You never saw me.' And that, indeed, was the last I saw of him. He had disappeared before I could respond to his statement.

***

When I finally opened my left eye in the watery daylight, I saw I was in the company of four men looking as dusty as I did. One of them later told me that when he arrived I was unconscious, and had been for hours. I did not remember anything, but I realised that I was a day behind in my counting.

It was about seven o'clock in the morning and the two guards were chatting away five metres from the entrance. A few sunrays filtered through the cracks in the grass walls of the hut. The door was a khaki sack that would have contained maize grain in normal circumstances. There was a four-inch gap between the ground and the sack, which swung to and fro as the wind blew in different directions. September, like August, was hot and windy at Tembwe Training Camp, in the remote areas of Tete Province in Mozambique. The smell of dry sand swept through the makeshift, loosely thatched hut. The faces of the four men were not wholly visible in the partial darkness, but I could see the misery on their faces. I tried to grin at each of them, but no one responded. I tried to examine them more closely – there was nothing else to do – but they quickly turned their faces away. They looked ghostly and frightening with their disfigured cheeks, lips, eyes and noses covered in grey dust.

One of them had a thick swollen sagging lower lip and a large swollen forehead that seemed to hang over his eyes, making him look like one of those long-distance cargo trucks with a raised sleeping cab. Another, who appeared to be the youngest, had eyes which, like mine, were heavily swollen. I could not tell whether he could see or not. He resembled one of those bullfrogs often found perching on rocks during the long summer months. I touched my own eyes, imagining that I must look like him, and then burst out laughing; we were two frogs, but I was sure I was the more beautiful. My laughter seemed to break the ice for, after a moment, everybody joined in, then the silence fell again.

***

The third man was the handsome one. He still looked good even with a nose like JoJo the Clown, the result of a one-sided boxing match with the security guard. The other prisoner kept his face turned from me: he seemed ready to pounce on anybody given the chance.

It was after nine when the Camp Security Commander came to visit us. He had a loud mouth, and never once do I remember him saying anything constructive or interesting. He used torturous language, and made vulgar jokes about the inmates. Vicious and cruel, he had not even completed his primary education when he was recruited into the liberation struggle. With nothing in terms of brain, he thrived on sadism and intimidation. Interrogation had to be accompanied by a slash on the buttocks with a whip or a slap on the face, but still he was called the Camp Security Commander. It was he who had to prove the innocence of every new arrival. Though it depended on his moods, which were erratic, you were deemed innocent if you were a man, and of his educational level or lower. If you were a woman, even if his intention was to sleep with you, he first had to fill you with fear; but if you were just a tiny bit more educated than he was, then you had to be thoroughly beaten. This made it easier for him to sexually assault you later, as he would say that he would throw you back in prison if you resisted. Since he was the man in charge, nobody, not even the Camp Commander, could challenge him.

***

It was the same man, Nyathi, who was later demoted from the front line, after several brave rural farmers complained that their women and children were being sexually abused in the base camps back at home. He took his revenge by defecting, and he later led a battalion of Rhodesian soldiers with armoured cars to massacre refugees at Nyadzonia, the unguarded refugee camp where he was known as a Commander.

***

On his arrival at the camp he blew the emergency whistle, which meant that everybody had to go immediately to the assembly point. Seeing the military trucks, most of them thought that at last Frelimo had provided transport to transfer them from the camp, in which they were bored, ill and starving, to another camp for military training. Nyathi waited until most people had made their way from the water points, the barrack construction area, cooking and cleaning tasks. An emergency whistle meant that even the sick had to get themselves to the parade ground.

Nyathi stood at the front, sloganeering and having some of the refugees sing revolutionary songs while waiting for everyone to arrive. Two latecomers ran straight past the armoured cars and immediately noticed that the men behind the wheels were whites who'd painted up, but forgotten the backs of their ears, which still showed a startling white. Bravely they ran on, right through the crowd shouting over Nyathi's voice. 'Run, run, run away, comrades! It's not Frelimo! It's the Rhodesians! Run away! Run away!'

Nyathi's response was to jump off the platform on which he was standing and instruct the Rhodesians to fire. People, *en masse*, were simply mown down, blood gushing from them like so many burst pipes. Among the strewn and bleeding bodies Nyathi observed a few who had begun to wriggle away from the mayhem on their bellies, and sadist that he was, he instructed the Rhodesians to drive their cars over the bodies so as to crush the survivors. The battalion moved in tandem, as if they were ploughing a field, crushing the dead and the living. Anyone who tried to run away got a bullet in his back. A woman who survived said she had rolled herself back to lie amongst those who'd been crushed, and covering herself with blood, lay and watched Nyathi and his Rhodesians complete their mission.

Of course the lucky ones ran into the bush as fast as they could. Many of them never returned to see what had happened. Those who survived often did so surrounded by the dead and wounded, terrified that if they were to stand up, they would be shot down. The woman I knew shouted for help the following day, after Frelimo had arrived.

***

Hearing Nyathi's voice, loud and strident, I recalled immediately how I had come to be in prison. When they arrived at a military camp, recruits were required to write a brief synopsis of their lives; if they couldn't write, they had to tell someone who would write it down for them. If you had made your own way, you had to explain why you had decided to join the struggle; if you had been recruited by the comrades and brought across the border into Mozambique, you generally escaped interrogation. The process was called 'three check ups', but I have never known what it meant. If the security commander was satisfied with your biography and explanation you would go free, but if not, or should he want you for other reasons, you found yourself in prison.

Nyathi had asked me to write my autobiography and give my reasons for deciding to join the liberation war. I asked him whether I should do this in English or Shona.

'Whatever,' he said. 'I am trained to read all kinds of languages through the word.'

I wrote down the story of my life, in Shona, innocent and excited.

I was one of three: there were two women with me who had been assisted across the Zambezi by a comrade. Without even looking at their papers, he told them that they were free to go and join the others at the barracks.

When it came to my turn he snatched my piece of paper from me, pretended to read it, and asked what grade I had done at school. I told him that I'd left in Form 3, a year before writing my O-levels, and he went crazy.

'You haven't written the truth,' he shouted, and knocked me onto his grass double bed. I saw stars in broad daylight. I was so shocked that I did not shed a tear but stared at him, my eyes wide like a zombie. 'Why would you leave school and all that comfort to come to place of suffering and dying?' He gave me no chance to answer, but slapped me eight times, first on one cheek then the other. Then he told me he was going to take me to Mbuya Nehanda, where the spirit medium would learn the truth. I knew all about Mbuya Nehanda, the spirit medium who was executed in Salisbury in 1898 for fighting against the colonisers. I was relieved – I felt frightened and hurt by Nyathi's anger and blows, which had come as such a shock. Little did I know that there was no spirit-medium, just a prison.

I followed Nyathi to his hut, which was empty. Fingers of fungus hung from the wood, suggesting that the place had been deserted for more than a few days. No Mbuya Nehanda, just a guy sitting five metres from the hut doing nothing. Nyathi had thrown me into the hut, where I sat doing nothing, and was not able to sleep. Tears had followed, when I remembered the eight serious claps on my cheeks, when all I thought I'd done was do what I was told – write my life history. The hut felt a long, long way from the liberation struggle of my dreams. Sounds of martial music came from a distance as the comrades marched to the kitchen for lunch. Food was scarce, good food didn't exist. Sadza was a delicacy, especially accompanied by real beans, not the bush beans we used to call *ndodzi*. Our main meal was maize grain boiled in salt, which made us thirsty, or just *ndodzi* in salt, or a mixture of *ndodzi* and *mangai*, boiled maize grains. But we prisoners always had food. One of the guards would go to the kitchen, jump the line and bring us our food; other companies might just be told: 'The food is finished,' before they had even been served. If they were lucky, they might get served first at the next meal.

There were two meals a day except for the commanders, commonly known as *chefs*, and sometimes they even had tea with *pao*, Mozambican bread. The commanders had a separate kitchen with different cooks. It was a privilege for your company to be on duty at the commanders' kitchen, for even if you were never chosen to cook, someone might sneak some leftovers into the barracks. I was never selected to cook in the *chefs*' kitchen, since I had been branded a suspect. They said those who had been interrogated and imprisoned as enemy suspects might poison the *chefs*. Paranoia was rampant, even then. Suspects did the hard tasks of fetching grass and poles for construction, digging toilets and weeding in the camp fields.

Food was a serious but interesting issue because of the tactics that people developed to try and obtain more. If you were caught, you were beaten until you called out all the names of the relatives you had left behind. Beating, however, did not stop anybody; there were even people who were known for their skill in acquiring extra food. There were a few Mozambicans in the surrounding villages, and people would sell their clothes, or clothes they had stolen from others, for a cob or two of maize, *pao*, tobacco or sadza. Very rarely we ate meat, and when a wild animal was killed, nobody ever asked what kind of an animal it was.

Singing and dancing formed part of our daily activities. We sang for food, when we were waiting for the *chef*, when somebody was being beaten, or when we were waiting for announcements. Music was a survival strategy, dancing kept our morale high. We sang and danced out our problems to avoid despair. There were of course times when one might take time to compose music, or sing with real joy; but mostly music was an outlet for our pain.

***

When Nyathi walked into the hut everybody suddenly became alert. He ordered the guard to bring him a small bench, so he could sit and talk to us. The sack door was raised and two other men came in with him. 'Yes, gentlemen and lady! Are you ready to tell us the truth now?' I lay on my side, my hands supporting my body since my buttocks were swollen from the previous beating, which had caused me to black out. 'E! – e! – e! – e! e! sit up properly, prostitute! Don't act funny here, I also know that you were bitching around with those Frelimo soldiers before you got to *batalio*!' shouted Nyathi. I had to sit upright and pretend I was not in pain, and that my body was not swollen.

'I have brought my two associates whose job it is to deal with any one of you who decides to waste my time,' said Nyathi as he picked his nose. 'I want each of you to narrate your story as it should be: no lies, no exaggeration and no withholdings. My name is Nyathi, the charging buffalo. I do my work as work.'

But before the first person could utter, a comrade came running over and told Nyathi that he was urgently wanted by the camp commander. He left, and the two men accompanied him. I knew it was not the end of our suffering, but it provided temporary relief. Moreover, his presence had helped to stimulate some communication among us. We started asking each other our names, and made jokes about the way in which our faces had been disfigured.

One of the men had nicknamed himself Che Guevara after the famous Bolivian freedom fighter who worked with Fidel Castro. He had been in his second year at the University of Rhodesia, and had been thrown out after a students' demonstration against the Smith regime. He had read about socialism and capitalism, and had a better understanding of general political issues in and outside Zimbabwe than any of us. Che whispered, 'You're the only woman here. When we were brought in, we thought you were dead because you were unconscious for such a long time. The security guard told us they had just done a good bashing, and warned us that if we didn't tell the truth the same would happen to us. Now listen carefully, Ticha, you have to create a story, otherwise they will pound you to mincemeat.'

'Have you created a story?' I croaked. He stared at me. I had lost my voice and could not remember how. I had cried a lot, but not out loud, so I wondered how my voice had gone missing.

The other prisoners listened carefully but none of them contributed. Che said he had been beaten enough, and could not take it any more.

'My parents never once slapped or pinched me. So to join the war and find my own comrades beating me for no good reason is more than I can take!' Che fell silent.

'Ticha, you must cook up a story and tell these guys that you were sent by the enemy, otherwise you will die in this small thatched hut.' I shook my head without saying anything. I still thought it was wrong to tell lies. 'Have you made up a story?' I asked hoarsely for a second time. Che just nodded his head, but did not explain what it was. I asked the others whether they would do the same, but they just stared at me like zombies. I could not tell whether they understood my question or not, but I knew that they heard what I said because they all looked at me.

Nyathi came back after lunch, and began by telling the guard that four men who had tried to slip back into Rhodesia had been caught and brought back to Tete by Frelimo vigilantes. He said they would be beaten until they passed out. Che looked at me as if to say, 'You see! I told you these people will kill if you don't do what they want.'

'All right! All of you sit up straight and receive your warm-up before we get into serious business!' shouted Nyathi as he sat back on the bench. 'Give each of them five strokes on the buttocks, Chombo. Take the bigger stick.' Chombo, his assistant, knew the procedure. We were not allowed to protect our bodies with our hands. If you did you would get an extra one. They said the party needed hands for carrying guns to shoot the enemy, and if you broke your hands you would become a burden that had to be carried by other freedom fighters.

Che was the last one to be beaten. After two strokes he shouted that he had something important to tell them so they should stop beating him. Nyathi instructed Chombo to stop, and even we, with pain still sinking slowly into our nervous systems, were forced to listen. The interrogation was not private. Chombo took a pen and paper and started taking notes. 'Speak it loud and clear. I don't want to keep saying, "What did you say?"' Nyathi said nastily.

Che began narrating his well-cooked story. 'My name is Che, and I was born in 1955 in Rusape. I was sent here to do some reconnaissance and see how the comrades are organised, where they stay, what they eat, how many there are and what kind of weapons they use. I belong to a party called CHARM, that means Communist Hurricane African

Revolutionary Movement, which is led by one black professor at the University of Rhodesia. We have over ten thousand soldiers with five thousand being trained in the Soviet Union, three thousand in Romania and two thousand in Cuba. So far none of the soldiers are yet in the country.' After this Che started crying. Tears just ran down his cheeks and could not stop. I didn't understand why he was crying, because we knew he was lying since there was no such party. 'Maybe he feels guilty about lying,' I thought, wondering how anyone could possibly believe in a party called CHARM. The more I thought about it, the funnier it seemed, and a sudden burst of laughter escaped from my body.

'Give her two strokes, Chombo. Take that scissors and make a cross through her hair from ear to ear and from her forehead to the back of her neck and then let's see if she thinks she is beautiful. Do you think you are anything special? What are you laughing at? Do you think this is a circus?'

'No! No! No, comrade, I am sorry, it just happened.' I still received the two extra strokes and a hairstyle with four portions; but Che was excused his beating although he was not allowed to return to barracks.

Che was in his second year at university. He understood something about communism, and certainly more than they did. He had been detained because he told them that he had been a university student. Naively he had thought that his literacy would be of use to the liberation army. Instead he suffered for it and never even rose to section commander.

***

Three days later the five of us, Che included, were taken before a parade of eight thousand people. We were told to stand on the platform and we each had to tell the comrades how we had been sent by the enemy to destroy them. Each one had to tell their own story and then ask for a pardon. I was lucky because I still had no voice, so Nyathi had to tell my story on my behalf. Since I had insisted that I was innocent, he told them that I was still under investigation but my other crime was that I had been going out with Frelimo soldiers in Tete. 'Instead of coming to fight for Zimbabwe, she came to sleep around with Frelimo. We are making examples of these people as we have done before, and will do again, because everyone is the eye of the party, so keep checking. Watch these people, and watch out for other spies and traitors.' From that moment I could not take the security department seriously. All I knew was that they hated anybody who had gone to school, and only felt comfortable with illiterate comrades.

Little did I know that only a month after I was released from prison, that same beast Nyathi would break his way into my vagina and escape with my virginity, though after fifteen minutes' fierce struggle I managed to spit out a piece of flesh from his right thigh. Nyathi had a big black penis whose erection got harder with resistance; little did I know that either. I was fifteen, and I cried as I felt blood run down my legs on my way back to the barracks in moonlight. For years my body reacted to the memory, and it was years before I felt whole again.

***

The last time I met Che, on the streets of Harare, I nearly cried. He recognised me, but nothing he said made sense, and I realised that he was mentally ill. I am sure it arose at that special place: the place that many people in this world will never know or understand.

(ii)

Gukurahundi

4

Torn Posters

Gugu Ndlovu

In 1984 I was too young to vote, yet that didn't stop me from performing my patriotic duty with razor-like precision. The early mornings were best for our raids. My small but fierce guerilla squad would trudge through Sanki's lucerne field, the dew dampening our brogans as we closed in on our unsuspecting targets. Crouching as we neared, not to be discovered by the sentinels, we waited. Watching for the right moment to strike. Just seeing 'PAMBERI NE ZANU PF' emblazoned on their bloody posters, we were engulfed by a bitter rage. It rose like bile in our throats erupting as earsplitting war-cries, roused us into action, and we ran screaming across the field with weapons raised to encounter the enemy.

We ripped into their flesh, stabbing and tearing at it, slashing their principles, punching holes in their policy. Each blow killing HIM and his fat greedy ministers. We surveyed the scene with arrogance. Damage Report: for me and my comrades, a few scratches, a splinter, scraped knees, an undone ribbon and some grass stains on our uniforms: mummy won't like that. The enemy was another matter – they lay indifferent, confettied at our feet.

Treason is punishable by death. Must hide the evidence! Drag the carcasses, stuff them into the anthills. A place where anything from aborted babies to bewitched panties ... disappeared forever. Swallowed whole by the earth.

This was our contribution to the elections, our duty to our country. However trivial it may have been, it filled us with an ironic sense of pride. Like the comrades we'd seen on TV, we lifted our fists and shouted, *'Amandla awethu!'* for the cameras. For now our mission is far from complete. School is still another two kilometres away, our hands stained with the hopelessness of the mutilated posters, our eyes peeled for more that carry the poisonous message.

***

News from distant realities far far away, trickled into our daily conversations. In the villages of Matabeleland: entire homesteads abandoned, pots still on the fires; huts set ablaze with sleeping families inside them; mass graves in abandoned mines; mothers stripped naked and forced to watch their children's throats slit; elderly women beaten, raped, and killed for their blankets. From what we were told, an unsettled group of Ndebele army men whom the government called 'dissidents', were plundering villages and killing their occupants.

'It's Him,' our father would say quietly, lighting a cigarette. 'He's killing us.'

Filling up his and Uncle Dan's glasses with more whisky, we could feel the tension in their bodies and voices. Uncle Dan was planning to leave for the UK. Apparently, these weren't dissidents, but soldiers employed by Him to disguise themselves as dissidents and kill the people of Matabeleland. (Many years later we found out that the army, consisting of approximately 20,000 soldiers, had been given orders to kill a minimum of 100 Matabele people each. The exact figure of how many were killed is still unknown.)

'That's where they start, the villages, I'm telling you Georgie he's coming for us next,' Uncle Dan would say after a couple of glasses.

'I can't run anywhere, Dan. How can you run away from home? From what's yours?' Daddy would say, opening his hands out.

'Would you rather he kill you?' Uncle Dan would ask, concerned at my father's stubbornness.

'Agh man he won't kill me – maybe arrest me, yes.' He would say taking a sip, then he'd turn to Uncle Dan to tell him what he always did. 'Dan, you're not a politician, you're not a soldier, you are a businessman, you know how to make money. So go to England and make money. Me, I'm a politician, this is a chess game. I can watch his moves … he's trying to make us angry at our people's expense, and he's doing a bloody damn good job of it; but as long as I'm alive he won't get his checkmate; maybe he'll get pieces, yes, but never checkmate.' Uncle Dan left for England. Our father stayed and continued his game.

Disguised soldiers' fires continued to light dark Matabele nights as they burnt villages. The cries of women and young girls also filled the night air as their bodies were violated. People's hearts were heavy with grief for their losses. That grief quickly mutated into a dark bitterness, as we all tried to make sense of it. As children we inherited that bitterness as a predisposition. Only after they came and took our fathers did it become truly ours.

***

In my dream, a large truck was trying to run me down. There was no one in the driver's seat. I was running, but I couldn't run fast enough. Mummy was standing on a hill calling my name. Her voice was getting closer and closer, and then I fell. Mummy called my name again. I opened my eyes to her concerned face.

'You have to get up, honey,' she said softly.

'It's too early,' I croaked sleepily.

'I know but we have to get up … get your shoes and come,' she said as she moved on towards my sisters' and my cousins' beds.

They came in the morning. Before the sun was up. There were a lot of us living at home then, seven of us kids, an uncle and our parents. My five-year-old brother, who'd been up for at least half an hour, came running into the room. He was holding his Lego spaceship, which he'd made the night before.

'There are huge trucks outside, guys,' he panted excitedly. 'And they've got real soldiers in them, with guns,' he added, obviously still intoxicated after seeing a dozen or more AK-47s. My heart sank to the bottom of the Zambezi River – they'd finally come for father.

A cock crowed ...

'Is Daddy here?' I wanted to know urgently.

'Yes, he's outside talking to *them*,' Mum said calmly.

'What do they want?'

'They want to know if we have any weapons, so we have to go and sit outside while they search the house,' my mother said, as she turned to wake up another small sleeping body. I cracked the front door ajar to get a peek of what was going on outside. It looked like an episode of the A-team, an action television series we'd once loved: two dozen or so armed soldiers, scattered amongst half a dozen army trucks of different shapes, sizes and purpose, burdened our front yard, imprisoning flower beds and small trees, digging large muddy skid marks across the lawn. Under a broken peach tree, in a far corner of the garden, Butho's tricycle was a mangled mess of metal. I walked out of the door, angry and ready to fight … I was only twelve, what did I know, but I had attitude.

We sat outside on the verandah as the sun came up, while they pillaged our home using our parents as guides. The dogs had been barking all night. Now, they sat around us panting, licking, sniffing and growling. Arrogant, bloodshot eyes gazed uninhibitedly at my budding breasts. We just smiled politely, even shyly, because we were still in our nightclothes, by far our favourites, Snoopy and Charlie Brown, that our Canadian grandmother had sent last Christmas; but even their cheerful happy cartoon faces couldn't soften the arrogant gaze. At least Thandi and Siphiwe were hidden behind the thick matching flannel pyjamas they had on.

A few cradled their AKs and tried to make friendly conversation, 'Wot grrede rr u en?' 'Wot es yowa nem?' Their English with a heavy

Shona accent felt like they were insulting us.

Then they piled back into their trucks and drove off, taking Daddy and Uncle with them.

We went back into the house, now empty with loss and heavy with sadness. Scattered papers, overturned mattresses, emptied closets, overturned furniture – clothes everywhere ... summoned tears that somehow wouldn't fall but turned into thorns that stuck in our throats.

Butho

Daddy said he's going to buy me a new bike, because the soldiers drove over my old one. Mummy says they are bad. Thandi was in a bad mood again. Because her egg was too soft. Gugu got angry and threw it in the dogs' dish and Mummy shouted because that really was a waste. It's boring when she shouts. These days she's always shouting. I wish Daddy was here, then she wouldn't shout. She needs all the National Geographics *in the house so she can take them with her. She's going to see Daddy. He's in jail (whisper). But he didn't do anything bad. Mummy said he said something the bad guys didn't like ... but not cursing, like FUCK or SHIT. Mummy says we aren't allowed to go and see him. Only she's allowed to visit. That's what 'they' (the bad guys) say. Themba and I played 'dissidents' today. He's my best friend. This time they were red ants, we killed them, every single one of them – squashed their heads off and chopped off their legs. They took Themba's Daddy too.*

Mummy

After endless letters and meetings about the abuse of our human rights, we finally got the okay for the kids to see George. Only I couldn't take all of them. It's only a small step, but I'm already exhausted, and we still have to get him out.

We took the night train up. The three girls shared the top bunks, which pulled out from a wooden panelled wall. Butho and I had the lower beds, which served as seats when we weren't sleeping.

Honestly! Can you believe that six years later the sheets

and blankets still have NRR (National Rhodesian Railways) imprinted on them? It's as if this government of vultures, holding court in their Victorian robes (with the white wigs), are nostalgic for the colonial era, only this time, they are in the driver's seat inflicting the pain.

We marvelled at the refined fitments of the compartment – a wash-basin that could also be a side table, ashtrays hidden in the arm rests, reading lights that were noticed in walls once the beds were pulled out. Although they generally didn't work, and probably hadn't since Independence, though they still looked functional to an innocent visitor – an ironic and glorified reminder of our colonial past. As a new country of only six years, most things of the colonial era had reached a stage of mechanical dysfunction but were still left in place. Their empty symbols littered and mostly cluttered our lives.

Thandi

We're on the way to visit Daddy. He's staying at Chikurubi Maximum Security Prison. It's a jail. Mummy says he's been there for thirteen months. That's a very long time. Because I'm in Grade 3 now, and Gugu had to give me her old tracksuit which doesn't fit her anymore. Siphiwe and Thembi couldn't come because they aren't Daddy's children, they had to stay home. Gugu said they put Daddy in jail for constipating against the govament. But I think she's lying, she doesn't know what she's talking about. She wouldn't let me bring my Dada (that's my best blanket) on the train. And I always take it with me, even when we go to see Gogo. She said I'm a big girl now and I don't need it. But I don't think I'm that big. Maybe just a little bit, 'cause I did help make the cake for Daddy. I hope he likes it. I put the icing on, it's chocolate, his favourite.

Mummy

Bloody Hell! Are they lined along the entire track from Bulawayo to Harare? Who can sleep with the eternal sound of singing crickets?

The solid darkness rushes by. Broken only periodically by wisps of homestead-hearths and animal smells. In the day it is flat open grasslands, dotted every now and then with clusters of mud huts. Ideal land for cattle grazing. Quite evident, as the scent of dung rushes in through the window as we pass by a siding. George would have loved that smell. It would have taken him back to his childhood, to his days as a cattle herder. It bothers me that it is only in these recent years that he has begun to share his boyhood with me. I think he was ashamed. I sense that in time it will be his pride.

***

The train moved slowly into the bustle of Harare's morning rush hour. Vendors, marketing everything from newspapers, boiled eggs and second-hand books to stolen watches, moved mindfully through the tangled congestion of slow-moving traffic. Money exchanged for goods through open windows. Bicycles wove in and out of the chaos. Like scavengers, the vendors swarmed the train as it inched into the station.

Marion stood near a group of women wearing white, who sung a welcoming hymn to one of our fellow passengers. Living in Matabeleland, I'd never heard Shona sound so beautiful. The clapping and ululation of their song floated in through the windows of the train, welcoming us all. A newspaper billboard on the platform read GOVT CLAMPS DOWN ON MATABELE DISSIDENTS. I could feel the thorns rising inside my chest. I was afraid as we stepped onto the platform. We had arrived in enemy territory: Mashonaland.

'Wow, you guys have grown!' Marion remarked, rubbing the top of my brother's head.

'Look, I built an ammunition demolisher,' he said, shoving his latest Lego contraption in her face. 'It's to kill the dissidents,' he said loud enough to catch the glances of several passers-by. He winced as I jabbed him in the ribs.

'Ow! … Mummy, Mummy,' but she pretended not to hear as she floated deeper into conversation with Marion.

I liked Marion Douglas. She was tall like me. It felt comfortable standing next to someone my height. At twelve I already wore a size eight shoe. My fast-growing body felt awkward and disproportionate, especially my feet, which felt like a clown's. Somebody had told me that the size of your feet relates to your height. Maybe … I hoped, maybe, my feet were smaller than hers.

'You guys are going to love my car, especially you, Butho,' she said as we all climbed in. Marion drove a Citroen. It worked on hydraulics. You had to wait until the car rose up before you could drive it. The rumble of the car's engine vibrated through our bodies as we waited silently for it to rise. Like the colonial artifacts, it excited us.

'Cool, just like a spaceship,' my brother said in his loud voice.

My sister quietly sucked her thumb. She was grumpy because I wouldn't let her bring her Dada. She's too old for that at seven. It's actually becoming a bit embarrassing.

We smelt of train and needed to bathe, but Mummy didn't want to waste time. Marion drove us straight to Chikurubi. Our sleepy faces betrayed our frightened, racing hearts. We hadn't seen Daddy in over a year. The thought of seeing him frightened us. We had heard that he had been unwell. What did that mean? Could he walk? Was he eating?

***

A huge grey concrete wall surrounded the prison. We had not expected the trimmed hedges and manicured lawn of an English manor house as we drove through the gates towards the buildings. Older prisoners in brown khaki uniforms and shocking white tackies, silently weeded, trimmed and watered the grand manor garden. Eerily, almost in unison, they momentarily stopped to watch as we drove up the road to the prison buildings. We stared back, earnestly looking for him among them. He wasn't.

At the office they told Marion she wasn't allowed in. 'She eesn't a family member,' they said arrogantly. She had to wait in the car.

We walked, frightened and excited, our arms overflowing with gifts of books, magazines, baked cakes, yoghurts, school report cards, cigarettes and bed-sheets.

In the room it was us against them. Twelve or so policemen and the four of us.

Their smiles were not kind, but amused.

'Poot yowa things heeya,' one barked, indicating a table with a baton stick. While they carefully examined our gifts, they spoke amongst themselves in Shona. In the midst of their loud conversation we heard ours and Daddy's names mentioned.

They emptied packets, opened letters, paged through books, and opened yoghurt containers. My sister yelped painfully as one mutilated her beautifully iced cake with a penknife. 'Security purposes,' he said stiffly, shoving it to the side of inspected goods. Thorns threatened. I held her hand tightly.

We stepped through metal detectors and were body-searched, then led to the 'receiving room'. It was a bare room, nothing but a wooden bench and a highly polished red floor.

We waited, fidgeting and shifting.

***

Are we going to see Daddy now? Are we going to see Daddy now? When are we going to see Daddy? Is he still coming? Are we at the right place? When are we going to see him?

***

Thandi

Butho drove his toy car on the floor. When he got up the knees of his pants were red from the polish on the floor. I told Mummy, but she ignored me. She was quiet and angry. I was already sad because the policeman chopped up my cake for Daddy. He said it was for security purposes. I don't know what that means, but I cried. Gugu wanted to cry but I think that's why she's angry.

We are waiting for them to bring Daddy. We've been waiting a long time.

***

We heard footsteps and jangling keys. The door opened, a policeman led him in. For a moment our eyes deceived us, we didn't immediately recognise him. A shrunken older man with white hair and in a brown khaki prison uniform shuffled in. His skin had assumed an unhealthy ashy hue. He had lost a lot of weight and the uniform hung on him. He looked at us and smiled, we recognised him through his eyes, which shone as they always did. We gasped, 'Daddy!' and ran to him.

'How are my savages?' he laughed, opening his arms to receive us. 'Savages' was his pet name for us. After tearful hugs and kisses we sat down, briefly intoxicated with happiness, as he hugged and kissed Mummy.

We spoke over a painful silence, hoping that our stories about school and various family members would stop it. The silence got louder. We soon couldn't hear ourselves, so we raised our voices up a notch to deafen it, but it was no use. Only the silence could be heard, bringing up thorns that cut at our throats. It became so painful that we no longer spoke, we surrendered to the warm relief of tears. We cried for our father, for his absence. We cried for all the fathers they had taken.

'Don't let them see you cry,' Daddy said wiping the tears away. A wing had fallen off of Butho's ammunition demolisher; he sat on the floor unaware of rising thorns and falling tears, trying to fix it as he prepared it for 'war'. We wiped our tears, while the thorns still clawed.

'If they see you cry they will feel they have won over you.' I thought of the torn posters buried under the earth in the bellies of ants. My patriotic duty was not to cry, but to crush the ants that had digested those toxic words. I decided, echoing my father's words, that there would be no checkmate while I was alive.

5

WHEN THE MOON STARES

Christopher Mlalazi

The sound of a car engine in the village has always been a noise that makes people, both adults and children alike, stop whatever they're doing and watch the road, as if a good spirit is about to appear. It's a sound filled with the nostalgic reminder that we're a people filled with hope, and that we are not alone in the world.

But today the sound of the approaching vehicle elicited a different response. Mother grabbed my hand and we fled into the bedroom, where she quickly closed the door and locked it. I sensed the old determination of a woman who is firm on decisions and reassuring to have around.

'Quick, let's push the wardrobe against the door, Rudo!' she cried.

The wardrobe, which stood at the far wall, was heavy, but we managed to push it across the small room and lodge it against the door.

Still breathing heavily from the effort, mother said we must hide under the bed, and we crawled underneath it. Then she pulled the blanket over the gap between the bed and the floor. Darkness enfolded us. The sound of the truck had increased to a steady frightening roar, as if it was right outside. Mother's hands were tight around me. We were not talking, but just listening intently. Finally, the sound receded, and died away. Silence descended on the hut again.

Outside I could hear chickens cluck-clucking, and their chicks chirping. The sound of birdsong seemed to have increased in intensity suggesting that the sun was setting.

***

We seemed to have been under the bed for a very long time. Then I fell asleep. I had a dream. A soldier was carrying a long spliced stick, and in the splice were cut-off hands and the fingers were wriggling like worms, making all kinds of shapes; then the biggest hand, which had a silver ring on its ring finger, beckoned me nearer; all the hands were now crooked at me, all beckoning me to come, and suddenly the hands were mice and they jumped off the stick and clambered over a soldier; he tried to beat them off as one would beat off flies, and then the mice became Sithabile and the other girls who had disappeared all those weeks ago after I'd left them with the soldiers; and now they were all screaming in one long-drawn-out scream.

I woke up with a start. My heart was beating fast. Mother's hands were still tight around me. It was pitch dark under the bed, but I could smell mother's comforting scent, that of wood smoke overlaid with sweat. The scream that had been in my dream was still there, and now it had become a wail, long and drawn out, like a person grieving. It was a woman. Mother's hands grew tighter around me, but it was not she who was wailing. Then, faint and far off, we heard more wailing, which almost sounded like echoes of the first. And then there was this one wail that seemed to be right outside our hut.

'It's Auntie,' mother said, her voice cracking. '*Mwari wangu!* What is happening to us!' Mother speaks fluent Ndebele, but when she is tormented she reverts to the Shona she learned as a child.

The wail outside had become continuous, whilst the other far-off wails were still there as if accompanying it.

Suddenly mother released me from her embrace, her movement sharp. 'No,' she said, 'this can't go on, or we're all going to become mad.'

She inched herself out from under the bed, and I followed her. The room was now as dark as it had been under the bed, save for a beam of moonlight stretching through the small window by the door, and lending the room a little light. Mother, in a crouch, moved to the window, and I could see the shape of her head outlined against the moonbeam as she peeped outside.

My parent's bedroom has a sharp smell of mothballs, which are put in the wardrobe to protect our clothes from termites. Maybe it was the lack of light, or the sense of gloom that pervaded the room, but the aroma of mothballs seemed very intense at that moment, as if they had been ground with a stone to release their scent.

Suddenly, mother began pushing at the wardrobe with her back. I moved to help her and we pushed together. The wail outside was maddening. The wardrobe screeched as we managed to heave it aside to expose the entrance again. Mother unlocked and opened the door and cautiously we went outside.

A full moon sat in the sky, like a thoughtful eye. The yard was revealed clearly and sharply in the moonlight. The wails still hung around the village, like a choir of witches. There was no one in our yard. Then mother headed for the front gate, and I followed close behind her.

There is a small hillock in front of my home that hides our hut from the road. Tonight it seemed like an upraised warning finger and we walked around it, following a path. On the other side of the hillock are the homes of Uncle Genesis and Uncle Francis. I walked with trepidation because mother had told me that my two uncles and their families were all now dead. But I couldn't imagine them dead. I had never seen a dead person, though I had been to homes where wakes for the dead were being held, and have never liked the gloomy atmosphere.

Uncle Genesis's home is on our side of the big road, and Uncle Francis's home is on the other side. When you get off at our bus stop, which is called Dlodlo Bus Stop after our family name, you get off directly in front of Uncle Genesis's home, and then if you walk around it you pass the hillock and get to my home.

As we rounded the hillock, we heard the wailing voice, which I had thought sounded in our yard when we had been in the bedroom. It was now louder. Other wails still filled the air from around the village. Then we came to the gate of Uncle Genesis's homestead. Beyond the gate was nothing but five round shadows indicating where the huts of the homestead had once stood.

A figure, lit by the moonlight, was kneeling before one of the dark shadows and what remained of the foundation of a hut in the yard. The wailing was coming from this figure. I felt a cold shiver run through my body.

Mother walked into the yard, and I followed close behind her. A strange scent of roasted meat caught my nose, but I didn't turn my mind to it as I was concentrating on the wailing figure. Before we reached it, we had to skirt the bodies of three dead dogs, Skelemu, Danger, and Basop, which had belonged to Uncle Genesis. One couldn't approach his home without them barking, even if they knew you, and Skelemu had been the most dangerous of them all, just like our dog, Gadi. Now, we would hear their familiar barking no more.

We reached the kneeling figure, and mother stopped behind it. Then the wail became a voice: 'Oh Genesis my brother, Oh Genesis my brother!' The voice kept repeating itself. The smell of roasting meat had become stronger.

It was Auntie. And as my eyes adjusted to the scene in the moonlight I noticed that the foundation of the hut Auntie was kneeling before had once been the bedroom of Uncle Genesis. In the middle of the floor stood a dark mound, like burned sacks piled on top of each other.

'They are all dead, Mamvura,' I heard Auntie's anguished cry. 'Even Francis and his family. What did they do to anybody? Why are they dead now and so painfully like this? Oh they are all gone *Nkulunkulu wami.*'

Mother gently put her hand on Auntie's shoulder.

'There is nothing we can do now Auntie,' I heard her say. 'They have gone to join our ancestors.'

'Genesis and Francis never did anything to anybody, Mamvura.' Auntie was still wailing, but the sound had diminished. 'They were not dissidents, but just simple parents who were looking after their families and their livestock.'

Still kneeling, she turned and pressed her face into mother's skirt. Mother placed both her hands on Auntie's shoulders. Auntie sniffled wetly, before breaking into a fresh outburst of sobs.

Mother did not say anything, but her hands lay still and warm on Auntie's shoulders. The more distant wailing from the village still echoed around us. I felt a hot lump stick in my throat.

***

Mother and Auntie have always argued, especially when Auntie has had too much to drink. Sometimes I think they don't like each other, but I could be mistaken. When Auntie is drunk she sometimes says mother and I are rat-eating people, and she says so in a ridiculing voice. When she does this mother never argues back, but just tells her that Shona people do not eat rats, but mice, which are delicious. I still remember one day long back when I was in our maize field with mother and father, and father had caught a mouse in a trap and mother had made a fire and roasted it. We had eaten the mouse right there, all three of us sharing the parts of the tiny animal, and it had been nice-tasting, like roast chicken. I had asked father if we couldn't catch more mice to take them home for supper but he'd laughed and said, 'Do you want Auntie to call us rat-eaters?' I've also sometimes had this dream of walking with my mother across a valley of tall dry grass, and walking with us is a man carrying a long, spliced stick with rows of mice on it. One day I told mother about this dream and she said it was not a dream, but that back in Mashava, when I was a child, she used to go with me and her father, my grandfather, hunting for mice in the bush, and the man in the dream was grandfather, who is now deceased.

But now Auntie is pressing her face into mother's skirt, seeking comfort, and mother has her arms around Auntie's shoulders, giving her this comfort. Then I cocked my ear. I could hear the faint sound of a child's cry. I quickly shut it from my mind, thinking that it was a trick of my imagination, for after all this was not an easy day.

'The soldiers came to the clinic and burned it down, too,' Auntie said in a muffled voice, her face still pressed into mother's skirt. 'I'd just left and was hiding in the bushes. Then they ordered the nurses to undress and they drove away with all of them quite naked.'

'So much has happened today,' mother was crooning. 'Put it out your mind for now, Auntie.'

Auntie's shoulders heaved, indicating a fresh outburst of sobbing.

Then I heard the faint cry of the baby again. I saw mother's hands freeze on Auntie's back.

'Did you hear that?' Mother suddenly asked.

'Hear what?' Auntie asked, and a hyena laughed in the night, as if in answer. 'You mean the hyena?' Another hyena laugh responded to the first one.

'No,' mother replied. 'I thought I heard the sound of a child crying.'

'I heard it too,' I said. 'At first I thought I was imagining it.'

Then we were all silent. The wails from the village continued, as if they had always been, just like the moon and the stars. Our ears were cocked for the cry of the child. Mother gently lifted her hands from Auntie's shoulders, and Auntie's face turned into the night and away from mother's skirt. The moonlight fell on her face, sparkling on the tears streaked on her cheeks.

Suddenly, there was a burst of gunfire, and we quickly looked around as it seemed to be all around us, although also far off, but we couldn't see any gun flashes, or the streak of bullets across the sky. Moments later the gunfire died away, and the distant wailing voices had also fallen silent.

Then the cry of the baby came again.

'I can hear the baby now,' Auntie said, standing up.

There was a mortar and a pestle lying next to the ruins of the kitchen. Mother walked over and picked up the pestle and then walked toward the charred mound in the middle of the hut. The pestle was about her height, and as thick as her arm.

I was watching mother in surprise, wondering what she wanted to do. The cry of the child returned again, this time it was unmistakable, but it was hard for me to tell where it was coming from. I saw mother push the pestle into the charred heap, and the pestle sank through the remnants of the blaze. Then she tried to lever the pestle up, but it was too heavy for her. Auntie moved towards her, and the two women levered the pestle up, and the charred lump broke where the pestle was inserted into it, and I nearly ran away in fright.

The charred lump was a mass of human bodies, burnt together. I could now see charred limbs, bones shining white in the moonlight, grinning skulls; the smell of roasted meat was very intense. It had come from these bodies. My stomach heaved and I quickly knelt down. Bile came gushing out of my mouth, even though I had last eaten early in the morning when I'd thought of going to school, when I thought it was a normal day. I heaved again, then spat and looked up at the women through tear-blinded eyes.

Mother and Auntie were attacking the charred lump. They heaved again, and more charred bodies toppled awkwardly over to the side.

Uncle Genesis had two wives and nine children, including Sithabile. This charred mass of bodily remains was all that was left of them. Finally, only one body remained on the floor, prostrate in front of mother and Auntie. This body was not as burnt as the others on top of it. Its legs were charred up to the knees, but the upper body was still intact. It was Auntie maDube, Uncle Genesis's eldest wife, and also Sithabile's mother. She was lying on a sheet of asbestos. I remembered these sheets. They had stood for a long time against the wall of Uncle Genesis's bedroom and Sithabile had told me that the asbestos sheets would provide the roof of a five-roomed modern house that her father was planning to build one day.

The cry of the child, though muffled, was louder than ever, and it seemed to be coming from underneath maDube's body. Then I saw mother and Auntie lift up the asbestos sheet on which maDube's body lay, and put it to one side. The cry of the baby increased. Auntie maDube had been lying on ten other sheets of asbestos and carefully, one by one, mother and Auntie laid them all to one side. The last two were badly torn and they just shoved the pieces aside, to reveal the floor from which protruded a metal handle. Mother and Auntie both pulled at it and it came up with a trapdoor that had been covered with grime and ashes to reveal a hole in the floor. A blast of fresh screaming resounded from inside it.

I knew about this hole. Uncle Genesis had it dug in his bedroom floor as a safe into which to put his important things, especially money during the time he had his store, to hide them from thieves, Sithabile had told me that. Normally there would be a small table standing over the hole, but it too must have been burnt to cinders along with everything else in the house.

Mother reached down with both her arms and drew out a baby.

It was screaming. Mother shushed it and then she stepped back towards me. I had remained kneeling all this while not far from where I had puked, but I now stood up, and wiping the tears from my eyes, I looked at the baby in wonderment. It was Gift, Uncle Genesis's lastborn child, and born from Uncle Genesis's youngest wife, maNgwenya. About a year old, he was dressed in cream wool jumpers and a matching hat that covered his little head.

'*Mwari wangu,*' mother was saying. She was inspecting the baby. 'He seems not burnt,' she announced. Tears were flowing unchecked down her cheeks.

A hot lump was now sitting in my throat, and threatening to burst.

'But what about under his clothes?' Auntie asked, her cheeks still glistening with tears. Gift was still crying in mother's arms but his cries were diminishing to soft whimpers.

'It's dark and we can't remove them,' mother replied. Then Gift stopped crying. 'But I don't think he has any burns. Otherwise he would still be crying and he would squirm in my arms.'

Mother then removed her breast from her blouse and fed it to Gift, and the baby immediately started suckling hungrily. I have always wondered when the milk will stop coming out of mother's breasts, but of course I have never asked her, not yet, because the wound from the baby she lost two months back is still fresh.

With Gift still suckling, mother dropped down on her knees, and asked us to do so.

We all knelt. The moon still sat in the sky, as if was worried about what was happening to us. The night was silent without even a breath of wind, or the trill of crickets.

'*Mwari wedu,*' mother started praying. She was looking up at the moon, and the moonlight glinted off her tears. 'We thank you *Mwari wedu* for keeping your little baby alive in the middle of a fire, and without your kindness this would never have happened. We thank you *Mwari wedu* for being our father when we are in need, and we ask that you show us the way to safety so that our children can also live and grow up to be adults. We pray to you *Mwari wedu* to look after all the dead. We ask for protection in this dangerous time *Mwari wedu*, in the name of the son and the Holy Spirit. Amen.'

(iii)

Whose Land is it?

6

The Trek

Lawrence Hoba

The old scotch cart makes its way slowly along the beaten-down track: 'J. J. Magudu, Zimuto' is scribbled on each side against the dark rotting wood in black paint. The inscription must be as old as the wood on which it lies. I do not know who wrote it. Even Baba does not know because one day I asked him who'd written it and he said that only his father had known about it. The old metal wheels are brown with rust and make a squealing sound as they turn; the axle is cracked.

Baba sits on the edge of the cart, brandishing a long leather whip he occasionally cracks to urge on the cattle pulling the cart along. It is the cow that is the problem. She stops frequently to feed her calf. The ox, black with a white patch on its head and long horns, walks energetically; it has no suckling worries. It stares straight ahead, wearing the same expression as Baba, tired and bored. Sweat trickles down Baba's face. Perched on his head is a broad-brimmed straw hat. Mama has one like his on her head. I also have mine, only baby Chido doesn't. I know Mama will weave her one when she is old enough. Baba wears a pair of *manyatera*, and yellow overalls with 'NRZ' on the back. He never worked on the railways, he just brought them home one evening. Mother once asked how he got them and she ended up with a swollen eye.

Mama sits with her back to father, staring at the road behind, her face expressionless. She does not even smile at baby Chido playing gleefully on her lap. She just holds her tight to keep her from slipping. Mama always goes to church on Sundays.

The church is an old building with a thatched roof that leaks when it rains. The roof should have been repaired long back, but there are not enough men, believers, to do the job. The pastor is an old fellow with broad square-rimmed spectacles and a head that makes him look like a he-goat. I do not know why women cry when he preaches.

The sun is hot, Chido wails, Mama plants one big breast into her mouth and she sucks happily. I am also hungry. Mama gives me a gourd of sour milk to drink. Some pots and plates lie clattering in a corner. I hate the noise. A sack of maize meal, almost empty, sits next to the pots in a twenty-litre tin. Mama uses it to fetch water from the well every day for washing Chido's old nappies, for cooking sadza and *muriwo*, and for father's bath. I always go down to the river to bath. A wooden stool and some straw and hide mats sit in another corner. Father always says women and children should never sit on stools. Sometimes when he is not at home, I sit on the stool, and it shakes and squeaks. He must be afraid that we will break it.

An old mattress lies rolled up with blankets inside, tied together with tree-bark fibre next to the mats. There is no bed base; father always erects one with sticks dug into the ground. My own bed, which we left behind, had a mattress made from sacks filled with soft straw. Mama must have emptied the sacks and put them somewhere, because I cannot see them from where I sit next to her.

Some old sacks lie next to the mattress; they contain all our clothing. A few old nappies for Chido, mother's dresses, father's trousers and shirts, and my torn shorts and T-shirts. There is also Baba's old suit that he wears on special occasions.

A plough sits at the far end of the scotch cart, looking new. Mama bought it last year with money from her groundnuts. Mama always works hard, but I prefer playing with Chido and Baba favours the calabash. Two hoes lie next to the plough. Mama's hoe is worn from use, Baba's is still new and clean: the inscription 'Master Farmer' is still visible. The only use Baba's hoe ever gets is when it rubs against his shoulders as he goes down to the fields to inspect the crop.

A metal board leans against the plough, with the inscription 'Mr B. J. Magudu, Black Commercial Farmer; Farm 24' crudely painted in white gloss. I had never known that Baba wanted to be a commercial farmer. One day he had come home, after he had been away for several weeks, and told mother that he had been given a sugar-cane farm, together with the farm house. They had been acquired by the government. Mother had listened solemnly. I think Baba should have written 'Mrs Magudu' instead of Mr Magudu; he never works in the fields, the farm will be Mama's to run.

I sit staring forlornly from side to side. Baba does not want me to sit next to him; he says I will fall off the edge. The sun wearies on towards the hills, where it will soon disappear behind them, and vast expanses of sugar-cane, green and tall, appear on both sides of the road. We pass a farm gate, with 'R. W. Whyte. Farm 23' worked healthily out of metal. I know the next farm will be our own. My back is now sore from sitting.

Tomorrow we will all be busy. Chido and I will be discovering our new home, Mama will be exploring her fields. Papa will be gallivanting, searching for the farmer who might have brewed a few drums of thick, rich *masese*.

***

I jump off my big bed. Mama always tells me that one day I will break my legs. I wonder if the *murungu's* children didn't jump off the bed like me. I have their photographs under my mattress. I stole them from the pile Baba wanted to burn. Besides, I can't get off slowly because Chido is wailing. I have to run and tell her to shut up before Mama comes. She isn't a baby anymore but she just won't stop crying. Chido cries when no one has hit her but Mama didn't cry when Baba hit her with his hoe handle.

Now she can't weed the fields anymore. Only *sekuru* works leisurely among the sugar-cane. Sometimes I go with him. There is no school here. There are no other children. They all went away with their parents when Baba couldn't pay them. Only *sekuru* didn't go. I asked him why. He said he had nowhere to go. He looked away when he said this. His voice is funny. Mama says he is from a faraway country called Malawi and that's why it's like that. I asked him why he didn't go and get his own farm like Baba did. He did not reply. He just put his hoe down on a pile of dried sugar-cane.

It's last year's sugar-cane. We harvested it when we arrived. Mama has forgotten the old priest now. She doesn't go to church anymore. No one tells her to reap only where she sowed. There are heaps and piles of it. The whole farm. Baba couldn't find a tractor to take it to the mill. He says the *murungu* should have left the tractors. I wonder why he left everything else. Even the dead *mesidhisi-bhenzi*. That's what Baba said it is called, under the big mango tree next to our scotch cart. Baba says everything is now ours, so we won't need a rickety, wobbly scotch cart and cattle. Everything belongs to us.

I go through the sitting room. Mama has moved the sofa so as to leave the door open. The door still doesn't work after Baba broke it to let us in when we arrived. There is a man sitting on the leather sofa that Baba always sits on. I don't know when he arrived. He is staring blankly at the TV. It is not on. It hasn't been switched on for a long time now. Like the stove and the machine that always went hoo-hoo-hoo – sucking in all dirt from the carpet. Mama knows all these things. She once worked for a *murungu*. But it's been a long time since the man in a van came to switch off the electricity.

I don't have to go to Chido's room anymore. She is quiet now. Mama is looking at the man. She raises her head to look at me and then looks down. There are tears in her eyes. Once I asked *sekuru* why Mama never cries. I know I don't cry because I am a man. Baba said only women and girls should cry. One day he beat me up for crying when I fell off the scotch cart. He never beats Chido. But *sekuru* said old people cry only when something very bad has happened.

Baba has not been home for a week now. Mama once said that beer will be his death. So maybe he has finally got himself killed. Is that why she is crying? Now maybe she can go and fight *sekuru*. With her plaster cast on the left hand I know she can beat him. She blames him for all our misfortunes. She says it's because he liked the *murungu* too much. So now he doesn't want us to become rich and is using his medicine to make our sugar-cane fail to grow. She told me that she once met him walking naked in our backyard in the middle of the night. I wonder where she was going because her own room doesn't face that way.

The man looks at me. He stands up to go. He takes his hat, which I had not seen from where I stand, and perches it on his head. It has a star stuck on its front. He takes one more look at Mama and after scanning the whole room with squinted eyes, makes for the door. He stands there for a moment and then tells her to be ready tomorrow morning. Mama doesn't say anything. I want to run after him and ask him why he has come. But Mama won't let me. Her eyes tell me to go out and follow the man.

I know *sekuru* is in the fields. Maybe the man went to him as well. I have to go and talk to him. The sun is very hot. It is still early in the morning. It hasn't rained for a long time now. The soil is dry and parched. Even in the sugar-cane fields there are big cracks on the ground. If only Baba had come home with money he got from selling our three oxen and the cow. The calf was stolen. We all grieved for it – Mama, Chido and I – but not Baba. Maybe if the engines were working, there would be enough water to irrigate the fields. There might even be fertiliser, that's what *sekuru* said the crops needed to grow.

Sekuru is working in the sun. He is working harder than he ever does. Sweat trickles down his head and his thin shirt is already wet from it.

He does not stop to look at me when I arrive. He has an opaque beer container next to him. I never knew that he drank beer. But who brought him the beer?

I tell him that Mama is crying. He looks at me scornfully. He does not say anything. I watch him as he goes on working furiously. He is repairing the canal, putting the loose blocks in order. Someone must have told him to do this. But it isn't mother. She hasn't come to the fields for two months now. He continues working. I want to cry. He doesn't want to listen to me.

...

The sun is hot. Baba still hasn't come back. The policeman says he will come after us when we are gone. Chido is playing close to Mama. At first she wouldn't get into the truck the police brought to carry our things. I don't know why they brought guns and big helmets with glasses on them.

Mama left most of the things she had packed when she saw them.

Baba is a problem. But I know if they come like this he won't even say a thing. Only *sekuru* remains on the farm now. And as we pass by the vast expanses of our stunted sugar-cane, I can see him working furiously. He does not even raise his head to look at us and he seems unperturbed by the big black *mesidhisi-bhenzi* parked beside the field. There is a man with a pot-belly standing beside it. Maybe if Baba worked hard, he would get to take the *murungu's* things.

We pass by the farm gate. The driver does not stop. I want to take the metal board with our name and throw it far far far away. But we are heading for home now. Tomorrow we will all be busy. Chido will be wailing as usual. There will be school for me. But above all, the old he-goat priest will come visiting, with some scriptures for Mama.

7

The Sins of the Fathers

Charles Mungoshi

Everyone had gone and they were now alone, Rondo Rwafa and his father, the ex-minister. Unknown to the father, the son – who'd never handled one before – had a gun in the inside pocket of his jacket. By the end of the day he would shoot – or not shoot – his father.

They were sitting at the dying fire under the green marquee stretched out over a corner of the big yard of Rondo's house in Borrowdale. Metal and bamboo chairs were ranged haphazardly round the huge fire that had been kept going for almost a week now.

Rondo hadn't been there when the accident occurred but his mind had been repeatedly going over what he imagined could have happened that day. He could see his father-in-law, Basil Mzamane, singing his song to the two girls, the one that he had been singing earlier that day to him, Rondo. Just as he had joined in to accompany the old man – Mtukudzi was also one of his favourite musicians – he could hear his children singing, '*Todini*/What shall we do/*Senze njani*'. He imagined a lot of laughter in the car, the old man so involved in singing and the joy of being with his granddaughters that he forgot to pay attention to what was on the road. As he thought it through again, Rondo still couldn't let his children see what was going to happen to them in the next few seconds. Only the old man saw it – too late – and his '*Maiwe-e zvangu!*' didn't register on the children's minds. Or so Rondo preferred – wanted – to think. He couldn't bear to imagine what would have gone through the children's minds if they had seen it coming towards them. Probably – *it is just possible* – that they did see it, but couldn't understand what it meant. It is also possible that they might even have cheered the behemoth coming towards them, towering above them. The sight of it moving inexorably – so Rondo wanted to think – might just have made them unaware of its destiny. So, after all, they just might have died happily – or, at least, obliviously. Rondo was trying to erase the pain, trying to come to terms with it as it coursed through him again and again.

He was sitting on the same sofa he had sat on for the past week, chin lodged in the heart-shaped cup of his hands. He had only left the sofa at the insistence of his workmate, Caston, who, under the pretext of buying groceries for the mourners, was really trying to take Rondo's mind off things a bit. For the whole week he had been hearing the low continuous buzz of murmuring voices, broken now and again by the keening and wailing of some female new arrivals, as the mourners came in and out of the tent; sitting with them, the bereaved family, or leaving to attend to some urgent personal business, but always coming back again later to keep them company, to mourn with them. Of course, Rondo was not unaware that all these people came for different reasons: some out of the genuine awareness of neighbourly goodwill, some out of respect and some – well, you could see it in the way they stared into the cameras as they shook hands with the old man, the ex-minister, Rondo's father. These photos would open doors in the future. People would be remembered. Rondo had seen the crowds milling all over the place. He had heard their voices, low and consoling, but sometimes also, loud and laughing, seemingly having forgotten why they were gathered at this house. (These loud voices seemed more honest than the low ones.) And then he heard all the voices as one, a strong hushed roar – wild beasts on the rampage? A distant river in flood? Only it was July, height of the cold dry season. Some voices had found lodging in his mind and he had heard – and understood – that they were all talking of what had happened in his home. It was not natural, they were saying. And then there were the songs. The haunting songs that the women had sung all night, every night, throughout the whole week, and that were now echoing back to him as he sat there across the fire from his father.

They sat like that for some time in silence. Rondo started, as if waking from a deep sleep. He was certain that something had roused him, touched him physically, but he couldn't immediately tell what it was. He looked up. He turned his head right and left. He was surprised to find that his father was now sitting beside him, on the sofa. The thought that his father had changed places without his being aware of it, scared him. He also noticed that his father's hand was resting on his knee. Despite the fire and the general warmth in the seat, Rondo felt the coldness of that hand through the thick material of his jeans as if shards of ice had been deposited on his flesh.

'Your grief will pass away like dew in the morning sun. One day you will be grateful, glad that this has happened now and not later. You will remember me and thank me.'

'*Why*, Father?' Rondo's mind was elsewhere. His voice sounded strange to him. They were not talking about the same thing.

'You will hear people talking. They will try to give you all sorts of advice. It's lies. Don't listen to them,' his father was saying, but Rondo found himself straining his ears, only to hear a silence settling down inside him, heavy as a huge stone, in that space which his children's voices would have filled. He felt his father's fingernails digging into the flesh of his knee as if he were trying to make him understand something that he couldn't say in words.

Rondo's eyes fixed on his father's. He saw, in the older man's eyes, the glow of the dying fire. A little flame flared up, flickered and died. Slowly, almost contemptuously, Rondo removed his father's hand from his knee. His father's eyes opened a little wider, in surprise, then quickly he gave a sad little laugh. 'Nothing lives for ever. You are still young. You can have other children.' Without another word, the old man rose and shuffled towards the house. Rondo heard him coughing horribly; then the cough was abruptly cut off as the door to the main building banged shut behind him.

As his father entered the lit area in the veranda, Rondo had thought his shoulders looked narrower and droopier than he had remembered them. With more intensity, the thought which had begun to visit him with almost daily frequency since the accident, came once more: I must have been afraid of just a shadow. His wife, Selina, might have been right after all. To admit that she might have been right, that she could possibly be right, was not a pleasant thought for him to entertain: You are always in the shadow of your father. She'd even gone as far as saying: I could do better in your pants.

In the shadow of my father, he reflected again, as his thoughts grew clearer. Exactly what am I doing to myself? His mind moved on to his colleagues in the journalistic fraternity and their attitude towards him. While they didn't exactly laugh at him to his face, they certainly didn't take him seriously. They might have wanted to, but Rondo was one of those people who at any gathering inadvertently became a laughing stock. And the worst of it was that Rondo, feeling defenceless, would join in their laughter, as if to say: Well, if you see me as a fool, I'll be one. In short, everyone seems to be telling Rondo to 'Grow up. Get a life,' and yet …

There was the scrape and squeak of a door opening. Rondo looked up and back at the house. Silhouetted in the doorway, with the light behind her, so that he couldn't see her face, stood his wife, Selina. They looked at each other like that for a long moment and then Rondo turned his gaze back into the fire. He realised he was expecting to hear again the squeak and scrape of the door, to tell him that his wife had gone back into the house. He didn't feel he could endure company at the moment.

Then he heard the snap of a twig very close to him and he looked around. It was Selina. He restrained himself from shouting at her – which would have surprised her. He hadn't heard her footsteps as she approached him across the thick lawn. This thought, combined with the earlier one of his father changing places, alarmed him as he realised the possibility of many things, things to do with life and death, that were happening to him without his being aware of them. But this thought quickly melted away when he felt – gratefully – the warmth of Selina's hand on his frozen shoulder. He could smell the wool of the blankets she'd risen from, recent sleep still lingering on her. Without looking at her, he raised his hand and laid it on top of hers on his shoulder. Then, her fingers cracking as he squeezed them in his, he was trying to say something to her that couldn't be said by word of mouth. And also trying to get from her something which was more than body warmth. He let his head rest against her belly, his skull just nudging the underside of her breast.

'You haven't slept a wink for the whole week,' Selina said in a very low voice, as she crouched by the fire, knocking several pieces of wood together into a blaze.

'I feel as if I have been asleep all my life,' he said, at the same time wondering whether she understood what he meant. He sank his fingers into her dreadlocks.

'I finally managed to sleep last night – thanks to your mother.'

Selina was silent for a moment, then she went on, 'All night, every day, we sat side by side. Then last night – I suppose she saw me nodding off, and she just took my head and put it on her lap. I hadn't realised how exhausted I was. And how I needed a mother to hold me just like that.' Another silence. Then, unexpectedly, 'A great woman, your mother.'

Because he was thankful or confused – Rondo said, 'And my father?'

Selina tensed: 'What do you mean?'

'Oh, nothing.' Now he was – as always – on the defensive. Of course, he didn't mean *nothing*. What he really wanted to know was what his wife really thought about his father. So far, she hadn't said anything at all about anything, not since the accident in which her own father and their – his and her – own children had perished. It exasperated him that she always seemed to hold herself above everybody else, as if passing judgement on them – and him – as weaker mortals. Subconsciously, what irked him was that she hadn't said anything – good, bad or indifferent – nothing that would, at least, indicate a direction for him to take. Although he might have not known it throughout their life together, he now seemed to have an inkling that she had always made all the decisions. (A fact which had been quickly commented – and acted – on by his father.) Now, how he was to handle his father largely depended on what she, Selina, said about the old man. But now she was behaving as if she ... Rondo wondered if she knew. He could never tell with his wife. Or, possibly, his own mother could have told her – they were inseparable, his wife and his mother. The two of them also knew how to get information. Rondo had always been surprised – he would burst into his, or his mother's, house with what he thought was something neither of them would have heard. But the thing about them was that they wouldn't embarrass you by letting you know the 'news' was old hat. They would look kindly at you and from that look you would know that they had been hiding the information from you for the past month – or even a year. They preferred not to offer 'news'.

'Very strange', Rondo said to Selina.

'What?'

'This accident.'

Selina stiffened. Then she turned her head slowly away from the fire and looked at him. She stood up, took both his hands in hers, and gently pulled him up, 'Come on. You need rest. Let's get you some sleep and then I will prepare you a big breakfast. I can't remember when I last cooked you something since we started employing a housemaid. Come on. I don't want to lose you as well.'

'Lose me?'

'To the maid.' But she suddenly let go of his hands as if she had remembered something else she would rather forget. She put her face into her hands and gave one big heave of the shoulders.

Rondo put his arm round those shoulders.

'I think I'll accompany Papa's body to Bulawayo tomorrow,' she said after she had stopped crying.

'We will go together.'

'No.'

'Why? Are you blaming …'

'No No No Noooo!' She didn't quite scream, but she put her hand to Rondo's mouth and then rushed off across the lawn and into the house, crashing the door shut behind her.

He looked after her at the closed door, feeling the way she'd gone. She'd realised he'd been about to say something, he thought. Something that hurt only him – but would later filter out to those near him. She was always telling him that he apologised too much. It was a form of selfishness, she said. But he had been brought up in a different world: she had been brought up by people with 'long hearts' – people who forgave others – all this he understood now – and he? Rondo remembered telling Selina about his first disappointment – and the first sermon from his father, who was then – he didn't know in those days of political troubles – but, of course, his mother knew. Anyway, an uncle had given Rondo an old guitar. He was only four then. His father had come home – in Old Canaan, Highfield, then – and found him strumming away tunelessly on the instrument. His father had broken the strings and thrown the whole contraption into the fire, saying, 'No Mick Jaggers or John Whites in my house! Scum! They have no sense of responsibility, those people. Flowers of the sun. Playing and singing on trains with no destination in mind. Railway followers. Tch. Tch. Tch. Rolling Stones. No son of Rwafa has ever been a rolling stone ….'

He had been only a child – and he didn't have any idea who Mick Jagger or John White were. But he had remembered the fear that had been planted in him then. (He'd peed in his shorts – he'd told Selina!)

And he had told her all this because he loved her and he was about to lose her because his father, a full-blown bhuru rokwaNyashanu, would not let the Rwafa family be demeaned by an effeminate son who wanted to marry into an ignominious muDzviti family. And he would have lost her if she hadn't stood by him – she, her father and his own mother. The flames of that burning guitar had gutted all the courage out of him.

It had always brought tears to his eyes to see his mother and wife together – while his father frowned – and even spat – at the relationship. And throughout, Rondo didn't know what was behind all this – tension – in their relationships. Once, his mother tried to simplify it for him: 'Your father is Zezuru-Karanga and, once-upon-a-time, they were raided by the maDzviti-Ndebele. Well, in those days or even in these days, if you have a war, you have a war. It does bad things to people's minds. So, they will always remember the pain of the scars rather than the relief of the healing. Your father, *mwanangu*, is one bombed-out battlefield of scars. And his deepest scar is that he cannot forgive: not just his enemies. You. Me. Anyone.'

It hadn't meant anything to him then, but it had been easier to accept than, 'Well, my son, give me a grandson, to whom I can leave all this.' All this was, Rondo thought, his cars, houses and money. And his charisma – because, though he might have been afraid of him, Rondo really thought that his father, his *Daddy*, was the greatest. In his nightmares, Rondo would have done anything for him.

But after the ignominy of marrying a *muNdevere*, there was the further ignominy of having a granddaughter with *Ndevere* blood as first in the family. And then a second granddaughter. After all this, there was nothing that could have appeased Mr Rwafa, the ex-minister, Rondo's father. It was as if his son Rondo had been written out, written off, disappeared.

But the problem was that Rondo was an only son, and an only child.

As an only son, a lot of things were done for Rondo by his father, of which the young man was not aware. And because he was not aware he did not show his father enough gratitude, or respect. Rondo's father was, therefore, a very disappointed man. At times so disappointed that his wife had to do a lot of humiliating things to cool him down. She might have enjoyed their affluence as one of the members of the small ruling elite in a newly-independent government, but Mrs Rwafa had very deep fears about the future of her only child. His father loved himself so much, he was prepared to destroy his son in his endeavour to have – a duplicate? an heir? Mr Rwafa, as Minister of Security, seemed to have pursued his duties so zealously that he hadn't been able to distinguish Party from family. And people had suffered. Especially Rondo, to the extent that never, throughout his life, had he been able to answer any one of his father's questions. He had developed a stammer. His mother could have told him that lots of people developed a stammer whenever their father asked them questions. It had taken Rondo a very long time to realise what his father's job was, although he knew that he was somewhere high-up-there. And Rondo's mother was caught in between the sensitivity of her husband's job and the sensitivity of her son's nature. In a way, each of them lived locked in their separate cages.

Rondo always thought his father must be right; he was too diminished to think otherwise, and he was afraid for his mother whenever she had to oppose the old man. He loved – or thought he loved – his father, but the topic was too charged to consider deeply.

Maybe he loved him because he always did everything for him? His mother did a lot too – the more intimate things like underwear and peanut butter – but his father was out and up there with Batman and Superman. Yet he couldn't tell in exactly what sense. And Selina? It seemed the first time she came into their house she had understood the whole situation: Rondo's father had asked, 'Who are her people?' and the moment Rondo told him, his father had walked out. He had stayed out of sight for the whole day, yet Selina later told him it was the most enjoyable day she had ever had in her life. From day one, Selina had – so it seemed to Rondo – taken to his mother like her own, or like an old friend.

Rondo loves both his mother and his wife but now he is wondering whether they, too, are not laughing at him. Like his colleagues at work.

Rondo Rwafa knows very well that he is not a brilliant journalist. In fact, he couldn't even remember how the job had come about. One morning his father came into his room and said, 'Slob, wake up. Time you earned your own keep.'

'Slob.' His father's language exactly. None of the words he used to address Rondo had any respect in them. It seemed that there wouldn't ever be anything that his son could ever get right. And Rondo suspected that in her less I-love-you moments, Selina saw him in this same light: less-than-me. Only his mother seemed to see him as whole.

So, Rondo had found himself at the Clarion, the city's daily paper, among people who seemed to start laughing at him the moment they set eyes on him. Yet – yet – they held him in a kind of awe. He had been presented to the office by no other than Rwafa himself. They flocked round him. They asked for favours – which, of course, they got (although at times it meant a few uncomfortable minutes in his father's office at home). Yes, his colleagues laughed at him, he knew, but – now, he didn't know – could it be malicious? He gave them money – advances – at the thin times of the month, and not a few had used his name to get something or other from finance houses, credit stores, legal firms and so on. But – was it possible that all the time they had been laughing at him?

Recent events were driving Rondo's thoughts down avenues he was not accustomed to. More than mere recent events were making

Rondo see something else in events that he'd always taken for granted.

Of his workmates, Rondo could say Caston Shoko was the closest to him, although not quite a friend. Caston wasn't very popular with the rest of the fraternity because he behaved as if he knew all the answers. Maybe, because of this, he saw the company of Rondo as the lesser of the two evils. Anyway, Cas loved to talk and drink and Rondo had lots of money and a guileless face.

A long, long time back, Caston had asked Rondo: 'Do you know what your father does?' Rondo had shrugged the question off. A second (or another) time, Caston had asked again, 'Have you ever wondered about the Second Street accidents?' And again, Rondo had shrugged his shoulders.

'Do you even know what they are?' Caston asked.

'No. What are they?'

Caston had laughed: Rondo would always be a naive clown.

Rondo had laughed because he didn't know and he didn't think it mattered. Now, after this accident, thinking things over, Rondo had a better idea of what Caston had often tried to tell him. And Caston more than confirmed it when, on one of their several trips in the past week to buy food and firewood for the mourners, he said, 'This is your story. It would be a betrayal if we wrote it up, since it involves a colleague.'

Silence. Then, looking at Rondo, he said slowly and conclusively, 'This is a typical Second Street accident.'

Rondo stared at Caston like a trapped animal. He felt terror, and in that moment accepted that he had always refused to think about why his father left the house in the morning and what he did before he returned in the evenings – or the following week, for that matter.

Caston observed his friend quietly. There would never have been a good moment ... He put his hand on Rondo's shoulder. 'You can't be a child forever, Rondo.'

They walked slowly to the car, and drove back to Borrowdale in silence. Caston stopped the vehicle. Rondo sat motionless in the passenger seat; his friend looked at him for a moment, and said quietly, 'We're home, Rondo.'

Then, as Caston began unpacking the goods from the boot, he

said, 'In case, you need it, there's a gun in the glove locker. It's loaded.'

***

Rondo had not been used to living his life from deductive or logical thinking, but now the accumulation of events and the history behind them had made him so numb he was almost a zombie. And Caston wouldn't leave him alone.

According to Caston, this whole story had to be seen from the point of view of Rondo's father.

'What happened at the birthday party?' Caston had asked.

Rondo couldn't see anything wrong with the party except that two old men, his father and father-in-law, had made speeches that seemed to have turned sour. His mind seemed at times to have an amazing way of getting rid of the details of an experience.

'No,' Caston had said. 'Only one old man made a speech. And that broke up the party, didn't it Rondo? Don't you remember that?'

And Rondo remembered. He even remembered other incidents that Caston didn't know anything about. Rondo recalled what had happened at the birthday party, but a day before the party, there had been – a quarrel? A misunderstanding? – between his father and father-in-law. There had always been a tension between the two men but the episode at the party had rendered it dramatic.

Although he thought he loved his own father, Rondo had always sensed that if he had to choose, he would pick out his father-in-law as his father. It was just a feeling, not defined, not absolute. Nothing about his father-in-law's demeanour showed that he was a very successful businessman and the MP of a constituency in northern Matabeleland. When he was with his father-in-law, Rondo always felt that the space around him had expanded. He didn't know exactly how to put it but he felt he could – and he would be allowed to – do anything he wanted. Only on very rare occasions had Mr Mzamane mentioned his differences with Rondo's father, and even then, he would conclude, 'Of course, he is free to think as he likes.'

So, at one point in their married life, Selina suggested that they invite every relative and friend for a joint birthday celebration for their daughters, Yuna, six, and Rhoda, five. Mr Mzamane had married again after Selina's mother had died and Selina didn't yet feel comfortable with her stepmother. So, in the invitation to her father she had alluded to this. She knew that her father would understand, and he did, he came alone. He also came a few days before the celebrations as he had business to conduct in Harare.

Mr Rwafa – surprisingly – drove to Rondo's home to see Mr Mzamane on the morning after his arrival. He seemed quite cheerful, which was also very unusual in Rondo and Selina's house, but more especially in the presence of Basil Mzamane. Not least because the bill for the couple's wedding celebrations had been met by Mr Mzamane. The larger part of the expenses anyway: Rondo's mother had helped too, in tears at times, because her husband had told her, 'Who did you say is wedding?' and had conveniently left town 'on State business' for two weeks. Selina couldn't believe that this was just a courtesy call, a friendly gesture towards her father. However, the ostensible purpose of this surprising visit wasn't kept secret for long. As with other high-ranking officials in the ruling party, Rondo's father had had his eye on a certain farm in the Ruwa area, which was presently owned by a white man, a Mr Quayle. Rondo had driven to the farm on several occasions because he had a natural love for the outdoors: the trees, the hills, the open vistas. On the first occasion, he had gone out to the farm with his father; subsequently, Selina had accompanied him. She seemed to like the Quayles, too.

Indeed, they seemed very nice people. Each time he visited the farm they presented him with some of their farm produce: milk, honey, apples – whatever was in season. They had to force the bounty on him since he was too shy and embarrassed to receive gifts from people.

Rondo learned from Mr Quayle that the relationship between him and his father 'went years back … when we worked together in a bookshop in town … but it's now mostly sustained by our passion for duck-shooting.'

Rondo hadn't bothered to find out anything more from his father about this relationship. He didn't even speculate on the possibilities that it could go beyond just duck-shooting.

'Ever shot duck, Mr Mzamane?' Rondo's father asked Rondo's father-in-law that day before the birthday celebrations.

'No, why?'

'Because I'd like you to watch some duck-shooting today. Sad you can't shoot yourself. It would have been more fun.'

'One can always learn,' Mr Mzamane said.

'Isn't it a bit late in the day for you?'

Mr Basil Mzamane had laughed his uproarious laugh and said something that had made Rondo laugh as well. But Mr Rwafa seemed to disapprove. He was a man who laughed little.

They drove out towards Ruwa in Mr Rwafa's Pajero. Rondo had wanted to sit alone in the back, to give the two elderly men a chance to talk – same-age-boys stuff – but Mr Mzamane had declined to do so saying, 'I suffer from vertigo.' Rondo had had to sit in front with his father, wondering what vertigo had to do with anything.

At the Mabvuku turn-off they found an open truck parked by the roadside. It was full of youths singing chimurenga songs and waving ugly-looking clubs. Some even had bows and arrows and spears.

Immediately they passed the truck, it fell in right behind their own car.

'Your duck-shooting posse?' Mr Mzamane asked.

Rondo laughed. He hadn't thought about it at all.

'Damn right,' Mr Rwafa had replied and Rondo stopped laughing at the chilly tone of his father's voice.

'They must be pretty good marksmen to hit flying ducks with those clubs.'

'Not at all. We hunt *sitting* ducks.'

Mr Mzamane gave another of his uproarious laughs, 'That's pretty good. I must tell this to Radhebhe.'

There was no more talk in the car, but looking behind him Rondo wondered whether his father hadn't been telling the truth after all. The truck was still behind them. When they stopped for some drinks at Ruwa, it stopped at some distance on the road ahead. And it fell in behind them again when they passed it.

As they turned off the main Mutare road to the farm, the truck also turned off.

'Now, tell me. Is this just coincidence or what?' Mr Mzamane seemed a little dark – with fear or just worry?

Rondo's father didn't bother to answer. Rondo didn't even think that there might be something ominous about the truck trailing behind them with its load of club-wielding, slogan-chanting youths. He was preoccupied by the sudden beauty of the land they were driving through. He did, however, wonder briefly whether the boys in the truck saw the same things that he saw in the countryside. If they saw anything, their minds probably wouldn't register it or were fermenting with thoughts of what they were going to do wherever they were going.

As they drew closer to the farm, the singing – chanting almost – grew louder, more intense, menacing. It was no longer just ordinary singing. There was something elemental in it, the naked, unashamed raw lust for blood. Not that Rondo didn't like the singing. He had been brought up on these songs, although in peacetime the words would be different. And he found himself wishing that the youths were using peacetime words.

Right now, right here where they were just leaving an area of bush – musasa, mutondo, mususu and an assortment of wild fruit trees – and coming into the open of the valley towards the river, the land provided a breathtaking view of its immensity. Across the river lay some low granite hills, with dark forests and mountains in the blue distance. It was just after midday, yet something affected the atmosphere so that the heat seemed subdued and the air acquired the dark colour of old memories. Rondo thought: any moment a duiker will disturb the tall grass and dash across the road. And more from a forgotten or unknown memory rather than a remembered reality, his nostrils were filled with the smell of fresh water.

Soon, they were rolling down to the stream – with very little water in its bed – and crossed a narrow concrete-and-stone bridge into the scrub on a low hill. They kept on driving up, then round a bend in the road, almost a blind turn, and there they came upon a jeep, stalled to the side of the road. Its hood was open and a white woman was bent under it, looking into the engine. She looked up as Rondo and company came to a noisy, dusty halt beside her car. The lorry with the chanting youths pulled up behind Mr Rwafa's car. The woman stood, frozen, her dirty hands gripping a greasy spanner.

There was a moment of silence as the woman looked at the men in both vehicles and the men looked back at her. For a few painful moments, neither side seemed to know what to do with the other. Then the woman brought down the hood of the jeep with a loud bang, moved quickly to the open door of the jeep, reached in and pulled out a rifle.

The youths in the truck jumped out at that moment and advanced towards her. Rondo hadn't heard the sound of the door open nor Mr Mzamane getting out but suddenly there he was, standing with his hands raised, the woman behind him and the mob before him.

They all froze. Mr Mzamane spoke in a calm, fatherly voice: 'Let us all remember we are human. This lady probably needs our help. Even so, if there is something you had planned to do, I don't want to be a witness to it, because I am not part of your plans. I am a stranger to this part of the country. Is this how you treat visitors in your homes? Would you like me to tell the people where I come from that this is how you treat people here?'

There was a stunned silence, and a slight tremor of knobkerries being lowered by a degree or two.

Then an impatient voice rang, 'Chef? Who is this man?'

All eyes turned on the young man. That was when Rondo realised that his father had sneaked out of the car and disappeared.

Quickly, Mr Mzamane assessed the situation and said, 'You see? He gave me word that today is cancelled. Go home. He is going to contact you. I am his Bulawayo comrade. We are in the same work, same rank.'

For no reason that Rondo could see at all, the men lowered their clubs and got back onto the truck grumbling. They drove off.

'Thank you,' the woman said, but she continued to clutch her rifle. And that was when Rondo recognised her.

'What seems to be the trouble with the car?' Mr Mzamane asked.
'It just seized.'

Rondo felt that he should have done something to help, and because he hadn't, he kept his head very low out of embarrassment.

Mr Mzamane opened the hood of the jeep and fiddled with the engine and said, 'Try her, let's see'.

The car started on the first kick.

The woman thanked Mr Mzamane profusely. She gave him her name. Mr Mzamane said it didn't matter. She asked if they had time so they could drive to the farm, it wasn't far, for a cup of tea. Mr Mzamane joked, saying that they had to hurry and catch up with the singing boys in the truck before they got up to some other mischief. The woman thanked him again and said that if in future he was ever in that area, he should drop in for a cup of tea. Or he could make an appointment with her husband for duck-shooting. She gave a small laugh, thanked him again and drove off.

Less than two minutes after the woman had driven off, Rondo's father appeared from behind a bush. He didn't say a thing. He got behind the wheel and they drove back the way they had come.

About thirty minutes of total silence in the car seemed unbearable to Rondo. Also, he felt terribly oppressed and morally bound to say what was bothering him. One of those very rare occasions when fear of his father was less than the pain inside him.

'That was Mrs Quayle back there,' Rondo said.

'Is she your mother?' his father snapped.

'Do you know her?' Mr Mzamane asked.

Rondo looked furtively at his father. Mr Rwafa concentrated on his driving.

'I am asking you, Rondo', Mr Mzamane said.

'We often drive to the farm. Father sometimes …'

'Traitor,' Mr Rwafa spat the word out under his breath.

'Shoots duck with Mr Quayle?' Mr Mzamane offered, laughing. 'Nothing to worry about, Rondo. They – or at least she – seem good neighbourly. You heard her invite me to tea? I am sure you too have had tea with her or them?'

When neither Rondo nor his father answered, Mr Mzamane told Rondo that he had to grow up and see people as they were, as individuals. He talked of how some are good and some are bad and how sad it was that the majority of people seemed keen on seeing only the bad in people. He told the story of a white farmer in the Manhize Mountains who was – well, not exactly a spirit medium, but who believed in vadzimu. Whether he believed or not, Mr Mzamane said, was not the point. But it seemed to help his prospects. The story behind the story is that his grandfather settled in the area of the Pazho people, thus taking possession of their sacred pool, Kapa. Not only did the sacred pool come under his farm, the ancestral graves, the forests, the beehives – everything that had given the Pazho sustenance, was on his farm. Well, might is right, a fact of life. But three years after Kakuyu – that's the name the locals gave this settler – three years after settling on the farm, he couldn't prosper. Every year several head of his cattle died from an unknown disease. Baboons, wild pigs and birds played havoc with his grain crops.

'He was thinking of selling the farm and calling it quits when the headman of the Pazho people told him what to do. You see, although Kakuyu now owned what had been these people's ancient land, he allowed them to make use of the sacred pool and pray to their ancestors. So, the headman thought, why not help him as well? So, he asked him to buy a *retso*, the black-and-white cloth of *vadzimu*. He told him what to do with it every morning at the sacred pool. He told him the words to say. And that he had to leave a handful of grain from the land.

'The man had a bumper harvest the following season. Only one cow died, and that could easily have been from old age. That man was the grandfather of the farm's present owner. The Pazho people enter and leave the farm as they like to attend to the graves of their ancestors, pray at Kapa, set up beehives, mousetraps, birdtraps, termite traps …'

'Shut up, traitor!' Mr Rwafa shouted, his voice icy, and he rammed his foot on the brakes of the Pajero.

'There is more to the story than …'

'If you respect me …' then he started the car and they were off again.

***

Rondo wouldn't have tried to see what lay behind this incident if Caston hadn't asked him to remember what happened at the birthday party. And what had happened at the party?

It had turned out be a great party, at least at the beginning. No one paid attention, at first, to the two elderly men, the politicians, who were quite conspicuous by their keeping as far apart as possible. If you didn't know the score, or didn't look closely, you wouldn't notice the tension behind their tight smiles and loud laughs, as they seemed to compete in entertaining the groups of children and young parents that formed and dissolved around them. Basil Mzamane could have won the contest easily if he hadn't been too aware of being 'away from home'. At one point, Mr Rwafa managed to raise some eyebrows when he referred to Mr Mzamane as 'The Honourable MP'. There seemed, at least to an innocent ear, no innuendo of sarcasm or irony in his voice. A number of people were so moved that they observed a few seconds of silence. It was an unusual admission from Mr Rwafa and it revealed a rare chink in his armour, people thought. There was a noticeable relaxation all round after this. Selina and Rondo even allowed themselves to think that this was what they had wanted all along. A moment like this with their parents, all their parents; Selina felt the party had served its purpose.

But then, out of the blue, someone – Rondo couldn't later remember who it was – probably one of the dreadlocked crop of reporters – said, 'Mr Minister' (they still called Mr Rwafa 'Mr Minister' in deference to his past glory – and, well, his age), 'Why don't you tell the children a story, Sir?' 'Yes!' another one shouted. 'We haven't heard you tell us about what you did in the liberation struggle.'

Someone should really have stopped the whole thing at this point but nobody did; and Rondo later remembered having the feeling that he used to have as a boy, when he embarked on something that he knew was not allowed to do, and yet the very thought that it was not allowed, fuelled his action.

It was quite a peaceful scene: the children chasing each other and screaming and squirting water into each other's faces and firing crackers; Rondo and his friends minding the braai, standing around and joking, glasses of beer in hand; and the women in their own corner of the garden – it looked as if nothing could possibly disturb the equilibrium of things. But then someone had asked that question – and already it was too late to do anything about it, when Mr Rwafa raised his voice and said, 'Are you sure you really want to hear about that?' 'Yes!' Quite a number of voices shouted back. No one noticed Basil Mzamane wandering quietly away, pretending to be admiring the plants in Rondo's garden.

Mr Rwafa made all the children sit cross-legged at his feet. Rondo and his friends made themselves comfortable in sofas, legs crossed, beers in hand, forming a protective outer circle around their children.

Mr Rwafa talked of betrayals. He talked of traditional enemies of the people since time immemorial. Enemies of the state. Enemies of the clan, of the family. Looters and cattle thieves. Personal enemies. People who spat in the faces of their own people. Child thieves. Baby snatchers. He talked of his waking up to his mission. He talked without any shame of his personal prowess. Of his achievements. The obstacles he had to overcome to get where he was. 'The obstacles were nothing,' he said. The main thing for them to remember was that, 'No son of the Rwafa family would ever play second fiddle to anyone's lead. A Rwafa's place is always up there, at the top, out there, right in front of the crowd. No one who carries Rwafa's blood should carry anybody's pisspot!' He raved on, foam flecking the corners of his mouth, his eyes an incandescent red. His voice rose higher, hurt – terribly, terribly hurt – by effeminate, spineless sons of the family who marry into the families of their enemies, poisoning the pure blood of the Rwafa clan.

Rondo couldn't look at his father. Guests started leaving, silently, one after the other, grabbing their children by the hand and hurrying them to their cars where they summoned their wives. Rondo was rooted to his seat, an untouched drink in his hand, unable to look up or to wave goodbye as his father carried on and on like one possessed. At some point, his father had rapped the ground so hard with his favourite hard-wood walking stick that it snapped cleanly in two. His father had looked at the broken, ornamented stick, a gift from admirers in Mozambique, as if it were the death of a well-loved heir and only child. He had wiped bitter sweat off his brow.

Rondo listened to his father, sensing that something terrible was happening, or had already happened, but unable to tell exactly what. Everyone had gone and only he and his children remained. Rondo looked at the children, six and five years old. He looked at their open-mouthed, wide-eyed innocence as the old man rambled on: 'They need to be smoked out, flushed out, blasted out of their hiding places, the impostors!'

***

Remembering all this, Rondo had been reminded of another incident that he had almost forgotten. He wondered how he could have done so.

It was the day he had helped himself to some ripe mangoes from the neighbour's garden. He hadn't seen anything wrong in that but the neighbour had come upon him, pulled him down by the leg and given him a thorough thrashing with a green peach switch. And when his mother heard him howling, she had come running out and lifting her skirts in the man's face, she called him a child-murderer. The man went on shouting 'Whore!' and called Rondo 'Woman's child'. And then his father had come into the neighbour's yard with his thick elephant-hide belt and without even bothering to find out what the matter was, proceeded to thrash Rondo. Even after all these years, the sight of his mother dragging herself on her knees from one man to the other, back and forth, begging them, clapping her hands to spare her only son, her only child, that alone gave him a very uncomfortable feeling, and he just didn't want to remember. He had never told anyone about it, not even his wife. At that early age, he was only eight, although he didn't have the words, he must have understood what *powerlessness* meant. Yet his mother had always insisted, 'Your father really loves you. He just doesn't know how to show it.'

It was that same feeling at the birthday party, Rondo remembered. After the party, things couldn't be expected to remain the same. There was a tension in the air. Mr Mzamane tried to joke a bit but gave it up, saying he had to sleep early for the long drive to Bulawayo the following day.

That was when he had asked if Rondo and Selina could let his two beautiful granddaughters accompany him. It had been a long time since he had given them a real treat. Rondo and Selina had said they saw nothing wrong in that. But Rondo also remembered a seemingly insignificant thing that had happened soon after they had given their consent.

Rondo's mother had asked, 'Did anyone of you see where my husband went?'

People had laughed. Remembering it later, Rondo was not sure that this should have been ignored.

***

Rondo stood up from the fire in the marquee and walked to the guest room that his father had been using throughout the week. He didn't knock. He found his father reading a magazine, sitting on a sofa.

'What took you so long?' his father asked without taking his eyes off the paper. Rondo didn't answer. He pulled a folded piece of paper out of his pocket and handed it to his father.

After reading it, his father looked up and said, 'Did you ask one of your more intelligent friends to write this for you?'

Rondo didn't answer. It was all he could do to stand there, unblinking. His father hadn't asked him to sit down.

'I wouldn't have believed that you had it in you,' his father laughed harshly. But his laughter caught in his throat when a gun appeared in Rondo's hand. But something was wrong. Rondo had the butt of the gun pointing at his father, as if he was offering it to him.

His father's eyes opened wider still and a great flood of sadness washed through him. He looked wearily into the face of his one and only son. He searched all over his face for a foothold of manhood, for a handhold of hope, 'So, the whole thing is your idea then?' He took the gun out of Rondo's hand and pointed it at his head.

Rondo could have been a rock for all that he felt. It wasn't courage. Just numbness. Stupidity, his workmates or friends would have said. He understood them now. Somewhere inside him, a deep wish emerged that his father should shoot him. That would simplify matters. He would be taking care of things as he had always taken care of the things of his life.

'I haven't used a gun before,' Rondo said calmly. 'I thought you'd do this thing better than me. After all, this is the story of your life.'

Slowly, his father put the gun on the floor, reached inside his jacket and took out his own service pistol. Rondo watched all this as if it were happening on the screen. Then, unexpectedly, his father hissed, 'You two get out of here and shut the door!'

Rondo obeyed and as he turned, he saw Selina in the doorway – with a gun. She didn't resist when Rondo pushed her gently out closing the door softly behind them.

The sound came as a soft muffled plop.

But Rondo was looking at the gun in Selina's hand. She read his thoughts, and said, 'Your mother gave it to me.'

Rondo bent his head in silence.

8

Trespassers

Chiedza Musengezi

Chembe lies on his bed, floating between wakefulness and sleep. It is May. The chill of an approaching winter stirs him awake. He slides under the blankets and stretches out an arm to put out a candle, crushing the burning wick between thumb and forefinger. A smell of candle fumes lingers. He fluffs up a pillow, positions it, but before he lays his head down, there is a confident rap at the door. It is nine o'clock in the evening. Outside a full moon rises.

'Who is it?'

'It's me.'

It is Jailos. Chembe can tell from the timbre of the voice. Jailos assists with security duties on Chapisa Farm. He's on duty tonight. Chembe waits to hear what the matter is.

'Two men want to talk to you. They want to see only foreman.'

Chembe reaches for his overalls that hang on a chair beside the bed. He wears his boots, pulls a woollen hat over his head and picks up a baton and torch from a corner. The two men stride along a path one behind the other. Jailos leads the way at a fast pace. Chembe thinks the young man is either afraid or excited.

'Who are these people?'

'Don't know. They won't speak to me.'

It is a clear night with a star-studded sky. Definitive shapes of farm buildings are visible; the farm school, tobacco barns, empty horse stables, garage and tool sheds. The torch beam sometimes falls on the thatch of a cooking hut or on the asbestos sheet of a farmhand's main house as they go past the farm compound. They head towards a locked gate. Two figures stand near the stile as if ready to climb over the fence. One is tall, the other of medium height. The rosette of light turns this way and that before Chembe focuses on the two strangers. A woollen scarf with brown stripes is wound round the neck of the taller one. The short man wears a beret at an angle on his head. Both have their hands in their jacket pockets.

The taller one speaks. 'Hey, switch off that thing. We're not thieves.'

Chembe tries to take the sting out of the stranger's words. 'Good evening, my brothers.' He directs the torch light to the ground. 'How can I help you?'

'You the foreman?"

Chembe nods his head.

'Just the man we're looking for. Eh, we want to come and address the workers some time. You arrange that for us, old man.' It is more a command than a question.

'Old man.' Chembe heard the slight sneer of disrespect in these two English words. The old would not be part of this new order. Were not expected to either understand or appreciate it. Still, he politely informs them that he cannot allow strangers onto the farm. They have to seek permission from Mr Winterson, the farm owner. The young men have no interest in what he says. The short one has the last word before they melt into the bushes.

'These *vaenzi* will be back *chop chop*.'

Chembe realises perhaps he should not have used the word strangers, but that was the rule – no strangers without appointment – and the young men's attitude had not encouraged him to think they were men of good will.

Nonetheless, Jailos still complains, 'Mudhara Chembe, *hini ndava*? You talk like you're born out of the same womb. They could be thieves, troublemakers, vandalisers. We should have…' Jailos completes the sentence with a crossing of hands at the wrists mimicking a handcuffed person. Both Jailos and Chembe were issued with handcuffs after training with a security guard company in Harare.

'I know, but not so fast. They've not stolen or caused trouble. Better wait. See what they're up to first?'

'Up to no good,' insists Jailos.

Chembe thinks it's unwise to annoy strangers, especially at night. They follow the fireguard that runs along the perimeter fence for about two hundred metres checking for loose strands where the barbed wire may have been cut. All is well. Jailos remains behind sitting by a fire in the small wooden shelter near the stile. Chembe returns to his house. He decides to pass by the farmhouse for a quick check. He strides through a windbreak of pine trees and up the slope of the hill where the house stands. He finds the security lights shining bright and the tall gate locked. Thwacks of electric current reassure him that the farmhouse perimeter fence is undisturbed.

***

One early morning, thirty-five years previously, Chembe arrived at Chapisa Farm. He had travelled forty kilometres from Harare by bus along the Mutoko Road then walked five kilometres along a dusty strip that branched off to the left of the main road. He waited at the farm's main gate among a group of people from the nearby Chikwaka Communal Lands looking for seasonal work. The farmer needed extra hands to help out with the tobacco crop. Experienced tobacco pickers and graders were selected. Chembe was not among them. However, he'd caught the attention of the white farmer and his assistant because of his seemingly underage appearance. A boy of medium height, slight of build, a hint of puppy fat underneath smooth face skin and upper arms without the firm bulge of hardened biceps.

'What farm experience do you have?' Mr Winterson stared down at the boy with his pale blue eyes.

'Me, I'm a grader. Fast grader of oranges at Mazowe Citrus Estate.' Chembe had been laid off at the estate because acreage under citrus plantation had been reduced to make way for maize growing.

'We grade tobacco here not oranges. What else did you do?'

'Me, I clean, wax and pack…o..oranges.' His confidence crumbled.

'I see. You have only worked with oranges.' Feeling empathy for the youth, he thought that he was being illogical to expect work experience out of a boy who was still a child. 'How old are you?'

'Eighteen.'

It was a guess. His father, who originally came from Malawi, had left the citrus estate for the mines, where wages were said to be double what he was getting. He did not register the birth of either of his two children through ignorance or irresponsibility, who knows? When Chembe reached school-going age, he could not be enrolled in school without a certificate. His mother, who had never been to school, paid a man of Malawian origin to pose as the father at the Mazoe District Office. The hired father retained the first names of the children but gave them his surname. He stood before the clerk, presented the children along with his proof of identity. He plucked birthdays out of the air and the children acquired birth certificates and an identity, enabling Chembe to go to school, and later, to leave the citrus estate and seek a job elsewhere.

By ten o'clock in the morning it was warm. Chembe watched the farmer roll up the sleeves of his khaki shirt to his elbows, exposing arms with veins that stood out like chords. He pulled at the wide brim of his hat to shield his eyes from the sun as he checked the identity documents of the job seekers. Recruitment of the temporary workers was close to complete, and Chembe still stood outside the gate. Mr Winterson was not an unkind man, and there was something about the youth's quiet persistence, which struck a chord with him. Impatience is not a virtue in a farmer.

Mr Winterson called for his assistant and instructed that the youth be employed in the vegetable section. Fifteen acres of Chapisa Farm was under market gardening. Chembe would be watched for three months before being confirmed in the position.

The young man turned out to have the strength of an ox. He turned up early for work every day and was never absent without good reason. He sorted, cleaned and crated potatoes, tomatoes, butternut squash, cabbage, aubergines and cucumber. Always ready to help the new recruits Chembe impressed Mr Winterson with his social skills and eagerness to embrace new arrivals. He kept the young man at the back of his mind for when there was a more responsible post to be filled.

Chembe shared a two-roomed house in the farm compound with another young farmhand. In five years he grew taller and his body filled out. He sported a beard on his chin. Well-liked by the rest of the farmhands, some mothers expressed the view that he would make an ideal son-in-law.

So it was that Chembe met Snodia, a seasonal worker from Chikwaka Communal Lands, which border the eastern side of Chapisa Farm. He liked her dark complexion and her big eyes set in a round open face that made her seem as if she had no secrets. Once she accepted his proposal for marriage, Chembe did not waste time. He wanted to be introduced to her family immediately, but the visit to Snodia's parents was a not great success.

Chembe spoke Shona fluently but with the inflections of Chichewa, his mother tongue. He and Snodia were sitting in the grandmother's hut with members of her family who had come to meet their son-in-law-to-be. They found, or pretended to find, his speech hard to understand.

'Huh? What did you say?' Snodia's aunt, mother, grandmother or uncle would ask when Chembe spoke. Sometimes Snodia would intervene to clarify a point or provide an appropriate word or its pronunciation. She was eager to make him blend in with the rest of the family. He masked his embarrassment with contrived cheerfulness and laughter. It was also an uncomfortable moment for Chembe who had to talk about his family history, which he had little knowledge.

'So where is your family? Snodia's aunt wanted to know.

Chembe talked about his mother and sister. The mother had died and his young sister was a junior wife to an older man who had journeyed with his father from Malawi to what was then Rhodesia. He hardly had any recollection of his father who had left for Jumbo Mine when he was four years old. When his mother had followed his father to ask for money towards maintenance of the children, he was no longer there. Some of his friends said he had been seen on a ranch in Plumtree in the south west of Zimbabwe driving a herd of Brahmans to the feeding troughs. Chembe's mother gave up. She had neither money nor energy to chase after him.

'My father works in Matabeleland,' was all Chembe could say.

At the end of the visit, when some relatives saw them out of the hut to the bus stop on the Harare-Mutoko Road, the grandmother tactlessly pulled Snodia aside.

'Throwing yourself away to a foreigner like that?' she whispered loudly. 'What's wrong with the local men? *Xnaa*! You're not wise.'

Snodia was taken aback by the old woman's outburst.

'It is better to settle down with someone you know, who has grown up with you. What is wrong with Togara, Misheck, Obey?' the old woman named the eligible young men in the village. 'And what do you know about the ways of your man's people?'

Snodia loved Chembe and she was going marry him, but she didn't want to upset her grandmother so she simply responded that he was a hard-working and honest man, much respected by the other farmworkers.

But her grandmother would not let up and carried on as if all Malawian people were one. '*MaBrandaya anotetereka*. They are drifters cursed with running away from their own people. They travel not to reach a destination.'

'Grandmother, you have never travelled further than Juru Growth Point,' she said, pointing at an eclectic conglomeration of buildings in the distance, the communal lands' main contact with the outside world. 'How do you know about people who live in other parts?'

Snodia was upset; she rejoined the rest of the group. The grandmother turned and walked back at an uncharacteristic pace for one who walked with the aid of a walking stick. She too was upset that her wise counsel had not been well received by her own kith and kin.

Sharing her grandmother's concerns with Chembe strengthened his resolve to marry her. He approached Mr Winterson and told him about the imminent marriage. He hoped Mr Winterson might let him buy two old cows that he could put towards lobola. The cost would be deducted from his wages little by little. The farmer was not agreeable.

'I'll be setting an example. Opening floodgates. Before I blink every bloody farm worker would want a *mombe* from me. Out of the question.'

'But you're a father to me. I've grown up under your care. Most of what I can do on the farm you taught me.' Chembe knew Mr

Winterson's bark was often much worse than his bite, and he was quietly conscious that he had successfully replaced the blue gums with indigenous trees; he could plough the fields, cure and grade tobacco as well as grow all the vegetables from seed. 'Who else would help me build my family?'

And Chembe was right. Mr Winterson had three grown sons who had emigrated to South Africa, and not much outlet for his paternal instincts. So, on reflection, Mr Winterson agreed to help, but only if his wife concurred.

'Give the young chap a chance. You always talk about what a good worker he is.' Mrs Winterson did not often go down to the fields but she knew Chembe from the clinic she ran on the farm and from the many times he brought vegetables to the farmhouse. She knew her husband felt affection for the young man founded on mutual trust, his work ethic and his admirable character. He would like Chembe to be happy, with a family of his own. He felt he deserved a chance at life.

Once Chembe had paid *lobola*, his standing with his in-laws improved. Of the three young men who had married into the family he was the only one who had paid off the bride's wealth. Being a farm hand the in-laws found him helpful around the homestead. He was especially attentive to the grandmother who had finally warmed to him. She had a ready list of chores for him when he visited: logs to be chopped for firewood, a broken garden fence to be mended or a door to be put back on its hinges. And Snodia's grandmother knew how to show her appreciation. Chembe often walked out of her yard on a full stomach, a fat pullet under his arm, a gift for his family at the farm. Sometimes he would bring saplings of *musasa, mubvee*, duikerberry and other local trees he was planting on the farm, to the pleasure of his father-in-law.

***

The years passed generally peacefully and productively, and the couple had two children, Maladitso and Mayamiko. When they reached school age, the pressure from Snodia's family for Chembe to build a house in Chikwaka began to make more sense, especially as it meant that the children could go to the local Anglican mission school that had qualified teachers. The pre-school on the farm had been good. Snodia had participated, and taken a course run by Save the Children, but the primary school still depended on O-level school leavers.

And so it was that over several years, with small loans here, and hard work there, Snodia and Chembe built a brick house in Chikwaka with five rooms and a corrugated iron roof. The woman had begun to live there with the children long before the final nail was struck. And while Chembe missed them, his work on the farm as foreman kept him fully occupied from dawn to dusk and he always joined the family at weekends, cycling fifteen kilometers each Friday on a bicycle laden with packets of potatoes, onions and tomatoes. And sometimes she and the children would return to the farm, especially during the school holidays, when Maladitso loved to ride the tractors, everyone turning a blind eye, given Chembe's position.

But all good things come to an end. Maladitso returned one day from school with his clothes dirty, and covered in cuts and bruises. 'Whatever have you done?' his mother asked, hastily filling a bowl of cold water. 'Hondo called my father a foreigner, a white man's lap dog. He said that soon he would be out of a job, and that his own father would have land on Chapisa Farm. He said Mr Winterston is a thief and must go back to England.'

Snodia felt the struggle, which had been on the lips of every market woman for weeks now, coming right into their home. She took a wet cloth and bathed the cut on Maladitso's forehead, as if he were a small child, and not a young man. She wondered what she should say to him. She knew people were jealous of her and Chembe because of the loans they had been given by Mr Winterston, because of all the free vegetables and firewood. But hadn't her husband worked for it over almost two decades now; didn't he deserve the respect of his employer? But she knew too that when the chips were down, the fact that he'd been born in Zimbabwe would count for nothing. People would turn on him, and call him a traitor, a Malawian dog. Should her son receive the same treatment?

Maladitso looked at her. 'ZBC says we should go and take the farms, drive out the white man. Do we not need land? I fought Hondo because he insulted my father, but I am not defending the farm.'

Snodia felt that she should go and see Chembe; the only way was to talk to him. Her heart was filled with misgiving. But he should be back home in two days – that is if he came on Friday, as usual. She decided that it would be best to wait, and that if he did not come, she would go to the farm on Sunday.

On Friday Chembe had been unusually late to arrive, Snodia had been out twice to the bus stop, looking for him. Her anxiety built with the noise of the dogs barking, a familiar sound but one that grated against chafed nerves. Then someone with a familiar scent stepped into the yard. '*Fusek! Choka,*' she heard Chembe mutter, shooing away their two dogs. Once he'd settled, Snodia served him sadza and dried mushrooms in peanut butter. Afterwards she heated up bath water for her husband who was washing down his dinner with heavily sugared black tea from his favourite tin mug. He disliked china cups that he said were so small they could not hold a mouthful.

They were in bed when Snodia brought up the subject of trouble on the farms.

'If I were you I would leave the job.' Snodia's voice was low.

'Why? And do what? Watch my family go hungry?'

'It's not your farm. Keep out of it.'

'Keep out of what?'

'You told me there are strangers about?'

'Ah, nothing new. People wander from the reserves to cut thatch grass, collect firewood… Winterson doesn't mind, so long as they ask.'

'They don't ask these days. They say it's their land. Haven't they already invaded the neighbourhood farms – Norfolk, Serui, Nyabira … You *must* know this.' Snodia's firm voice trailed away. 'Don't chase them, setting dogs after them like you do. You'll only invite trouble for the family.'

Snodia did not reveal that their son had already had a fight with a group of youths who had come under the influence of the local councillor. How long would it be before he joined them. He was at that very impressionable age. Her best friend had told her that she could do nothing with her own son who was being paid to join the invaders, and he's given *mbanje*, the woman said helplessly. 'Nothing can I do, not when he's been smoking and drinking – and we need the money.' Snodia felt she knew better than her husband how these invasions were going to break up families, break up communities. When something was free, everyone would want a share of it.

'You're living in a cocoon,' she told him. 'Here in Chikwaka everyone is talking about these invasions. People are divided, but they all want land.'

'Yes, but they want food, jobs, firewood too,' said Chembe, refusing to hear the anxiety in her voice. There'd been troubles before. They would pass.

'Winterson is not a politics man, only a farmer.' Chembe laughed the way he did when he thought an idea was far-fetched, though deep in his heart he worried too.

***

Back on the farm Mr Winterson asked Chembe to increase the patrols. There was an upsurge of people who wandered across the lands without permission. Chembe, as foreman, was asked to double up as head of security. He found a way to cut down on moving up, down and across the farm. He climbed the *musamvi* tree that grew on a rise of the fifty acres of local trees. It was a big, tall tree with great limbs; its leafy boughs formed a wide thick canopy. Where the trunk divided, one branch grew up and outwards then curved on itself into the shape of the letter L. Chembe followed the branch and sat in the bend, his legs resting on the smaller branches beneath. With his head partially hidden in the foliage he would sit quietly and people could walk past underneath without noticing him. Climbing trees was a childhood habit. His position gave him an excellent observation point. From this height, Chapisa Farm spread out like a map beneath him. He could see the red of the farmhouse roof, the dam that shone like a sheet of glass to the south of the vlei and the dairy herd grazing. Besides being a look-out, it gave Chembe real pleasure. He enjoyed the solitude of the woods: the breeze stirring the leaves and twigs, and the cracking pods and the many birds that came to feast on *tsamvi* fruit, the pea-sized sweet figs, which he also sometimes ate.

Chembe was in the *musamvi* tree when two men walked past beneath him. He recognised the tall man with the striped woollen scarf. The strangers were back. Chembe quickly and quietly climbed down the tree and followed them at a distance. He saw them talking to Jailos, who was watching over the women from Chikwaka whom Chembe had granted permission to cut thatch grass. He strained to catch snippets of the conversation. The tall one seemed to raise his voice deliberately as if he knew he was being followed, and as if he wanted to be sure that Chembe heard his every word. This being the case, Chembe strolled up to them, and nodded.

'The white farmer is going to leave,' the stranger continued with barely a glance in Chembe's direction. 'He has already had our letter. It's now twenty-one years since the country got its independence. He has made enough money. Now, it's our turn. We are going to parcel out the farm in ten, twenty, thirty and fifty acres for people to farm.' Jailos glances at Chembe with eyes that say the idea is sound.

'I would say a man who owns land is a free man, Mudhara Chembe. You grow your own food. Feed your family. You go to the fields in your own time. Nobody shouts at you.'

The strangers smile, nodding in agreement. Chembe reflects. It is all very well for a young man like Jailos to talk like this. He has no family. What would stop a young man from trying a new life? His position is different. He has a family. Mr Winterson has been good to him. It would be better for him to live with the difficulties that he knows. What other hazards might lie ahead? Has Jailos been seeing these men secretly? It's a discomforting thought.

'Experienced farmers like you, we give thirty acres of good land.' The tall one points at the ploughed fields. We will give you a plough, two oxen and maize seed. What more can you ask?'

'But who are you? You have no permission to be here. Now you talk about taking over the farm. I have to tell Winterson.'

'You'll soon know. But go ahead and call him.'

Chembe hurries towards the farmhouse. A plume of smoke rising where the women are cutting grass halts him. He changes direction, trots towards them. He is angry that the grass-cutters are acting against the rules, starting a fire that can easily spread. Chembe confronts them, but the women are unperturbed. They have to eat and they need to cook because they will be cutting grass for the next three days.

Chembe is taken aback.

'I'm going to call Winterson. He has to see for himself.'

The women laugh and jeer. 'What can your white man do?' says one.

It's clear that what has been happening in the neighbourhood has finally arrived at Chipisa.

Chembe hears a crowd in the distance. Shouting and singing '*Jambanja jambanja*,' and armed with machetes, knobkerries and bicycle chains. One holds aloft the signpost that has been uprooted from the farm entrance. The inscription reads 'Chapisa Farm. Trespassers will be prosecuted.' The crowd heads towards the forest of indigenous trees close to where the grass cutters are. The women put down their sickles and join the crowd ululating and dancing. Chembe winces at the thuds of axes felling trees that he has tended for years.

One of the workers alerts the farmer who phones the police. He drives twenty kilometres to Goromonzi Police Station to pick up the officers because they have no vehicle. He brings back three officers. The senior one sits in the front with his hat on. He has a baton in his lap and drums on it with his thumb. The younger officers share the back seat, which smells of dog fur. There is silence in the car. The Land Rover swerves as the farmer hastily takes corners on the strip road. The senior officer instructs the farmer not to rush.

When they arrive the farm workers have gathered to watch what is happening. The tall man encourages them to join in. Chembe spots Mayamiko in the crowd. Their eyes meet. The son looks down, averting his father's gaze. He looks rough and smells rougher. His eyes are red and tired. His hair is uncombed and his clothes have the sickly tang of old sweat. Chembe is shocked, embarrassed, angry and sorry for his son all at once.

***

The police officers do not restrain the crowd. The senior officer turns to the white farmer. 'This is outside our control. You have to talk to each other and reach a compromise. The farm belongs to all of you. These are their ancestral lands too.'

'I will not.' The farmer is now red in the face. He turns to the farm workers. They look passive and cowed. He clears his throat. He shuts his eyes as if to make everything disappear. There is a silence. Heads drop. The workers look at each other's face's, covertly. The farmer's inner ear replays the police officer's words: 'This is outside... ancestral lands.'

Tension makes the white farmer's words tumble out through a half-open mouth. 'The land grabbers are here ... you're welcome to join them ... if you wish.' Anger shakes his voice and halts his speech. 'If you think they've come for land ... I'm afraid you're mistaken. They're thieves, sniffing round my property like a pack of wild dogs. They're after my dairy herd, my cured tobacco, my farm equipment ... You can go with them ... Go on!'

Muffled sniggers came from the invading crowd followed by a wave of shock that ripples through the gathering of farm workers. A shuffle of feet draws his attention. Jailos and a small group of farmhands saunter away towards the group that has come to the farm.

'We're for land.' Jailos's speech is loud, slow and deliberate.

The farmer interrupts the cheers and whistles, a show of support by the incomers for the farmhands that have joined them.

'Good riddance to all of you, if you go. Do you think those people care about you? You'll be on your own. And God help you because I won't. No more free school for your children. No more free rations of maize meal, beans ... No more free clinic when you're sick. And in a few years, when all the trees are cut down, this land will be barren.' He points at the acacia tree-clothed anthills beyond the ploughed wheat fields, the designated burial ground for farm workers. 'No more decent burials when the time comes ... ' He pauses.

In the silence a few of the farm workers turn their eyes to the anthills where remains of their relatives lie beneath mounds of earth with upturned battered ceremonial dishes on the top and planted crude wooden crosses bearing the name of a baby, mother, brother or grandparent in the spidery scrawl of those who have not gone beyond the second grade of primary school. He too looks at a clump of white flowering bougainvilleas that cover up the graves of three generations of the Wintersons. Tears unexpectedly well in the farmer's eyes. He chokes with emotion. Not just years, but a century of work and investment. Chembe moves close to him. The police officers glare at the farm workers who murmur protest.

'We can call for riot police,' the senior officer tells the farm workers.

'You have twenty-four hours to leave the farm. Out! *NomuBrantyre wako*. Foreigners!' the tall man shouts. 'And that includes you, Chembe. You're a Malawian, a white man's poodle. Get out. Go! We're better off without you!'

(iv)

Gender Relations

9

MAININI GRACE'S PROMISE

Valerie Tagwira

Sarai's mother had concluded that it was not the three successive funerals but her own subsequent illness that finally did it.

Since her disclosure, things had gradually changed. In time, the subtle had become obvious. The extended family seemed to have conveniently forgotten about their existence. Prior to that, their visits had been increasingly shrouded in an aura of something parallel to embarrassment and detachment. Then they had become erratic, before ceasing altogether. For Sarai, dropping out of school to become her mother's carer was inevitable. She felt as if the family had washed their hands clean of all responsibility, before dumping it carelessly into her fifteen-year-old lap.

Her vivacious and capable aunt, Mainini Grace was the only one who kept in touch. She sent money for groceries from Botswana and wrote encouraging letters, filled with promises that she would visit. She also promised that she would bring tablets for her ailing sister, as well as arrange for Sarai to go back to school.

Occasionally *mainini's* list included the gloves that Sarai had requested for her mother's bed-baths, the bra that she wanted so much because girls of her age had started wearing breast support; and sanitary pads because there were no pads or cotton wool in the shops.

While the letters had become a beacon, little by little the fruition of Mainini Grace's promises became questionable. In the eleven months since the last funeral, she had not returned from Botswana. Despite this inconsistency, the letters continued. Sarai would read them avidly, over and over again, longing for her aunt's return, and wishing for her to be the one to share this experience with her.

In her replies to Mainini Grace, Sarai always expressed these sentiments, just stopping short of hinting that the money that she sent was never enough. Because of the shortages, grocery prices on the thriving black market were always exaggerated.

***

After the most recent letter, Sarai allowed herself to be optimistic. Previously, it had always been, 'Soon, my dearest.'

But the imminence of *mainini's* arrival was given life with her assurance of a date of her arrival was expected on Wednesday, the 17th of July.

In the morning, Sarai woke up very early and tidied up the shack. She wrapped her hands with pieces of plastic and gave her mother a bed-bath, just as the nurse had taught her to do. The raw bedsores did not seem as daunting as before, and her mother's muted groans of discomfort when she rolled her over were not as heart-rending. She needed no encouragement to eat up her maize meal porridge that was tasteless from lack of sugar or peanut butter. On that day, spasms of pain did not contort her face as they normally did when she coughed.

It was a day with a difference, and they spent it in happy anticipation of Mainini Grace's arrival.

But by early evening, Sarai knew that the coach from Botswana had long passed Kwekwe, and was probably in Harare already. Mainini Grace had not come.

'Do you think she will ever come?' she asked her mother, disheartened.

The older woman's brow creased for a moment, before she said slowly, 'There must be a good reason. I know my sister. I'm sure she will come soon.'

Sarai looked at her mother, astonished by this lack of anxiety. She did not appear to be disturbed by her young sister's slipperiness, although she was supposed to have brought life-saving medication from Botswana. What good reason can there be for Mainini Grace to make these false promises when mother is so ill? Sarai felt deceived and confused.

She wondered why she had been foolish enough to expect anything different. Misery was predictable, while its opposite was simply out of reach. Her aunt was not coming. Though her own desire to go back to school was not as urgent as her mother's need for medication, Sarai wondered, Will I ever sit in class again? At that moment, she felt fleeting resentment against Nhamo, a former classmate who she knew to have assumed her prior position at the top of her class.

Despite her apparent complacency, Sarai's mother was generally more unwell than she had ever been. Nothing seemed to help relieve her cough. Not the bitter juice from boiled gum-tree leaves that had given her husband temporary relief. Not even the lemon tea and the Vick's chest rub. She needed proper medication to ease the cough, but there was none. It was three months since the last bottle of cough mixture had run out.

***

Although she was deeply tired, Sarai knew that she could not sleep before her mother nodded off. To do so would have been callous. Impossible, in fact. Her place was right there, sitting next to the older woman, who now lay huddled on a reed mat spread out on the floor.

It was a place that she had no desire to surrender. Only Mainini Grace could have shared this place with her. Her heart ached with love, and with profound loneliness.

Once again, she mopped the older woman's brow with a slow, gentle movement. Beads of sweat reappeared, no sooner than they'd been soaked up by the cloth. The older woman's forehead continued to glisten in the dim light.

Sarai sat back in the silence, overcome by a yearning for happier times. Searching her heart, she failed to summon any such memories. Reality swooped back swiftly to fill the temporary emptiness of her mind.

Her eyes strayed to the soot marks staining the wall. She made a mental note to scrub it down first thing in the morning, or else risk suffering the landlady's wrath. Mai Simba's legendary rages were guaranteed to instill fear into any living soul, and for Sarai, eviction was a real and immediate threat.

She constantly received reminders about how compassionate Mai Simba had been to take in the likes of her and her mother; and she had been warned several times about the hazards of fire in the shack. She now took care to make a great show of cooking outside before sneaking the fire indoors for her mother at night.

Just yesterday, the home-based care nurse had looked at the soot marks with obvious displeasure. 'You had a fire in here?' It had been an accusation. 'How do you expect her cough to get better?' she had demanded, with a gesture that enclosed the cramped, airless shack.

Sarai had been immediately contrite, but she had wondered, What else can I do? Her disobedience came out of necessity, rather than wilful intent. July was cold, and starting to get windy. Her mother's body was hot, but she often complained that the cold gnawed relentlessly into her bones, robbing her of what little comfort remained. Sarai understood her discomfort. It was winter, after all.

***

Why aren't you here with us, Mainini Grace? Sarai stared blindly at the dying fire that mirrored the demise of hope. Her mind did not really register the red embers that lay glowing among grey, powdery ashes.

She had an illusion of seeing through them into a vast, colourless place where she was held suspended at the edge of a precipice. She shook off the surreal vision with a shrug and stretched out her stiff, cold limbs.

The room was dimmer, now that the fire was almost out. Cold air was starting to creep in. She shivered. Just as they had used up the last of the firewood, they were also using the last precious candle whose lone flame looked as feeble as its source.

Mai Simba's main house had electricity. When she was in a good mood, she often promised to connect an electric light bulb to the shack, but it never happened. If only Mainini Grace had come, maybe she would have brought a few candles from Botswana. Sarai's thoughts wandered again to her elusive aunt.

Her mother's eyes seemed to be summoning her, pleading for something that was not hers to give. She dragged herself forwards to wipe her forehead again. The woman's withered hand rose, trembled, and dropped abruptly.

Sarai strained her ears, at once reluctant and fearful of what she would hear. Instinctively, she knew the words before they were spoken.

'Be strong, *mwanangu*. It will happen soon. I know it.' A wavering croak, barely a whisper, 'Be strong. Be strong.'

The words seemed to hang suspended between them, and then they fell like the fading notes of an echo. A repetition was whispered through bouts of coughing. Her mother's voice was muffled by thick phlegm, but still her wish seeped into Sarai's awareness. The words seemed to reverberate like a haunting refrain. They would be with her forever. She was certain of it.

'Find Mainini Grace. She will put you back in school. Don't end up like me.'

Please don't say that, *Amai*. Don't say that. She willed her mother to stop and reached out to hold her hands, dismissing thoughts of Mainini Grace. She should have been there with them as promised, but it was simply inane to wish for her now.

The feverish hands quivered in her grasp, now so claw-like and wasted they could have been a child's. Sarai remembered holding her young brother's hands in the same manner and thinking then that they were like the feet of a tiny bird – puny, but with sharp pointed nails. She wished she had remembered to trim her mother's nails, if only to avoid these painful comparisons.

Her young sister's small hands had had a similar feel. Little birds' feet. The two little birds had flown, one after the other. But her father's journey had been slower and more agonising, almost like her mother's.

Sarai steadied herself. Her voice was strong but gentle when she spoke. 'Don't worry. Don't worry *Amai*.'

In preceding years, she had perfected the modulations of these same words. Don't worry, Mary. Don't worry, Tafara. Don't worry, *Baba*. Over and over again, she'd repeated them tenderly; the pitch of her voice suitably attuned to encourage and soothe. Always. And now it was, Don't worry, *Amai*. She was the untouched; destined to be the survivor, the comforter.

However, despite her exterior calmness, a muddle of emotions wracked her. Fear and resentment at looming abandonment. Desire for her mother to live, to be well again, so that she could love and protect her, as it should be. Uneasy relief that finally it would all be over; her mother would find reprieve, and not before time … Her heart thudded and her thoughts withdrew to the day before yesterday.

***

It was only two days since they had discharged her mother from hospital. Only two days, but the bleak medical ward and its horribly caustic smells were already a distant memory. As if too embarrassed to show itself, a prescription lay concealed among numerous hospital cards in a tattered paper bag behind the door. There had been no medicines in the hospital pharmacy. It was the same last time, Sarai thought bitterly, making an effort to hold imminent tears of anger at bay.

'You will have to look after her at home. Our outreach nurses will support you. For now, we have done everything possible,' the doctor had said sombrely, his voice firm and authoritative. His demeanour had been that of one who took pride in his work; one who believed his words had the power to miraculously restore Sarai's confidence in a system that had failed her before. Several times.

The words had fallen empty and meaningless, soothing phrases that were no doubt reserved for the near-to-dying. Sarai had been so angry that for one manic moment, she had seen herself grabbing the man's neck and strangling him.

Clearly, her mother was no better than when she had been admitted into hospital a week before, if not a little worse. At the recollection, anger peaked swiftly again and collapsed. She now knew it to be a futile and exhausting emotion, and she needed her reserves.

Yesterday's follow-up visit by the home-based care nurse had been no compensation. The woman had come empty-handed. Although she had counselled Sarai and told her what to expect near the end, denial had been so much easier to embrace. The reality was unbearable.

Making no attempt to disguise tactlessness, or simply lacking the skills to do so, the nurse had explained that there would be no need to call an ambulance; if she should be so lucky to have one coming out at all. The hospital no longer had anything to offer.

Nothing.

Nothing.

Neither had Mai Simba or the neighbours, who had sometimes come to their aid. In the dead of night, Sarai knew that they only had each other. The wind howled eerily. The candle flame appeared to swirl and dance; merry and oblivious.

The nurse forgot to tell me about the pain I would feel. She forgot about me. She forgot about me … In spite of her determination to be strong, Sarai found herself weeping silent, clandestine tears. She inclined her head, almost immediately resolute once more, thinking. Her mother should not see the tears that shimmered in her eyes or the drops that rolled down her cheeks.

With a quick duck of her head, she furtively wiped her face on the blanket. Its roughness scratched her cheeks, causing a slight stinging sensation. Her mother appeared not to notice.

Though much quieter now, the insistent whisper continued, 'Do not end up like me. Find Mainini Grace.' Sunken eyes glowed unnaturally in the dim candlelight.

Sarai caressed her mother's hands in hers, keen to reassure her but no longer confident of her ability to do so. Her bemused thoughts raced, unwillingly returning to Mainini Grace. Why isn't she here?

Silently, she nodded and squeezed the wizened hands, almost ready for acceptance. Hadn't they been preparing for this eventuality together? They had been through enough to make them courageous. Words that her mother would never hear formed a lump in Sarai's throat.

The older woman had closed her eyes. She now lay quiet, her breathing rapid and increasingly shallow. Her words kept ringing in Sarai's head, distressing but at the same time strangely comforting because she knew that her mother wanted the best for her. She allowed herself to hope once again that Mainini Grace would come. *Mainini* was a strong, lively woman who had a way of taking charge and making things happen. Sarai knew that if anyone was capable of putting her back in school and giving her a bright future, that person was Mainini Grace. She would do everything possible to make sure her life did not reflect her mother's. She owed it to her.

***

As Sarai sat, she heard from a distance the hum of a car engine. The sound became louder as it approached the dwelling. Then there was a brief silence followed by the resonance of doors banging. A dog barked and a few distant yelps of solidarity ensued. She heard hushed voices, mingling with the thud of footsteps. Her mother stirred and tugged weakly at the blanket.

Sarai wondered if the landlord, Mai Simba's husband, was back from one of his cross-border trips. He often arrived late at night. She pictured his children rushing out of the main house, falling over each other in their eagerness to welcome him back home. Jealousy surfaced. They had a father who was alive, when hers was not.

A soft knock on the door interrupted her musing. Her mother's eyes flew open. 'Who is it?' she asked in a breathless whisper.

Sarai shook her head, puzzled. Who could be calling so late? She hoped it wasn't Mai Simba coming to spy for evidence that might suggest that they had broken yet another household rule. Reluctantly, she stood up and dragged her feet towards the door. She pulled the handle.

The bizarre vision that she encountered was that of her mother standing at the doorstep. The right side of her body was concealed in shadow; the left side was harshly illuminated by the glare of an electric bulb shining from Mai Simba's veranda.

Sarai stood frozen in shock as she took in the sunken eyes, the gaunt cheeks, and the emaciated form that was dwarfed by an oversized coat. At her mother's feet were three suitcases. She shook her head, light-headed and confused by this peculiarity. She remembered weird stories of how dying people sometimes said goodbye to their loved ones in the form of apparitions.

'*Amai*? How did you …?' Her voice trembled in query and died in her throat.

The woman held out her hands and stepped forward. 'Please don't tell me she's gone …' The voice was fearful. It was not her mother's voice. It was familiar, but unexpected. Certainly not like this. Not coming from this spectre.

Sarai found herself shaking uncontrollably. In that moment, she understood everything, and her unanswered questions immediately found answers. Reality and reason merged, eliminating the need to demand an explanation.

And then came the realisation of what must surely have been fate's calculated conspiracy against her. All her expectations collapsed in that instant. She felt as if something had exploded in her head, and a strident buzz was triggered somewhere deep inside her.

'No-o!' Screaming, she launched herself forcefully on the woman. She grabbed the scrawny neck and squeezed. They fell backwards in a writhing heap on Mai Simba's cabbage patch. The woman struggled and gasped. 'Sarai … please… no …'

Sarai thought she heard her mother calling out to her, but she felt something stronger compelling her to focus on squeezing harder. The buzzing in her head grew louder, drowning out everything.

It was her anguished hysteria that severed the stillness of night summoning Mai Simba and the neighbours. She felt hands pulling her from all directions, trying to break her hold on the woman who now lay on top of crushed cabbages, apparently lifeless, her eyes glazed as a small moan escaped her.

'Why you too? Why you too, Mainini Grace?' Sarai sobbed brokenly as they led her away to Mai Simba's veranda.

10

Message in a Bottle

Isabella Matambanadzo

I felt the sinews of my mind stretch. And rip. This feeling took hold of me and wouldn't let me go. It came every time I thought about my mother and the things that happened to her that year. They'd tried to hide her from me, but we had our own special way of communicating. It had always been so.

I was accustomed to coming home to a neat, empty house. My key, like a precious pendant on a leather thong around my neck, clicked easily into the lock of the side door. I reached my hand inside the security gate and pulled at the switch that let me in. Once inside, I put my exhausted book bag on the floor. It has seen better days. Achemwene, the tailor who'd come to our neighbourhood from Malawi, had patched swathes of denim into the very worn sections where the armbands rubbed against my shoulders. He had smiled a big, toothfull grin and reassured me that it was as good as new.

I pulled off my brown lace-up shoes, together with my white ankle socks, and let the cool concrete floors soothe my tired feet. We'd had athletics at school that day. The teacher was in a foul mood, so we ended up running long-distance laps. I looked down at the grey floor, waxed to a brilliant shine with Cobra. Again, I thought about the things I would do for Mama when I was grown up and working. I'd make sure she had her dream kitchen and pantry with the floors done up in those cobalt blue Talavera tiles she loved so much.

I slipped on my flip-flops and moved to change into my home clothes.

My single bed, pushed against the wall, was draped with a faded mint-green duvet. A teddy bear Mama had given me for my birthday rested its frayed head in the hollow of my pillow. She'd bought it from a lady who lugged sacks of second-hand toys from Mozambique. The psychiatrist had a similar bear, only new. He also had a mother, so how could he be sitting safely behind his big desk asking me how I felt?

My routine was familiar. I would wash my hands with water stored in a green plastic jug, which was easy for me to lift from under the sink without spilling. That's where we kept the drums of water, which we collected in our wheelbarrow every weekend from the community borehole; it'd been put in by an international aid agency so that we wouldn't get cholera. Our small home, though it didn't use much of it with its modest proportions, hadn't had water run through its taps for more than a decade. Now I'm fourteen, but I can't remember how water flows through taps. I've never stood under a shower of warm water or known the luxury of carelessly washing twice a day with no care for the labour involved in gathering water. Don't get me wrong, I'm not complaining. It's just that I am curious about why it is this way.

At our small wooden dining table, I would first say my grace for the food that Jesus had put on our table. I'd never met Jesus because he was busy all over the world suffering for everyone's sins. When I was small, I really wanted to meet him to say thank you for the food because that was the polite thing to do. Instead, I ate the peanut butter on brown bread Mama left in a lunch box on the table for me. I always ate my afternoon snack alone. Then carefully filled a small glass with UHT milk. Even though there were lots of cows in our country, the days of fresh milk were long gone.

The milk gurgled down into my stomach like the joyful laughter of the little brother I often imagined. All the other children at school came in twos or threes. In our family it was just me. And Mama. Then just me.

I did my homework meticulously. Maths first, because I always struggled with simultaneous equations. Then science, which I enjoyed.

And finally, geography. It fascinated me, the mysterious, unseen and ultra-powerful world of tectonic plates. I imagined them moving. Maybe as slowly as a tortoise. My plan then, was to become an astronaut. I wanted to go to university and then fly to the moon. I could not wait to walk on its bouncy surface, which somehow reminded me of the sweetness of the marshmallows Ma used to buy me after she'd been paid.

We'd stopped shopping for luxuries a few years ago. We now only ate meat once a week. Other days our meals were mostly *sadza ne muriwo*, the green vegetables that have an endless life and grow in our small vegetable patch at the back of our house. Or sugar beans. Or kapenta: dried fish so small it disappears in one easy swallow.

On Sundays we had chicken. Mama would catch one from her coop. She usually nabbed a youngish rooster whose meat she said was still tender, and cooked it her way. With a thick onion and tomato sauce. On Sundays, she went all out with the cooking because she didn't go to church, though she made sure that I went.

Every Sunday morning she walked me to the gate of Our Sisters of Penance Tabernacle. It was like an outing for us. We discussed the things that had happened in the previous week and our plans for the time ahead. Often, Ma came home when I was already in bed. Had I stayed up for her, I would've realised that she'd started forfeiting her evening meal, so that we had enough milk and bread for the next day's morning tea. Our mornings went by in a rush of getting out of the house on time. Me to school and she to work. Unless we shared the bucket wash together, we seldom managed a hug. Now I wish we'd dawdled. Slowed those days down. I had no clue that they would be so few.

Mama would be waiting to pick me up after the service and we'd walk home hand in hand, chatting. My Bible was a hardback with a picture on the front cover of Abraham. He was the prophet who was told to sacrifice his son; the priest said the story explained the importance of faith. Of suffering. And I liked those stories. Especially when the suffering ended and the people in the Bible were triumphant. Like when Isaac survived.

When they thought I wasn't listening, people said those like my

Mama were not allowed in our country. In the beginning I wondered if it was because I didn't have a father. That's when I considered myself an illegitimate child, born out of sin. Later, I learned that it was for a different reason.

Ma never responded with Amen after I'd said grace for our Sunday lunch, which was always chicken, rice in a juicy peanut butter sauce and cabbage salad with a small spread of mayonnaise. She did not even close her eyes. I knew this because I would peep and see her looking longingly at our gate as if she was expecting someone, and unsure if they'd come. Unlike the neighbour's houses, ours very seldom had visitors. When people walked past our home, they looked away and scampered by as if in a hurry to get away.

Aunty Zina, who called Mama *s'thandwa sami* had a pierced nose, a high-pitched voice and smoked hand-rolled cigarettes with a wickedly sweet smell. She was Ma's only girlfriend, and our regular visitor. Apart from the very tidy chap with a clipboard and ballpoint pen who every month came from the municipality offices to dutifully read the water meter for the water that never came. She arrived in her flowing *shweshwe* skirts that swished before her as she eased herself from the taxi, which had picked her up at the airport. She always arrived with delicious gifts that were of little practical use. If Mama had asked her to bring us a small solar panel, so we could have light, she came with scented candles and long-stick matches claiming they were more romantic. When Aunty Zina was with us, we used two-ply toilet paper, and washed with bubble bath. Actually this didn't make much sense because we only ever had bucket baths.

During Aunty Zina's visits we went to town in taxis, not squashed in a kombi. She spoke animatedly to the flower vendors at Africa Unity Square, asking after their families and how their children were doing at school. She knew them all by name. There was Felix, who used to be a certified accountant at a big firm that closed down in 2002. His wife was now a nurse in the UK, sending money for the new house they were building in Bloomingdale. Obvious, an engineer by profession, had worked as a project manager at a construction business whose owners had shut down and moved to live in a gated community in Jo'burg in 2003. His wife was in Perth, in Australia, near the beach working in the Army and waiting for her immigration papers to allow her to bring him over. No-Matter had worked as a clerk in a bank that had gone bust in 2006. His wife and children had managed to get into Canada before the citizenship rules changed. His wife hadn't been able to come home for her mother's funeral and No-Matter had buried his mother-in-law with a sense of aloneness and shame. He couldn't afford the cow for the funeral feast. He'd entered the U.S. diversity visa lottery through an Internet café-based pimp, to whom he'd paid $50.00, as he didn't know it was a free lottery.

It was like that with Aunty Zina. We walked stall to stall from Third Street to Second Street – it's now Sam Nujoma Street – but she always referred to it by its old name.. She spoke to everybody with ease and familiarity. And she bought bunches of overpriced long-stemmed roses, without haggling, leaving hefty tips in the vendors' hands. 'Wunderbar' she would say, cradling the flowers as a mother does a new baby, and slipping into the German she'd learned in Munich. It didn't matter to her that I didn't always understand what she was saying. She spoke to me in a mish-mash of her musical click-click language, German, and very grown-up English. She did not treat me in the way other people did, as if I was too young to comprehend. I tried to teach her Shona, but the only word she was interested in was 'beloved'. She used it when she spoke to my mother. 'Mudiwa', she would say giving Mama the roses, which we placed in empty peanut butter jars.

She drank too, Aunty Zina. There were always cans of beer, whisky and bottles of red wine in her suitcase. And when she drank she said it made her feel good. That's when she liked to take all her clothes off and dance around our living room in her matching underwear. I had never seen underwear that matched before. Her panties and bra were always co-ordinated. She played Miriam Makeba's music loudly on a small battery operated beat box that she always had with her. She came from Cape Town, where she drove a drop-top convertible BMW, which she had brought back with her from Germany. She said her apartment had a view of the mountain and the ocean.

Mama always smiled when Aunty Zina was around. The three of us would hold hands and dance to the music which had a lot of click-

click sounds that came from deep in the throat. I fumbled along with Miriam Makeba:

> aHiyo Mama, ahiyo Mama ya,
> nants'i Pata Pata
> aHiyo Mama, ahiyo Mama yoh,
> nants'i, Pata Pata
> Saguqa sath'ahi ti
> Aaah saguqa sathi nantsi...

Aunty Zina gave me one of her decadent laughs. It made me feel joyful. She said I was off-key and sang like a tenor rather than an alto. Her grown-up English always hit me in the right place.

She once gave me a packet of tissues that had the smell of a rose garden and I wanted to keep them around me forever. But the scent faded a few days after she left us.

The two of them slept in Mama's big double bed and drank filter coffee, which Aunty Zina had brought, from one cup. In the small kitchen they squeezed between each other, broad hips rubbing a generous bum, as one of them chopped and the other stirred the pots that sat on the two-plate gas cooker. Aunty Zina's groceries should have included tinned sardines, which lasted longer and were more cost effective, but she always brought us salmon and prawns; vacuum packed on ice. She said that sodium and preservatives, which were found in tinned foods, were bad for our health. Sometimes Aunty Zina would stand behind Mama and wrap her long arms around her stomach, resting her head on her back. Even with these most mundane of chores like cooking, together they turned life into a dance.

> aHiyo Mama, ahiyo Mama ya,
> nants'i Pata Pata
> aHiyo Mama, ahiyo Mama yoh,
> nants'i, Pata Pata
> Saguqa sath'ahi ti
> Aaah saguqa sathi nantsi...

Zina was not her real name. It was the name people called her by. Her passport had her full name, Ntombizine. I loved the way it made my teeth grind against each other. She travelled all over the world and always sent us letters, photos and postcards as well as boxes of dark chocolate.

Afterwards the psychiatrist gave me pills to stop Mama showing me what had happened to her that year. But the pills did not work. They only made me sleep, even during the day. Maybe if they had been the bigger ones that I saw other people get they may have had an effect. And as she always did, Mama came to my side and told me what had happened.

She was walking home from her job as a civil servant. There'd been no pay since October – that was in 2014, but every day she woke up and diligently went to work. We had a miserable Christmas that year. We couldn't go shopping for new clothes or eat chicken and rice with peanut butter sauce or ice-cream with fresh mangoes. Usually we ate until our stomachs hurt. Instead we had *sadza ne muriwo* from the little garden, which was now very dry because the rains hadn't come so we couldn't water it. We didn't feel too bad though because everyone was doing the same.

The weeks went by and still in February 2015, there was no rain. Or pay. Ma had that look in her eyes. The look of suffering. She was not the only woman who had that look. All the mothers in our street had the same expression. There was no laughter in our neighborhood.

When there was electricity we'd watch the Minister for the Treasury on the television. He always looked very cross about the pay issue. I wasn't sure why, particularly at being on TV, which was so cool. Instead he foamed at the corners of his small-pursed mouth and spit always followed his words in a shower.

Mama got off the taxi late at night because her department was working long hours on some important papers that were wanted by the boss of a big, rich organization called the MFI. Ma said they gave loans and money to countries all over the world, but I didn't think it was fair that Ma and her colleagues had to work for months without pay because there were too many ghosts in the civil service. Until then, I thought the only place to find ghosts was at the community cemetery. That's why we never hung out there at night time.

By the time she turned the corner and reached our neighborhood the lights were out. Because she didn't have her torch with her, Mama walked the journey homewards in the hardness of the dark. The dark is always at its worst just after the lights go, before we fumble for the matches to light candles or remember where we left the solar lamp. That's when the thing happened. When Mama was looking downwards, not sure of where there was a shadow in the path that would trip her up, or if the stray dogs would chase after her, confusing her for a thief. The only thing she saw was the ripples in the pools of water that filled the pot holes. They looked like mirrors shining intermittently all over the streets. It perplexed us to see so much water flowing when it never came through our taps. I had by now lit the candle we kept near our veranda so that she could see her way from the gate. I was not allowed to leave the house when it was dark.

It was month-end and I think Mama had many things running through her head. Perhaps her feelings for Aunty Zina. But mostly she was doing calculations. Adding up how she was going to pay the rest of my school fees because the head teacher had written her a final letter of demand. I also knew the tin where we stored our maize meal was running very low. Instead of sadza, which used more maize flour, we'd started eating a very thin porridge. I didn't understand the head teacher's logic. She was also in the civil service and knew that there had been no pay since last year, so why did she bother to write rude letters to all the mothers demanding fees that did not exist? The school bursar said it was for the audit trail. Grown-ups use big terms when they think children shouldn't understand what's going on. But we do. I thought it was just a waste of paper. But grown-ups don't like to listen to kids, even when we're right, so I didn't say anything.

Mama didn't notice the small gang of people that had formed behind her. Maybe they were walking very softly. Or maybe her usually clear mind was too confused by how we would cope. I don't know. Next thing she was on her knees in a puddle, her skirts swirling in mud and one shoe missing.

One of them kicked her to the left of the head as if he were hitting a penalty. The thud brought her face down in the mud. And she swallowed the rusty water in a cry for help that no one heard. Mother was strong. But the gang had taken her by surprise. That's why she had no power to fight back. They drowned her in the puddle, right there in the water of the pot-hole that was very near our home. And then they pulled her underpants down to her knees. One of them reached for the quarter bottle of Krango and broke its plastic base off. He thrust the neck end up between her legs.

Inside the bottle was a message. *'Ngotchani! Ngwembe!'*

'Burn in hell'.

Though there were fingerprints on the bottle that provided evidence, the police didn't open a docket. Conservative officers were reluctant to rock the boat. They said it would be a messy case that would affect their superiors.

The Psychiatrist doesn't believe me when I tell him I know what happened. He says I am prone to flights of fancy. But Mama shows me everything when I'm asleep. She does not lie. I tell the Psychiatrist that they came to her funeral. The gang of quiet-footed people. I saw the mud on their shoes. They reached their hands out at me in false sorrow for my loss and hung around for the free food. Some of them even wanted to carry my mother's wooden coffin to the graveyard, which was not far from our home. They sang the choruses of the funeral songs.

Because Mama didn't go to church she was buried by her funeral policy from a firm called 'The Comforters'. The government policy was broke. The CEO had withdrawn all the money from the bank and built himself a four-storey house with an elevator and a heated swimming pool. For some bizarre reason Ma had chosen 'The Comforters' insurance that came with a singing choir.

> *Jehovah anotipa*
> *Chisepe misi yese*
> *Nekutitungamira*
> *Mutsembwe dza Satani*
>
> *Zvotanga takasungwa*
> *Ndizvovo tinotenda*
> *Chisepe chenyu Baba*
> *Ndi Jesu Kristu Tenzi*

If she hadn't done that it would have been a very quiet funeral, like a white person's where no one really cries or sings.

And that is how the feeling started. For a long time, the postcards arrived from Aunty Zina, who didn't know what had happened. My mind would spin with too many voices that chit-chattered over each other. They would tell me that if the MFI had paid my mother, rather than wasting its money investigating ghosts, maybe she'd have been able to buy one of those little Japanese cars and come home safely.

11

GOLD DIGGER

Albert Gumbo

Kukara walked confidently into the offices of the Fear Water Company, a white-water rafting outfit based in Mosi-oa-Tunya. He had planned his passport out of poverty for months and getting a job at Fear Water was simply step one. It would give him access to his visa: A white Scandinavian female tourist!

Unemployed and living in Chinotimba Township, Kukara watched other youths his age flaunt their white girlfriends in the neighbourhood. Fascinated, he had heard of so-and-so striking gold and taking off to live with his girlfriend in Scandinavia. Kukara had failed to find employment with his nine D-grade O-levels, but he had one thing going for him. He had been the school's top athlete and his physique had benefited from his exertions on the sports field. The pretty student teacher who'd taken sports in his final year would willingly have testified about the boy's attributes if she'd been allowed to. Kukara only had one failing: he could not swim, and the Zambezi river was not a particularly attractive practice venue. However, the power of vision does wonders for any human being and it helped to have a cousin who was a waiter at one of the local hotels. Intensive swimming lessons followed for a month in the dead of night and being a gifted athlete Kukara was soon declared a worthy swimmer by his cousin. He was ready to apply for a job at Fear Water!

Wearing a vest and sandals as just about every local lad does in Mosi-oa-Tunya, Kukara waited patiently while the receptionist called the manager to announce him. He smoothed his growing dreadlocks once again to make sure he looked presentable and tried to calm his nerves. He was used to this from the sports field and knew that the adrenalin rush he felt when his name was called out simply meant he was ready to achieve phase one. His cousin had coached him well on what to say and what to avoid. 'Can you swim?' This manager did not waste time at all!

'Yes, Sir,' came the confident response.

'English?'

'Yes, Sir. I got a D for my O-levels but I speak better than I write because I worked as a waiter at the Chiefdom Hotel every school holiday. My cousin is a waiter there and he found me a job.'

'Any other language?'

'I did French up to JC level but our teacher left because we had no textbooks. I can speak simple French like the greeting, introducing myself, and I know all animals' names at Mosi-oa-Tunya in French.'

'Say something in French.' Kukara smiled and with his best nasal accent replied: *'L'éléphant est très grand.'*

The manager liked this confident young man. He seemed to be genuine as opposed to the hundreds of others he had interviewed who only seemed interested in sleeping with as many white girls as possible. They were of course only responding to the high demand from sex-hungry white girls chasing the black virility myth. The manager preferred to call it white guilt. The most common bumper sticker in Mosi-oa-Tunya was 'ONCE YOU GO BLACK, YOU CAN'T GO BACK.'

'That is very good. There are two hotels in this town that have French partners and a lot of French people are coming into town.' The manager seemed to have made up his mind. He briefly outlined the job description: Take tourists down to the river below the falls, put them in a raft, spoil them and bring them back alive. On the way to and from the hotel, point out all the animals and say something extraordinary about them.

The manager's face broke into a naughty smile. 'For example, you can tell them an elephant is so big it drinks as much water as the Titanic!' He laughed at his own joke while Kukara tried desperately to remember what a Titanic was from his high school years. It must be an army truck he concluded, quickly joining in the laughter.

'You've got the job, young man. You start on Monday with some training on how to handle a raft in white water. Welcome aboard and try not to fall off.'

Phase one, sorted, thought Kukara to himself. As he walked out of the Fear Water offices, the thought of flying to Europe in the near future if all went according to plan drowned out the sound of the smoke that thunders.

***

Kukara walked quickly towards the Chiefdom hotel in the direction of the Mosi-oa-Tunya falls. He could see the plumes of spray rising out of the dense rainforest that fronted the Falls. He never ceased to marvel at the beauty of his town. Already at nine o'clock in the morning, it was very warm: half-clad, dirty overlander tourists were already emerging out of what used to be the town council chalets. Equally half-clad curio vendors were waiting to ambush them with unbelievable price offers. Everyone looked relaxed. Mosi-oa-Tunya moved at its own pace and felt like a little country unto itself. Kukara waved at a tour guide from the township, as he drove by in an open-roofed safari Land Rover. The tour guides had a superior attitude towards the rest of the township boys and had acquired a mix of American, Australian and Scandinavian accents. Superiority seemed to be determined by two things: how well you spoke through your nose and how many white tourists you had slept with.

Kukara's cousin, Anoronga, was still serving breakfast and so the young man waited in the courtyard of the Chiefdom observing the Land Rovers and minibuses that were waiting to pick up tourists. One of the guides walked over to him, 'Yes, *mfana*. *Uri* right?'

'*Mushe.*'

'Looking for a job?'

Kukara knew exactly what he meant. The tourism industry was on the wane and the hotels were struggling. There was tremendous competition for jobs and a lot of turf protection by the locals albeit in a very friendly manner. It was not unusual these days to see a touring company's 28-seater minibus with only one Japanese family on board.

'I have already got a job with Fear Water.'

'Oh. Well done, *mfana*. It's a good company.'

'Take that,' thought Kukara to himself. He watched the guide walk back to his Land Rover. They all looked alike, the guides that is. Dark, muscular, always dressed in shorts and a vest and what appeared to be a compulsory dog tag. Some went for full dress and wore wristbands as well to complete the local version of the Out of Africa effect. An hour later, Anoronga emerged from the majestic hotel with a broad smile.

'So, how did it go?'

Kukara smiled back as he shook hands with his doting cousin.

'I got the job!'

Anoronga whooped with delight. 'This calls for a celebration. Follow me.'

The two quickly walked towards the service entrance where a security guard stepped aside in return for breakfast left-overs that Anoronga had arranged minutes earlier. They sat in a corner of the vast kitchen and Kukara narrated the short interview that had just taken place, while they devoured a full continental breakfast. When they had finished, Anoronga grunted with satisfaction and proceeded to tutor his apprentice in the art of seducing Scandinavians.

'Now that you can swim, we must work on your understanding of these white women. First, you must understand that these girls feel very guilty about what their ancestors did to Africa. So they are rebelling against their societies by coming here and sleeping with as many black boys as possible. But they do not sleep with just anyone. I can sleep with a white girl but my manager cannot. He is too polished, too educated and the biggest sin of all, he wears cologne.'

Anoronga laughed at his analysis. The laughter drew an audience as all work stopped in the kitchen. The head chef was still upstairs playing his looking-important-and-sophisticated act in the restaurant.

One of Anoronga's workmates added to the advice. 'You see *mfana*, these women like you when you smell a little bit. They love the dark smell of Africa. It is like an aphro … ehh, aphrodi, ah whatever, it's like *vuka vuka* for women!'

More laughter followed as Anoronga, leaning closer to his young cousin, continued the lesson.

'You must not appear too clever. You must agree with everything they say. You also hate George Bush, you hate the war against terror because it is all a conspiracy. You believe in fair trade and you think animals must not be put in zoos. Just agree with everything and make sure they understand you are poor because of your white boss. By then they are ready for bedding. Put on a great performance over the two nights that they usually stay here. On the second night, you must sigh loudly several times and when they ask why just say they must not worry it is nothing. They will ask you why over and over again and then you reluctantly tell them all you want is to start a new life in another country. One of them will bite like a Zambezi bream! The rest, as they say, will be history!'

Wild applause followed. Anoronga was not nicknamed 'teacher' for nothing! Kukara left feeling heady. He was grateful to his cousin and was determined to make it overseas so he could get a good job in a factory and send money back home to his extended family through the Homelink money transfer. As he walked through the dusty streets of Chinotimba, past his old school, he looked at the plastic shacks in people's back yards where many of the young people stayed as lodgers trapped in the vicious grip of poverty. Kukara thought these young people were the most optimistic in the world. Despite the fact that tourism was in the doldrums, they grimly hung on to this town in the belief that the good times would be back.

Kukara walked into his mother's house and told her the good news. She gave him a hug with joy. Her husband had died years ago and she had laboured hard to send her five children through school.

'My son, well done. You must work hard and maybe they will make you a manager one day and you can drive one of those Land Rovers. But be careful of these white girls. I do not want you to die of AIDS like Mrs Mawara's son.'

'Don't worry, Mum. I am not like that.'

Kukara hid his discomfort at his mother openly suggesting he would sleep with a white girl. It was true that a lot of young people were dying of AIDS and the phenomenon was linked to the propensity for the young people to want to experience the real thing with a white girl. You could not truly claim to have slept with a white girl if you had used a condom. As the saying went: Contact! A typical conversation between two tour guides would go as follows: '*Shamwari*! What a night last night.'

'With who? I saw you with a Dutch girl at Explorers.'

'The very one! Boy did she scream.'

'Contact?'

'Definitely!'

The peer pressure was great and the guys who lied about making contact were still alive while a large number of those who had succumbed were on their sick beds. Almost every household had lost a son or a nephew to contact sport.

Kukara pulled out his old French textbooks and began to polish his French. 'Le lion est dangereux.' Five days elapsed before the first booking came in for Kukara's team. A group from Sweden! Kukara could not tell from the booking sheet how many were male or female although Inga certainly sounded female. He got into the back of the Land Rover and headed with his team straight to the launch site. The tourists would arrive in half an hour and Kukara and his team had to prepare the raft.

While they waited, Kukara dabbed some Vaseline onto a bicep here and a shoulder there. The others laughed and did the same. A glistening muscle went a long way in the courting ritual. Kukara was not wearing any deodorant, his hair was twisted into the beginnings of a dreadlock and he was looking cool in his imitation Ray-Bans that his cousin had organised from a Zambian who in turn had bought them in South Africa. Zambians didn't need visas to go there. Kukara was ready for take-off.

The mini-bus arrived at 9.30 precisely and the team swung into action. Three girls only! The hunt was on as the five guys tried to establish eye contact while very professionally helping the party to put on their lifebelts. The more experienced guys had outmaneuvered Kukara and he found himself helping a male tourist.

'Damn!' Kukara thought to himself. 'I need to move faster next time.' He resigned himself to getting the job right as they all moved to the front of the two rafts for the instructions from the Fear Water supervisor. One of the women raised her hand as Kukara's team simultaneously tried to avoid recoiling in distaste. She had a thicket under her armpits! 'Fuck! Kukara thought. 'I'm not accepting a visa from that one!'

'Yes, miss?' The supervisor waited before starting his brief.

'No speak English.'

This was an awkward moment. Kukara dreaded what was going to come next.

'German?' asked the guard.

'No. French?' suggested thickets.

'No,' replied the guard shaking his head as if to say another long day in the making.

'Yes!' Kukara heard himself say and regretted it at the same time.

Thickets smiled, the guard frowned. That was all he needed, the rookie to steal his thunder. Kukara stepped forward and reached out his hand trying to avoid staring at Thicket's armpits.

'Je m'appelle Kukara.'

'Inga.'

Paradise regained!

Kukara translated telegraphic style in his schoolboy French as the guide explained the safety instructions. The other guides who could not speak a word were amazed at how fluent he was. Inga seemed to be happy as well because she nodded and smiled a lot. Soon enough it was time to launch the rafts. Kukara and Inga got into the second with a nervous looking Swedish couple and another guide. The roar of the Zambezi rushed over their voices and laughter as the tourists developed an adrenalin-induced hazy look of exhilaration that apparently always came at the start of a white-water rush. As the raft bobbed to and fro, from side to side, up and down in the foaming water, Inga would steady herself against Kukara's solid frame with one hand while she held on to the side with the other. Kukara enjoyed the temporary contact despite his aversion to her thickets. He was beginning to convince himself that she liked him when the raft slid off a massive rock and flew into the air. Time seemed to stand still for a couple of seconds while Kukara stared down Inga's tonsils as she screamed silently, wide-eyed. The noise roared back as the raft slammed itself back into the angry waters and went over on one side because Inga had dived into the safety of Kukara's arms just before impact. The next thing was the sound of gurgling water, kicking and scratching as Inga panicked and tried to use Kukara as a platform out of hell and back into oxygen. Kukara's lungs screamed for air as he tried to both stay calm and steady Inga while still underwater. He made it back to the surface in time to see a rock loom ahead of them and pulled Inga back down to save her head. Inga screamed even more silently, this time because her mouth was full of water. The French-speaking guide was trying to drown her! Before she could perish the thought, he was grabbing her round the waist with his strong left arm and hauling her out of the water.

'Why doesn't he use both arms?' she thought in a brief moment of sanity and Scandinavian logic as his unseen arm remained firmly gripped around the raft, which appeared on the verge of righting itself. Before she could think of something sarcastic, she was swept half into the air and tossed back onto the raft like a used rag and was too grateful to complain. The last thing she saw before passing out exhausted was the face of her benefactor looking down at her, smiling, muscles glistening in the hot African sun – she had met her first angel and by God he was black! Two weary hours later, the team made it back to the top of the gorge.

'Merci. Merci beaucoup.' Thickets was grateful and it showed in her gushing thank you. Eternally grateful would not have been an overstatement at that point. 'I am staying at the town council chalets,' she continued in a mix of bad French and even worse English. 'Can I buy you a drink?' The last sentence seemed to come out of a tourist phrase book.

'Ce n'est pas nécéssaire.' Kukara held his breath. Anoranga had advised him not to appear too eager if offered a drink, a joint or some hanky-panky.

'J'insiste.' Inga wanted to thank her saviour who had snatched her from the jaws of death in the cauldron of the Zambezi. During the long walk up the unnatural stairs carved out of the cliff she had shuddered at the thought of crocodiles feasting on her naked corpse.

'Okay,' Kukara hid his smile. 'So this is what filling in a visa form feels like!' he thought, as he pointed out the way to Explorers bar. They agreed to meet at nine that evening and Kukara walked back to the Fear Water office via the pharmacy. He could not afford the expensive Durex condoms and so he bought two packets of the Protector brand. Besides, they were stronger and bigger than the Durex! The locals called them Peugeot: The car made for Africa!

The rest of the day passed uneventfully and the manager was very pleased to hear about Kukara's conduct from the tour leader who grudgingly gave an objective report, knowing that if he didn't the other tour guides all eyeing the same promotion into his job would not hesitate to quietly correct the record with the boss. After work, Kukara strolled down to the Chiefdom and narrated his first adventure to his cousin while he feasted on left-over lunch. Once again there was an audience.

'It was incredible. I saved her life and she wants to buy me a drink tonight!' A lot of congratulatory backslapping followed as Anoranga prepared to dispense more life skills to his young apprentice. 'Right, *mfana*. You say she is a thicket? Do not forget to say how you find that sexy later on. But first make sure you offer to buy the first round. She will not let you because of this white guilt thing.'

'She will say you are badly paid but do not get offended and show off what little money you have!' The eager beaver from the last time added his two cents worth. 'Exactly,' affirmed Anoranga.

'Do not be too proud to spend her money. It is her proud and rightful contribution to the fight against third world poverty and she will find another poor victim to help if you do not play the part!'

Armed with this advice Kukara prepared to leave as eager beaver shouted a final instruction at him. 'And remember not to bath!' Loud laughter followed young Kukara out of the service entrance of the Chiefdom.

The sun was setting over the Zambezi as Kukara ambled slowly home. He was tired but his body was aching with excitement. He had come this far, he could not mess up. He stopped at the local STAR store and bought some cheese courtesy of Anoranga's advice. Cheese was apparently good for red bull type performance. He would need lots of energy later, because apparently Scandinavians always asked for more.

***

When he arrived home, he told his mother about his day.

'I saved a client from drowning today.'

'My brave son,' she smiled broadly showing white strong teeth. 'Was your boss happy?'

'Yes, he is buying the whole team drinks tonight,' Kukara replied casually, before adding, 'Do not wait up for me, Mum. I think I'll be back late. The guys tell me these celebratory drinks last a long time and we are not allowed to leave before the boss leaves the pub.'

'OK, son. Just take a bath and eat something before you go.'

'Yes, Mum.'

Kukara knew how fussy his mother was about hygiene. He boiled some water onto the stove before pouring it into a large basin and carrying it into the bathroom. He made a lot of noise splashing and singing 'Leaving on a jet plane' for about fifteen minutes before emerging after stopping himself from masturbating. He would need all his boys on duty tonight! He deliberately avoided his mother and told her he would take a nap and eat just before going out. He went to his room and set the alarm for 8:45 and took a nap in his underwear. He knew that if he were half naked his mother would not bother him.

***

At nine o'clock. sharp Kukara walked into Explorers wearing his Ché Guevara shirt. Revolution was in the air! He was going to leave the country if he played his cards right! He was tired of the economic and political crisis that had robbed him and thousands of young people his age of their dreams. Now he longed for a better life in a foreign land. As usual the music was loud and the tourists were outnumbered two to one by eager young men and women seeking visas out of Mosi-oa-Tunya.

'My saviour!' Thickets spotted Kukara before he saw her and she pushed her way through the crowd in the narrow bar and gave him a big hug. Other young adventurers who had been eyeing Thickets sighed with disbelief and turned their attention elsewhere. They had been trying to get her attention for close on half an hour and she had not even given them the time of day, but soon everyone knew why, as the older Swedish couple from the raft narrated the narrow escape on the river.

'Good to see you again!' Thickets had to shout in her bad French to be heard over the din. 'I like your T-shirt!'

'Thanks!' Going well, thought Kukara to himself. 'What can I get for you to drink?'

'No! No! Drinks are on me tonight.' Thickets was clearly in her element and her eyes were particularly alive in the soft light of the bar, or so it appeared to Kukara.

'You look happy!'

'I am happy to be alive!' They smiled at each other as the barman handed over two cold beers. Soon enough, the crowd wanted to move on to Wild Thang at the Chiefdom as the custom dictated, where there was space to dance, but Kukara had other ideas.

'Let's just walk and talk,' he suggested with a serious look on his face.

'Is it safe?' she asked. 'I do not think it's a good idea. Let's go back to the chalets. We can take a few beers with us.'

Kukara hid his smile. This was too easy to be true! They walked out holding hands while he carried three beers in one hand and she carried the other three in a STAR supermarket carrier bag. She fumbled for the key from her jeans shorts, pushed open the door and headed straight for a small cloth half-hidden under the bed.

'Do you smoke wisdom weed?' Her eyes lit up even more as she teased him. 'It is Malawi gold,' she added.

Kukara had always been a naturally gifted sportsman. The athlete in him screamed no! The refugee in him thought otherwise.

'Of course!'

They lay back on her bed and began to smoke the marijuana and soon they were both giggling about their adventure on the river, before attempting to solve the world's problems.

'What do you think of George Bush?'

'I think he should be sent to fight in Iraq!'

'I agree. The fascist bastard belongs in Guantanamo Bay!' Kukara had not been coached on that. Not even by Anoranga. The only bay he had ever heard of was Montego Bay in Jamaica and that through a couple of reggae songs. He tried to steer the topic to issues of poverty.

'You know Bush has imposed sanctions against Zimbabwe. He gives travel warnings and people like you do not come anymore.'

'It is criminal! They are causing the people to suffer.' Inga's eyes flared with anger.

'Yes, and you know we get paid on commission and with the low number of tourists nowadays, I have a very small salary. I have to support my mother, my brothers, sisters and some of my cousins.'

'It must be hard for you.' Thickets was clearly concerned. 'I only have one brother and he is studying the mating habits of the North Sea clam. We have to save our clams, you know.'

'We have to save our pangolins and we cannot without income from tourists.' Kukara heaved sigh number one.

'What's the matter?'

'Nothing. Have another beer before it gets warm.' They drank and smoked in silence for a while Thickets played with his budding dreadlocks. Kukara sighed again.

'What's the matter, honey?'

'It's just that I wish I could leave this country. Work hard and raise money to start a foundation for the survival of the Zambezi pangolin. It's endangered, you know.' Thickets hid her smile behind the thick blue smoke. She hated marijuana but it was well worth it. So it was true what the girls returning from African overland safaris said. If you wanted a great sex life for the rest of your life, go to Africa, don't bath for a while, grow your armpit hair and pretend you hate George Bush and they fall for it! She was especially proud of her drowning impression earlier today. For the first time she did not resent the strict education back home that made swimming compulsory at school. The system worked! All she had to do now was reel in her catch and offer the ticket. He would accept after a day or two of pretence and they would fly off home. Once there, he would have no choice but to stay with her because it was very difficult to get a job for foreigners and she would have the ride of her life! And he could not argue about her shaving her armpits once she was back home. It was fool-proof.

'You know,' she said casually. 'I have saved quite a bit of money from my first year of work. I could buy a plane ticket for you …' Kukara's smile was hidden behind a plume of blue smoke. Unbelievable! Anoronga would be impressed! 'Let's talk about that in a moment, he said as he began to caress her. Anoronga had said he must give her a sneak preview before cementing the deal. Just in case she changed her mind! As they reached for each other, they smiled into each other's eyes as if to say, 'Gotcha!'

(V)

Money Matters

12

A Land of Starving Millionaires

Erasmus R. Chinyani

The millionaire staggered towards the long line of tuck shops. The stagger of an inveterate beer-drinker after one bottle too many. Only he hadn't gulped anything for quite a long time. Four days to be precise. Not even a sip of tap water, due to the unpredictable water-cuts in his part of the city. He hadn't eaten anything either, or nothing but the national staple, they now call the air-pie – a euphemism for one big slice of *nothing*!

Hunched under the weight of a huge plastic sack, the millionaire had the look of a man who carried the world on his back. He stopped staggering when he reached the first shop in the row and heaved the sack onto the counter. Someone once said that the only good thing about hitting your head against a brick-wall is the relief when you stop. Still, there was only a blank look on his face: the look of a punch-drunk boxer at the losing end.

'*Mudhara*! I said how much is in that bag of yours?'

'One million three hundred thousand dollars in single notes. And I want a loaf of bread and a packet of sugar.'

The shop-keeper emitted a mirthless chuckle. 'Old man, don't you read the papers? Or haven't you got a radio? The prices of foodstuffs quadrupled this morning. *Half* a loaf of bread now costs one million five hundred thousand. Forget about the sugar. It's just not for your class anymore. Don't even ask how much. It will give you a heart-attack. Sugar is now strictly for the super-class.'

Mr Usury Chimbadzo doubled back as if he had been dealt a swift upper-cut. He thought of his huge family. The youngest of his three wives had just given birth to – believe it or not – triplets and his other two wives were explosively pregnant. He hadn't finished paying *roora* for the third wife and his in-laws were baying for his blood. All his school-going children had been sent home for non-payment of fees. The cumulative amount ran into *billions*. And the million in his plastic sack, which he was now being told could no longer buy half a loaf, was all he had. That and the now useless three hundred thousand.

***

Back home, his children were collectively wailing like some multiple-sounding siren. All twenty-nine of them. There was a time when he was very proud of his offspring. Then, he used to boast that he was the father of not one but *two* 'football teams' and their match officials. He used to grin when they nicknamed him Baba vaAlphabet. That was before the bolt-from-the-blue arrival of the hungry triplets. Together with their older siblings, they now formed one ear-blasting choir that Baba vaAlphabet could well do without. A choral outfit made in hell. The combined sounds of their non-stop shrieks set his teeth on edge, and spun his head like some planet that had strayed wildly out of orbit. They transformed the home's once-tranquil atmosphere into one brain-exploding, funereal din.

The cacophony was such that, even if he hadn't pawned his radio, cassette player and old black and white TV to alleviate the tooth-gnashing hunger haunting his house, he could never have used them because of the collective din deafeningly produced by his children. At first their hungry cries were directed at the mothers: '*Mommy, Tadha-a! Mai, chaja-a, AMAI TIRIKUDA SADZA-A-A!!!*'. The three mothers would, in frustration, either scream back at the kids or worse, they would direct their counter-attack at the man-of-the-house, Baba vaAlphabet. But now, lately the children seemed to have taken a cue from their mothers and directed their shrill demands at the man himself – Baba vaAlphabet, the millionaire with his stash of useless dollars. And now even these had run out.

Indeed, that very morning he'd left his home – actually escape would be a more appropriate word – to, he said, 'Try and borrow money from some bank.' He'd been lying of course. The truth of the matter was that he was out to collect two long-standing debts owed to him by two rascals, who happened to also be impulsive borrowers.

Although they only lived nearby, the two had been playing a cat-and-mouse game with him for a long time. In all his decades-long career as a no-nonsense money-lender, he was yet to encounter any clients as elusive as these two. So skilful were they at eluding him that he'd almost decided to give up the chase. But now, with an army of problems mustering against him, he felt he had no choice but to track them down, and wage an all-out war of his own. They'd borrowed a total of five million dollars when times were good; when a million was still a million and a person with a million in his possession could rightly and proudly call himself a millionaire without a pang of guilt. Now thanks to the hyper-inflationary environment threatening to submerge the nation and its once vibrant economy, times were bad for all of them.

Tough luck. The guy who had borrowed over three and a half million dollars, had committed suicide, and there was a low-key funeral going on when he arrived. Judging by the low-key attendance, the low-key ceremony, and the absence of food, Mr Chimbadzo could see that it would be futile to ask any of the mourners to pay the deceased's dues. Their starvation-masked faces told a big story.

He wondered how long it would be before they joined their departed relative on his underground journey. So Chimbadzo kissed his money goodbye in an unprecedented fashion.

Jumping up and down, he yelled unprintable obscenities at the coffin as if he was addressing a living person. Yelling and hollering about the coffin's 'mother' and 'father' and their reproductive anatomy and much, *much* worse, Chimbadzo was in an uncompromising mood. A funeral is supposed to be a very sombre occasion, where respect for the dead is upheld. Under normal circumstances, any person desecrating such an occasion in the way Baba vaAlphabet was doing risked being violently upended and unceremoniously ejected. But there was something wild and menacing about the old man in their midst that froze the mourners into inaction. Something that told them to let the money-lending demon vent his fury at the motionless coffin rather than provoking him into acting it out on one of them. There was a murderous glint in his eye as he unleashed volleys of vulgar, homicidal insults, which convinced them. A person prepared to 'kill' a dead man in his coffin can be a real terror to the living.

Anyway, after Baba vaAlphabet had shouted himself hoarse, he ran out of steam, and reluctantly ambled off while stopping now and again to sneeringly take a backward look. The mourners heaved a collective sigh of relief, as he went off to look for debtor Number Two. Sadly for Mr Chimbadzo, his next port of call wasn't fruitful either.

For his next debtor, a renowned pleasure-loving womaniser, who owed him one and a half million, had long contracted the HIV virus, and though he'd looked fit all along, his condition had now bloomed to full-blown AIDS. The man was on his death-bed, looking in such a bad way that even the hardened debt-collector had to calm down. One typically hot word from an enraged Chimbadzo would have seen him go out like the flame of a dying candle. For a while he just stood there, motionless, speechless before the dying man.

Then an idea struck him.

Although the place smelt of death and poverty from floor to roof, his money-lender's instinct rose to the fore and he could see how to squeeze some money from the already grieving family. Experience had taught him that distressed relatives would often be willing to do anything to save themselves from another death; trade anything in exchange for their dying relative's life – even their own souls. Old Chimbadzo made a few sympathetic noises, before saying, 'You know, Kutamburahuda here is my *very* best friend.' He lied, knowing the sick man was too weak to open his mouth and set the record straight. Even the dying man knew that *money* was Chimbadzo's only friend. Kutamburahuda tried to lift one of his twig-thin arms – apparently in a gesture of protest – but then his limbs slumped back on the makeshift bed. Chimbadzo continued, 'I can't let my friend die just like this. I know a man who can save his life. He's the best *n'anga* in the business. His name is … is …,' he stopped to punch his head in an apparent attempt to jog his memory.

He was getting old. Lying, to him, had always come as naturally as breathing. In the past, non-existent names of non-existent people would just pop out of his mouth from nowhere. '… his name is … Dr Target Super Actelic Chirindamatura Dust. '*Phew!*' Now there is one hell of an *n'anga*. The best! He can cure anything, I tell you! AIDS? What AIDS? This man can cure a coffin and cause it to cough out its corpse …' He caught himself just in time. 'Well, I've seen worse cases than my friend Kutamburahuda here, cured. This *n'anga* is something else I tell you! Dr Target Super Actelic Chirindamatura Dust can do anything!'

'Oh, really?'

'Where is this man?'

'How much does he charge per session?'

Expectant looks brightened up the faces round the sick man's bed. Everyone knew that funerals were expensive these days.

'This man lives … well, you wouldn't know the place. He keeps his surgery a closely-guarded secret. But I know, because he's my uncle … my father's father's … yes – my *uncle*! For only five million my friend here will look as fresh and healthy as a newly-born baby …' Again he caught his tongue just in time. Newly-born babies are not always healthy. He thought of his perpetually screaming triplets, as if all their health lay in their wailing.

Not unexpectedly, the relatives did not have much money and could not raise the five million, but they ran around and as luck would have it, they managed to come up with the exact money their sick relative owed him – one million three hundred bucks. They had put the money – in its several denominations – into a plastic sack. Lifting the heavy bag to his shoulder, he purportedly headed for the great *n'anga's* surgery.

As he left, the old debt-collector might have worn a triumphant grin after miraculously recovering his million-plus dollars – that is if times had been normal. But he was only conscious of having to buy food for his howling family. The journey home via the tuckshops, and without the relief of a kombi, was long, and the bag was heavy. Heavy, but worth it – or so he thought. Indeed, had he been paid a few months previously, Chimbadzo's million and a half might have solved a few of his problems.

So that's why we found him staggering towards the long row of tuckshops, a few hundred metres from his home. After the shocking news of the latest price increase, Chimbadzo stashed the hundreds of bills back into the sack before trying the other shops. But in most instances, the news was worse.

His head was whirling and spinning like a tiny scrap of paper caught in an August whirlwind. He wondered what he was going to say to his three expectant wives and battalion of children. Preoccupied, he reached the corner of his street. Perhaps his ears had been too deafened by hunger, his mind too loaded by the sack full of poverty and his eyes too blinded by rage and despair, that he neither saw nor heard the sudden emergence of the local MP's car.

Like a fiery bat straight out of hell, the legislator's blood-red luxury Mercedes turned the corner in the typical fashion of a well-fed politician with inexhaustible amounts of fuel to burn. Baba vaAlphabet flew into the air on impact, his sack of money with him, dying long before he hit the ground. His bag burst and the dollars flew into the air, scattered like colonial propaganda pamphlets dropped from a plane. And when they did flap down to join their owner, who lay prostrate on the ground, no one rushed to pick them up.

13

The Donor's Visit

Sekai Nzenza

Just after dawn today, Ndodye stood on top of the anthill and woke the whole village up. He was shouting: 'A message to old ladies, widows and orphans! *Chiziviso ku chembere, shirikadzi ne nherera!* Today the donor is coming only for you. Get up and go to Simukai Centre to get your food handouts. If you do not get up now, you will die of hunger in your hut.' Ndodye's voice rules the mornings. Voices travel fast before sunrise.

Every day Ndodye stands on top of the anthill near his house and announces all the village meetings and events. Last week he shouted that the donor was coming. Chiyevo and I got up early and started the journey to the food distribution meeting. Halfway there we met *Sabhuku*, the kraal head. *Sabhuku* said that was not true. There was no donor coming. Ndodye got the days wrong. We turned and went back home. Ndodye has a big voice. He used to be a soldier. Because his rank in the Rhodesian army was very low, he never had a chance to shout and order people to do anything. Now he got his chance at last: Ndodye is the village crier, neighborhood police officer and ZANU-PF village chairperson.

I say to Chiyevo, Ndodye was drinking *chi one-day* beer at your mother's house till very late last night. When did he get this message and how do we know it is true that the donor is coming? Chiyevo tells me: 'Last week he called all family heads. Today his message is only for old ladies, widows and orphans. It is a special day for them.

Ndodye cannot get the message wrong again.'

We get up and start the long walk to meet the donor. Chiyevo walks in front of me. Chiyevo is my granddaughter, *muzukuru wangu*, one of my late son's daughters. She accompanies me on long journeys like this and helps me carry whatever the donor gives us. This year Chiyevo will be turning eighteen. She only passed two subjects in Form 4 last year. How could she pass? She missed many days of school because we did not have the money for school fees. I sold my goat, her mother sold two chickens and we made enough money for her term fees, books and uniforms. Then the river was in flood for days and days and Chiyevo stayed home. When she went back to school, the teachers were on strike. Teaching has no money, they said. The government is not paying us enough. We are teaching your children only because we are merciful. Chiyevo got her results at the beginning of this year. She passed only two subjects out of eight. Her mother did not know what to do with her anger: 'I wanted you to become a teacher or a nurse. But you failed. You only passed Shona and Religious Knowledge. Where does that take you? What will you do next? You want to be someone's maid? You want to be a second or third wife to a sugar daddy?'

As usual, Chiyevo shrugged her shoulders, smiled and said nothing. Her mother shouted at her. Called her names and said she had wasted her chickens and her goats paying school fees for a dumb and lazy girl. You do not have a brain, her mother said in anger. Your head is full of nothing but water.

Chiyevo cried and I said she should not cry. She was not the only one who didn't pass at Simukai Secondary School. Many children failed.

Chiyevo and I stop at the river for a wash. It is still morning but it is already quite hot. Cicadas are singing. They promise good rains, I tell Chiyevo. She laughs and says, 'Mbuya, last year you said the same thing. Cicadas mean good rains. And did we get good rains? No. Last year we had the worst drought ever.'

Chiyevo is right. Last year was bad. We harvested very little. The donors did not come at all. This is September and our granaries are already empty. The rains will only come at the end of next month – if they come at all.

There were times, *muzukuru*, when we were never hungry. We harvested more than we could eat. Even these forests gave us wild fruits and mushrooms, I tell Chiyevo. She gives me one of those smiles that say: I do not believe you. What do they believe, the young people? You tell them that there was a time we sneaked out at night to feed Mugabe's men, the comrades. We risked being killed by Rhodesian soldiers. During the day, aeroplanes flew so low that you could see the white soldiers and their helmets. They could have easily thrown a bomb on to our compound and destroyed us all, as they did in some villages. I also tell her that her aunt, my first-born daughter Emma, her husband and two sons were killed in one night and thrown inside a cave. Their bodies stayed there, untouched, for several years.

'I have heard that story before. Is that really true?'

Truth. How much truth and how many times should we tell them what happened? How much truth should we leave out? Some people say Emma and her family were sell-outs and they got killed by Mugabe's soldiers. Others say they belonged to Sithole and they were killed by Muzorewa's forces. All I know is that they were not killed by white soldiers because those who were present at the *pungwe* said they did not see any white men. During the liberation war, more than thirty years ago, I lost a daughter, a son-in-law and two grandsons. They were singled out from the crowd and shot dead. In public. All in one night. I will never know who killed them. But what does it matter now? They all died. I can only thank the ancestors for keeping all their bones safe so we could give them a proper burial after independence.

Unlike her older sisters and some of her cousins, Chiyevo is a decent girl. She will be a good wife to someone one day. Chiyevo goes to church and works in the garden. Every day she comes to help me collect firewood, cook and fetch water from the well. If these were the old days and men were still strong, I would have gone to look for a husband for her. But these days, where would I look? Everywhere all you can see are skinny men. Even those who call themselves bachelors do not look healthy at all. Some of the widowed men are just looking for a younger woman to care for them until AIDS snatches them away, as it does. The only healthy men I have seen are those who work for donors, ZANU-PF, MDC, the churches and the Chinese clothing merchants. Business men are also healthy. They drive big cars and they have big stomachs. These men will take Chiyevo as a second or a third wife. But I will not let Chiyevo go with these men. They will treat her well at first until they find another beautiful girl to replace her. I tell Chiyevo that money can buy beautiful women. She should be patient and avoid situations with men that will lead to sex. One day a single good man will come along. Chiyevo does not say anything. All she does is listen to me, nod her head and do as I tell her.

In times of plenty, *mumaguta*, Chiyevo is normally fat, beautiful and strong. At present she is skinny. We all are. We are hungry. This is a bad season. When I was her age, I was fat and already married with two children. My father wanted more cattle so he married me off to VaMandiya, Chiyevo's grandfather. I was his third and youngest wife. I came to this village before I had my first period. I was not a woman yet. *Vahosi*, VaMandiya's senior wife made me sleep behind VaMandiya's back to keep him warm. After my first period, I became his wife. He loved me and called me VaNyachide, meaning I was his beloved.

Chiyevo, do not walk so fast. I am not your age, I tell her. She slows down. I used to be a good walker. Once I accompanied my mother from Hwedza to Mazowe for a *bira*, the ancestor worship ceremony. We passed through Salisbury on foot. Then when the liberation war came, curfew stopped us from going anywhere far. After the war, the numbers of buses coming here from Harare were so many. But everything changed when white farmers were forced to leave the land. Then Tony Blair and George Bush put sanctions on Zimbabwe. They kept the entire diesel and the petrol to themselves. During the past ten years no buses come as far as the village any more. Because of Tony Blair and George Bush, we have to walk many miles to Simukai Centre to get a bus to Harare. Everything begins and ends at Simukai Centre – ZANU-PF and MDC meetings, burial society, council meetings, agriculture meetings and now the donor's visit.

Chiyevo increases her pace again and pulls my hand: 'Mbuya, if we walk like *kamba*, the tortoise, by the time we get there, the donor will be gone. Look, Sabhuku's two daughters just passed us. They will be way ahead of us in the queue by the time we get to Simukai Centre.

Come to think of it, they are not widows, where are they going?'

I will not answer Chiyevo's question about Sabhuku's daughters. Talking while I am walking tires me. The message from Ndodye was an invitation for widows, old ladies and orphans. Sabhuku's daughters should not be going to the donor for food handouts today. But who can stop them? Sabhuku is the kraal head. He writes the names of those who qualify to get food. We all know that Sabhuku's daughters went away to Harare to work as maids. Some years later they came back with five children between them. Who is going to tell the donors that Sabhuku's two daughters are not widows? And his five grandchildren are not orphans? The donors do not know who we are. We do not know who they are. We just know that the donors are merciful white people from overseas. Every year we get donors with a different name. Most of them are Christians. They have plenty of food in their countries and they do not want us to die of hunger. They give us food through their workers – the local donors who live here.

We are at Simukai Centre now. My legs are sore and my back hurts. The donors are already here. Ndodye was correct. Last time I was here, a year ago, there was one lorry. We waited for a very long time to get one bag of beans per family. One bag of beans. That was all. Today is different. There is a big lorry covered with a tent. Behind the lorry are two trucks. The lorry is full of sacks. Food. There are many people here. People I have not seen since independence! Jakobho, the Anglican pastor from St Peters is here too. We are the same age. He has lost all his teeth and his back is all bent. Madaka, the war veteran who lost his leg when he stepped on a landmine. They gave him an artificial leg and when he is wearing trousers, you cannot even tell that he has one leg. I heard that he married a second wife with his war compensation money. His son is a strong member of the MDC. What a shame to the family that is. MDC did not give us land. Mugabe did. This is why I carry my ZANU-PF card and my *chitupa* tied at the corner of my head scarf.

When we left home this morning, Chiyevo said, 'Mbuya, you only need your *chitupa*, not your ZANU-PF card.' I told her that you never know when they will ask for the ZANU-PF card. I am always ready with it. She laughed and said, 'Mbuya, both your cards tell lies about who you are. Your date of birth on both cards say you are sixty years old now. That is not possible because my father would have been fifty now if he was still alive. And he was the last of your eight children. Also the card says your name is Enifa. Your name is Makumbi.'

What does it matter what year I was born? I ask her. Who was writing the time and the day of my birth? Enifa is my Christian English name, given to me when I was baptised as a young girl and I became an Anglican. I kept the same name when the comrades said I should change and support the Catholics during the liberation war. They said Catholics supported the fight for our land. Anglicans did not.

Chiyevo never learns. She leaves home without her ZANU-PF card all the time. Last time some youths at Simukai Centre asked her to produce her ZANU-PF card. She did not have it so they said she was a Morgan Tsvangirai MDC supporter. It was just luck that Ndodye was getting off the bus when he saw them harassing her. He told them that Chiyevo was from Chimombe kraal and as they very well knew, there is not a single MDC supporter in Chimombe. He, Ndodye, would not allow that to happen. They let Chiyevo go. I keep telling her that she should just keep both cards with her in different pockets. Right pocket for the ZANU-PF card and left pocket for the MDC card. That way she will be safe when youths from either political party ask her for a card.

This food distribution centre is noisy and chaotic. A policeman is shouting: 'We want order. *Chembere* one line! *Shirikadzi* one line! *Nherera* one line!' My legs are burning. It is hot. The donors are standing further away near the cars. Three men and two young women. One white woman. They are talking and laughing while drinking water from bottles. I am thirsty.

'If you do not stand in line, there will be no food distribution to anyone!' shouts the policeman. Someone needs to tell the policeman that the lines are all confused. Who says an old lady cannot be a widow and a widow cannot be an old lady? I belong to both lines. Orphans cannot stand in line on their own unless an adult stands with them. Some adults accompanying orphans are widows and some of them are old ladies. How do we know which line to go to?

The policeman is getting impatient. He is holding a whip. I think he is close to whipping some people into line. Under the *muchakata* tree, all the headmen are having a meeting. One of them goes to speak to the policeman. After listening to the headman for a short while, the policeman changes his orders: 'Everyone must stand according to their kraal!' I am pushed into the Chimombe kraal line together with Sabhuku's two daughters and their five children. Ndodye helps us, and within a short time our line is straight, long and orderly.

We have been standing in line for a long time. Nothing is happening. My back is very sore and my knees are shaking. Chiyevo comes to tell me to go and sit under the shade of a tree. She will stand in line for me. When she gets closer to receiving the food package, she will call me. I rest under the shade and take my snuff. After a while I feel the need to go and pass water. There are Blair toilets here. The rude nurse from the clinic is walking around shouting and telling people to use the public toilets. I have never used public toilets. Never. Who knows what disease you can pick up from those pit toilets? Their smell is worse than a dead skunk. The bush is cleaner than the toilets at Simukai Centre. I disappear behind the bush. The rude nurse sees me. She shouts at me: 'Imi Gogo, listen, we do not use the bush here!' I ignore her. I am only passing water. Since when did she start telling people what to do with their private waste? That is not her job. She should be inside the clinic giving injections. She is only shouting like this to get some favours from the donors. Maybe she will get free aspirins to sell once the donors leave.

When I come back from the bush, Chiyevo is nowhere to be seen.

'Have you seen Chiyevo?' I ask Ndodye. He is smartly dressed in a blue jacket, brown trousers, black shirt, a yellow tie and a big brown hat. On his jacket are several war medals, probably stolen from dead soldiers. He does not stand in line because he is managing security here. Ndodye will get a double food package as reward for his services later on. He tells me that two donor women took Chiyevo away from the line. He points to the direction where he saw them going. To a car parked under a tree a bit further away from all the activity. I go there to ask Chiyevo why she let them take her away. Now I have missed my place in line. They have given her a chair – the type that can be folded up. Chiyevo is drinking water from a bottle. Two young donor women, one white and one African are talking to her. They are both wearing pants.

'This is my grandmother,' Chiyevo tells them. The white woman smiles at me. She extends her hand for me to shake it. The last time I shook a white woman's hand was Mrs Janet Smith, the wife of the Rhodesian Prime Minister, Ian Smith. That was many years ago, long before independence. It was at the Agricultural Show at The Range. Mrs Smith wore gloves to greet us, just like the Anglican missionary women. I shake hands with both donor women, the white woman and the African. They have soft hands – hands accustomed to holding a pen, not a hoe.

'Gogo, we want to interview your granddaughter for a project we are working on with the youth,' the African one says. 'She will be back in time to get her food handout.' I do not know what she means by a project. I thank them and go back to the line. It has moved much closer to the food lorry. Sabhuku's girls and their children allow me to go in front of them. When my turn comes, a young clerk shouts: 'Enifa! Enifa Bako! Chimombe Kraal.' A boy born only yesterday calling my name as if he is calling a schoolgirl. Ah, how this hunger takes away all respect for age. I get my bag and wait for Chiyevo under the tree. The bag is heavy. Inside is a bottle of cooking oil, a packet of red beans and a big bag of bulgur. I like bulgur because it is like wheat and a bit like rice. It is easy to cook. In 2008, three years ago, when we were very hungry, bulgur saved us. Chiyevo said she read that bulgur came from America and it was meant for horses. But what did it matter? It was food. Starving people ate bulgur and within a couple of weeks they gained weight. Village women's bottoms became prominent again.

The donor women gave Chiyevo a small plastic bag with something in it. When I saw the bag, I felt happy: at least Chiyevo had not been interviewed for nothing. Sabhuku's daughters look at her with envy. I do not want them to know what gift Chiyevo got from the donor women. I will wait until we get to the river, then see the special gift. Maybe they gave Chiyevo biscuits, sweets, a packet of powdered milk or even sugar. Or some US dollars. We need some to pay for the grinding mill. Chiyevo carries my food bag on her head and holds the smaller bag with the gift in her hand. I walk behind her. We stop at the river to rest and drink some water.

Tell me what the donor women wanted, I ask Chiyevo.

'They said they were doing a research, an investigation. They want me to be part of a project to do with measuring the number of girls able to use protection when having sex.'

'Sex with a man? What man? You do not have a man.'

'That is true Mbuya, I do not have a man.'

'So, what do you protect?' I ask. I am puzzled. But I wait. I am expecting her to show me something to eat. Or maybe the gift of money. After all, the women she was talking to are donors. They come here to give.

'They gave me this,' she says. Then she pulls out several plastic tubes from the bag. I recognise the tubes immediately. Condoms. I have seen them at the clinic before. They are disgusting. Chiyevo takes another small packet out of the bag. She opens it and says, 'And this, Mbuya, is a female condom. You put it inside yourself before meeting a man.' She hands it to me to have a look.

'Chiyevo, you do not even know what a man feels like. So you want to feel a tube first before you feel a man? And how are you going to have a baby if you put that tube inside you? No, I do not want to touch it.'

Chiyevo shrugs and smiles. Then she says, 'In this packet are thirty condoms for the men and in this other one are thirty female condoms. They are all for the study. The donor women want to know the number of girls able to tell men to use condoms. They also want to know the number of girls able to use the female condom. Once a month I am required to tell the sister at the clinic the number of times I use protection and what type of protection I have used. She will write that number against my name. Mbuya, the donors said I must be prepared to protect myself when I meet a man. A man can't always be in control of what happens.'

Chiyevo is smiling. Is this Chiyevo talking? I shake my head. I feel anger rising inside me.

'Chiyevo, you disappear from the queue. I stand until my legs and my back hurt so much while you sit in a chair like some educated lady, drinking water from a bottle and talking about sex with strangers. Do you eat condoms?'

'Mbuya, this is just a just a study. Nothing else.' Chiyevo says, shrugging her shoulders.

'Instead of asking for sugar, a bar of soap, or just one dollar for the grinding mill, all you do is sit there answering questions about sex. What do you know about sex? Then you walk away with a bag of condoms for men and condoms for women. Can't you see what these women are doing? They hide behind the food truck so they can snatch you from the crowd and give you condoms. They are encouraging you to have sex before you get married.'

Chiyevo shrugs her shoulders, smiles and says nothing. I say to her, 'Chiyevo, go back to the donor women and tell them we do not have sex before marriage. Tell them condoms are not food. Tell them only those with full stomachs have time to think about sex. Tell them we want food, not sex. Go back now.'

Chiyevo looks at me as if I am mad. I am not mad. Why should the donors visit us and encourage our children to have sex? Even Chiyevo's mother does not tell her anything about sex. I do. It is my job as Chiyevo's grandmother to teach her about sex and marriage. What is the use of age if I cannot teach my grandchildren our culture, *tsika dzedu*? We are hungry, we are poor, but we still have a culture to follow.

Chiyevo walks back. Slowly.

I sit by the river and wait for her. After a very long time, Chiyevo comes back. She is accompanied by Ndodye. And she is still holding on to the packets. 'What happened? Why did you not give them back?' I ask her. She says the donor women were already gone when she got there. Ndodye's smile tells me Chiyevo is lying. 'So what are you going to do with those?' I ask.

I want to grab the packets of condoms from her and throw them into the river. Ndodye speaks with a soft polite voice: 'Mbuya the donors come to give food and they also give us condoms. We need both to stay alive. You cannot stop change. Let her keep the condoms. It is dangerous without protection out there.'

Then Chiyevo nods her head and giggles. 'Mbuya, I want to keep them,' she says, looking at Ndodye. Everyone says this daughter of my son is beautiful. What they do not know is that her head is full of water. Chiyevo's mother is right: this girl does not have any brains. She listens to the donors doing a project on her and accepts what they give her. Now she is listening to Ndodye who wants some of those things for himself. Today the donor's visit has given me food. But it has also taken Chiyevo away from me. I cannot tell Chiyevo what to do anymore.

14

The Rainbow Cardigan

John Eppel

Ugogo Mpala lived with her grandson, Benson, and her great granddaughter, Siduduziwe, in a derelict swimming pool in the low-density suburb of Hillside, Bulawayo. It was the cheapest apartment on the property of the Honourable Barnabas Simba MP, cheaper even than the converted chicken run, and the old tool shed made from slatted creosote planks. Altogether the Honourable MP had 27 tenants living on his property. The rentals were reasonable considering the dire shortage of accommodation in the City of Kings. Benson had scavenged some rusty galvanised iron sheets and some treated blue gum poles, and had erected an A-frame roof above the swimming pool. Ugogo was finding it increasingly difficult to climb up and down the original iron steps in one corner of the pool, so she seldom left the deep end where her informal business was established. It was one of Siduduziwe's tasks to take orders from and convey finished products to her great grandmother's customers.

Ugogo supported her last remaining family by knitting. Her clientele were middle class mums with babies and toddlers. There was a steady demand for booties, bed socks, onesies, and rompers; and there was an occasional demand for dressing gowns. She also knitted for her dependants, and her crowning glory was a cardigan for Benson made out of carpet wool. She had discovered a batch of the multi-coloured yarn at a church fete, and had purchased it for next to nothing. The cardigan had a floppy collar and six large buttons, only two of which were matching. It was stiff and scratchy but these minor discomforts were worth it for the attention this kaleidoscopic wonder brought to Benson, who wore it day after day, come hell or high water. Nothing like it had been seen since the time of the Biblical Joseph. He was known by his drinking chums as The Rainbow Nation.

Times were so hard that Ugogo could no longer afford to keep both children in school. It was agreed that Benson, who had failed his O-levels two years in a row, would leave while Siduduziwe, who was bright and hardworking, and only in the first year of high school, would stay on. Benson had heard from his drinking chums that there was a fortune to be made in the alluvial diamond fields that had recently been discovered near the city of Mutare. He determined to go there and try his luck. He decided to walk the several hundred kilometres, hoping for lifts on the way. Ugogo and Siduduziwe accompanied him to the Harare road. In a plastic bag he carried a spare shirt, a bottle of water and half a loaf of bread. They said their goodbyes and watched the young man slowly disappear into the distance. Because of the visibility of his cardigan, it took a long time.

Siduduziwe had lost her parents to AIDS-related illnesses. She often thought about them as she walked down Cecil Avenue and up Fairbridge Drive on her way to school, comfortable in her knitted white socks, not so comfortable in her knitted green jersey, which she wore even on the hottest days. This was to conceal as much as possible of her threadbare uniform, which was not likely to survive many more washes. Siduduziwe was a gentle soul, vulnerable to peer group pressure and to overbearing school teachers. She loved nature's creatures, in particular birds. She was forever rearing a fledgling that had fallen from the nest, or rescuing hapless doves from domestic cats. Her father had been a Parks and Wildlife ranger, and he it was who instilled in his daughter a love of nature. Her mother had been a primary school teacher, and Dudu, as she was affectionately known, was determined to follow in her footsteps. Meanwhile she was completely dependent on her paternal grandmother, Ugogo Mpala.

Benson in his cardigan, now showing signs of wear and tear,

returned from his stint in the diamond fields bearing good and bad news. The good news was that he had acquired 12 high-quality diamonds the size of marbles, the bad news that he was on the run, a) from the authorities and b) from a criminal gang. Before he could be properly welcomed by his doting relatives, he informed them that he would leave that very night, making his way south-west to Botswana. He had friends in Francistown who would help him sell the diamonds to a kindly Lebanese business man. As soon as he was settled, either in Botswana or South Africa, he would send for Ugogo and Dudu so that they could live together in prosperity. They would never again want for anything. Ugogo would have her own TV; Dudu would have a brand new twelve-speed bicycle; he would go to church every Sunday in a three-piece suit. He asked his grandmother to prepare some *isitshwala* and tea to help him swallow the diamonds. Dudu watched in awe as her uncle wrapped each gem in thick paste and downed it with a gulp of sweet tea. The first half dozen went down quite easily, the last half dozen not so. He gagged a few times. During this ritual Ugogo stitched a few holes in the cardigan, which was now so stretched, it could be used as a blanket – as long as Benson kept a foetal position.

He bade them goodbye with the reassurance that he would send for them as soon as he was rich and settled. They watched him disappear into the night, a fading rainbow. They did not hear from him again.

Years later, when Siduduziwe was about to enter her final year at Hillside teachers' College, her great grandmother had a stroke known as hemiplegia, which paralyzed her down one side of her body. This meant she could no longer knit and this in turn meant that Siduduziwe would no longer be able to attend college. It was a bitter double blow for the young woman. When the first term opened she was not there for registration. One of her lecturers, Mrs Mbambo, contacted her at the converted swimming pool and commiserated with her. There was much clicking of tongues and shaking of heads. Mrs Mbambo had lectured Siduduziwe since first year, and well knew the student's worth. She had arranged a class outing to study rock art and geological formations in the Matobo communal lands some 40 kilometres south of Bulawayo. She particularly wanted to show her students the way different fault lines produced very different looking granite hills. She vowed to sneak Siduduziwe on to the bus. If the authorities found out she would be severely reprimanded for setting a precedent, but she knew how fond the other students were of Siduduziwe, and she was sure none of them would spill the beans. She felt it was the least she could do for this unfortunate young woman.

The day for the outing arrived. The cassias along Cecil Avenue were in full bloom, and they gave off a lovely fruity scent. Beneath the tree where Siduduziwe waited for the college bus, a party of cackling red-billed hoopoes was feasting on termites. The young woman felt wretched. How could she face her erstwhile fellow students without hiding her head in shame, not just because she had failed to come up with the college fees but because of her ragbag appearance? She heard the singing before the bus stopped for her to get in. It was one of her favourite gospel numbers, 'Siyabonga Jesu', composed by Solly Mahlangu:

> *Wahamba nathi, oh wahamba nathi*
> *Oh wahamba nathi, siyabonga*
>
> *Siyabonga Jesu, Siyabonga ngonyama yezulu*
> *Siyabonga Jesu, Siyabonga ....*

The song and the jovial faces helped her relax a little; the welcome applause led by Mrs Mbambo, as she climbed into the bus encouraged her to lift her head and smile shyly at the passengers. She was motioned to a seat next to the lecturer, and soon she joined in with the next song:

> *Thando luka baba*
> *Thando luka baba*
> *Lubanzi lujulile lumnandi nsukuzonke....*

After the first verse the bus went quiet. Every single student looked expectantly at Dudu. She knew what to do; she had always been the soloist, and her heart expanded with her lungs as she poured out God's love for the wretched of the earth, while her comrades chorused:

> *O lumnandi ekuseni bo*
> *lumnandi*
> *Emini bo*
> *Lumnandi*

Ntambama
Lumnandi
Lumnandi nsukuzonke.

By the time they turned off the Old Gwanda Road in the direction of the communal lands, dear Dudu had almost forgotten her threadbare clothes and her empty purse. She and the others were fascinated by a pair ground hornbills, iNsingizi, who were hunting some distance apart, calling to each other every now and then. They were amazed by their deep, booming voices. Mrs Mbambo explained that these birds played an ambiguous role in Ndebele culture: 'Its call, if made early in the morning, is a harbinger of rain, but if it comes too close to a villager's hut, it is a harbinger of death. It must be chased off.'

The first granite hills came into view and Mrs Mbambo pointed out two distinctive formations: the whaleback or *dwala*, and the castle koppie. Whalebacks, the students learned, have predominantly horizontal fault lines, while castle koppies have predominantly vertical fault lines. The metaphors are quite appropriate. Dudu could not take her eyes off a magnificent black eagle soaring above the lichen pocked granite hills.

The bus came to a halt near a cavernous overhanging rock, which displayed some faded Bushman paintings of what seemed to be a hunting party: stylised humans with sharpened throwing sticks chasing a realistically portrayed eland bull. The lecturer explained that the Bushmen, Zimbabwe's first human inhabitants, had a sophisticated notion that art not only imitated life, it possessed life. 'That's why the humans in the rock paintings are unrecognisable as individuals, while the animals they hunt are perfectly recognisable. There are two issues to consider here. First, why are the humans not recognisable as individuals?'

'Like voodoo?'

'A bit. If you draw or paint the likeness of an individual, you will have control over them. This was a most civilised understanding among these people. Second, why are the animals portrayed so realistically? Anybody?' No one? Okay, well... when the Bushmen killed an animal for food and clothing and tools, they expressed their gratitude by recreating that animal on the walls of their caves. In this way they brought them back to life. Don't you see?'

'Isn't that an ostrich over there?' ventured one of the students pointing at a shape to the left of the hunting party.

'It is indeed,' the lecturer replied. 'Can any of you suggest why the ostrich might have been an important bird for the Bushmen?'

'To make feather dusters,' said the class joker.

'Mmm… that would be somewhat anachronistic. Anybody got a sensible idea?'

'Didn't they use ostrich egg shells to store water?'

'They did indeed. In times of drought they would store them under the ground. What else?'

'Protein?'

'Plenty of that – in the eggs as well as the flesh.'

Siduduziwe then suggested that they might signify something magical for the people. 'Good point, my dear. The ostrich is indeed a legendary bird. It was the Bushmen's Prometheus. What do I mean by that?'

'It gave them fire?'

'It gave them fire. It has enormous strength. It doesn't fly. It sits on its eggs to cool them, not to warm them. To the Bushmen it came back to life after it died. These unique characteristics, for a bird, placed it in the realm of the magical where animals can metamorphose into humans and vice versa. Look at that creature there,' she pointed to another site on the overhang. 'See, it's got the body of a human and the head of… some creature.'

'It is birdlike.'

'It is. Now, I want a couple of you to go into the cave area – mind your heads – and see what you can find in the dirt.'

Two of the young men took up the challenge. They soon returned with excited expressions on their faces. They had found sharp bits of flint, which would have been used as scrapers and cutters, bits of broken pottery, and beads. The others gathered around to witness the treasures.

'Look carefully at those beads,' Mrs Mbambo addressed her students, 'what do you think they are made of?'

'Egg shells,' someone replied.

'Quite right, my dear, ostrich egg shells. The Bushmen believed that wearing ostrich eggshell beads either around their necks or around their waists would protect them from illness. They would also pulverise the shells and rub the powder into their bodies, even eat it. You see, the ostrich is a bird that had great potency for the San people. And birds are significant for other cultures too. Think of the soapstone birds from Great Zimbabwe. They seem to be eagles. What do they tell us about the Mwenemutapa kingdom and the Karanga people? Birds fly…'

'Not the ostrich.'

'No, not the ostrich; but most birds fly. They also seem to appear out of nowhere, and disappear suddenly. These characteristics make them symbolic of the link between heaven and earth. And birds of the night, like owls, can extend that connection to the underworld.'

'So when a shaman puts on a bird's head mask…'

'He is merging with the spiritual world. He is metamorphosing, becoming.'

'Angels have wings.'

'Fairies too.'

'Let's not get carried away, shall we?'

During their tea break, in which Mrs Mbambo provided Dudu with a packet containing egg and tomato sandwiches and an orange, an excited little boy from a nearby village, ran among the students crying, *'Buyani uzobona, buyani uzubona.'*

He wouldn't tell them what it was he wanted them to see, but motioned them to follow him along a narrow path. Some of the students, including Siduduziwe, after getting permission from Mrs Mbambo, who indicated that they need not hurry back, she fancied a nap, followed the barefoot child. He kept a few metres ahead of them and repeatedly looked back to see that they were not going astray.

Finally they came to a clearing where a single buffalo thorn tree stood covered in birds' nests. *'Khangelani,'* said the boy pointing at one of the nests. Because of the midday glare, it took the students some time to focus. No one heard Siduduziwe gasp. Certainly no one heard her heart pounding. This nest stood out from the others because it had been partly woven with wool, brightly coloured wool – rainbow colours. This was a colony of bickering white-browed sparrow weavers with their untidy westward facing houses of straw. The students expressed curiosity but soon began to wander back to the bus where the driver, still in his seat, was, between snoozes, poring over that day's edition of the *Bulawayo Chronicle*. They spread themselves on the ground basking in the shade of the trees, enjoying the respite.

Alone now with the boy, Dudu thanked him and gave him her orange and the remaining sandwiches. She sent him on his way, and then she began her search. She started at the edge of the clearing and walked slowly around it keeping her eyes peeled for tell-tale signs. Once she completed a circuit she rippled out a metre and began again. For the first time she noticed harvester ants scurrying back and forth with bits of dried grass in their mandibles. She looked up to the sky and saw clouds billowing in the direction of neighbouring Botswana. Too early in the season, she thought, for rain.

After several fruitless circuits of the bush surrounding the clearing, Dudu began to get despondent. She had to try another approach. She decided to return to the nests and watch the birds. She counted a party of seven, but only two of them seemed to be working on the nests. After careful observation it dawned on her that they were building different nests, one with grass-stems and the other with bits of wool. She had to focus all her attention on the latter.

It seemed ages before that bird flew off in a certain direction where an anthill was just visible. It seemed ages before it returned with a wisp of rainbow-coloured wool in its beak. Dudu's heart began to pound again. She watched the bird weave the wool into its nest, watched it chase a subordinate that had flown too close, and watched it fly off again in the direction of the ant hill. This time, cautiously, she followed it. She saw it dip over the rise, out of sight. She waited for it to reappear, and it did, after a minute or two, with another wisp of wool in its beak. There was a lot of thick bush round the base of the ant hill so she had to give it quite a wide berth before returning to the point where the bird had gone down.

There he lay, prone, skull crushed, still wearing what was left of Ugogo's cardigan. The skeleton was no longer intact. Scavengers must have visited it in its shallow grave in the ant hill. Dudu looked around for other items of clothing but saw none. Tentatively she approached her uncle's remains. The bird had returned for some more wool and was making a commotion. Tentatively she touched this bone, and then that bone. 'Benson?' she said, as if waking him for a cup of tea… 'Benson?' Then at last the sobs came, chest-heaving, heart-breaking sobs, sobs that collapsed into inexpressible cries of desolation. *'Umdala omncinyane! Umdala omncinyane! Maye! Maye!'*

Suddenly, drops of rain began to fall about her. A few landed on his pelvic girdle and she made a move to wipe them dry. That was when she noticed, below the still intact rib cage, a cluster of small dirty stones. She sat back on her haunches, disbelieving. Her heart racing in her chest. Then she took a few deep breaths. This was not a moment to give way to emotion. Leaning forward, carefully and respectfully, without upsetting the skeleton, she removed them, counting them into the empty lunch packet. There were twelve in all. Her breathing slowed down. She said a quiet prayer: *'Siyabonga,* Jesu, *siyabonga. Siyabonga,* Benson, thank you my Uncle. Thank you my ancestors.' Then she gathered a handful of sandy soil and let it sift through her fingers onto her uncle's remains, ensuring that some of it landed on the rainbow cardigan. Finally, she looked up at the fluttering sparrow weaver and said, *'Siyabonga inyoni,* the wool is yours.' Then stuffing the packet into a pocket of her ruined dress and turned to rejoin her companions at the college bus. And not a moment too soon for echoing through the bush she heard the impatient sound of a hooter.

Back on the bus, she hardly heard her companions chatting noisily with each other. She gazed out of the window at the brown veld, hardly seeing the familiar hills. Her grandmother knew someone who knew someone – a friend of Uncle Benson's – who would help her sell them.

(vi)

Social Relations

15

THE MUPANDAWANA DANCING CHAMPION

Petina Gappah

When the prices of everything went up ninety-seven times in one year, M'dhara Vitalis Mukaro came out of retirement to make the coffins in which we buried our dead. In a space of only six months, he became famous twice over, as the best coffin maker in the district and as the Mupandawana Dancing Champion.

Fame is an elastic concept, especially in a place like this, where we all know the smells of each other's armpits. Mupandawana, full name Gutu-Mupandawana Growth Point, is bigger than a village but it is not yet a town. I have become convinced that the government calls Mupandawana a growth point merely to divert us from the reality of our present squalor with optimistic predictions about our booming future. As it is not even a townlet, a townling, or half a fraction of a town, there was much rejoicing at a recent groundbreaking ceremony for a new row of Blair toilets when the District Commissioner shared with us his vision for town status for Mupandawana by the year 2065. Ours is one of the biggest growth points in the country, but the only real growth is in the number of people waiting to buy coffins, and the lengthening line of youngsters waiting to board the Wabuda Wanatsa buses blasting Chimbetu songs all the way to Harare.

You will not find me joining that queue out of Mupandawana. When the Ministry dispatched me here to teach at the local secondary, I was relieved to escape the headaches of Harare with its grasping women who will not let go until your wallet is empty. Mupandawana is the perfect place from which to study life, which appears to me to be no more than the punchline to a cosmic joke played by a particularly mordant being.

So I observe life, and teach geography to schoolchildren whose only interest in my subject is knowledge of the exact distance between Mupandawana and London, Mupandawana and Johannesburg, Mupandawana and Gaborone, Mupandawana and Harare. If I cared enough, I would tell them that there is nothing there to rush for; *kumhunga hakuna ipwa*, as my late mother used to say.

But let them go, they shall find out soon enough.

Mine is not a lonely life. In those moments when solitude quarrels with me, I enjoy the company of my two friends, Jeremiah, who teaches agriculture, and Bobojani who goes where Jeremiah goes. And then there are the Growth Pointers, as I call them, the people of Mupandawana whose lives prove my theory that life is one big jest at the expense of humanity.

Take M'dhara Vitalis, the coffin maker.

Before he retired, he worked in a furniture factory in Harare. He had been trained in the old days, M'dhara Vitalis told us on the first occasion Jeremiah, Bobojani and I drank with him. 'If the leg of one of my chairs had got you in the head, *vapfanha*, you would have woken up to tell your story in heaven,' he said. 'The President sits in one of my chairs. Real oak, *vapfanha*. I made furniture from oak, teak, mahogany, cedar, ash *chaiyo*, even Oregon pine. Not these zhing-zhong products from China. They may look nice and flashy but they will crack in a minute.'

On this mention of China, Bobo made a joke about the country becoming Zhim-Zhim-Zhimbabwe because the ruling party had sold the country to the Chinese. Not to be outdone, Jeremiah said, 'A group of Zanu PF supporters arrives at the pearly gates. Saint Peter is greatly shocked, and goes to consult God. God says, but ruling party supporters are also my children. Saint Peter goes to fetch them, but rushes back alone shouting they've gone, they've gone. How can the ruling party supporters just disappear, says God. I am talking about the pearly gates, says Peter.'

We laughed, keeping our voices low because the District Commissioner was seated in the corner below the window.

M'dhara Vitalis had looked forward to setting down the tools of his trade and retiring to answer the call of the land. 'You don't know how lucky you are,' he was often heard to say to the fellows who idled around Mupandawana. 'You have no jobs so you can plough your fields.'

He had spent so much time in Harare that he appeared not to see that the rows to be ploughed were stony; when the rains came, there was no seed, and when there was seed, there were no rains. Even those like Jeremiah, who liked farming so much so that they had swallowed books all the way to the agricultural college at Chibhero, had turned their backs on the land, in Jeremiah's case, by choosing to teach the theory of farming to children who, given even an eighth of a chance, would sooner choose the lowliest messenger jobs in the cities than a life of tilling the land.

M'dhara Vitalis was forced to retire three years earlier than anticipated. His employer told him that the company was shutting down because they could not afford the foreign currency. There would not be money for a pension, he was told, the money had been invested in a bank whose directors had run off with it *kwazvakarehwa* to England. He had been allowed to keep his overalls, and had been given some of the tools that he had used in the factory. And because the owner was also closing another factory, one that manufactured shoes, M'dhara Vitalis and all the other employees were each given three pairs of shoes.

Jeremiah, Bobo and I saw him as he got off the Wabuda Wanatsa bus from Harare. 'Thirty years, *vakomana*,' he said to us, as he shook his head. 'You work thirty years for one company and this is what you get. *Shuwa, shuwa,* pension *yebhutsu*. Heh? Shoes, instead of a pension. Shoes. These, these . . .'

The words caught in his throat.

'*Ende futi dzinoshinya*, all the pairs are half a size too small for me,' he added when he had recovered his voice. We commiserated with him as best we could. We poured out all the feeling contained in our hearts.

'Sorry, M'dhara,' I said. 'Rough, M'dhara,' said Jeremiah. 'Tight,' said Bobojani. We watched him walk off carefully in his snug-fitting shoes, the plastic bag with the other two pairs dangling from his left hand.

'Pension *yebhutsu*,' Jeremiah said, and, even as we pitied him, we laughed until tears ran down Jeremiah's cheeks and we had to pick Bobojani off the ground.

For all that he did not have a real pension, M'dhara Vitalis was happy to retire. Some three kilometres from the growth point was the homestead that he had built with money earned from the factory, with three fields for shifting cultivation. Between them, he and his wife managed well enough, somehow making do until the drought came in two consecutive years and inflation zoomed and soared and spun the roof off the country. M'dhara Vitalis went back to Harare to look for another job, but who wanted an old man like him when there were millions unemployed? He looked around Mupandawana and was fortunate to find work making coffins. M'dhara Vitalis was so efficient that he made a small contribution to the country's rising unemployment – his employer found it convenient to fire two other carpenters. And that was how he became known as the coffin maker with the nimblest fingers this side of the Great Dyke.

***

We had seen his hands at work, but of his nimble feet and his acrobatics on the dance floors of Harare, we had only heard. As the person who told us these stories was the man himself, there was reason to believe that he spoke as one who ululated in his own praise. As Jeremiah said, 'There is too much seasoning in M'dhara Vita's stories.'

All his exploits seemed to have taken place in the full glare of the public light. 'I danced at Copacabana, Job's Night Spot and the Aquatic Complex. There is one night I will never forget when I danced at Mushandirapamwe and the floor cleared of dancers. All that the people could do was to stand and watch. *Vakamira ho-o*,' he told us. We laughed into our beers, Jeremiah, Bobojani and I, but, as we soon came to see, we laughed too much and we laughed too soon.

M'dhara Vita's employer was the Member of Parliament for our area. As befitting such a man of the people, the Honourable had a stake in the two most thriving enterprises in the growth point, so that the profits from Kurwiragono Investments t/a No Matter Funeral Parlour and Coffin Suppliers accumulated interest in the same bank account as those from Kurwiragono Investments t/a Why Leave Guesthouse and Disco-Bar. And being one on whom fortune had smiled, our Honourable could naturally not confine his prosperous seed to only one woman. Why Leave was managed by Felicitas, the Honourable's small house, a generous sort who had done her bit to make a good number of men happy before she settled into relative domesticity with the Honourable. As one of those happy men, I retained very fond memories of her, and often stepped into the Guesthouse for a drink and to pass the time. She always had an eye out for the next chance, Felicitas, which is how she came to replace me with the Honourable, and she decided that what the bar needed was a dancing competition.

The first I knew of it was not from Felicitas herself, but when I saw groups of dust-covered schoolchildren at break time dancing the *kongonya*. Now, the sexually suggestive *kongonya* is the dance of choice at ruling party gatherings, so I thought that they must be practising for a visit from yet another dignitary. Later that evening as I passed the Guesthouse I saw another crowd of children dancing the *kongonya*, while another pointed to the wall of the building. Intrigued by this random outbreak of *kongonya* in the youth of Mupandawana, I approached the Guesthouse. The youngsters scattered on my approach, and I saw that they had been admiring a poster on which was portrayed the silhouette outline of a couple captured in mid-dance. The man's back was bent so far that his head almost touched the ground, while his female partner, of a voluptuousness that put me in mind of Felicitas, had her hands on her knees with her bottom

almost touching the ground.

Below this enraptured couple were the words:

**Why Leave Guesthouse and Disco-Bar
in association with Mupandawana
District Development Council
is proud to present the search for the:
Mupandawana Dancing Champion
Join us for a night of celebration and dancing!
One Night Only!!**

Details followed of the competition to be held a fortnight from then, and the main prizes to be won, the most notable of which was one drink on the house once a week for three months.

Mupandawana is a place of few new public pleasures. In the following two weeks, the excitement escalated and reached a pitch on the night itself. In their cheap and cheerful clothes, Mupandawana's highest and lowest gathered in the main room of the Why Leave Guesthouse and poured out into the night: the lone doctor doing penance at the district hospital, the nurses, the teachers, the security guards, the storekeeper from Chawawanaidyanehama Cash and Carry and his two giggling girl assistants, the District Commissioner in all his frowning majesty, the policemen from the camp, a few soldiers, the people from the nearby and outlying villages. Tapping feet and impatient twitches and shakes showed that the people were itching to get started, and when Felicitas turned on the music, they needed no further encouragement.

The music thumped into the room, the Bhundu Boys, Alick Macheso and the Orchestra Mberikwazvo, Andy Brown and Storm, System Tazvida and the Chazezesa Challengers, Cephas 'Motomuzhinji' Mashakada and Muddy Face, Hosiah Chipanga and Broadway Sounds, Mai Charamba and the Fishers of Men, Simon 'Chopper' Chimbetu and the Orchestra Dendera Kings, Tongai 'Dehwa' Moyo and Utakataka Express, and, as no occasion could be complete without him, Oliver 'Tuku' Mtukudzi and the Black Spirits. They sang out their celebratory anthems of life gone right; they sang out their woeful, but still danceable, laments of things gone wrong. And to all these danced the Growth Pointers, policeman and teacher, nurse and villager, man and woman, young and old. There was *kongonya*, more *kongonya*, and naturally more *kongonya* – ruling party supporters in Mupandawana are spread as thickly as the rust on the ancient Peugeot 504 that the Honourable's son crashed and abandoned at Sadza Growth Point. Bobojani was in there with the best of them, shuffling a foot away from the District Commissioner, while Jeremiah and I watched from the bar.

The Growth Pointers did themselves proud. The security guard who stood watch outside the Building Society danced the Borrowdale even better than Alick Macheso. Dzinganisayi, widely considered to be the Secretary-General of the Mupandawana branch of ZATO (aka the Zimbabwe Association of Thieves' Organisations) proved to be as talented on the dance floor as he was in making both attended and unattended objects vanish. Nyengeterayi from Chawawanaidyanehama Cash and Carry got down on hands and knees and improvised a dance that endangered her fingers, given the stomping, dancing feet around her.

And who knew that the new fashion and fabrics teacher could move her hips like that? As I watched her gyrate to Tuku, a stirring arose in my loins, and I began to reconsider the benefits of long-term companionship.

Then, out of the corner of my eye, I saw M'dhara Vita enter the room.

He was dressed in a suit that declared its vintage as circa 1970s. The trouser legs were flared, while the beltline that must have once hugged his hips and waist was rolled up and tied around his waistline with an old tie. The jacket had two vents at the back. He wore a bright green shirt with the collar covering that of his jacket. On his head was a hat of the kind worn by men of his age, but his was set at a rakish angle, almost covering one eye. And on his feet were one-third of his pension.

'*Ko*, Michael Jackson*ka*,' Jeremiah said as we nudged each other.

M'dhara Vitalis gave us a casual nod as, showing no signs of painful feet, he walked slowly to the dance floor.

And then he danced.

The security guard's Borrowdale became an Mbaresdale. Dzinganisayi's movements proved to be those of a rank amateur. Nyengeterayi's innovations were revealed to be no more than the shallow ambitions of callow youth. M'dhara Vitalis danced them off the floor to the sidelines where they stood to watch with the rest of us. He knew all the latest dances, and the oldest too. We gaped at his reebok and his water pump. He stunned us with his running man. He killed us with his robot. And his snake dance and his break-dance made us stand and say ho-o. His moonwalk would have made Michael him- self stand and say ho-o. The floor cleared, until only he and the fashion and fabrics teacher were dancing.

M'dhara Vitalis was here.

The teacher was there.

The teacher was here.

M'dhara Vitalis was there.

M'dhara Vitalis moved his hips.

The teacher moved her waist.

M'dhara Vitalis moved his neck and head.

The teacher did a complicated twirl with her arms.

M'dhara Vitalis did some fancy footwork, *mapantsula* style.

The teacher lifted her right leg off the ground and shook her right buttock.

And then Felicitas put on Chamunorwa Nebeta and the Glare

Express. As the first strains of Tambai Mese Mujairirane filled the room, we saw M'dhara Vitalis transformed. He wriggled his hips. He closed his eyes and whistled. He turned his back to us and used the vent in the back of the jacket to expose his bottom as he said, '*Pesu, pesu,*' moving the jacket first to one side and then to the other.

'Watch that waist,' I said to Jeremiah. '*Chovha* George!' said the District Commissioner. 'If only I was a woman,' said Jeremiah. That last dance sealed it, the fashion and fabrics teacher conceded the floor. By popular acclaim, M'dhara Vita was crowned Mupandawana Dancing Champion. It was a night that Mupandawana would not forget.

***

This was just as well because the one-night-only threat of the poster came true in a way that Felicitas had not anticipated. Two days after M'dhara Vita's triumph, the Governor of our province summoned our Honourable MP to his office in Masvingo. A bright young spark, one of the countless army of men who are paid to get offended on behalf of the ruling party, had taken a careful look at the poster and noticed that the first letters of the words Mupandawana Dancing Champion spelled out the acronym of the opposition party, the unmentionable Movement for Democratic Change. Naturally, this had to be conveyed to the appropriate channels.

'What business does a ruling party MP have in promoting the opposition, the puppets, those led by tea boys, the detractors who do not understand that the land is the economy and the economy is the land and that the country will never be a colony again, those who seek to reverse the consolidation of the gains of our liberation struggle,' so said the Governor, shaking with rage. I only knew that he shook with rage because Felicitas said he did, and she only knew because the Honourable told her so.

The upshot of this was that there were no more dance competitions, and M'dhara Vita the coffin maker remained the undefeated dancing champion of our growth point. He took his a one-drink-a-week prize for what it was worth, insisting on a half-bottle of undiluted Château brandy every Friday evening. 'Why can't he drink Chibuku like a normal man his age?' Felicitas asked, with rather bad grace, to which I responded that if he had been a normal man of his age, he would not have been the dancer he was.

To appreciate his skill is to understand that he was an old man. They had no birth certificates in the days when he was born, or at least none for people born in the rural areas, so that when he trained as a carpenter at Bondolfi and needed a pass to work in the towns, his mother had estimated his age by trying to recall how old he was when the mission school four kilometres from his village had been built. As befitting one who followed in the professional footsteps of the world's most famous carpenter, he had chosen 25 December as his birthday, so that his age was a random selection and he could well have been older than his official years. What was beyond dispute was that he danced in defiance of the wrinkles around his eyes.

Even if he had not got his drinks on the house, many of us would have bought him, if not his favourite brandy, then a less expensive alternative. There were no competitions and no more posters, but we began to gather at the Guesthouse every Friday evening to watch M'dhara Vita. Fuelled on by the bottom-of-the-barrel brandy and the *museve* music, his gymnastics added colour to our grey Fridays.

It was no different on that last Friday.

'Boys, boys,' he said as he approached the bar where I stood with Bobojani, Jeremiah and a group of other drinkers.

'*Ndeipi* M'dhara,' Jeremiah greeted him in the casual way that we talked to him; none of that respect-for-the-elders routine with M'dhara Vita. He cracked a joke at our expense, and we gave it right back to him, he knocked back his drink, and proceeded to the dance floor. Felicitas had come to understand that it was the Congolese rumba that demanded agile waists and rubber legs that really got him moving. So on that night, the Lubumbashi Stars blasted out of the stereo as M'dhara Vitalis took centre stage. He stood a while, as though to let the brandy and the music move its way through his ears and mouth to his brain and pelvis. Then he ground his hips in time to the rumba, all the while his eyes closed, and his arms stretched out in front of him.

'*Ichi chimudhara chirambakusakara,*' whistled Jeremiah, echoing the generally held view that M'dhara Vitalis was in possession of a secret elixir of youth.

'I am Vitalis, shortcut Vita, *ilizwo lami ngi*Vitalis, danger *basopo. Waya waya waya waya!*' He got down to the ground, rolled and shook. We crowded around him, relishing this new dance that we had not seen before. He twitched to the right, and to the left. The music was loud as we egged him on. He convulsed in response to our cheering. His face shone, and he looked to us as if to say, 'Clap harder.'

And we did.

It was only when the song ended and we gave him a rousing ovation and still he did not get up that we realised that he would never get up, and that he had not been dancing, but dying.

***

As M'dhara Vitalis left Why Leave feet first, it was left to Bobojani, with his usual eloquence, to provide a fitting commentary on the evening's unexpected event.

'Tight,' he said.

There was not much to add after that.

We buried him in one of the last coffins he ever made. I don't know whether he would have appreciated that particular irony. I am sure, though, that he would have appreciated making the front page of the one and only national daily newspaper.

The story of his death appeared right under the daily picture of the President. If you folded the newspaper three-quarters of the way to hide the story in which was made the sunny prediction that inflation was set to go down to two million, seven hundred and fifty-seven per cent by year end, all you saw was the story about M'dhara Vita. They wrote his name as Fidelis instead of Vitalis, and called him a pensioner when he hadn't got a pension; unless, of course, you counted those three pairs of shoes.

Still, the headline was correct. 'Man Dances Self to Death'.

That, after all, is just what he did.

16

Maria's Interview

Julius Chingono

Maria arrived at No. 28 Shava Road, a house at the top of a hill in the plush suburb of Highlands to the north of Harare, to find an unwelcoming entrance. She looked closely at the wooden plate posted on one of the brick pillars that held the rusting steel gate. The plate read O and S Ga.adzi.wa, the paint was peeling and letters were missing. She put down her two green canvas bags and noticed that they were already blotched by red soil. The gate was not locked but a big key hung on a chain from the gatepost that tilted a little inside the yard. There was no one in sight. A driveway of concrete blocks stretched away from the gate and was flanked by huge jacaranda trees. Maria, stretching, stood on her toes and peered through the overgrowth of trees and shrubs, squinting in the haze of the hot afternoon. A white house peeped through the fading green of trees and wilting flowers. But Maria did not dare walk through the gate. She feared dogs, although she saw no sign of life beyond the gate. The yard was hot and lifeless, except for the faint twitter of birds, and the drone of vehicles behind her on the access road.

With difficulty, Maria shook the chain strung around the gatepost. It was the only way she could draw the attention of the people in the house, if there were any there. Then she hit the frame of the gate with the hanging key, and the metal clanged through the air, disturbing the birds in the cool shadows of the trees.

She took a handkerchief from the hip pocket of her faded blue jean skirt and blotted the sweat that ran down behind her ears and above her eyes. She rubbed her bare arms. She straightened the cheap pendant that fell from her neck, arranged her skirt and brushed away the loose strands of her permed hair with her palm.

A girl in a green tracksuit appeared in the driveway. She stopped when she saw Maria and stared at her silently. She wore rubber slippers of different colours and her hair was uncombed. She was about eighteen years old, Maria's age. Maria raised her hand. She did not find the strength to shout. The gesture shook off the girl's hesitation and she walked towards the gate.

'Can I help you?' she said abruptly, standing well back. Maria wondered how the girl was managing in the glaring heat – a zipped-up track-suit, goodness she must be hot.

'Good afternoon, I would like to see Mrs Gahadzikwa.'

'Is she expecting you?' The girl looked at Maria, shading her eyes from the sun with the palm of her hand. She shrugged lightly when her eyes shifted to the big bags lying beside Maria. She did not seem to like visitors whom she could not recognise.

'I hope so.' Maria's voice was shaky. She moved nearer the gate, moistening her lips with her tongue.

'She is not in.'

'I have got a letter for her.' The girl stretched out her hand to receive it but Maria did not give her the letter that was tucked in the hip pocket of her skirt. Instead, she tried briefly to explain how she happened to be enquiring about Mrs Gahadzikwa.

'I understand Mrs Gahadzikwa is looking for a housemaid. My previous employer referred me to her.'

'Okay, you can wait. She'll be coming any time from now,' the girl said. 'She is somewhere in the neighbourhood.'

'Thank you.'

Maria watched the girl walk away fast, wiping her face with the front of her track suit jacket, and disappear at the bend in the driveway. She hoped her manners were not those of her prospective employer's.

She turned and found herself some shade below a big gum tree across the road. The late September heat was dazzling to the eye above the tarmac. She sat down on her handkerchief, spread over the resinous leaves of the tree and inhaled the aroma of mint. Her bags kept vigil at the gate. She whiled away the time by combing her hair behind her ears and touching up her dark face with a brown powder and red lipstick. She waited. The traffic droned up and down the access road. She thought of the reference letter from her previous employer. She felt it was written in the right language and tone to impress her prospective employer. Hardworking. Honest. Reliable. Mrs Mukoko, her previous employer, had given her the letter to read before she sealed the envelope. She smiled at herself in the small mirror of her handbag. The job was hers, she thought.

A tall fat woman without an evident waistline approached the gate. She wore a baggy blue flowery dress. A big straw hat tilted to one side of her head blocked Maria's view of the woman's features. Her body seemed to sway with the effort of walking. Reaching the gate, she observed the two large bags and, raising the front brim of her straw hat, looked around. Maria rose and swiftly carried her 4 foot 2 inches of height across the road towards the woman, trying quickly to close her handbag as she moved, but leaving her handkerchief behind her.

'Good afternoon.' Maria's voice was more than polite.

'Afternoon. Can I help?' The woman quickly proceeded through the gate, then half-turned and spoke to Maria through the rusty bars, eyeing the bags as she did so. Maria suspected that this was her prospective boss, though she seemed strangely unreceptive. Her voice was barely audible. Sweat dripped heavily from her chin, in the afternoon heat.

'Mrs Mukoko sent me with this letter.' The woman arranged her hat to shade her face, then she rested her hands on the gate and immediately jumped back with a cry. The metal was burning hot. She seemed entirely preoccupied, as if Maria was no more incidental than a fly. The girl fumbled in the pocket of her skirt and pulled out a crumpled envelope. She curtsied as she poked the envelope through the bars. She needed the job. She had left her previous place of employment without being paid her last salary and she badly needed money, let alone food and accommodation. She knew how interviews for domestic employment were conducted. Politeness and servility were often key.

'Let's see.' The woman did not take long with the letter; Maria watched her fat fingers grasping it and observed the woman's bare plump shoulders rippling under her skin. She concluded that she did not resemble any of her previous employers and she would have to tread carefully.

'Uhm, come through!' The woman sounded pleased but she did not open the gate; instead, as if she was expecting Maria to follow her, she began to make her own way up the drive, the open letter and torn envelope pinched between her fingers.

Maria threw the bags inside the gate and forgot to close it when she hurried after the woman. The woman did not look back as she swayed heavily up the drive, her brown leather slippers pattering steadily ahead of Maria.

'What's your name?' she called out.

'My name is Maria.' Maria trotted up behind to fall within hearing distance. The weight of her bags grew heavier on her small arms. She fell in behind the woman listening hard for any further questions as she struggled to stop the bags from dragging on the ground.

Beyond the bend in the driveway, the white house exposed itself. It was evidently bigger than the one she worked in before. The white paint on the walls and the blue of the gutters appeared new. She hoped white was not the woman's favourite colour. Maria's eyes did not dwell much on the garden. A quick look showed that it needed work: the shrubs were overgrown, the wilting flowers needed water, the lawn wanted cutting, and ant-hills sprouted in the red earth A big *munhondo* and another *musasa* tree stood tall in the front yard.

But Maria did not pay the garden much attention. She hoped there was a gardener. There was certainly work to be done. She stumbled up the steps of the porch, staggered forward and fell on her bags, but the woman did not turn to investigate the cause of the slight commotion behind her. She opened the door and walked into the house. Maria picked herself up and quickly squeezed herself and bags through the door before it closed.

'Take a seat.' Maria sat down on a sofa near the door. The woman disappeared into a passage that led into a room where Maria could hear children playing. Their noise was interrupted by the voice of a woman, but Maria did not hear what she was saying, though she recognised the voice of the girl who came to the gate.

The women did not take long. She came back holding a baby boy aged about two, Maria thought. A wet towel hung around the woman's neck. The woman fell into a sofa directly opposite the one that Maria was sitting on. She switched on a big blue fan that ran noiselessly behind her. Maria observed her quietly. She seemed more yellow than brown with thin lips that slanted downwards. Her nose was small below a pair of sleepy eyes. When she breathed she let out a slight whistle. She had no visible eyebrows and her hair was tied into a ball at the back of her head.

'By the way what's your name, Sisi?'

'Maria Mhofu.' Maria sat at the edge of the sofa pulling her mini skirt that was exposing her young thighs. 'I will not mind if you call me Sisi.' Her voice felt unnecessarily loud and she looked at the women with concentration. She knew the interview was still in progress. She did not want to miss a word uttered by the woman's discontented mouth.

'Okay, that makes it easy for the kids. Have you been to school?' While she waited for Maria's reply she introduced her light brown child, whom she called Di. The child was only wearing diapers. He played with his mother's big straw hat. The mother stretched the child's hand towards Maria. 'Say Sisi … Sisi!' Her tone was English and the baby laughed, looking at its mother with interest and waiting for her to repeat the unusual sound. 'I passed two, two O-level subjects, English and Fashion and Fabrics,' Maria said without regret.

'You are the girl I am looking for. You may as well call me Amai.' Maria thought with relief, 'the job's mine'. Amai stared at Maria.

'I will,' Maria replied looking down at her bags.

'What I would like you to do is talk and teach my children English – I mean, your medium of communication should be English.' A smile slid down her slanting lips.

'I will.' Maria nodded her head slowly thinking that if Amai was now giving instructions the job must be hers. She liked her new boss's manner of recruitment, it was at least fast. 'I can show you my certificate when I have unpacked.' Maria did not keep her school certificates handy because she never expected anyone to ask to see her educational qualifications. Most prospective employers bothered about experience and nothing else.

Amai handed Di to Maria. Then she struggled to rise. She held on to the armrest of the sofa with both hands and pushed her body upwards; standing, she panted and complained about the heat, wiped her face with the wet towel and moved towards the kitchen. Maria thought she must be about thirty years old, though her feet were swollen – maybe she was suffering from some overweight disease. She embarked on an English lesson with Di.

'Say Dhe e..e..dhi?' She lifted the child by his armpits and plonked him securely on her knees facing her. Di was too heavy for his age. 'Say siii si.' Di found Maria's tone interesting.

The child laughed and waited, looking at Maria for more funny sounds.

Amai returned cuddling a smaller baby, one about nine months old. Maria's heart sank. Amai sank down on her sofa and started to breast-feed the child, who was called Kuku. The baby sucked noisily, as if she was not finding enough milk.

'Your other duties will be cleaning every room in this house. We have four bedrooms, a kitchen, a dining room and a lounge.' It sounded like an achievement. Maria took a brief look around the room they were in. There were four big black Dralon sofas, a colour TV and a video set. A big brass flowerpot with an exuberant green climber popularly known as 'money-maker' sat at the back of the door to the porch. Its branches trailed around the top of the windowsills. The leaves were covered with dust. A mahogany display cabinet with glasses and ornaments occupied half the width of the room behind Amai. The furry carpet was brown, brilliantly decorated with flowers that blew out from the centre. The radio, stereo, a table with a vase of plastic flowers, a coffee table, three stools, and a small table for the telephone, were scattered around the rest of the spacious lounge. Two big photographs hung on opposite walls: one of Amai, in colour, and one of a bearded man of about thirty-five years of age in black and white.

The room was too big for Maria's liking. She sighed and arranged her skirt, which had slipped to her pelvis. Amai noticed and glared at Maria. She did not utter a word but her glare said it all. That such dressing was not acceptable.

'After cleaning the house …' Amai stopped: the manner in which she emphasised 'cleaning' showed that she had a keen taste for cleanliness. Maria imagined that the girl in a tracksuit must have been doing the cleaning, because one could not expect Amai to do much, given her weight. The room appeared tidy but she knew that she was expected to do better, judging from the voice of her new employer. 'The household linen and clothes.' Obviously Amai did not own a washing machine or a hoover. 'We will appoint set days for the laundry – washing clothes and household linen.' Amai closed her sleepy eyes as if she were trying to remember some more instructions, while giving her breast a good squeeze for the still-sucking Kuku.

'I hear, Amai.'

'Sisi, you must be very careful – how you handle the different fabrics.' She opened her eyes and stared at Maria.

'I will – er – I know.' Maria stammered, nodded and looked away shielding her face with Di.

'Sisi, if you are not sure of something, please ask.' Amai had forgotten that Maria passed Fashion and Fabrics at O-Level.

'I will.' Her tone was that of a bride exchanging marriage vows.

'My husband has a mammoth appetite for well-prepared food. He does not just complain but he refuses to eat badly prepared food. And I do not want him to go to work or to bed on an empty stomach.' From the kitchen Maria heard the clanking of a spoon and the spatter of frying meat. Maria imagined the girl in the tracksuit sweating before a hot stove.

'Is that meat cooked, Munya?' Amai swallowed, and then shouted in a voice that managed to be heard. She seemed fond of abbreviating names: Kuku, Di, Munya. Maria bit her lip when she imagined how Amai would shorten her own name. Her mind trailed away to her previous employer who never believed in taking short cuts to anything.

'I boiled it for an hour.' The girl with the husky voice appeared at the lounge door. Her tracksuit jacket was unzipped, exposing a pair of small, upright unbrassiered breasts. Her face was moist from the heat but her dark skin seemed to have been in some cold shower. Maria watched the girl she then knew as Munya hold the spatula like a cricket bat. She had a very forgettable face. The smell of frying beef seeped through the door where she stood.

'You know your brother-in-law – how he is with food?' Amai glared at the girl but her voice was low.

'I know he is a toothless hyena.'

'Let him hear you call him names,' Amai shouted to her retreating back. Munya gave a loud chuckle as she disappeared back into the kitchen.

'Sisi, what's in your bags? Are they both yours?' Amai's glare fell hard on Maria, who talked from behind Di.

'Yes, my blankets and clothes.'

'Sisi, you will have to open your bags – and show me what you have brought.'

Amai's eyes grew larger and her slanting lips were pursed. 'Sisi, put Di down on the floor and unpack.' Maria stared at Amai from behind Di in disbelief. How could the woman make such an order?

'It is not my fault. A girl I engaged last year stole from her previous employer and hid the clothes in this very house when the police were after her.' Amai's voice grated. Maria moved backwards in her seat. She did not put Di down.

'Here? Now?' Maria's voice was faint.

'Yes. I do not want to get up over such a petty matter. Place the child on the floor. And unpack so that I can see.'

The order was accusing.

The nipple of Amai's breast slipped out of Kuku's mouth but Amai did not realise it. She latched her eyes onto the bags. 'Open your bags.' She pointed. Her voice had gained volume.

Maria bit her lip, set the child on the floor like a doll and tore open the first bag, near to her. Her hands trembled. 'Tse.' The angry sound escaped her. She threw out her clothes, one by one, shaking each one with trembling vigour. Blouses, skirts, dresses, petticoats, knickers, bras, shoes, sandals. Some of the items fell into Di's hands and Di pulled them with his sticky fingers. Ha. This was fun. Birth control pills. Sanitary pads. Cotton wool, soap, two towels.

'How old are you?'

'Eighteen.' So what? Maria's stare did not distract Amai. She seemed to be looking for something in particular, as if Maria was already a thief. Then a small bottle appeared.

'Perfume. Let's see.' Amai reached out for the tiny bottle with both hands. 'Did you …?' she asked when she held the three-cornered miniature bottle above her head, glaring suspiciously at the name. 'Narcisse', she read the faint label on the bottle. A triumphant smile replaced her suspicious glare. Maria did not look up. She produced another bottle. It was even smaller. It appeared more expensive than the first, the label was new. Amai temporarily forgot about Kuku who slept buried between her thighs. She was turning the first bottle round and round and viewing it from all sides, and then seeing that Maria had produced another one, she lunged forward and seized the small glass bottle by its golden top. Amai placed both bottles in the palm of one hand and observed them as if they were rare jewels. 'Mrs Mukoko gave them to me because she could not pay me off.' Maria's voice choked.

The first bag was empty and Maria pulled the bigger one, and unzipped it, but Amai's attention was consumed by the perfume that she was inhaling from the second bottle. She breathed in the scent as if she was drawing in a life-saving vapour.

'How could she pay you with such expensive perfume?' She did not look at Maria, who threw her blankets out, oblivious to the fact that they fell on Di.

'She did not have the money and I did not like the dresses she offered.' Maria talked fast; she did not care whether Amai heard or not. Di cried forlornly under the weight of blankets but Amai took no notice. Maria pulled the small boy out from under the blankets.

'How much did she owe you?' She inhaled the scent again from the bottle, closing her small eyes. A heady aroma filled the room as it was dispersed by the fan.

'One thousand three hundred dollars'. Maria said quietly. She had finished removing her blankets from the second bag. Amai did not look down at the floor that was now covered with Maria's belongings.

'How many months?' Amai took another deep breath from the three-cornered bottle. It seemed she thought of perfume as the physic of perpetual life.

'Two.' Maria sat back and watched Amai go through another ritual of drawing in the scent with her eyes closed, and releasing her breath with her eyes transfixed by the two tiny bottles in her hand. There was silence. Di was attracted by the blue plastic pack of birth control pills; he reached across and seized the packet and then tried to open it with his teeth. Very little attention was accorded to him behind the heap of clothes and blankets.

'I will have to check on you.' Amai put the miniatures carefully on the floor. She laid the sleeping Kuku on the sofa and heaved herself up from her seat. Seeing what Di was up to she grabbed at the packet of pills. Di screamed. She thrust her breast back inside her dress. 'I will have to phone Mrs Mukoko.' She walked heavily past Maria towards the phone. Maria watched and waited. She felt blank. Di continued wailing. Maria seemed not to hear. But Amai expected Maria to care for the child. The child rose, grabbing at a chair leg, still crying.

Maria did nothing. She did not even look at it. 'Get a hold of that child, Sisi,' Amai ordered, but Maria looked away. She was not concerned any more. Job or no job. She only wanted Amai to discover her innocence. And then she would leave. 'Maria, mind the toddler.' But the child made its tearful way over to its mother and clung to her leg. 'Yes,' Mrs Mukoko was available. The niceties of housewives' chat were briefly exchanged.

'That girl is here. But I find she has valuables. She has some very expensive perfume.'

'Perfume? Ah you know how it is with girls, and this one has a fancy for expensive things.' Mrs Mukoko's voice echoed faintly down the line.

'Yes, but did you give her the two perfumes?'

'Yes. I gave her.'

'I just wanted to check, you know what happened to me last year.'

'No, she is okay, I – I – gave her – no problem.'

Mrs Gahadzikwa thanked Mrs Mukoko for sending the girl Maria, and put the phone down. She picked up Di who was now anchored to the lower part of her dress. She moved very slowly.

'All clear, Sisi. Before I sit let me show you your room.' Maria did not look up. She remained huddled in her seat, her hands crossed at her knees. 'Here you are, Sisi.' Ama tried to hand the two perfume bottles to Maria. The girl rose and took them. Tears escaped from her eyes.

'I did not want to be paid in perfume.'

'I have to be careful…' Amai's voice faded as she left the room, but Maria did not follow. She began slowly repacking her clothes.

17

DINNER TIME

Bongani Sibanda

Aunt MaMoyo is dishing up, and we're standing before her: me, Musa, Given and Grandmother NaJeremiah. We've hardly eaten anything in the past few days, and we're starving hungry. When she finishes, she quietly pushes two bowls towards our feet, and then puts a few more on a wooden tray and exits with Grandmother NaJeremiah following behind her. She's carrying food to the elderly people in the front hut.

Given hastily picks up the bowl of sadza. Musa picks up the okra. We squat near the door and start eating.

A little while later, aunt MaMoyo hurries in mumbling as usual. She sits down on her hide rug near the window and begins eating, telling us while she chews that she emptied the pot of sadza, so there won't be any left-overs. We ignore her and concentrate on the food, noisily munching and swallowing.

A constrained cough at the door disrupts our concentration. Our eyes dart towards the noise, and we see Grandmother NaJeremiah at the entrance, her brown basket slung over her right shoulder like a handbag. We don't know why she's come, but whatever the reason we're certain it doesn't bode well. She looks us over like one of the Sabbath prophets. Then she takes two paces towards the hearth.

'My white hen laid an egg this afternoon.' She coughs and adjusts the white scarf on her head. 'I've just checked the nest and the egg's missing.'

To her it's a question, but to us it's just a statement. The schwam schwam and ngwim ngwim noise produced by our munching teeth and swallowing gullets continues undisturbed as we lower our hands into the bowls, raise them to our mouths and lower them again. Predictably this stretches Grandmother NaJeremiah's nerves.

'I'm talking to you children! Can't you hear me? MaMoyo!' she bellows.

Aunt MaMoyo is always calm. She chews a mouthful of sadza, swallows, and without even looking up from her bowl replies that she saw no egg.

Grandmother NaJeremiah then turns her wrinkled eyes on me, Musa and Given. Our mouths are too full to speak, but we cannot slow down, so we look up at her, shaking our heads while praying that she does not press us for answers, since it's considered bad manners to answer an older person with a shake of the head.

Grandmother NaJeremiah takes two paces towards the hearth, calming herself down as she does so.

'Whoever took my egg and placed it somewhere safe is innocent. But if you refuse to tell me where it is, or give it back, well, Baba won't like that at all. You have okra for relish but you know your grandfather does not eat okra. And,' she speaks very slowly, 'he can not eat sadza without relish… so … whoever took my egg, I want it back. Now!'

With that, she turns and shuffles out. Her exit multiplies our devouring speed. We re-fill mouths, re-load hands and never let-up, like we're rushing somewhere. Then we hear NaJeremiah's squeaky voice shouting Musa's name from the front hut. Musa can't answer because her mouth is full. Only after Grandmother NaJeremiah has shouted her name several times does Musa respond. Grandmother NaJeremiah orders her to bring Grandfather SaEfi clean water in a jug.

Musa hastily lowers her thin hand into what little remains of the big bowl of sadza, grabs a morsel, dips it into the bowl of okra and drops it into her wide open mouth.

'Don't eat while I'm gone,' she dares us angrily. Then, signaling aunt MaMoyo to watch us in her absence, she goes to fetch the water.

Seconds turn to minutes and the minutes feel like hours as we gaze at the small portion of sadza left in the bowl. By the time Musa returns we're nearly screaming with impatience, but we say nothing and the schwam schwam, ngwim ngwim noise resumes, blending with the veee veee whistle of our fingers scraping the bottom of the bowl. We begin eyeing one another with talking eyes as we reach this unavoidable moment in our everyday lives. Today it's my turn to ask for *ingoroyi*. Musa and Given are already staring at me as if I needed a reminder.

I look towards aunt MaMoyo with a silent prayer because sometimes she scrapes *ingoroyi* for herself.

'We're not full,' I say. She remains silent, forcing me to repeat myself.

'I told you I emptied the pot.'

'We want *ingoroyi*,' I say, my manners forgotten.

'The *ngoroyi* is mine. I cooked for you.'

My eyes turn to Musa and Given. We're looking at one another, thinking, we want *ingoroyi* more than anything, even more than being loved and considered good children. My stomach still feels empty, like I haven't eaten anything for days; the desire to have something to fill it feels like an obligation, a kind of credit that I owe myself, a need that is 'as essential as oxygen in human life', to quote Ncube, my teacher.

I look at Given, my younger brother, squatting before me, licking his lips and audibly swallowing saliva. I look at his dusty head, the blotches on his face, his stomach that's bigger than everyone else's at school, his dirty khaki shorts with a small tear in the front through which peeps a small thing like caterpillar, and my heart sinks. Given is the only person I care about in the world, he's the only one I feel for when Grandfather SaTimoty is whipping us because the goats have broken into the maize field and plundered the crops while we were eating. I would even leave him my sadza if he asked, but he doesn't know that, so he doesn't ask. Musa is my cousin and I don't care much for her.

Given coughs as if he were clearing his throat. Musa rises and then quickly sits down again, why, I don't know. Aunt MaMoyo glances at us, unsmiling. She then lifts the pot of sadza closer to her, wrenches off the lid, and shoves her veiny hand inside. It emerges with some rich brown scrapings which she piles into her bowl. Without a word or glance, she pushes the empty pot towards us. We quickly begin to do what we're very good at – scraping, munching and swallowing. And in just a little while we're done.

Given rises and bolts out. Musa and I follow. We're heading to the front hut where we find the grandmothers still eating.

Musa squeezes herself beside Grandmother NaJeremiah, Given beside Grandmother NaTimoty. Myself, I sit opposite, on one side of the hearth, and in this position I can see the grandmothers' bowl of sadza is still full. They eat so slowly that it's as if they don't want the food; like it wouldn't matter if I seized their bowl and ran away.

Thoughts of how small our share of sadza alway is and how unfair this is, invade my mind. This happens every day when I see the grandmothers' sadza. Aunt MaMoyo cannot rob them because she knows they'll complain. One day, I remember, there was very little mealie-meal and aunt MaMoyo dished out a smaller than usual share for Grandfather SaTimoty, and she was summoned and warned. It was Grandmother NaJeremiah who spoke. She told her that Grandfather SaTimoty works so hard that if the sadza is not enough, it is better for us children to get little.

I'm still engrossed in these thoughts when I see Grandmother NaTimoty handing Given a piece of sadza. She didn't even dip it in the okra. Given, who's sometimes greedier than all of us, instantly swallows it, his eyes traversing the distance between Grandmother NaTimoty's hand and her mouth, expecting more. Musa expects grandmother NaJeremiah to make a similar gesture and stares at her with beady eyes. But Grandmother NaJeremiah disappoints her. She just rolls a piece of sadza slowly in her hand, dips it in the relish, bites it and chews. And then she looks around, up, and sideways, her small eyes fleeting past me before settling on the glowing fire.

'We've heard many stories about mischievous daughters-in-law,' she says. 'But this … it's unspeakable! Totally unheard of!'

My heart thumps. I'm in love with gossip, elderly people's gossip. It's the only entertainment I can get. It frees me of sad memories, fills me with energy, and makes me forget about all the bad things elderly people do to us.

But something holds me back, stops me from indulging fully in this episode. It's the bilious look I see on Grandmother NaTimoty's face. What's with her, I wonder, as she leers at Grandmother NaJeremiah, her eyelashes fluttering as if they would fly off her face.

'Last year a two kg packet of potatoes disappeared from my house,' Grandmother NaJeremiah continues, unperturbed. 'And the Christmas groceries our children bring in December are reported finished within two weeks. I don't even want to mention the mystery of the watermelons. The empty shells we found buried in the sand …'

She breaks off, her face a picture of concentrated anger.

My heart leaps. I feel like pawing the white out of the moon. I dash out for more firewood so the hut is better lit; I can hear the gossip better in the bright firelight. The hut starts to shine when I have added some logs. And I begin to see Grandfather SaTimoty, who has only been a shadow until now. He's not eating, slouched in his folding chair, his white head bent over his thin arms, which are crossed on his bony lap. Beside his lidded bowl on his food table is uncle Enoch's small radio, which is played every day at eight o'clock for Spot FM news.

'A leopard never loses its spots,' Grandmother NaJeremiah continues. 'That's for sure. And understand that I'm not saying this to spite a child because she's married to a son who is not mine, while all my sons are not married, as someone cynical might say. All I want is that we look into the matter and make a right decision. That's all. And to make a point clear, I'm not recommending any action against her. It's up to you. She's your son's wife, NaTimoty.'

Grandfather SaTimothy raises his white head, then lowers it again.

Grandfather SaEfi finishes eating, rinses his hands, puts down the dish of water, and then hauls back his three-legged stool to sit near the door. He turns his old face up and runs the fingers of his left hand through his bushy beard. 'Thank you, Dubes,' he says.

'Are you really thanking us for this day-to-day okra, Babomncane?'

'It's better than eating nothing, NaJeremiah. Since the weldi division has been delayed by three weeks now at Bango, if they don't come within a week, I don't think many people will make it.'

Grandmother NaJeremiah swallows and smiles, revealing her white teeth. In the orange firelight, I notice, her white scarf looks cream, her black face brown, her white hair, peeking underneath the scarf, looks sandy, and her small eyes are sleepy.

Given, Musa and I are now staring at the yellow piece of sadza in Grandfather SaEfi's bowl. We're praying that Grandmother NaJeremiah doesn't take it as usual and declare it hers, that someone descend from heaven and command that it be given to us, we poor grandchildren of this homestead, we who work so hard planting and harvesting and watching crows while elderly people shirk.

'We live in hard times, Babomncane.' Grandmother NaTimoty utters her first words. She leans back, and balances her left hand on the floor.

'Nowadays it's quite better,' Grandmother NaJeremiah cuts in. 'Do you remember how many people died in the early two thousands. Do you remember NaTimoty that SaMoffart's homestead is now a desert because of hunger? I mean, those children wouldn't have survived, would they? Not with whatever gifts might come from hungry people like us. Certainly not.'

'Long ago everything lay in men's strength,' says Grandfather SaEfi, yawning, his big mouth widening into a chasm. 'But today you fail even if you are strong.'

Grandmother NaTimoty agrees. 'If you had enough seeds and a good span of oxen, you knew you had everything. But not nowadays. You can't make rain. You can't cool the sun.' She shovels a handful of sadza into her mouth and begins to chew.

So far Grandfather SaTimoty has said nothing. He now raises his white head, looks about him with sleepy eyes and finally fixes them on me.

'Can't you boys go and *tsopi tsopi* the goats for me?'

'The goats were milked at sunset, Baba,' Grandmother NaTimoty says with sadza in her mouth.

Grandfather SaTimoty claps his hands like a woman expressing surprise. 'Today I'm going to sleep on an empty stomach. You people made a mistake by wasting the weldi division peas. The weldi division gave us plenty of peas. You ate without providence.'

Grandmother NaJeremiah says that when she's done eating, she'll fetch some dried cabbage from her house. It's a little packet she brought when she visited her sister at Mazwi at the last of last month. She'll fix it for him although she was saving it in case things got worse.

Just then, aunt MaMoyo hurries in to collect the dishes. She pauses when she sees the grandmothers still eating, and whispers that she thought everyone was done. Noticing that Grandfather SaEfi has finished, she steps towards his table, and kneels on the floor to collect his dishes, but Grandmother NaJeremiah grabs the bowl with the remaining piece of sadza, muttering that it will help her tomorrow morning since there'll be nothing for breakfast. Aunt MaMoyo rises with a dish of water. Her long, white dress sweeps the dusty floor as she turns towards Grandfather SaTimoty's dining table. Grandmother NaJeremiah casually tells her that Grandfather SaTimoty has not yet eaten. Aunt MaMoyo then marches out, her big stomach leading the way.

A brief silence follows, ending when Grandmother NaTimoty asks Given and I if we have bathed. Musa answers for us, telling Grandmother NaTimoty brightly that we washed after she reminded us. Another silence follows, and then Grandfather SaTimoty tunes in to Spot FM.

Meanwhile Grandfather SaEfi orders me to wake up very early tomorrow morning and pump his bicycle. It has a slow puncture, he tells me. And he reckons it will be flat by morning. He would like to arrive at Bango village before twelve.

'…Headlines tonight…' a stern voice on the radio announces, '…lack of commitment on the electrification of rural areas a cause for concern, Home Affairs Minister, Hermingway Ncube says.' Thus, the news begin, but I stop listening, as my stomach forbids it. My eyes refuse to leave the bowl of sadza left by Grandfather SaEfi, which Grandmother NaJeremiah has carefully placed near her dirty, brown skirt. I find myself thinking of grabbing it and running away. It's not the first time I've had such thoughts. I know that Grandfather SaTimoty will pull his belt off and flog me, but wouldn't that be okay in exchange for filling my stomach?

Sometimes I think of seizing other people's sadzas and getting whipped every day. A whip never kills. Grandfather SaTimoty would curse the day our mother, Lethiwe, left us in his care to find a job in

Johannesburg. A Satanic child, he'll say as always does. He takes after his unknown father. But I'll close my ears to his insults. Besides, who ever died from curses and whips?

On the news they're now saying something about the NASA and the glaciers discovered on Neptune. Next is a buzz about an Indian actress presently in the country. And then they talk about a record million-dollar move by one of our country's top footballers to an English club.

The news ends with Grandfather SaTimoty promptly turning the radio off. Nobody says anything. Nobody cares about the news. It's become traditional to listen to it because of uncle Enoch, but he's away.

'My opinion is that Luke should be told,' Grandmother NaJeremiah says, rising with difficulty and putting the bowl of sadza left by Grandfather SaEfi in her cane basket. My heart bounces when I see her do this. 'He'll decide what he does with her. We cannot continue living with a child whose people didn't teach her that stealing is a bad thing. And we can't send her back to her people ourselves because we don't have that power. If it wasn't for this cabbage I got from my sister, baba was going to sleep hungry.'

She turns and trudges towards the door, handling her basket carefully so as not to upset the bowl. In my imagination I've sprung to my feet, and seized the basket from her, but in reality I'm still seated, wishing I had the nerve to do so and knowing that one day I will.

(vii)

Exile

18

THE LETTER

Farai Mpofu

A voice was heard in
Ramah, lamentation,
Weeping, and great mourning,
Rachel weeping for her children,
Refusing to be comforted,
Because they were no more.

'From the information I have gathered, I want to make the punishment of this foreigner an example to all would-be offenders. I sentence him to twenty sjambok cuts for crossing the border into our country illegally.' Juba's heart pounds like the speaker of a disco machine ... A cold trickle of sweat meanders down the contours of his frightened face.

'I also sentence you to another thirty sjambok cuts for making one of our children pregnant.' The chief stares at Juba in disgust; his face has the expression of a constipated man. He continues, 'These people steal our hard-earned property, our cattle; and they bring immorality and incurable diseases into our community.' Juba looks at his bare, cracked feet with shame, feeling like Lucifer at the highest tribunal on judgement day. 'As for you, foreigner! Our daughter has refused to be married to you. We shall deal with you ruthlessly and then hand you over to the police.'

At that moment, the chief makes a covert gesture and two strong men, the chief's bodyguards, grab Juba in a vice-like grip. He is too weak to struggle. They strip him naked, tie his hands and force him to sit on an anthill. They stamp on an army of red ants, the inhabitants of the anthill, and in a natural act of revenge the ants bite at Juba's bare thighs, buttocks and genitals. Juba screams. He hears the crack of a whip; the villagers swallow in anticipation. Blood splutters into the air. The villagers swallow again. Juba screams. The guard generously beats another stroke and the young man moans … another and another … His tears roll into the dust.

There is a loud bang and Juba's head hits the metal walls of the van. He realises he must have fainted. A headache strikes at his cranium like a bolt of lightning. His body is aching, swollen and bloodied. He looks up and sees two Tswana policemen conversing. Their language sounds like gibberish. He tries to smile. One policeman notices what he assumes is a sarcastic grin and kicks Juba's head like a footballer in a World Cup final. Juba's world goes round and round as he descends into the dreamy realm of the unconscious.

***

Unknown Cell
Block B Prison
Francistown
Botswana

Dear Mama,
This is a letter to your lonely unmarked grave in the

heart of Matebeleland. Mama, I still have nightmares about the day you left me. I remember the drones of the helicopters, the sound and smell of the truck tyres, the sound of marching boots ... I remember they were looking for father. They said they knew he was a member of the opposition. You told them that he had gone, had already escaped to Botswana. They got angry Mama, and started kicking your belly - you were pregnant. They laughed, scornfully, saying that they would kill the dissident in your womb. One of them took a knife from the kitchen and slit through your stomach. I saw my little sister - Malaika, as I have come to call her - fall on to those savannah sands. I call her Malaika because she is the angel that never had to endure this horrible existence. You fell on your knees holding your stomach, but it was too late ... I remember your smile and your last words, 'Kuzolunga mtanami.'

All that time the other villagers were forced to ululate and sing songs denouncing you, the sell-out. I was later forced to dig a grave for you and my sister and I buried ... I ... buried you both. The letter I write you is without ink or paper. A letter without an envelope or stamp. A story written in my heart and sealed with tears. They put me in a filthy cell, a maternity ward for rats and cockroaches, and there were twenty other guys. I felt like a matchstick in a tightly packed box. I cried out but they closed their eyes and ears. I was coughing badly. I think I have TB. At last I bravely knocked at the heavy metal door and the guard angrily opened a small window on the door and asked who had knocked. I told him I needed medication, at least painkillers, and he told me to get them in Zimbabwe and left. I cried, Mama, and he laughed. I thought he was kidding me. But he left and never came back ...

For days I longed for a gasp of fresh air. But all I breathed was the humid, stale smell of greasy armpits, *groins, dirty mouths, urine and diarrhoea in the unflushed pit. We starved. Occasionally, they gave us left-over food from the Tswana prisoners' refuse bins. On lucky days we are given their sugarless, smelly, sorghum porridge. I refused to eat their shit. Nobody gave a damn and I also did not give a damn anymore. I felt as if I was slipping away to the peaceful lands beyond the River Jordan. I began to wish that I could die and meet you. I refused to bath in their cold water. I refused to smile at them. I refused to be dehumanised.*

Mama, today I'm gonna sing to the stars because humanity has a blind cruelty. I'm gonna sing that I need a life, a dignity and, like the elites of this world, I need good food: three-course meals in five-star hotels. I need VIP security – bodyguards in dark glasses. I need a prestigious education at Western universities like the children of the elite. I need to see myself seated in an expensive Mercedes Benz sipping expensive foreign wine surrounded by the most beautiful girls. I'm gonna sing to the stars as they twinkle at me like diamonds on a huge black cloth, above the stuffy prison cells of Botswana. Your loving son, Juba

***

On the fifth day they are released from the detention centre. They are grouped and herded into a lorry like cattle going to the auction grounds. The lorry is locked, once everyone is inside. The Tswana immigration and prison officers chatter amongst themselves. They sign documents and laugh with a brotherly love. Juba and the other prisoners peer through the meshed windows, admiring the Tswanas' clean, neatly ironed white shirts and navy blue trousers. One of the officers is munching at a juicy looking grilled chicken. They wonder why the Batswana never speak in English. Is it patriotism? Is it vanity? The officials shake hands and wave at each other as the gigantic truck roars into life. Back to Zimbabwe, in the truck, the prisoners-turned-deportees sit on the floor with dazed expressions on their faces. Juba sees the fading town of Francistown and watches the dry scrubland, wondering how this desert country is ironically very rich. Some say they want to dig jewels in the desert. He heard about the poor desert-folk who were relocated into townships – to live the urban life of darkness, prostitution and thievery; everyone is a thief in the city.

He also remembers home. He no longer has a home in Zimbabwe. He remembers Gorata, the Tswana girl he loved so much. He knows she loved him. If only it were not for the man-made boundaries, their love would have flourished. If only it was a free world. He knows her mother pressured her to refuse his hand in marriage. She could not bear the prospect of having a *mukwerekwere* son-in-law. He thinks of the baby and wonders what will happen to him or her? It will grow up fatherless.

The Batswana are building a two-hundred-and-fifty-volt electric fence on the border. They say they want to stop cattle diseased with foot and mouth from contaminating their healthy herds. The truck hums along and reaches the Plumtree-Ramokgwebana border post. Juba sees the long queues of Zimbabweans entering Botswana. He knows most of them will either overstay or simply throw away their passports as soon as they arrive. Many of these Zimbabweans, with their degrees and diplomas, end up as prostitutes and thieves. There are no jobs. Maybe the Botswana authorities are right. A man should stand up and protect his children when their resources are under threat from aliens.

Juba resolves that as soon as he is released he will begin the great trek back to Botswana. Then he imagines the new electric fence and realises that if the Batswana close their borders, at least the Zambian, Namibian, Congolese, Mozambican, Angolan and South African borders are still open. It is always better to be treated like a dog in a foreign country than to be treated like a dog in your own.

19

Shamisos

NoViolet Bulawayo

'These white creepers? They must be taken out. I want them gone.' Method taps his hoe and watches her hands gesture towards the flowering creeper. Her face is ablaze. Method swallows his surprised question, the words drowning in his throat.

The jasmine is in full bloom, the fragrance reminding him of Shamiso, the girl in 3C1 class at Njube Secondary School. Method wrote love letters to her and slipped them into her TM Hyper plastic bag, careful not to sign his name because he didn't think she would ever look at a boy like him. He calls this lovely creeper Shamiso because it brings back memories.

'We'll put red roses in their place,' his madam smiles. Method forces a smile in return.

'It'll be just perfect, you'll see,' her voice is suddenly cajoling. Method nods even though he's sure that roses cannot compare to the beauty of the jasmine in full bloom. Shamisos.

'But these are beautiful too, Madam.' Method speaks quietly when he addresses her because he knows the importance of sounding respectful.

'Are you sure you really want them gone, Madam?'

She nods her head vigorously, placing a finger over her lips as her cellphone is ringing. When she talks to Method she uses simple English, as if she were speaking to a small child, enunciating every word slowly and carefully as if she were counting money. With other people she sounds normal, and Method imagines her tongue darting around her mouth, dodging her teeth, with speed and precision.

Now she speaks in English laced with French, which Method studied for three years before the university was forced to close. *Right now. Yes-yes. Hell no, I'm not doing it myself, are you nuts? I fired the Nigerian, they're thieves. I mean things were just disappearing. Yes-yes. And I got rid of the Malawian, they're lazy, you should have seen the garden. No, I'll never employ any South Africans, Jesus! They think just because this is their country they're fucking entitled to everything. Yes-yes. No, in the house I have a Mozambican. An old man. Yes-yes. He has a temper but boy can he cook!* Then she switches to French: *Now I have a new gardener, a Zimbabwean. You too? Well, they're everywhere, like cockroaches. Yes-yes. So far so good. Looks unhappy though, not sure what his story is. I'll have to teach him to smile! Can you imagine? But he's hardworking. And you should see his head, it's like a fucking hammer.*

Method fidgets, wishing he didn't understand this language she's using to gossip about him as if he were invisible. He wonders that her mother did not teach her that one does not talk about people in their presence.

The woman looks up from the phone, meets his gaze, and flashes him a smile. Method beholds her coolly. She shoos him away and points vigorously at the creepers. He grabs his hoe and feels her watching him. He would love to get down on his knees and touch the Shamisos one last time but with her eyes on his back, he starts swinging his hoe.

A single hit and the first Shamiso is lying on the ground. He has no time to pick it up to examine the damage because she's somewhere behind him and so he swings, and keeps swinging. He does not want her to think him lazy. In no time he has a carpet of dying flowers around his feet, their fragrance suddenly thick in the air. Method looks toward the main house and sees the Mozambican staring at him through the kitchen window.

He does not know the man's name and he cannot see his face because of the distance between them, but he can tell from the way he's leaning forward that he's puzzled. Method looks away. He hardly knows the Mozambican because he works inside the house, like a woman. Now and then Method will see him taking out the rubbish, hanging clothes on the line, retrieving letters from the post box.

Once, when the Mozambican was hanging out clothes, he had stopped to talk to Method: 'My wife and children do these things for me back home, do you know that?' Method had shaken his head because it seemed the question was purely rhetorical.

'Yes, you don't know what it means for me to work like this, at my age,' the Mozambican continued, and Method nodded in a show of sympathy.

But still he could not help thinking the old man was being unreasonable; it could not surely be that bad, working in such a nice house: the lush cream carpets, the large TV, the deep sofas, the electrical gadgets. It was the home of Method's dreams – that is, when he made it big in South Africa. Then, his mother would live with him, waking up when she pleased to sit in front of the TV with her legs stretched out in front of her, smiling her brown-toothed smile and saying, 'My son, I am proud of you.'

***

'Hey you, Zimbabwean! What do you think you're doing?'

Method looks up at the sound of the brassy voice and finds himself staring at a bloodied kitchen knife. The Mozambican is waving it in his face.

'Are you mad? Can't you see you're killing the flowers?'

'I'm not killing them.' Method feels defensive.

'What's this then, air?' The Mozambican scoops up some wilting blooms and flings them at Method.

'Madam doesn't want them anymore.'

'She doesn't want the flowers?' the Mozambican's face knots in confusion.

'No. I mean, yes. She wants to plant roses, red roses instead.' Method is relieved he cannot see her anywhere; he would not want her to hear them talking about her.

'But they're beautiful.' The old man's voice is spent. Method looks at his white apron, clean except for a single red stain, and then at the butcher's knife, and wonders what animal the meat came from.

The Mozambican kneels down and cradles one small blossom in both hands. Method notices that he's missing two fingers on his left hand, and looks down, embarrassed by the sight of an old man mourning a flower. He's relieved when the man at last stands up and turns to leave, taking the flower with him. Method mumbles an apology, though he does not exactly know what for. Then he realises that he has spoken in his home language and assumes the Mozambican would not have understood him.

After the older man has disappeared into the house Method goes back to hacking. He is strangely upset, and can't quite explain why. He glances up to see the woman come out of the house and sit on the garden chair beneath the guava tree. She's still on the phone. He thinks of what she said about him, not knowing he could understand her. If he were at home, he would have grabbed her phone and slapped her with the back of his hand. But he's not at home, and besides, she's not a normal woman.

Method had thought they were sisters at first, the two women who shared the house, but one day, cutting the dense foliage behind the bedroom window, he had seen them sitting on the bed. They'd been arguing, and it was after their bickering had died down that he'd seen, from the posture of their bodies, from the way the one with a man's name, who never wore dresses, from the way that she looked at Madam, that this was not sisterhood.

Method had been stunned, then disgusted, remembering how such a thing did not even have a name in his country, how everybody back there knew that such people were not people, they were worse than pigs and dogs. If he'd been at home, he would have climbed in through the window and beat them senseless, especially that other one who wore men's clothes. He would have raised the alarm and people would have been happy to drag them out in the open and beaten them till they could not scream.

And if he had had a choice, Method would simply have spat in their faces and quit his job, but knowing how hard it was to find employment, he'd stayed. Meanwhile his mother's letters never stopped coming. *Dear Method, this is to tell you we are dying of hunger. My son Method, have you forgotten about us?* He had no choice but to stay and work for these two strange women, but he was always on the lookout, to see what they might do.

But they did not do anything, and nothing happened to him. They greeted him warmly when he came to work, paid him his wages fairly, and on time, made sure he was fed from their kitchen at lunch, and did not overwork him like some of his friends complained their employers did. Despite the fact that Madam occasionally spoke to him like a child, he was alarmed at how well they treated him. This baffled Method, how it was that these two, who were surely worse than animals, treated him as if he counted. He did not know quite when his disgust disappeared, but somehow it did, like a fart in the wind.

Method thinks of them lying close together on the bed; he remembers Mfundisi Gatsheni preaching about such sinners when he was a boy, and how they would burn in hell.

Now that he is older, Method knows there is no hell, knows that hell is here on earth, that hell is the terrible road he travelled to reach this country, that hell is the Limpopo River that he had to cross with his friend D. who never made it out because he could not swim, that hell is in the eyes of his neighbors who have lately been telling all the foreigners to get out of the shantytowns and go back home. This is how Method knows these strange women will not see hell, will not burn, so he wonders instead what it would be like to be in bed with Madam. Would she feel like any other woman? Has she ever been with a man?

Lost in thought, he strikes his big toe with his hoe. Crying out in pain, he throws the implement onto the ground, holding his foot in both hands. He does not hear himself, but he is calling for his mother; where he comes from people yell for their mothers when they're in pain. But it is not Method's mother who comes running, but Madam. She drops her cellphone and runs over to him; putting his wounded foot on her thigh, she examines it closely.

Method forgets the searing pain in his toe, suddenly ashamed by the sight of his dirty foot on her skirt; its calloused skin, the nails he has neglected to cut, which look like claws, the cracks in his heels. He is so ashamed that he wants to get up and run away but she is holding his foot firmly and tenderly, so tenderly something within him yields. He has not been held like this in a long time, and he likes the feeling so much that he wants to give her his other foot, then his legs, then his thighs, then his torso, then his whole body so she can hold it, hold him. He feels the pain in his toe ebb.

'It doesn't look bad, but you must be careful. How come you're not wearing shoes?' she asks, but he does not answer her, he does not know what to say when she is holding his dirty foot like this.

'Your feet are not too big, I'm sure you and Joe wear the same size.' She puts his foot down and scurries off. He wants her to stay, to call her back, but instead he strokes his bruised toe, which is now swollen and bleeding.

She reappears quickly, carrying a pair of blue sneakers in one hand, a small dish in the other. Over her shoulder, he can see the Mozambican leaning out of the kitchen window, his neck craned. She squats at Method's feet and begins swabbing his toe with some cotton wool; his blood is on her fingers. She dries his toe with a small cloth and applies a yellow ointment, then starts to unravel a roll of bandage.

'Can you wiggle your toe?' she asks. Method does so. She smiles.

'Good, you're lucky you didn't break it, Xolela,' she says, and wraps the toe with a bandage. Method hears the name she calls him by; she has difficulty making the –X sound.

Method wants to tell her that his name is Method; that Xolela is not his real name, but he knows he can't do so. Xolela appears on his South African ID; the picture is his, but the name is not. It was chosen by the tall thug Method paid for the document. An unkempt youth with a scar above his left eye, raking fingers through his long dreadlocks while observing Method with bloodshot eyes.

'Method? As in, what? A way of doing things? *Mara* what kind of name is that?' Method had not known how to answer.

'*Mara* you need a real name. One that makes you belong, y'understand? From now on you'll be Xolela. Xolela Mabaso!' And, just like that, as if he were picking something discarded on the street, Method acquired his new name, which he now used for all things official.

'There, I've bandaged your toe. Now try and see if you can put it inside the shoe, but please be careful,' she says. Method slides his injured foot inside one sneaker, which fits comfortably. He does not feel any pressure on his toe. He puts on the other sneaker, and then Madam is on her knees, tying his shoelaces. The wide cleft between her small breasts is not far from his face, so he looks away; he does not want to be caught doing anything wrong.

But she's too busy fussing over him, telling him about the importance of being careful, and soon Method begins to feel as if she were talking to him like a child, and he's overcome by a sudden feeling of annoyance.

'I have to go now,' Method announces, and stands up. He does not drop his voice and picking up his hoe, does not look to see if she is surprised that he does not thank her. Nor does he look up when he hears her on the phone again, but he knows, from the sound of her voice, that she is talking to the other one, the one whose shoes he's now wearing. She's telling her what happened, what she did for Xolela, the gift of the sneakers. Method swings his hoe angrily; he is blind to the Shamisos now, blind to their beauty. He hears her laughter explode and he swings and hacks to the sound, hacks like a madman.

***

The sun is sinking by the time Method gets home to Eden Park. Shacks surround him like hands encircling a throat, swallowing every inch of visible ground – sheets and sheets of corrugated metal stretching as far as the eye can see. Method finds the settlement tolerable in the sunset tinted sky; there is no need to avert his eyes as he does when he's at work; the growing darkness hides the puddles of murky water, the dirt, the armies of flies, the shit, the junk, the queues for water.

He picks his way through the narrow paths, past the Angolan quarter, the Mozambican quarter, the Nigerian quarter, the Malawian quarter; to walk through the settlement is to travel across borders, in and out of different countries. Method does not greet the people he meets. The journey to South Africa, to Eden Park, is a trying one so the foreign settlement dwellers regard each other with unspoken understanding because they know what has been endured. First, years of gathering courage, followed by painful partings and days or weeks on the roads crammed in the back of poorly ventilated trucks. Crocodile-infested rivers are fearfully crossed and hungry animals evaded in order to squeeze through barbed-wire fences while fleeing border agents.

In recent weeks the locals have told the settlers to leave, to pack their belongings and get back home. Regardless, the foreigners only observe the locals with amusement, shake their heads and smile. Only those who had not endured what they have suffered could open their mouths and shout, *GO BACK*, just like that. Go back, return to your own country – as if their dream was dispensable, forgettable, as if the scars on their bodies and minds counted for nothing?

Method stops outside the Somali tuck shop whose name he cannot read and contemplates entering. Inside, he sees the bent form of the storekeeper straighten up and turn to face the door. He cannot tell if the old man can see him, but he hears him begin to sing. Method does not understand the words, but he knows instinctively from the quiver in the old man's voice, that he is singing of his homeland.

Sometimes the old man will slip the name of his country into his songs, or the names of cities that Method can recognise: Mogadishu, Hargeysa, Berbera, Chisimayu, Jamaame. Method stands at the door, and the Somali's song fills the room with his forlorn voice until Method feels he cannot breathe from the sadness permeating him through a language he cannot understand. When the old man's voice lifts like smoke, Method feels the need to escape and turns quickly away.

When he passes the South African quarter his body tenses and his stomach knots. Lately, this part of the settlement has felt like walking through a forest of angry gods. There is something in the air, something unspoken; he can feel it even now, and in order to distract himself he tries to think of other things – the Shamisos, now lying in a pit at the corner of Madam's yard, the red roses, which he will plant tomorrow. When Method passes a group of women blocking his path, he moves out of their way because that is what is expected of him. He glances briefly at the group and catches the eye of a tall woman in a white 'I love Africa' T-shirt. In that brief moment he wonders fleetingly if he should acknowledge her with a nod, but her face darkens with a look that causes Method to trip over an abandoned log.

He quickly rights himself and keeps walking, but there is an unsteadiness to his knees. He has been given many looks in this quarter – dirty ones, blank ones, sympathetic ones, annoyed ones. For the most part, he has learned to tolerate those that can be tolerated, and ignore those that should be ignored, but the look this woman gave him is not a look one gives to humans but to flies, ticks, cockroaches, fleas; to a mound of excrement left in the open, one's stomach cringing in disgust, one's skin crawling in revulsion.

Method feels anger, then humiliation, then something nameless. If he were in his own country he would turn and confront the woman; but now he's hurt, wounded, a part of him wishing he were invisible. Breathing evenly, he walks with care, only lifting his eyes once he reaches his own quarters, among his own people. He proceeds to his shack. He could stop by Njabulo's, his neighbor, where he knows that men and women are already congregated to watch videos from home: Mukadota, Gringo, Kukhulwa Kokuphela, Neria, Paraffin. Yet, no matter the promise of good fellowship and laughter, Method does not join them. He knows these gatherings always end with men and women peeling off their clothes to show each other their bodies, touch each other's bodies with intimacy.

Their scars give birth to sad memories. Watching videos is a form of forgetting: the 2008 elections, the police with batons, the soldiers with guns, the militia with machetes. Do you remember? Buttocks burned. Limbs broken. Roofs blazing. I remember. Rape – Jesus, Jesus, Jesus, rape, not one not two but fifteen of them, one after the other. His sister, Sithokozile, why do you think she no longer speaks? Here, this eye, see it's blinded? Hit by a teargas canister on Main Street. This is where the machete cut, under the armpit, touch, don't be afraid, it only hurts a little now; just don't press too hard. Look, this, here, they say, in Njabulo's shack, their scars speaking in painful tongues. This is why Method does not go to watch movies with them; there are certain things from back then that he does not wish to remember.

He takes off his shoes and stands at the door of his shack, and beats them against each other to remove the dust. Satisfied, he retreats inside and holds the sneakers up to the light of a kerosene lamp. The leather is soft in his hands; he can tell they are very expensive shoes,

shoes he would never dream of buying. The black laces are streaked with gold. Method turns the shoes over and inspects the heels; there is barely any sign of wear. He holds them to his nose. He does not know what newness smells like any more, but perhaps it is a whiff of newness that he detects. He is suddenly overcome with gratitude, and he hates himself for not thanking Madam properly. Tomorrow, he will thank her, and the next time he sees that other one, he will thank her as well, yes, he must thank Joe.

***

After he has eaten a small supper of porridge, Method spreads his blankets on the floor. He reaches for the sack in which he keeps his things and fishes from it another sack, and from the second sack, fishes yet another. He unties the elastic band around the final sack and retrieves a stack of his mother's letters. *My son*, one begins, *Dear Method*, another, *Method*, still another, and another, *My dear son Method*. He straightens the letters one by one and slowly runs his fingers over her slanted writing, imagining his mother's face – her prominent cheekbones, thick lips, the lines of laughter at the corners of her eyes and around her mouth. This is how he remembers her.

Every day, after work, Method takes our these letters, reads and re-reads them and then talks to them, pretending he's addressing his mother. Sometimes he even imitates her voice as he imagines what she might say to him.

My son Method, how come you never write? Have you not seen my letters? He speaks, in her slow drawl.

I have seen them mother, in fact I read them every day. But …

But what Method, but what? He raises his voice as she would, her head leaning forward as if she were here, facing him.

And you have not sent any money Method. Do you think we eat air? Really tell me, do you think we survive on air?

No, *Mama*.

Then why, Method my son? What sin have I committed against Jehova to deserve this treatment? Method's palms are outstretched on his lap like those of a distressed mother, his fingers slightly curled.

Listen, *Mama*. Let me explain…

Sometimes Method's conversations with his mother last well into the night because he has so many things to say. But today, he is hopeful. He intends to surprise her now that he has been paid twice. He reaches again in the sack and fishes out a tin of snuff. He unscrews the red cap and retrieves a wad of folded notes. He glances at the door to make sure it is indeed locked, and then begins counting the money – $320 rands. On Sunday, his day off, he will go shopping for his mother.

He will buy her beans, rice, cooking oil, soap, candles, matches, a dress, vaseline, a pair of tennis shoes. His neighbor, Njabulo, ferries goods across the border, and Method has been saving to use these services. He puts his money back in the sacks. The letters, he places under his pillow and drifts off to sleep, thinking of the letter his mother will write after she receives the package from him. It will say, *My dear son,* it will say, *My dear, dear, beautiful son, I am so proud of you.*

***

Method is awakened by the sound of screaming. He tosses and turns, pulling the thin blanket over his head but he cannot shut the noise out. The settlement is never a quiet place; there are quarrels, parties, scandals, fights. One gets used to such things. Method tells himself he will not get up to see what is happening – tomorrow, he will plant the red roses, weed the lawn, and possibly knock down the anthill that is threatening to block Madam's gate. It will be a busy day and so he needs his sleep. He lies still and waits for the noise to recede. He knows it will eventually go away, it always does.

But today the noise clings, like skin, the chaos getting louder and louder. The voices throb, and Method can imagine the air outside quivering, and then parting, unable to hold still. Whoever they are, they are moving toward his shack. Then, for the first time, he can actually hear what they are saying, and he knows from their words that it is the locals.

> GO! GET OUT!
> LEAVE! GO TO YOUR COUNTRIES RIGHT NOW!
> YOU STEAL OUR JOBS, GO!

YOU TAKE OUR WOMEN, GO!
GO, GO BACK HOME, GO!
GO GO GO GO GO GO GO!

And then there are the screams for help, so raw, so scared, so desperate. Method props himself on his shoulders and tilts his head toward the wall. He concentrates on the sounds, listens closely to the intonations, trying to gauge the mood. He has never heard anything like this in Eden Park, voices so terrified, so anxious, so frantic, and others, so vicious, scathing, threatening. Method's head reels. What to do? What, exactly, has happened out there? What's going to happen now? He contemplates leaving his house but decides against it. He needs to remain quiet. Yes, that's what he needs to do, sit tight and remain quiet because who knows what he will find when he goes out there?

Method sees a long spear pierce the shack, and with one twist, his door is flung wide open. Outside, the sight makes his stomach turn. A weapon-brandishing crowd. Spears. Machetes. Sticks. Axes. Knives. Knobkerries. Fleeing bodies. Falling bodies. Bloodied bodies. Screams, pleas for mercy; please please please! And the shouting: Go, get out, go back to your countries! Go! Method does not move from underneath his blankets though people are inside his shack, screaming at him.

First, a machete cuts Method somewhere on the head. Blood gushes from the wound and his blanket is dark with blood. More and more weapons rain on him. The beatings hurt, and Method feels the pain deep in his bones, but he does not cry out. Then he feels something wet and the smell of petrol stings his nose. His heart pounds in terror. He does not know when the match lands on his shirt but suddenly he is on fire.

Burning sears throughout Method's body. He opens his mouth for the first time and howls. He gets up and runs in a big bright blaze toward the door, but now it is barricaded from the outside; they will not let him out. Outside, he hears a woman scream: Xolela! Xolela! And he bangs on the wall of his shack and screams his real name back. He knows he will not come out alive, but he wants to let them know that his name is Method. My name is Method.

20

A Secret Sin

Daniel Mandishona

Time is longer than rope, Jerry. Nothing lasts forever, except sin.

Thirty years lost in the diaspora. That was you, Jerry Machingauta. Your father was on his deathbed when you came back from England, a frail old man dying from an unknown illness that was slowly eating him from the inside. He had sores in his mouth and the power of sight had long gone from his eyes.

That first day you visited him in hospital he felt the skin of your face with the tips of quivering fingers and then asked you to sit on the edge of the bed next to him so he could feel the warmth of your body, the smell of your sweat. You and he had always been the same blood, the same flesh. Your lives had been tethered to a collective fate, your destinies conjoined.

In your tender years it was your father who encouraged you to pursue your studies, assured you that some day perseverance would engender its own reward. You were the only one amongst his three children who showed any promise, the only one who seemed destined for greater things. You dreamt of pursuing a career in medicine or engineering and your father's unwavering support enabled you to have a clear vista of your fate. And when you finally left for England your father warned you about the dangers of unknown cities, about the bright lights of Babylon camouflaging a deep internal rot.

In those early London days, you heeded his warning. You were constantly on your guard because in the war-torn townships you had left behind you had seen too many lives succumb to temptation. The roll-call of tragedy was inexhaustible, the departure of a relative or a dear friend always a catastrophic and incalculable loss. You went to the all-night funeral wakes, the late afternoon burials. You would dutifully stand, sometimes in the pouring rain, staring at the mounds of fresh earth marking the new graves and listening to the eulogies.

'Man that is born of woman has but a few days to live.'

Your mother died when you were young and the people who were closest to you from her side of the family were her three sisters – Esther Mushonga, Veronica Sendera and Sarah Mushita – maternal surrogates who gave you more love than you could ever handle in a single lifetime. At your mother's funeral it was these same people who wept the loudest, prompting your grandmother to sigh and shake her grey-haired head:

'If such furious lamentations cannot wake poor Hilda from the sleep of God then nothing else will.'

But your father was the one who was always there to guide you through those early difficult years, the beacon that shone bright at the end of your troubled journey through childhood; the one person who encouraged you to get through those difficult exams at the end of each term. Do whatever you want to do well or don't do it at all, he would tell you. Because an eel caught by the tail is only half-caught.

Those exams.

The desks lined up in rooms which seemed vast, smelling of the collective fear of an ill-prepared army aware of its fatal limitations, the soft rustle of crisp paper, the affected coughs of the candidates that betrayed something more than just nervousness.

'You may begin.'

Question papers fearfully torn out of their polythene covers and then the contents briefly scrutinised amidst silent howls of derision and relief. The ominous ticking of the clock on the wall, its two hands always split into a configuration resembling a mocking grin, the intrusive pandemonium of peripheral activities – of pencils and pens being readied for unknown battles, of desks and chairs being pointlessly repositioned, of handbags and coats clattering to the floor, and then the invigilator's voice booming like that of a drill sergeant:

'You have exactly five minutes.'

There was nobody waiting for you at the airport when you arrived because nobody knew you were coming. There was none of the incandescent jubilation that accompanied your departure; none of the wild ululating and cheering that followed your over-confident swagger towards the plane that balmy day in October 1974.

After completing the arrivals formalities, you sat alone in the back of a battered taxi, your route to the city centre taking you past the absurdly fortified houses of the southern suburbs and the hard-labour prisoners working on the verges of the road, pale and hunched in the morning mist like winter ghosts.

The telegram sent by one of your paternal aunts the previous week contained two terse lines that conveyed a grim message:

'Your father is very sick. You have to be here.'

How different it had been that day when you left, a starry-eyed nineteen-year-old with a grand vision of a bright future. It was the first time you had ever been on a plane, and it both excited and frightened you; when you looked outside the plane seemed to be floating on a mound of static fluffiness.

All round you clouds were suspended in mid-air like body parts floating in jars of preservative. And where the clouds were parted by the plane's heaving fuselage they hung in the sky like fat bubbles and the ground below seemed to spread forever in all directions, a disfigured and patchy mosaic with roads and streams spread out like arteries.

'Tell me about England, my son. Tell me about the land of the white man. The land of the BBC, The Queen, cricket and snow.'

And so you sat on the edge of the bed and told your dying father about those things, details he wanted to hear, an affirmation of lifetime myths that had adhered for so long they could now no longer be discarded. To delete the old man's perception of 'Overseas' would have been an unnecessary cruelty. You told him about the red double-decker buses as huge as suburban houses and the underground trains that moved with the stealth of serpents in the dark belly of the earth.

You told him about the tall glass buildings of the West End and the historic steel and concrete bridges of the River Thames that united opposite shores without touching the water, structures that ingeniously spanned space without ever seeming to belong to it.

You told him about the shopping malls of Wood Green and Croydon that were so vast and complex it took hours to explore all the shops, and about the same amount of time to locate one's car in the car park afterwards. You told him about shoppers scurrying up and down Oxford Street and Tottenham Court Road in numbers so great it was like watching the wildebeest and antelope migrations of the Mapfukunde valley.

'And your life in England? How was your life in England, my son?'

But certain things are better left unsaid, Jerry. Some revelations serve no useful purpose. Talk is cheap, word gets round. You couldn't tell your father about your secret life in the land of the BBC, The Queen, cricket and snow. You couldn't tell him about the numerous white girls you had gone out with, a secret sin that hung around your neck like a monumental yoke of shame now that you were back amongst your own people. You couldn't tell him about Zoey, Virna, Macy, Vaneshree and Mitzi.

First there was Zoey Bellingham, a bespectacled and loose-limbed teenager whom you met in a pub in 1977 and lived with for a whole year without her parents' consent. Her face wore a permanent wide-mouthed and goggle-eyed expression of mild surprise – like someone who had recently been revived by artificial respiration. She was always bumping into things, Zoey, as if her blinkered eyes were firmly glued to the sides of her head and she viewed the world around her through a monochromatic wide-angled aperture of confusion.

You couldn't tell your father that after Zoey there was Virna Fioravanti from Sicily, she of hair the colour of burnt sienna and the beguiling Mona Lisa smile. What you liked about Virna was that she didn't have any of Zoey's assorted psychotic manias. You liked her amoebic and phantom-like unobtrusiveness, her uncanny ability to become inconspicuous by imperceptibly diluting her presence.

Whenever some of your friends came over to discuss the worsening political situation in your country, Virna would be there, but not really there – like a chameleon that can adopt the colours of its background at will and disintegrate into a blur of anonymity.

On the other hand, she was into Chuck Berry and Little Richard and Howlin' Wolf, the raucous good-time music of Memphis and the Mississippi Delta, and the walls of her bedroom were adorned with shiny portraits of her idols in tight suits and pointed shoes. Every night she dragged you to a rowdy pub on the high street where an old Negro blues guitarist sang slow painful songs about slavery and emancipation and other associated ills of the black man's burden.

No, you couldn't tell your father about Mitzi.

You remember Mitzi?

Mitzi Rosenberg of the hoarse laugh and cherub cheeks. She was your second white girlfriend and you were her second black boyfriend. Her first African boyfriend was a bad-tempered Nigerian who beat her black and blue and left her after seven months with three broken teeth and a mind befuddled with bad memories.

It was a gloomy Thursday during the arctic winter of 1979 when you met Mitzi. The Liberal Party had funded a symposium on African Nationalism at the School of Oriental and African Studies. You went because some friends invited you. Mitzi went because her friend was one of the speakers.

You had met Mitzi briefly a few weeks before that, when you took part in some hospital's fund-raising marathon together and afterwards she joined you and your posse of home-boys on a riotous pub-crawl that took in its stride seven pubs and three wine bars across five boroughs. That night you and three of your mates ended up freezing to the bone in the cells of a South London police station for being 'drunk and disorderly'.

After the SOAS symposium there was a wine bar in the foyer. You mingled with politicians and academic celebrities. People you had only seen on television and in the newspapers. You spent fifteen minutes chatting to a plump breathless woman who did the weather forecast on one of the television channels. She had yellow teeth and terrible halitosis. She reminded you of Miss Penelope Leggett, your English teacher at St Phillip's secondary school.

The weather woman's name was Bridget and she told you in her spare time she wrote an agony column for a teenage magazine and kept a three-foot South American iguana in her bedroom. Your major disappointment was that in the flesh she seemed shorter than she did on television. When she put her hand on your thigh and asked you what you were doing later on in the evening you made your excuses and left discreetly.

Emboldened by the joint you had shared with a West Indian student in the car park you walked across to where Mitzi was and ensnared her with your Neanderthal charm. Shy at first, she told you she was an Archaeology student and had just spent the last two months of her gap year working with forty other students on an Inca dig in the central highlands of Peru.

She told you of her amazing travels on three continents during her year out. She told you of the rock cliff tombs of southern China, the ceremonial dancing grounds of ancient Polynesia, the fossilised bodies unearthed from ancient peat bogs in Europe. Lindow Man, Grauballe Man, Tollund Man. You told her you were studying Civil Engineering at Imperial College, that one day you would design a bridge to heaven to convey the souls of the newly dead. She laughed and said you were quite crazy.

That weekend you went to the Leicester Square Odeon and sat through two and half hours of 'Apocalypse Now'. Because you didn't really like war epics you lost the plot halfway through the film and spent the rest of the time giving Mitzi a feel under her crinkly polo-neck. Your kind of film was the one with the misunderstood tragic hero who barely makes it through the final reel. James Cagney in 'Angels with Dirty Faces', Jack Lemmon in 'The China Syndrome', for example.

Apart from the twice weekly doses of frenzied sex in her dingy bed-sit above a spice shop on the Fulham Road the two of you soon discovered you had very little in common. She was into female emancipation and nuclear disarmament and existentialist philosophy. CND, Germaine Greer, Søren Kirkegaard. You had little time for her exotic highbrow pursuits. The truth is, such things had never been central to your existence. You grew up in a dusty colonial outpost on a diet of cheap westerns, gaudy photo-action comics and two-reel 'B' movies. She couldn't understand your interest in John Wayne and Roy Rogers.

You always felt embarrassed to tell her about your past, your illiterate parents and your half-crazed brother Chamu who joined the army on a whim and came back with a calcified stump where his left leg had been. You didn't tell Mitzi about your younger sister Estelle who emerged from her rebellious teenage years burdened with the responsibility of bringing up three children from three different fathers. You didn't tell her about the ignominious shame your father felt at having to live with the eternal disgrace of Estelle's totem-less offspring. You never mentioned your aunt Peregrina Masuku who spent fifteen years in America and came back in 1973 with a Texan drawl and the clothes on her back.

One night, Mitzi told you about her family, migrant Polish Jews who had escaped the grinding poverty and hunger of their native country in the 1930s and settled in Central Europe. Half her father's family had perished in the gas ovens of Auschwitz. That day she opened a dog-eared picture album and pulled out a photograph of her great-aunt Tanya Rosenberg. The picture had been taken by one of the Soviet soldiers who had liberated the camp.

'There. That's my aunt Tanya,' she said, pointing to a forlorn scarecrow standing amidst a mound of bug-eyed skeletons.

'I don't hate Hitler for what he did,' she said, 'It wasn't his fault.'

You didn't tell Mitzi that when you were ten you started creating your own personalised nightmares, that you would visit your uncle Ephraim at the African hospital where he worked as a clerk and watch through a back window the daily ritual of white-coated mortuary attendants silently wheeling bloated cadavers to the post-mortem labs. That afterwards you would retch your guts out and go for days without eating or drinking until you became dizzy with hunger and dehydration.

You didn't tell her that when you were thirteen you wrote a story about a one-eyed giant who lived in the massive sewage ponds on the edge of the township and came out at night to prey on newborn babies. Miss Penelope Leggett gave you two out of ten and wrote 'See Me' at the bottom of your composition. You never did, because that was the week you spent at home bedridden with a convenient attack of mumps.

You didn't tell Mitzi that at fourteen you told your parents about the fire-eating demons that visited you at night and made you sleepwalk in ever-increasing circles until you fell down with exhaustion. You didn't tell her that on hot summer nights you had bad dreams that gave you nosebleeds and made you wet your bed, that you had a mortal dread of cockroaches and black ants, or that in your early teenage years you drew gory pictures that scared your siblings and so worried your parents they sought the help of your school's headmaster. He told them there was nothing to worry about; that it was just a pubescent phase that would soon pass.

You didn't tell Mitzi that as you grew older you couldn't tell the dreams from reality, that as the voices in your head grew louder the only way you could fight them was by staying awake all night. You became a creature of darkness, walking the township streets at night like a stray dog because you could not fight that which you could not see, could not touch, could not understand.

Your first suicide attempt was when you were eighteen, shortly before you went to England. You told your father it was the only way you could fight the demons. Fortunately for you, the malaria tablets nauseated you so much you vomited them. Your father called a priest who prayed for you and said the good Lord always watches over his flock.

You couldn't tell your father that after Mitzi left you because of your alcoholism you abandoned your studies and became a regular at the pubs in your neighbourhood frequented by self-made failures like yourself. The demons of your childhood had returned to haunt you. You quickly became the star attraction at the high street bars, daily showing off the little knowledge garnered in your nine months at university to anybody who bothered to listen. To make ends meet you got as job as a night-shift packer in a supermarket, but they made you redundant after four months. They told you there was an economic recession; last one in first one out.

Now officially an illegal immigrant, you went to live in a grimy northern town where the authorities couldn't track you down. And that's where you have been living for the past ten years, with a West Indian woman ten years older than you who took you in because she felt sorry for you. She let you share her bed and gave you a decent meal every day. When you left you told her you were coming back but deep down inside you knew you were not going to do so.

'Always tell the truth, my son. The good thing about telling the truth is you don't have to remember what you said.'

That was what your father always told you during your formative years. The truth passes through fire and does not burn. But certain things are better left unsaid, Jerry. Some revelations serve no useful purpose.

You couldn't tell your dying father that England was not the paradise of your teenage dreams. You couldn't tell him how you hated London, the bleak grey weather and the nauseating pollution; the aloofness of the city's disparate clans and the affected camaraderie of the shaggily dressed bohemian oddballs who frequented the students' union bar at your college.

And you couldn't tell him that in the thirty years that was your secret life in the land of the BBC, The Queen, cricket and snow you had achieved nothing. That like your aunt Peregrina Masuku you had wasted thirty years of your life and come back to your father's deathbed with only the clothes on your back and a baggage of bittersweet memories.

Time is longer than rope, Jerry.

(viii)

Resilience

21

SEVENTH STREET ALCHEMY

Brian Chikwava

By 5 a.m. most of Harare's struggling inhabitants are out of their hovels. They are on their varied ways to innumerable places to waylay the dollars they so desperately need to stave hunger off their doorsteps. Trains and commuter omnibuses burst with exploitable human material. Its excess finds its way onto bicycles, or simply self-propels, tilling earth with bare frost-bitten feet all the way to the city centre or industrial areas.

The modes of transport are diverse, poverty the trendsetter. Like a colony of hungry ants, it crawls over the multitudes of faces scattered along the city roads, ravaging all etches of dignity that only a few years back stood resilient. Threadbare resignation is concealed underneath threadbare shirts, together with socks and underpants that resemble a ruthless termite job. In spite of poverty's glorious march into every household, the will to be dignified by underpants and socks remains intact.

Activities in the city centre tend towards the paranormal. A voodoo economy flourishes as daylight dwindles: fruit and vegetable vendors slash their prices by half and still fail to sell. The following morning the same material is carted back onto the streets, selling at higher than the previous day's peak rates. In some undertakings the enthusiasm to participate is expressed in wads of notes; in some, simple primitive violence – or the threat of its use – is common currency. As the idea of ensuring that your demands are backed up by violence is fast gaining hold among the city's prowlers, business carried out in pin-striped suits is fleeing the city centre, ill-equipped to deal with the proliferation of scavenger tactics. Pigeons too have joined the new street entrepreneurs: they relieve themselves on pedestrians when least expected and never alight on the same street corner for more than two days in a row.

Even the supposedly civilised well-to-do section of the population, a pitiful lot typified by their indefatigable amiability, now finds itself anchored down by a State whose methods of governance involve incessant roguery. Instead of facing up to their circumstances with a modicum of honour, they weekly hurl themselves into churches to petition a disinterested God to subvert the laws of the universe in their favour.

At the corner of Samora Machel Avenue and Seventh Street, in a flat whose bedroom is adorned with two newspaper cuttings of the President, lives a fifty-two-year-old quasi-prostitute with thirty-seven teeth and a pair of six-inch-heeled perspex platform shoes. It has been decades since she realised that, armed with a vagina and a will to survive, destitution could never lay claim to her. With these weapons of destruction, she has continued to fortify her liberty against poverty and society. Fiso is her name and like a lot of the city's inhabitants she has conjured that death is mere spin, nobody ever really dies.

On the night a street kid got knocked down by a car it was a tranquil hour. A discerning ear would have been able to hear two flies fornicating several metres away. But to Anna Shava, a civil servant, soaked to the bone with matrimonial distress, the flies would have had to be inside her nose to get her attention. Her tearful departure from home after another scuffle with her husband set in motion a violent symphony of events. Security guards who scurried off the streets for safety could not have imagined that an exasperated spouse in a car vibrating to the frenzied rhythms of her anguished footwork could beget such upheaval.

Right in the middle of the lane, at the corner of Samora Machel Avenue and Seventh Street, a street kid staggers from left to right, struggling to tear himself out of a stupor acquired by sniffing glue all day. The car devours the tarmac, and in a screech of tyres the corner is gobbled up together with the small figure endeavouring to grasp reality. Sheet metal grudgingly gives in to a dent, bones snap, glass shatters. The kid never had a chance. His soul's departure is punctuated by one final baritone fart relinquishing life. Protruding out of the kid's back pocket is a tube of Z68 glue.

A couple of blocks from the scene, blue lights flashed from a police car while two officers shared the delicate task of trying to convince a grouchy young musician to part with some of his dollars for having gone though red traffic lights.

'You've been having a good time. That's no problem. But you must understand we also need something to keep us happy while doing our rounds,' one of the officers said with a well-drilled, venal smile before continuing. 'Since you are a musician we know you can't afford much Stix, but if you could just make us happy with a couple of Nando's takeaways …'

Anna, realising that they were not going to pay her any attention without some effort on her part, marched over to the officers. 'Will you please come to my help, haven't you seen what happened?' she said, donning that look of nefarious servitude that she often inspired on the faces of applicants at the immigration office. She knew better than anybody that being nice to people in authority could render purchasable otherwise priceless rights, and simplify one's life.

'We are off duty now, Madam, call Central Police Station,' one of officers yodelled over. Returning to her car and periodically glancing over her shoulder in disbelief she saw the offending driver stick out of his window a clenched handful of notes to pacify the vultures that had taken positions around his throttled freedom. His liberties resuscitated, he sped off in his scarlet ramshackle car.

Two days before, Anna, no less fed up with her errant husband, had followed him to the city's most popular rhumba club. She had found him leaning against the bar, with men she did not recognise. They talked at the tops of their voices in the dim smudged lighting. Her husband, who had been tapping his foot to the sound of loud Congolese music, recoiled at the sight of her. Befuddled, he grappled with the embarrassment of having been tracked down to a nightclub crawling with prostitutes. And then there was the thought of his mates saying that his balls had long been liberated from him and safely deposited in his wife's bra. His impulse was to thump her thoroughly, but lacking essential practice, he could not lift a finger.

'What do you want?' he asked, icily.

'Buy me a drink too,' she said brushing the question aside.

He stared at Anna as she grinned. Outrage lay not far beneath such grins – experience had schooled him. Reluctantly he turned to the bar to order her a Coke, struggling to affect an air of ascendancy in the eyes of his peers. He tossed a five hundred dollar note at the bartender, as if oblivious to his wife's presence.

Half an hour later, when Anna visited the ladies toilet, transgression would catch up with her husband. There a lady with greying hair, standing with what looked like a couple of prostitutes, cut short her conversation to remark innocently, 'Be careful with that man. He's a problem when it comes to paying up. Ask these girls. Make sure he pays you before you do anything or he will make excuses like, "I didn't think you were that kind of girl."'

Anna was transfixed, hoping – pretending – that the words were directed at someone else.

'You could always grab his cellphone, you know,' the woman added kindly.

That woman was Fiso, who at the time Anna ran into a street kid, was engrossed in the common ritual of massaging her dementia. Having spent a whole day struggling to sell vegetables – a relatively new engagement imposed on her by the autumn of her street life, she was exhausted and was not bothered by the screeching tyres down the road. It did not occur to her that what had registered in her ears was an incident precipitated by her well-meaning advice. Beside her, sharing her bed, lay her daughter Sue, a twenty-six-year-old flea-market vendor. In the midst of her mother's furious campaign against a pair of rogue mosquitoes, which relentlessly circled their heads before attacking, Sue came to the tired realisation that in spite of all the years on the streets, her mother still had undepleted stocks of a compulsive disorder from her youthful days. In the sooty darkness her mother blindly clapped, hoping to deal one or both of them a fatal blow. Precision however remained in inverse proportion to determination. The mosquitoes circled, mother waited, her desire to snuff out a life inflated. They would dive, she would clap. Sound and futility reigned supreme. At last, jumping off the bed, Fiso switched on the light. A minute later one of the mosquitoes, squashed by a sandal, was a smudge of blood on the president's face, but Fiso could not be bothered to make good the insignia of her patriotism. A few months before, she would have wiped the blood away. But the novelty of affecting patriotic sentiment in the hope of dreaming herself out of prostitution to the level of First Lady had long worn off.

The following morning Sue switched on her miniature radio, to be confronted by the continuously recycled maxims of State propaganda, which ranged from the importance of being a sovereign nation to defending the gains of independence in the face of a 'neo-colonialist onslaught'. Leaning against the sink, she failed to grasp the value of the messages to her life. She gulped her tea and went to the Union Avenue flea-market. There, among other vendors slugging it out for survival, she could at least learn where to get the next bag of sugar or cooking oil.

On the same Saturday afternoon that marked the climax to Anna's marital woes, Stix, a struggling young jazz pianist, had a call from his friend, Shamiso, inviting him to an impromptu dinner at Mvura Restaurant. Her friends and elements of her 'tribe', as she liked to refer to her cousins, were to be part of the company. With only the prospect of being part of a nondescript crowd at a glum, low-key music festival in the Harare Gardens, Stix committed himself to Shamiso's plans. At 7.30 p.m. he made his way to the restaurant. By midnight he had made a pathetic retreat to his flat, having shared part of his meagre income with two police officers fortunate enough to witness him driving through red lights. From his flat he had called Shamiso, and threatened to cremate her for inviting him to a restaurant where they would be saddled with a bill of over $15,000 each. That it was a restaurant with 'melted mars bar' on its dessert menu wickedly swelled his appetite for arson.

'So don't say you have not been warned about Mvura Restaurant,' Stix said to Fiso the day after the incident. 'If, however, out of curiosity you decide to go there, your experience will approximate to something like this: you get there, the car park is full of cars with diplomatic registration plates and there is not even space to open the car doors. At this point a security guard …' Stix pauses to light his cigarette. '… will run like a demon to find you parking space – but since you don't own a car, Fiso, you won't experience that bit.'

'So you're not going to take me there?' Fiso asks, but Stix ignores her and continues.

'You may be at a table where you sit back to back with the Japanese ambassador, and you will be confronted by a waiter wielding a menu without prices. By the end of the evening you will be sorry. Never assume that such restaurants price their food reasonably!'

Fiso listened, thinking what a curious person Stix was, and well aware that save for living in the same dilapidated block of flats, they did not have much in common. The nice restaurants, élitist concerts and well-dressed friends, existed only in the stories that Stix told her on their doorsteps on sluggish afternoons. They were just another spectral reality that Stix was fond of invoking. And after an hour or two of reciprocal balderdash, one of them would just stand up and walk into his or her flat, leaving the other to wean themselves from that hallucinogenic indulgence.

Defining one's relationship with the world demands daily renegotiating one's existence. So far-reaching are the consequences of neglecting exigencies imposed by this that those unwilling or unable to participate eventually find themselves trapped in a parallel universe, the existence of which is not officially recognised. These are the people who never die, Sue and her mother being a quintessential sample.

Sue has no birth certificate because her mother does not have one. Officially they were never born and so will never die. For how do authorities issue a death certificate when there is no birth certificate? Several other official declarations only perfect the parallel existence of most of Harare's residents. Officially basic food commodities are affordable because prices are State-controlled. Officially no one starves because there is plenty of food on supermarket shelves. And if it is not there, it is officially somewhere, being hoarded by Enemies of the State. With all its innumerable benefits, who would not want to exist in this other world spawned by the authorities – where your situation does not daily remind you what a liability your mouth and stomach are. It was therefore towards this official existence that Sue and her mother strove. Fed up with galloping food prices in their parallel universe, they took a chance and tried to take the leap into official existence.

It was an ordinary Monday morning when mother and daughter walked to the Central Registry offices hoping to get birth certificates, metal IDs and, eventually, passports. Sue had been told she could make a good income buying things from South Africa and selling them at the flea markets. But because the benefit of her deathless existence did not also confer upon her freedom of movement across national boundaries, she needed a passport. Fiso had decided to assist her daughter and get herself a passport too. Little did they know that they would find the door out of their parallel existence shut, and bolted.

By mid-afternoon Fiso was on her doorstep relating the events of the morning to Stix. Back in her humble flat, she felt better having spent half a day surrounded by the smell of dust, apathy and defeat. Such were the Central Registry offices: an assemblage of Portakabins that had outlived its lifespan a dozen times over. With people enduring never-ending queues, just to have their dignity thrown out of rickety windows by sadistic officials, inevitably a refugee camp ambience prevailed.

'If your mother and father are dead and you do not have their birth certificates, then there is nothing that I can do,' the man in office number 28 had said, his fat fist thumping the desk. He wore a blue and yellow striped tie that dug painfully into his fat neck, accentuating the degradation of his torn collar.

'But what am I supposed to do?' Fiso asked, exasperated.

'Woman, just do as I say. I need one of your parents' birth or death certificates to process your application. You are wasting my time. You never listen. What's wrong with you people?'

'Aaaah you are useless! Every morning you tell your wife that you are going to work when all you do is frustrate people!' Fiso stormed out of the office. Having learnt the false nature of authority and law from the streets, she was certain that he was her only obstacle. Men, she knew, could have the most perverse idiosyncrasies and at least one vice. In her experience, doctors, lawyers and the most genteel of politicians could gleefully discard their masks to become the most brutal perverts. It was a male trait, an official trait, and it accounted for her failure to acquire the papers she and her daughter needed.

Fiso's parents had died long back in deep rural Zhombe, where peasant life had confined them to a radius of less than a hundred kilometres, and where an innate suspicion of anything involving paperwork was nurtured. Back in the forties, stories of people having their names changed by authorities horrified semi-literate peasants such as Fiso's parents, who swore they would never have anything to do with the wicked authorities of that era.

'We were told to go to office number 28, but there was no one there. After about forty minutes, we went back to the office that had referred us, but there was no one there either. Returning to office number 28, and seeking help from an official who was strolling past we were told, "Look? Can't you see that jacket? It means he is not far away. Wait for him." So we waited – for three hours – only to be told to bring one of my parents' death or birth certificates.'

'Civil servants are like that, Fiso. They all have two jobs you know,' Stix said, mildly. Fiso was being too naïve for a seasoned sex purveyor, he thought.

'Look: a Japanese firm is making big money generating electricity out of sewage waste. All you have to do to bring your electricity bill down is shit a lot!' Stix, his eyes on the newspaper, was trying to steer the conversation in another direction.

That afternoon, it was Fiso who disappeared into her flat first, inexplicably regretting that she had let Stix have sex with her a couple of months before. They had been drunk, and she had found herself naked and collapsing onto Stix's bed, his fiendish shaft plumbing her hard-wearing orifice. 'Ey, you! That's not a good starting point!' was her only protest, and she cursed the alcohol that still swirled inside her head.

'If you'd been a virgin, Fiso, I would have washed my penis with milk, just for you,' Stix said after contenting himself. Fiso ignored the remark. More incensed with herself than with Stix, she simply decided to sleep over the anger in the hope that it would go.

In Harare, vegetable vendors can yield useful connections. After Fiso and Sue had failed to get their papers, a woman at the Central Registry was brought to the attention of Fiso by a fellow vendor. This woman, a relative, could assist her to get any form of ID for a fee. Because the vendor and her relative went to the same church, she suggested that this would be the ideal place to introduce Fiso.

Less than a hundred metres from the church building, a man of Fiso's age stood by a corner selling single cigarettes and bananas. Fiso, sensing her increasingly disagreeable nerves, sought to calm them down with a cigarette.

'Sekuru,' she addressed the man 'How much are your cigarettes?'

'I'm not your Sekuru. Harare does not have any Sekurus. They are all in the rural areas. If you desire a Sekuru then make one for yourself out of cardboard.'

'How much are your cigarettes?' she asked again, avoiding the contentious term.

'Fifteen dollars.'

She quietly retrieved three brand new five-dollar coins from her purse, handed them over and picked a Madison Red from among the many on display. Contentedly lighting the cigarette and avoiding eye contact, she heard the man ask, 'What time is it?'

'If you need a watch why don't you make yourself one out of cardboard?' she retorted, and walked away, victorious.

With what panache does fate deliver the person of a harlot into a church building? Cockroaches appear through the cracks in the walls and wave their antennae in response to an almost primeval call. The priest, beneath his holy regalia, shudders, aware of the relative paleness of his cloistered virtues in the face of a salvation cobbled together on street corners. Against the tide of attrition of the human condition, what man of cloth can offer a soul a better salvation than the sheer dogged will to live? In the priest's mind, however, such sentiments only manifested themselves in vague notions of jealousy and contempt. As Fiso strolled in, carefree, the holy man recoiled, the congregation's heads turned, and the devil chuckled. A Dynamos Football Club T-shirt, fluorescent green mini-skirt and six-inch high perspex platform shoes upstaged the holy word.

Destructive distillation is a process by which a substance is subjected to a high temperature with the absence of oxygen so that it simply degenerates into its several constituent substances without burning. After her silent confessions and having received the body and blood of Christ, Mrs Shava found herself subjected to destructive distillation by an ogling congregation. Like anyone being introduced to a person of dubious appearance on sanctified premises, she degenerated into her constituent attributes of self-righteousness and caution.

'The church services are short here – or was I late,' Fiso remarked after being introduced to Mrs Shava by her vending friend.

'No, we're not like those Pentecostal churches, we're less fanatical,' Mrs Shava said, unable to look Fiso straight in the eyes and bewildered, her mind whirling with an elliptical sense of *déjà vu* as she wondered where they had met before. She could also feel the stares of the congregation pecking at her back from several metres away. She resented them but neither did she like talking to Fiso. However, having listened to her plight, she agreed to help her out. Everyone had to live, after all.

'Eeeek, ahh, it's complicated.' Mrs Shava moaned, a technique that she had perfected after helping several people. 'It's no easy task,' she continued, wanting to justify her fee.

'I understand, but I must have a birth certificate. And my daughter cannot get one if I don't have one – and she needs a passport.'

'I can try, but it's a risk, I could lose my job.' Mrs Shava assumed a pious expression. Fiso knew that it was time to tie up her end of the deal. She understood what Mrs Shava meant when she said that success depended on a number of factors; Fiso knew it meant one thing only.

'I understand it's a big risk, but I intend to reward you for your efforts.' Fiso glanced at her friend for clues but the vendor's face was as blank as a hospital wall. 'I don't know what you would like, but I'll leave you to decide, my sister.' Mrs Shava's lips parted dispassionately to reveal her white teeth. 'Okay, call me on Wednesday and I will see if it's all right for you to come to my office. People at my workplace will be on strike but I can't risk my job. If it's okay, I'll give you the forms, you fill them in and I'll take them back. And don't forget my fee: $15,000!' She smiled for the first time and turned to walk away.

'Uhh, huh, your phone number at work?' Fiso stammered.

'Nyasha will give it to you, I have to see someone else,' came the reply.

Fiso turned to Nyasha, and they smiled at each other.

Contentedly walking off, Mrs Shava could not have guessed that in less than a minute she would be caressed by more poltergeistic echoes of a recent past. She was walking out of the church premises when Stix stopped by to pick up Fiso in his scarlet car. A shiver descended Mrs Anna Shava's spine as she recalled the night she killed the street kid. Fiso's face, though, defiantly refused to fit into the jigsaw puzzle, and Mrs Shava could only watch in bewilderment as the old harlot jumped into the car, which rattled away, accelerating sideways like a crab.

...

In a mortuary at the central hospital, clad in a blue suit, white shirt, and seemingly asphyxiated by the tie around its neck, lies a slightly overweight corpse. A cellphone is still stuck in one of the pockets and when it rings for the third time, it is answered by a being who, after years as a mortuary cleaner, picking his wages from its floor, has become indifferent to death.

'Hullo, Central Hospital,' he answers.

'Hullo, I'm looking for my husband, is that his phone you are using? Who are you? Is he there?'

'Aah, I don't know, but unless this is the body of a thief who stole the phone from your husband, your husband is dead. The police shot him in the head. They said he was rioting in the city centre.'

The previous night Anna's husband had not returned from

work. That he would have come to such a rough end, no one could have guessed. But being in the insurance industry he would have appreciated it, if he'd been told that the value of his life was equivalent to twenty condoms, and in all likelihood would not have contested such a settlement being awarded to Anna. His death, though, had consequences that reverberated through to Fiso, because on the day she was supposed to call Mrs Shava, grief and its attendant ceremonies had already claimed her. Then on Monday, having spent all night at Piri-Piri, the city's sleaziest night-club, Fiso decided to take the Central Registry juggernaut head-on. Suffering from a hangover, and caring not about consequences, she went straight to the Registrar General's office.

'I've been trying to get a birth certificate and can't, because your staff members only care about getting bribes!' The Registrar General's secretary remained calm, picked up the phone and dialled, but before she had uttered a word, the RG had emerged from his office. Being a constant target of ridicule by the press as the man heading one of the most inefficient and corrupt government departments, he was very sensitive to criticism.

'How can I help you, lady?' he demanded impatiently.

'I only need a birth certificate, but your staff is only interested in frustrating people into paying bribes!'

'Those are serious allegations.' The RG's interest lay only in smothering public objections.

'All I want is a birth certificate, Sir. My womanhood is an old rag. I've paid the price of living. Please do not waste my time, I'm too old for that.'

The Registrar nearly had convulsions. 'Sandra, call security!' he ordered.

The secretary fumbled, dropped her pen and spilt her coffee.

'Your staff members all want bribes. I come to you and all you do is get rid of me! I suppose you want a bribe too? What else can you do apart from sitting on your empty scrotum all day?'

In a little less than half an hour Fiso was behind police bars facing a charge of public disorder. The police, however, soon found their case stalling. There was no way of establishing her identity because she did not have an ID. After she told the investigating officer that she was trying to get just such an ID when she was arrested, the officer called the Registrar General who offered to quickly process an ID, if it was in the interest of facilitating the course of justice. That afternoon Fiso was bundled into the back of a Land Rover Defender in handcuffs and taken to the Central Registry to make an application for an ID. Predictably, she refused to co-operate, so she was later thrown back into the vehicle and taken to the police cells.

Two days went by, each bringing a new face into the cell she shared with six other women. On the third day two cellmates went for trial and never returned – either freed or sent to Chikurubi Maximum. Then a new inmate arrived. From her appearance one would have surmised that she was a teenager picked up from the vicinity of a village while herding goats. It was her carefree disposition that won her the attention of her cellmates.

'What are those for?' she asked, looking up at the left corner of the cell. The officer who had brought her had hardly locked up. No immediate answer came until the officer had disappeared.

'Those are CCTV cameras,' someone finally answered her.

'What is CCTV,' the girl asked again.

'Closed Circuit Television. It enables them to watch us from their offices all the time on one of their televisions.'

Later in the evening when another new face was brought in, the goatherd girl asked the officer: 'Is it true that you have a TV and that you're watching us?'

The officer just continued with his duty of locking up the gate as if nothing had been said. Goat-girl was, however, unfazed.

'I think you people are going to be in trouble when the president finds out that you are wasting TVs on criminals. I'm sure he would like to be watched on TVs too. Or watch himself so that he's safe from assassins and perverts?'

After five days in the cell Fiso was cautioned and released without charge – not even that of failing to produce an ID. The investigating officer, seeing that the case was going nowhere, had managed to convince his superior to release her with just one statement: 'It's only an ageing whore.'

22

THE GENERAL'S GUN

Jonathan Brakarsh

In downtown Gweru, there's an auto dealership, Dynamo Motors. It specialises in Mercedes. It is the place to go in Gweru if one wants a Merc.

One day, a normal day, with traffic moving at a leisurely pace down Main Street, a kombi pulls up with its engine running. It has the message, '*God Knows*' written across the top of the windscreen in silver lettering. The driver is stone faced – either angry or scared. It's hard to tell. He has a smooth face, a woman's complexion. There's a great deal of noise inside the kombi – chanting and loud voices. The door slides open and out leaps a mass of writhing energy. The Youth Brigade. People outside this country have often asked how one makes a youth brigade. The recipe is as follows:

Take one unemployed, poorly educated youth
Throw in generous amounts of chibuku *or* mbanje
Add some cash

… and you have what just jumped out of the kombi. Seventeen of them to be exact. They're singing revolutionary songs and waving pangas; then they all rush into Dynamo Motors, attracted like dogs to a steak supper, touching all the beautiful new cars – silver ones, gold ones, blue ones and black ones.

The big-bellied Manager, sitting behind his expensive desk, looks up at seventeen red-eyed, panga-waving, ragged-looking youth with nothing to lose. He turns pale and feels his aging process accelerating. The leader of the group, with a white toothpaste smile, high cheekbones and the smooth stroke of a master batsman, sweeps his panga through the air and embeds it in the manager's desk, which shudders in response. 'Next time *ndinonyatso kunanga zvakanaka!* My aim is good,' he said. 'Next time, it's you!'

The youth with him are toy-toying, singing, eyes blazing under the fluorescent lighting of the Mercedes dealership. On the walls are large posters of beautiful women posing on shimmering Benzes. With great excitement, the youth jump down into the showroom area. They love the cars. They open the passenger doors and sit behind the wheels, laughing gleefully. The youth leader pronounces, 'By order of the Governor, this *bhizimisi* is now ours. We want *mari* and your cars. Now!'

The Manager feels a large space opening up in the pit of his stomach. 'I have to make a call,' he croaks, his throat dry and tight. The youth leader raises his panga again and axes it into the wood of the manager's desk, leaving a second noticeable gouge on the beautifully waxed surface. The Manager calls a number, and waits, while the perspiring islands of wetness on his shirt slowly merge together. He talks quietly into the phone, taking rapid breaths, speaking in jagged sentences. You can hear the tension in his voice, and the hope. The man on the other end of the line, says, 'Keep them busy for thirty minutes and I'll be there.' The Manager hangs up.

'Well, gentleman,' he says to the crowd milling disconsolately around his desk. Some are already looking through his drawers, some are playing with trophies they have found – a letter opener in the shape of a Mercedes, a cigarette lighter resembling a girl in a bikini – and some are waiting as if frozen in time.

'Well gentlemen,' he says again, rising from his chair, always the salesman, always ready to sell to an interested customer. 'Can I show you around?' The group follows behind him, one of the youth intermittently giving him a hard push. He recovers his gait each time, pointing out this car and the next, proclaiming the wonders of owning a Mercedes. He enquires about the cars they presently drive. There is a silence, perhaps the hint of embarrassment and then anger. 'Shut the fuck up, white man,' one of the youth yells, hitting the

Manager between the shoulder blades with the handle of his panga. The Manager's body crumples momentarily but he pulls himself up, regaining his composure. 'Gentlemen,' he says, 'would you like to see our newest model?'

The morning is passing. One of the youth orders, 'Make us tea and don't forget the *mukaka*, sugar and *chingwa*!' The Manager hears this command. You can see him calculating, knowing he'll never have enough bread to satisfy the hunger of the group. He calls to the tea-boy, 'Be kind enough to make tea for everyone here, please'. There is an exchange of glances between them and the message is clear.

'I will have to go next door to heat the water as our kettle is broken,' the tea-boy says. The tea-boy, a man with neatly groomed hair, a grey moustache, and black shoes brilliantly shined, walks at an unhurried pace to the kitchen.

The Manager feels the increasingly sharp bites of panic. The youth leader feels that the Manager lacks respect. He shouts, 'Do you want to live or die fat man?' In this moment, as short as a click of the fingers or as long as eternity, the birds stop singing, the sounds of traffic recede into silence, all activity ceases. There's only this moment.

The Manager begins to cry, 'I have a wife and three children. I pay school fees for my maid and gardener's children. I am a good man.' He repeats more slowly, as if to himself, 'I am a good man.'

The youth leader laughs. 'This fat white man is a good man!' The crowd of youth laughs loudly and forms a circle around him. Each youth sings, as they take turns kicking and slapping him, 'The fat white man is a good man!'

The sound of cars, engines growling at high acceleration, wheels turning, can be heard in the distance. Three cars shriek up Main Street, on a sunny day before teatime in Gweru. They expertly glide into the parking bay. From the khaki-coloured army truck jump two rows of fully armed soldiers, bayonets glittering in the winter sunlight. From the two jeeps emerge more soldiers with truncheons and riot gear. And last, with a waddling stride, comes a man wearing an impressive khaki uniform with three rows of medals advertising his accomplishments. He has a barrel chest and a belly to match; a dark brown leather gun holster at his hip. His uniform is a work of precision: knife-edge creases and a flawlessly ironed uniform jacket. Middle-aged, he is still strikingly handsome.

The two rows of soldiers march into the Mercedes dealership with speed and discipline, taking up positions at all exits, gun pressed to shoulder and finger on the trigger, ready. The other soldiers follow. They lower the visors of their riot helmets and have their truncheons raised. The youth continue kicking and slapping the manager, oblivious to the activity around them. 'Here's something to help you, fat white man,' says another youth. Cackling, he gives the Manager a good kick in the rear end which propels him several metres across the floor. The other youth cheer and applaud appreciatively. 'Ronaldo,' one shouts. 'No, it's Messi!' the other shouts. They all laugh. 'The only white man you can trust is a dead white man!' They all start to clap in rhythm repeating this phrase over and over again, like a mantra.

The youth hear a distant knock on the door. The man in uniform with three rows of medals is knocking on the front door with the butt of his gun. It is a beautiful weapon catching the sunlight on its golden flanks, the top adorned with diamonds stretching down the length of the barrel.

'These cars are already paid for. Come back next week,' one of the youth shouts, not looking at the man at the door. The youth is preoccupied with the Manager, waiting for him to rise to his knees so he can take another kick at his backside. The army officer walks purposefully into the centre of the room and places his gun to the temple of the young man who is waiting for the Manager to rise up on all fours. The youth turns angrily toward the source of his pain, 'What the fu…!' Then he recognises the man in uniform. 'General Muvudzi!' he stammers in alarm. 'General Muvudzi!' the rest of the youth exclaim in terror.

The youth brigade looks at the soldiers blocking the doors, bayonets pointed in their direction. They see more soldiers with riot helmets on and batons raised. The General now speaks. 'You have two minutes to vacate the premises. Any stragglers will be shot and buried in an unmarked grave.'

'Weapons to the ready,' the General orders. The soldiers unlatch the safety mechanism of their automatic rifles, the sound of multiple clicks like gun shots. Each of the soldiers centres their rifle sight on their chosen target. The General takes his gun, the gleaming gold exterior evoking dreams of unlimited wealth and the good life, and places it within arm's reach on the Manager's desk. The onlookers don't know what he will do next, and inhale sharply. He smiles and looks at his watch. 'On your marks, get ready!' he announces. 'Go,' he says quietly.

Chaos ensues. Youths jump out of Mercedes, like termites scurrying from a termite mound which someone has accidentally kicked; others try to run to the exit doors only to be blocked and beaten by soldiers stationed there. Some smash through the plate glass window where white letters announce 'Dynamo Motors'. The discordant sound of glass breaking fills the air. There is screaming, yelling, and blood.

Looking over the heads of the soldiers, observing the scene, slender and well dressed, in tight fitting black jeans and a white shirt, is the kombi driver. He is looking at the General's gun. He's mesmerized by the General's gun. Two youth rugby tackle a soldier knocking him down, a victory, before six other army men pile on top of them, batons beating a bass rhythm to the screams.

At that moment a soldier comes barreling through to help his comrades, pushing the kombi driver into the showroom, a scene of mayhem. Several youth grab him, begging him to take them to his kombi, but he keeps running searching for a safe exit, darting in between the Mercs.

Then, he sees the gun, shimmering amidst the pulses of the showroom's fluorescent lights. He moves as if in slow motion, fascinated by the sparkle of the gun barrel as the diamonds reflect the light. They remind him of his mother's gold sequined dress glinting in the light of the sitting room as she danced. He feels the power of the gun in his blood. With this gun he would set all men free. He runs towards what he seeks, skirting around the corner of a life-size image of an African woman in a pink bikini draped over a silver Mercedes. She is smiling in the direction of the Manager's desk.

The General is entertained by the chaos. He remembers the words of his Chief Commander, 'Let the guns speak.' One minute has elapsed. He walks over to a soldier, points to the youth brigade leader and whispers, 'Shoot him!' Several bullets whoosh through the air and thump into the young leader, the impact slamming him into a wall. He collapses onto the floor. This event increases the activity level in the room.

Mr Mpofu, the elderly tea-boy, looks out from the kitchen and sees the General's gun. He sucks in his breath, imagining himself in the general's uniform. He pictures all the respectful ranks of soldiers in straight lines and crisp uniforms, ready for dress parade. He imagines what he would tell them to do. He imagines using the gun. Realising what he must do, Mr Mpofu wheels out the tea cart among the bullets and bodies falling. Nothing touches him. On the cart, there is a large tea cosy with nothing underneath it.

Across the room, one soldier in particular has his eye on the General's gun, while the rest of him rifle butts every youth who tries to make it past him. He's thinking how much he could sell that gun for. The Marange diamonds on the barrel are still worth a fortune. He could finally afford to feed his family, rather than live on bread and tea, while he waits for the monthly paycheck which always comes late. He's a soldier with a mission.

Time passes. The General's watch now indicates one minute and fifty seconds and the General is becoming bored. He motions to his men to begin shooting. There is still a group of youths determined to retrieve something of value, their eyes drawn to the Mercedes silver insignia rising proudly from the bonnet of every car. Suddenly, their bodies explode, lumps of flesh ricocheting off the walls.

It is over. He's unhurt. The Manager steps out of the metal utility closet where they keep the microfibre polishing cloths that Dynamo Motors proudly gives each customer to maintain the sheen of their new vehicles. He wants to shoot the asshole who beat him up. Shoot him in the butt. With a gun like that he could finally get some respect, quit this stupid job and make things happen. All he can think about is the gun.

During this pause in the atrocities, the kombi driver sees his opportunity and sprints to the back room, which is small with a two-plate electric stove, a half-full box of Tanganda tea, and a white Defy refrigerator. The back door is open and he runs out into the daylight, into freedom.

The soldiers haul off those still living to jail. Who knows when they will be released? Who knows if anyone will ever know they've been thrown in jail? If they have connections to people in power, they will be out within a day or two, ready to rejoin the Youth Brigade.

The General looks around the room with satisfaction and orders his men to remove the bodies and dump them into the truck. Then he turns to the Manager and says, 'In the beginning you whites fought against this Indigenisation Act that requires a fifty-one percent partnership with Zimbabweans. Now you can see that it's a good thing. Sir, tell your boss that I work hard for my fifty-one percent. Kindly send the profit check by the end of the month.'

Returning to the Manager's desk he reaches for his gun. His hand closes on air. 'Where is my gun?' he bellows. The soldiers look at each other, baffled. 'Find my gun, now!' the General shouts. The men begin to look in all the places a gun might fall in the heat of battle, pushing aside any body parts that might obscure the gun from view.

The kombi driver is breathing hard from what he has witnessed in the last two minutes of his life. Running to the kombi, parked nearby in a side alley, he removes a crumpled knapsack from under the seat. He pulls out a casual but fashionable dress, flat women's shoes, a padded bra and make-up. He quickly begins to change. His legs are smooth and hairless. The dress falls, appropriately, just below the knee and shows off the curves of the padded bra. He puts on the wig, secures it, and takes one last look at himself in the rear view mirror before closing and locking the kombi. The sun illuminates the silver lettering on the windscreen which proclaims, '*God Knows*'. She smiles, takes out a tissue and wipes a bit of lipstick from her front tooth. There is considerable room between her flat chest and where the padding of the bra begins.

The General will have his gun. It is the backbone of this country. But they cannot find the gun. In all his years of fighting, even post-independence, vanquishing the opposition, ensuring peace in this land, the General always had the gun by his side. It has never left him. The golden gun was a gift from his most trusted soldiers, honouring his years of leadership. He added the Marange diamonds when he was put in charge of security for the mine. This gun gave him a second honeymoon when he returned from two years in the DRC, co-ordinating military operations. His marriage had cooled and grown distant over those years. But when he showed his wife his golden gun, the barrel highlighted with diamonds, she fell in love with it and with him, again. In the bedroom, she would twirl the gun while seductively moving her hips. He must have that gun!

The General is whipping himself into a fury. And then, he remembers how the Manager had been captivated by his gun. Like a hungry man staring at food that he has no money to buy. He faces the Manager and looks him in the eye for several long seconds. 'Where's my gun!' he demands. The Manager does not flinch from his gaze. He orders his soldiers to search him. 'Where's my gun?' he repeats with increasing anger. The General receives no response, just the unflinching gaze of the Manager. 'You can usually trust a white man,' he thinks but his intuition tells him that if this man doesn't have the gun, he knows who took it. 'Handcuff him to the jeep,' he commands his soldiers.

As the soldiers roughly escort him from the showroom, the Manager halts in front of the General, 'What has this country done to us?' he says with a mixture of vehemence and bewilderment. Laughing, the General replies, 'You have it all wrong. What has this country done to you? Not us! I'm doing very well, thank you.' Thinking about who he will interrogate next, the General walks away.

Mr Mpofu, the tea-boy, observes the proceedings with an impassive face, hopeful that the General will never find the answer. The tea-boy has had enough. He calmly exits Dynamo Motors. He will not be making tea there anytime soon, he thinks to himself.

The soldier who had his eye on the General's gun is happy. He hums as he drags deceased members of the Youth Brigade from the car dealership and throws them into the truck.

The army continues to investigate, stopping and searching passers-by and kicking in the doors of various houses and flats in the neighbourhood. They carefully search all the restaurants and cafes in the area and anyone who'd stood watching the events that transpired at Dynamo Motors is dragged into the interrogation room.

The kombi driver, Tafadzwa, or Tati, as her transgender friends call her, walks leisurely down Fifth Street, her hips lilting in the sunlight. Tati doesn't want to draw attention to herself, but she has a lithe beauty that men notice. She makes a right turn into Chitepo Avenue, arriving at a rather dilapidated building. There's the bass sound of disco music emanating from three floors above. Tati begins to climb the stairs to the tiny flat. The lift has long ago stopped functioning.

There's a lively party going on at Tati's flat, though it is only two in the afternoon. A strobe light reflects off a red disco ball, creating the effect of crimson lightning. All her friends are there. Some have done a poor job shaving their faces, others have carelessly applied their make-up (Tati makes a note to sit them down for a make-over lesson), but they're all in their best party dresses so their dereliction can be excused. Some are slinky, some are bony, some are overly muscular, but they're all women. They revel in their gender. Some skitter across the dance floor on high heels, while others perform highly sexual moves.

Tati walks over to the group gathered in the lounge. She sits down. Removing an object from the space between her chest and her bra, Tati shows all her friends – the gun. It is surprisingly light for a weapon. One woman strokes the barrel, loving its smoothness. She compares the gun to the male organ which they all possess. 'I would much rather have the gun! And what I could do with those diamonds!' she says marvelling. Another woman puts out her hands, almost in supplication. The gun, a holy item, is placed in her two palms. She smells it, then licks the barrel, to screams of delight from the other women. They are cheering and effortlessly hoist Tati onto their shoulders while she swings the gun around and around in circles.

They're dancing. 'I got the power!' they sing. They are delirious with pleasure and laughter, singing louder and louder. They all worship the gun. There's a knock on the door. There is a volley of strong knocks on the door. There is the crunching sound of wood being splintered by rifle butts. Tati keeps dancing. They all keep dancing. All her friends singing together, 'I got the power!'

23

The Grim Reaper's Car

Nevanji Madanhire

My fingers are itchy. It must be the rats. I didn't wash my hands last night after supper; mother didn't notice. I wonder why? Mother has always said that if I didn't wash my hands after supper the rats would nibble at them all night. There are so many rats in our house. I see them every day, coming from under the cardboard box that contains our clothes. There is also a hole in the corner of our house. I saw them last night, darting in and out of it. All rushing towards my fingers. They were big. One was the size of a cat. It darted towards me, its whiskers long and sharp like a porcupine's quills. Its mouth was sharp too, with protruding teeth. They were long and sharp just like father's *okapi*. I couldn't scream or move away when its slimy tongue licked my fingers. It must be the witches that froze my muscles because why, otherwise, couldn't I scream?

But father should do something about the holes through which the rats come into our house. He only says the house is too old to be repaired. He accuses the colonialists for having built such houses for black people. But I think if only he could buy a bag of cement he could make a few bricks and plug the holes with them. Our house is no different from the next one, or from the hundreds of others that make up this place called Tafara.

Tafara. It means happiness. They say the place was given the name because so many years ago, before even my father's father was born, black people did not have houses to live in. I think they lived in shacks at mines or around the towns where they worked. Those who were lucky and worked for white people as cooks lived behind the white people's homes. They were lucky because they were also given food by the whites. So the story goes something like this: the whites saw that their suburbs were getting crowded so they decided to build a home for their workers. And when these houses were built and given to the workers, the workers were very pleased, hence they called this place Tafara. But that's many years ago.

They say in fact, in books, the place was originally called Single Quarters. That means the men who lived here were not allowed to bring their wives. So the houses are very small. It's only one room really but recently we were allowed to extend them. Mother added a small kitchenette but she does not cook in it any longer. It has become the children's bedroom. So she does all the cooking outside, in a shack made of plastic. But that is okay. Everyone has a similar structure in their yard. It has no windows, so when mother is cooking in it we children would be playing outside because, as she puts it, 'The air in here is not enough for all of us to breathe.'

But when it rains, as it is doing these days, she cooks in the house because it does not rain in the house.

I am not going to school today. It's because of the fever. Mother says I have got a fever. She says it's hot on my forehead but I don't see what's wrong with a little warmth because I am cold. But the rats. Why doesn't father trap them, or buy some of that stuff they say kills them. The tin even says 'Keep Out of Reach of Children'. If it can kill children surely it can kill rats. Father insists that there is nothing he can do about the rats. He says they have always been part of the house. Always, that is, since he was a child himself.

I think the rats come from the fields. Yes, they come from the fields because that is where we grow maize and rats love maize. Now that everyone has harvested their maize the rats follow us to our homes and eat the maize, or if they cannot find any they eat the mealie-meal. So we can't win. We harvest our maize so the rats cannot eat it but they follow us to our homes and eat our harvest.

They are not really fields. Just patches of land that the municipality has not decided how to use. We are not even allowed to grow crops on the patches of land. In fact there is a sign that says: 'Growing crops here is illegal. All crops will be destroyed.' Sometimes they destroy the crops but most times they don't, especially during the council elections which come every two years.

In rural areas they build grain stores away from the houses so the rats remain there. Only in rural areas they do not call them rats. They call them mice. They hunt them and eat them. They say they are delicious. I tried one and vomited so much mother had to give me a solution of sugar and salt. But she enjoyed them. She said that in her childhood she used to trap them in the fields.

We haven't been going to the rural areas recently. Father hates the place. He says it reminds him of poverty and witchcraft, but mother says it is because he failed to build even a hut because of laziness so he is ashamed because all other men of his age have decent homes. I don't blame father. I hate the place too. I think it's better to be poor in the town than to be poor in the rural areas. I don't know why.

Could father have been a child once? Without the beard? Without the ginger hair? Without the veins that stand out on his hands? With a set of clean white teeth and two white eyes? I think he is afraid of the rats himself. As scared as I am when they come nibbling at my fingers in my sleep. Because why for example did he open his okapi when we heard a noise behind the cardboard box the other day? It was only rats! But his eyes popped out like those of a rat that has been kicked against the wall and is dying.

Today is Wednesday. There will be an assembly at school today; I will miss that because we sing the national anthem on Wednesdays. God Bless our land which we won through the blood of our gallant fighters. Father says he was one of the gallant fighters but I don't believe it because he is so afraid of the rats. Scared of them as they come to nibble at his fingers. But father always cleans his hands after supper. And I will miss the assembly. The headmaster addresses pupils every Wednesday.

'Good morning, school,' says he.

'Good morning, Sir,' say we.

'How are you?' says he.

'Very well thank you and how are you,' we say.

I had a fever last Wednesday and my jersey was wet because of the drizzle.

I think I am oversleeping. And I haven't gone to the toilet yet. People must go to the toilet first thing every morning. Mother says the morning wee cleans away the demons of the night. But mine is hot, it must be because of the fever. Yesterday I nearly cried because of it. I am afraid I might cry. My stool, too, was hot yesterday, and watery and yellowish. It must be the demons.

Mother has gone to the market to sell tomatoes. She never puts tomatoes in our vegetables. She says they are all for sale. I wonder why she doesn't sell salted nuts. Amai Pupu does. They sell very fast. At the market people say they sell fast because she soaks them in her child's wee before frying them. They sell at a dollar per handful. Mother should do the same. She should use Tati's wee, or mine. But mine is so hot and yellowish I think customers would get the smell. Young kids' wee does not smell. If she doesn't want to sell the nuts herself, I will do so on my own.

The idea of me selling nuts is not bad. One dollar per measure. I would not know what to do with that money. I would buy myself a white dress like Pupu's, with lace all over, and a pair of black stilettos. Then, maybe, I would go to church. I would also buy mother a similar dress and similar shoes. For father I would buy a packet of decent cigarettes. American Toasted Milds. Then I would save a dollar a day.

Three hundred and sixty five and a quarter dollars per year!

The other day we went into town. Mother said we were going to see a doctor. But when we came out of the doctor's he had done nothing to me. No injection, which was a relief.

No pills either. Mother said the doctor was too expensive.

But, outside the doctor's was a beautiful shop. I did some window-shopping. I liked the TVs. We sometimes watch TV next door. The other day we saw the president. It was on Independence Day. The president fought for freedom, not father. If father is right that he too fought for freedom why doesn't he wear a black suit, a white shirt and red tie? I can imagine our president holding a big gun; like Rambo's.

We saw Rambo at the community hall last month. I think Rambo was just imitating our president, for how could he shoot so many people if he was not imitating our president?

The TVs were expensive. The smallest one cost $150,000. But if I sell nuts and save a dollar a day, we can still buy it. I won't give up until we buy the TV. Then we would see our president from our own house. I wish I could see him one day holding the big gun as he used to do when he shot all the white settlers.

I am a born-free. That means, when I was born, the president had already killed all the settlers.

Oh, it's still Wednesday. I slept and then I thought it was the following day. I woke because of the dream. There was a big black car, it stopped by and a man looked out through the window and said: 'Let the children come to me.' It was our president but why didn't he have eyes in his sockets? And I didn't like the look of his smile. It was too … toothy.

I have missed assembly. I should have seen all the Misses today in their colourful dresses. They dress best on Wednesdays. I don't know why. But I like Miss Ndoro's hair. She puts rollers in it every night and when she removes them in the morning the hair falls back in waves. I won't need rollers when I grow up. My hair is soft and wavy. I mean since the beginning of the year. I think I am growing up. And I am in Grade 5. Next year I will be in Grade 6. And then I will be in Grade 7.

I think I should go to the toilet now.

Mother hasn't returned from the market yet. I am not hungry but I haven't eaten anything since morning. Anyway this is not the first time I have felt that way. Mother forces me to eat when she comes back from the market but the more I force the food down my throat the more I feel like throwing it up. I think I am not hungry.

Father has not come back either. I don't know where he is. I don't know how he spends his days.

Tati is slung on mother's back and enjoying himself. I don't think he ever feels hungry because as soon as he begins to cry mother puts her breast into his mouth and he tugs at it with his hands and begins to suckle. Sometimes it's as if he is chewing the breast. I think it's made of rubber because Tati's teeth are sharp.

It's time to take my Cafenols. A few years ago mother used to give me the pink sweet ones. Now she says I am grown up, so I have to take the white bitter ones … they are bitter. Mother buys them in piles. They are always in packets of three. One, three times a day. At first I used to just close my eyes and swallow them down with water. Now they stick on my tongue. No matter how much I try to flick them to the back of my mouth they stick on my tongue and begin to melt. They are bitter. I tried another trick. I dissolved them in water and tried to gulp the solution down. It was terrible. I tried to wrap them in a morsel of sadza and swallow them, but they still stuck in my throat. Now when mother is away I just don't bother. I just throw them down the toilet. But when she is here … Oh. They say the tongue is what tastes stuff. I have never been able to avoid the tongue. I wish she would give me those pink sweet ones. I can't be that old, can I?

Mother must be coming any time now. This is about the time she prepares the evening meal. I think it's a trick. She does not want to cook the afternoon meal and the evening meal. She cooks sometime between the time she is supposed to cook the afternoon meal and the evening meal. It looks like everyone down the street has followed her example. Or, is it that she has copied everyone else's example? So mother is coming in any time now to prepare our lupper. I think the word lupper is known only in our street.

But I don't think I will have lupper tonight.

Father normally comes home a little later than mother. I think it's also a trick. He knows his meal will be ready and mother would have brought some money from the market. After eating he always asks for money from mother. She always says she does not have any. I don't believe her because the basket in which she carries the tomatoes and the vegetables will be empty, or almost empty. Then how can she say she does not have money? She does not look good with those black eyes.

But why can't father get a job? Pupu's father works. If father really fought and chased away the white settlers he should get a good job. The white settlers had good jobs, so we are told. I don't think father chased away the settlers because, otherwise, he would have a job.

Mother has just walked in. Long time back I would have run to her and taken her basket from her or at least carried little Tati. Now I don't have the power in my joints to do that. Mother understands. But she is always angry when she comes in. I can hear it in her voice.

'Have you taken your pills?' she asks with fire in her voice.

'Yes, mother,' I say, hoping they have dissolved thoroughly in the toilet bowl.

'If you lie to me and you have not taken those pills you will die,' she says.

She walks towards me and feels my forehead.

'Still hot,' she says. 'You are not going to school again tomorrow.'

Tomorrow is sports day. I will miss sports. I am good at high jump. I compete for my house. My house is called Tembwe. The others are Mugagawu, Mboroma and Chimoyo. Father says they are the names of great places. I don't believe him because in Geography the only great places are Great Zimbabwe, the Victoria Falls, Matopos and the Hwange National Park.

I would like to go to the Victoria Falls one day to see the angels flying to heaven.

Mother has lit the paraffin stove. I can smell the paraffin. It makes me feel dizzy. I can smell it in the food when we eat it. I can also smell it in my clothes and in the blankets. It makes me dizzy. Why can't we buy an electric stove that does not have the smell of paraffin? Why can't we buy anything?

Mother is going to cook dried kapenta again. I hate it. I think she should cut away the heads first before cooking. I think it's in their eyes that the smell comes from. And they stare at you so much as you eat them. I close my eyes whenever I bring them to my mouth.

She won't put tomatoes in the kapenta. She says all the tomatoes are for sale. The onions too, and the vegetables. She does not add anything because the kapenta is salted already. I think that is why she alone loves kapenta.

Father doesn't seem to like kapenta either. He is always cursing saying he wishes the war would come back. He says they used to eat nothing but chicken during the war. But where did he get the chicken in the bush? I think he will be lying. That is why I don't think he fought the war.

Mother wants to bathe me but the water is cold. She says she won't warm it because we will run out of paraffin and paraffin is so expensive these days. I hate cold water. I think my fever comes out of it. She says bathing is healthy and cold water is best for sick people. I don't believe it. I can't refuse to take the bath because she will become angry and slap me. I will wrap myself in the blanket afterwards and sleep. I wish they could give me an extra blanket.

I failed to eat the kapenta. Anyway, I am not hungry.

Father has already walked out. He did not eat too. He cursed and cursed.

'Can't there ever be just a piece of meat for the father of the house?' he said as he slammed the door shut.

'Do you want me to go and whore?' mother shouted after him when she was sure he would not hear her.

What is to whore? When I told her the other day that I needed another blanket she said, 'Do you want me to go and whore?'

I didn't have the bath after all. Mother said it would kill me because the water was too cold. But she boiled a cupful of water on the stove. She said that would not waste that much paraffin. She then soaked my towel in the hot water and dry-cleaned me. That's what she called it. She did the same with Tati. She herself had a proper bath with cold water.

I am all wrapped up in my blanket now but I am dizzy because of the paraffin. I can smell it everywhere. Mother is singing a lullaby for Tati. I think the song is funny.

I had good luck today
I picked a button on the road
etcetera

It is funny, the song, I mean.

I am sleepy. I think the lullaby is for me too.

I am cold. I think mother will give me an extra blanket.

I had dozed off. That man in the big black car came again and said: 'Let the children come to me.' He smiled. All those big white teeth and empty sockets. No eyes. But was it our president? I think so, but I am not sure this time. If I go into that big car, what happens?

Mother will give me an extra blanket. It looked warm in that big black car.

Father is holding a gun. He is shouting, saying he is fighting for freedom. Mother does not listen. She looks aside but father holds her shoulder and says: 'Can't you see I am fighting for freedom.' The gun is only Pupu's toy and shoots water. Of course he is not fighting for freedom; he just wants mother to give him some money so he can go and buy a scud. He shoots at mother, with water.

Tati crouches by the vegetable bed. His belly is full. It is big but nothing comes out of it. I think mother should give him fresh milk. I once drank fresh milk myself and I was able to go to the toilet. If I get into that big black car will Tati know? I think it's warm in the car. Father has bought himself a scud. He is calling me saying: 'Let the children come to me.' Of course no children like the smell of a scud. I won't come to you, father.

I am tired. I have been walking so long. But where am I going? I should be at school by now but this road is endless. I have been walking and walking. Perhaps I should go back home. Mother said I should not go to school today. I will rest.

I can hear sirens in the distance. It must be the president. The big black car is coming. I will just stand by and wave. I love the president. He set us free. I am a born-free.

The first motor-bike has passed, its siren blaring away. Then the next. Then the next. Then the black car. It stops. The president has stopped for me. But will Tati know? Will anybody know that I have gone with the president? The president opens up his arms; and smiles and beckons at me saying: 'Let the children come to me.' He smiles his toothy smile. His eyes are deep in their sockets. I am going. It's warm in the big black car. But will Tati know?

Annotations:
Comments, Study Tasks & Further Reading

01 *Queues* – Shimmer Chinodya

Notes

GMB: Grain Marketing Board.

Hazvina, Memory, Nontokozo: womens' names.

Chaminuka: pre-colonial spirit medium, remembered for predicting and trying to withstand the country's colonisation.

Nehanda: spirit medium (c. 1840-1898), active in the first Chimurenga (1896-7), remembered as an inspiration in the second Chimurenga (1966-1979). Cf. note 6 in our 'Introduction'; cf. also *Nehanda* (1993), a novel by Yvonne Vera.

Bedford: type of army truck.

hunhuism: a philosophical concept like to ubuntuism, which propagates a particular kind of African humanism. Cf. *Hunhuism or Ubuntuism: A Zimbabwe Indigenous Political Philosophy* (1980) by Stanlake J. W. T. Samkange.

Clopas Wandai J. Tichafa: is a character in Chinodya's novel *Harvest of Thorns* (1989), whose partially epistolary courtship of his wife illuminates an era with the precision and delicacy of a great comic artist.

freezit: a frozen drink sucked from in a thin pipe-shaped plastic bag.

Comment

Shimmer Chinodya's story 'Queues' weaves together two narratives: a 'personalised' history of Rhodesia and Zimbabwe from the mid-1970s to the end of the millennium and a story of a man and a woman falling in and, subsequently, out of love with each other. The former comprises a subjective version of the anti-colonial struggle with all its ideological tropes, the auspicious beginnings after the country's independence in 1980 and the slow, but apparently inevitable, downfall of post-colonial Zimbabwe. In the latter, two people, not young, but already in possession of a certain amount of life experience – a widow with a daughter and an unhappily married man with a family – are having what he describes as an 'affair', while the woman clearly expects more. Eventually, neither do the lovers' expectations match, nor do their personal circumstances allow a happy ending.

While these two narratives cleverly delineate the specific properties of the individual and the collective, the personal and the political as well as their precarious interdependence, the potential 'parallels' in meaning of the two processes are anything but obvious. One of the striking *literary* aspects of the text is Chinodya's use of rhetoric. More than once, he links the two narratives by means of diaphora: a word or an expression used at the end of one narrative is used again (or resumed) at the beginning of the other, albeit with a slight shift in meaning owed to the different context. For example:

I wondered if she was worth the effort, if she was not chained too much to propriety; why I needed to be with her, why she readily let me pay the bill, what it would take to make her unshackle *herself from herself.*

We declared independence, after that long bitter war, in 1980. In the late 80s we tried to **unshackle** ourselves from the past. Out went the chains of the old constitution and in came the new.

Or:

We **thirsted** for education.

I had begun to **thirst** *for her.*

Or:

Rudo [Shona: love] glowed with pride. She was happy to have me, to have Jean. To have **friends.**

After the thorny land business, we quickly lost our **friends.**

Although this procedure may appear somewhat laboured, it points to the wide range which language offers (and the complex limits it sets) its users in personal and group (for example, political) communication.

It is surely worthwhile pondering the difference between personal and political 'friends', between 'thirsting' for a person and something like education, but where, to what extent and in what respect do these concepts overlap?

Towards the end of 'Queues', another rhetorical means is employed to emphasise the monotony and, at the same time, the overwhelming complexity of the daily struggle to make ends meet, when the protagonist has to wait (to queue!) for a whole day to get 20 litres of petrol for his car. The anaphoric use of 'we talk about …' – seventeen times in one paragraph – impressively illustrates the host of problems Zimbabweans have to deal with: petrol, food, money, alcoholism, illnesses and so on and so forth.

The ending of the story appears to be resigned even gloomy. And yet, the lessons assigned to, but only partly and grudgingly learned by the male protagonist who clings to the liberation narrative, who feels spurred on as well as unnerved by his female other, who is willing to move on, can serve, personally and politically, as touchstones for a different (and, perhaps, better) life.

Study tasks

Politics in Zimbabwe has always been profoundly influenced by the ideologies of independence underpinned by over a decade of a bitter civil war, and government has never been able to shake itself free of the strugglist mantras.

- Consider some of the political divides that inform the outlook of these two different but not dissimilar protagonists.
- Compare the 'personalised', subjective history of Zimbabwe with the account provided in the Introduction. How do they inform each other? Which feels more real?
- Discuss what you regard as 'parallels' between the historical account and the lovers' story.
- Which aspects of the author's style and language are most effective, why?

Further reading

Beniah Munengwa's short article 'Chinodya's Queues still mirrors Zim's problems'. *NewsDay*, November 27, 2018 (https://www.newsday.co.zw/2018/11/chinodyas-queues-still-mirrors-zims-problems-15-years-later/), highlights the topicality of the story.

02: *Fancy Dress* – Alexandra Fuller

Notes

tutu: short, stiff, flared skirt, often made of net and starched, worn by ballerinas.

brookies: knickers; briefs, underpants.

Burma valley: an area on the border between Zimbabwe and Mozambique.

Pronutro: South-African whole grain breakfast cereal.

biltong: dried, cured meat.

Afrikaner: Afrikaans-speaking person, descendent of white Dutch settlers in South Africa.

cowardy custard: an epithet often used by children to accuse each other of cowardice, and sung as a rhyme 'Cowardy cowardy custard, you can't eat the mustard' etc.

under-rods: (slang) brookies for boys.

boomslang: tree snake.

picannin (piccanin): a small black child; originally from the Portuguese 'pequino', adopted into *Chilapalapa*, a bastardised simplified language drawn from different African language groups, and first used on the mines in colonial Africa. Seen as the 'language' of the oppressor who could not speak or learn any authentic African language.

ridgeback: a hunting dog first bred in southern Africa.

munt: (Rhodesian slang) derog. term for black African.

pukka British: (Anglo-Indian) truly, genuinely British.

Affies: (Rhodesian slang) derog. term for black Africans.

sis: (Rhodesian slang) epithet indicating disgust.

Pom: (Rhodesian slang) a 'Brit', someone from the UK.

Comment

This is a story about the class, cultural, language and racial barriers between individuals and groups of people – and if and how they may be overcome. It is narrated from the perspective of Alison, a perhaps ten-year-old little white girl who, however, is blessed with the ironic clairvoyance of an adult. The societal fault lines of 1970s Rhodesia are demonstrated in the context of a children's fancy-dress party. On the one hand, there is – with regard to skin colour – the white-black divide, on the other, even starker, the split between white and white. The latter manifests itself in various forms: richer whites vs. poorer whites and Afrikaner vs. British-born colonials. Alison, miserable from the very beginning because her mother bullies her into going not as a princess in pink, but as a rather bitter metaphor, whom surely no one will understand. Wearing a drum that once contained pesticide, and a wilting rose, Alison is mocked and ostracised by the other children, as she knew she would be. Meantime, the poison the drum once contained makes her skin itch and burn. The only person who recognises her plight and does something about it, is the Nanny, a practical black woman. The denouement is as swift as it is unexpected in bringing to the fore all the latent but powerful prejudices.

What we find so valuable in the story is its ostensibly artless, but at the same time charged atmosphere of a child exposed to the bigotries of the adult world, vulnerable but aware. It is this atmosphere that stays with the reader – as well as the perhaps unanswerable question if the price Alison has to pay for her act of courage is too high, acceptable or unimportant. Who can judge but Alison herself? But *can* she judge, being as young as she is? If not, how long should she wait? And if she waited however long, would she still have the courage she had when she was young?

Study tasks

- Try to describe the dilemmas Alison finds herself in when (i) she arrives at the fancy dress party, (ii) she is ostracised by the other

children, (iii) she is pitied by the very competent warm-hearted nanny, (iv) she is scolded by the hostess?
- What is the role and attitude of her mother?
- Develop alternative strategies for her.

Further reading

Partially as a result of the chimurenga war, and the necessity of all war to reduce the opposing sides to a simple paradigm, whites in Rhodesia and now in Zimbabwe are often understood as one undivided homogenous entity. To get a sense of this more complex whole, we suggest you read:

Don't Let's Go to the Dogs Tonight – Alexandra Fuller
Absent: the English Teacher – John Eppel
Those Lying Days – Nadine Gordimer (set in South Africa, it could well have been in Rhodesia in the fifties)
Mukiwa – Peter Godwin
The Grass is Singing – Doris Lessing

03: *That Special Place* – Freedom Nyamubaya

Notes

java-print dress: dress with a strong distinctive design, the word originally comes from the Indonesian island of Java.

Tembwe Training Camp, in the remote areas of Tête Province in Mozambique which borders on northern Zimbabwe.

JoJo the Clown: the name given to a clown who offers his services at children's parties, festivals, etc.

Frelimo: the Mozambique Liberation Front (*Frente de Libertação de Moçambique*).

Mbuya Nehanda: *mbuya*: grandmother; Nehanda: spirit medium (c. 1840-98), active in the First Chimurenga (1896-7), remembered as an inspiration in the Second Chimurenga (1966-79). Cf. also *Nehanda* (1993), a novel by Yvonne Vera.

Comment

Told from the perspective of a fifteen-year-old girl who leaves school to join the liberation struggle, it is a narrative of physical torture, sexual abuse and mental humiliation meted out by group of freedom fighters who are supposed to be 'liberating' the country from oppression. In this manner, the text is not just about torture and the temporary relief that food, music and timid human solidarity may offer, but rather about brute force and scheming violence of one person against another – represented here by the 'beast Nyathi', but active principally everywhere.

We wondered about the title: a special place can be a 'place of honour'; it may also mean an 'exceptional position'. We need to remember that there were divides within ZANLA[1], one of which manifested itself between those with education (even as little as two years of high school) and those without. It was all too often assumed that the educated cadre who joined the struggle was a putative Smith informer, and had to be hard-tested to ensure that he or she was not.

But the concentration camp-like situation at Tembwe Training Camp is diametrically opposite to any place of honour and if the prisoners occupy any exceptional position it is that of being treated as the lowest of the low. But perhaps 'that special place' is just that: a literal no-man's-land where no man or woman is allowed to exist, where goodwill and idealism cannot survive and where no human individuality is allowed to live.

Further reading

Guns and Guerrilla Girls: Women in the Zimbabwean Liberation Struggle – Tanya Lyons

For Better or Worse: Women and ZANLA in the Zimbabwe's Liberation Struggle – Josephine Nhongo-Simbanegavi

Women of Resilience: the voices of women ex-combatants compiled by Zimbabwe Women Writers

Mothers of the Revolution compiled and edited Irene Staunton

Echoing Silences – Alexander Kanengoni

---

1 The Zimbabwe African National Liberation Army.

Pawns – Charles Samupindi
Bones – Chenjerai Hove
Kandaya – Angus Shaw

Study tasks

- Try to feel into the protagonist's tale as much as is possible for you. Imagine how you would react if you were to meet the 'beast Nyathi' again, this time in the context of a hearing of a Truth and Reconciliation Commission.

- Could it be argued that the title is simply ironic?

- People who go to war to defend or free their country are often heroized on their return. How necessary is this? Is it subconsciously a way of protecting a wounded nation from having to relive the brutalities of war? Consider how long it takes in any society for hard, realistic novels about war to appear?

- How important is it for any nation involved in war to have a 'truth commission'? Some societies offer healing or cleansing ceremonies to help heal those involved in war, whether as victim or perpetrator; others expect people to find their own path. What role should a state play in a society recovering from the traumas of war?

04: *Torn Posters* – Gugu Ndlovu

Notes

Pamberi ne ZANU-PF: forward with ZANU-PF.

HIM: allusion to Robert Mugabe.

the elections: the first post-independence elections of 1985.

Amandla awethu!: 'amandla' is a Zulu and Xhosa word meaning 'power'. It was used, first and foremost in the South-African struggle against apartheid, in a call and response format, with someone shouting 'amandla' and the crowd replying 'awethu' (= ours), i.e. 'the power is ours'. In a more general sense it means 'power to the people'.

Matabeleland: a region in the west and south-west of Zimbabwe.

'dissidents': In late 1982, political resistance to the government led by ZANU-PF developed in Matabeleland (where the majority of the Ndebele live). It was met by brutal oppression when, over the course of five years, an estimated 20,000 civilians were killed.[2] This onslaught was called *Gukurahundi*, a Shona expression meaning 'the first rains of the year that wash away rubbish'.

AK-47: an assault rifle, developed in the Soviet Union after WW2 by Mikhail Kalashnikov.

'Wot grrede rr u en?' 'Wot es yowa nem?': What grade are you in? What is your name?

Chikurubi Maximum Security Prison: prison on the outskirts of Harare notorious for its inhuman treatment of inmates and degrading conditions.

'constipating against the govament': What Thandi probably means is that her father was thought to have been *conspiring against the government*.

Mashonaland: region in northern Zimbabwe.

eesn't: isn't.

'Poot yowa things heeya.': Put your things here.

Comment

This multi-vocal narrative is set in the context of the *Gukurahundi* massacres of the 1980s. It is told from the perspectives of (i) a twelve-year-old girl (Gugu), (ii) her siblings (a brother, Bhuto, and a sister, Thandi) and (iii) their mother. The text graphically illustrates how children experience and react to military harassment and institutional repression. They have to come to terms with the fact that their father, a hero in their eyes, is accused of conspiring against the government and, as a consequence, imprisoned. When, after a year, they are allowed to visit him – we do not learn whether he ever stood trial or was thrown into jail without any court procedure – they hardly recognise him. The prison atmosphere is experienced by the children is stifling and the visit ends in a flood of tears – which the father tries

---

[2] See http://hrforumzim.org/wp-content/uploads/2010/06/breaking-the-silence.pdf

to still by exhorting them to remember that if the guards see them cry 'they will feel they have won over you'.

Gugu concludes that it is her 'patriotic duty [...] not to cry' and that there would be 'no checkmate' while she was alive. While we empathise with Gugu's resolution, we wonder whether she had (or, perhaps, wanted to have, but did not know) any alternatives.

Study tasks

This is another story where the voices of children are used to explore a reality, and where the different perspectives illuminate and complement each other. Because children are innocent, vulnerable, the potential harshness or cruelty of the situation they are in is rendered with greater intensity.

- The author and her main narrator share their first name. Should we read the story as if it were autobiography? What might that add to our understanding? Does fiction allow for greater detachment and less self-centredness?
- Consider all the detail around the election, the arrest of her father, the *Gukurahundi* massacres, how much fear from the atmosphere do you detect in the story?
- Collect information on the *Gukurahundi* massacres from one of the following videos:

    (i) https://www.youtube.com/watch?v=aMojwBuTtXY (ca. 10 mins.) or

    (ii) https://www.youtube.com/watch?v=n5VpQQGawAM (ca. 60 mins.).
- Try to find information on Chikurubi Maximum Security Prison and the treatment of prisoners there. You could also read and discuss Petina Gappah's *The Book of Memory* (2015) which is set in the prison.
- Read *Running with Mother* by Christopher Mlalazi.

05: *When the Moon Stares* – Christopher Mlalazi

Notes

Mamvura: Shona name of the mother.

Mashava: village in the Masvingo Province.

Comment

This story also addresses the *Gukurahundi* massacres. It is told from the perspective of a fourteen-year-old teenager, Rudo (meaning love), who, together with her mother, had to hide from soldiers of the Fifth Brigade who killed most of their relatives and devastated their village. When the raid is over, mother and daughter find another survivor ('Auntie') and together with her discover in one of the burnt-down huts under the charred bones of their relatives a trapdoor in the floor and in the hole below a baby, crying but unharmed. They recognise it as the youngest member of the family, Gift, hidden by his mother before the raid.

What we find impressive about the story is that the author chooses to depict the acts of murder and mayhem not directly, but indirectly: the reader does not witness the actual killings of people and burning of homesteads, but is confronted with the fear and anguish of three survivors – and with their relief, joy and thankfulness when they discover the baby. The thoughts and feelings of Rudo add a distinct poignancy to the events described in the text, which might feel odd amongst adults, but perfect for this adolescent girl.

It may be worthwhile to reflect on the fact that most of the few stories dealing with the *Gukurahundi* massacres are narrated from the perspectives of children: in 'Torn Posters' of a twelve-year old and in 'When the Moon Stares' of a fourteen-year old girl. Is it just by chance or is it, rather, that if an adult had narrated the story, the author would have had to avoid the criticism that the story was too melodramatic, sentimental and didactic, while a child's voice allows for innocence and ingenuousness?

Study Tasks

- In order to make certain points the authors works with repetitions. Find out where and when and how they work to enhance the text's meaning.
- What do you make of the title of the story?
- Christopher Mlalazi developed his story into the novel *Running with Mother* (2012), whose reading we would recommend. There is an informative interview with Mlalazi in *The Guardian* (https://www.theguardian.com/world/2013/aug/16/zimbabwe-running-with-mother-robert-mugabe).
- 'The war begins. A curfew is declared. A state of emergency. No movement is allowed. The cease-fire ceases. It begins in the streets, the burying of memory.' This is from Yvonne Vera's novel *The Stone Virgins* (2002) which also deals with the massacres. Discuss the tone of this sequence of sentences. Where is its climax? What does it mean?
- The most recent findings on *Gukurahundi* are to be found in a *Guardian* article of 2015: https://www.theguardian.com/world/2015/may/19/mugabe-zimbabwe-gukurahundi-massacre-matabeleland.

06: *The Trek* – Lawrence Hoba

Notes

trek: a journey or a trip, usually involving difficulty or hardship; the Great Trek: in South African history, the movement of Boer (originally Dutch) settlers between 1835 and 1845 from Cape Colony to escape British rule and settle in Natal and Transvaal. More generally speaking, in colonial times, the journey by white people to seize and settle African lands originally occupied by Africans. In an interview with *Munyori Literary Journal* (October 30, 2013), Lawrence Hoba reminds us that the land reforms of 2000 began with people going *en masse* onto the farms, normally organised in groups of villagers, townspeople and war veterans.

Annotations: Comments, Study Tasks & Further Reading

Some walked, some drove or were driven, some travelled in scotch carts. In one sense it was a reverse trek. Whereas the 1900s had seen the indigenous people fleeing the land, the early 2000s saw the whites being threatened and fleeing and the blacks resettling on land their forefathers used to occupy. This was more like the pioneer column which had trekked into the land in the late 1800s and invaded the same land (cf. http://munyori.org/lawrence-hoba-talks-about-his-short-story-collection/).

Zimuto: village in Zimbabwe's Masvingo Province; the Magudu family moves from there to the sugar farming belt in the low-veld region of Chiredzi.

NRZ: National Railways of Zimbabwe.

Black Commercial Farmer: Cf. http://www.cfuzim.org/~cfuzimb/index.php.

Malawi: landlocked country in southeast Africa, bordered by Zambia, Tanzania and Mozambique.

Comment

'The Trek' illustrates, from the perspective of a child narrator, what the land question (the fast-track land redistribution programme of 2000) involved on the level of an individual poor family whose head is 'given' a farm. While there is some spurious pride in re-possessing the land, the Magudu family is ill-equipped to take charge of the farm allocated to them. As they do not have any resources of their own and are not given either financial or institutional help, they cannot but fail in the endeavour. They are ejected from the farm and have to return to their former home.

With dry but gentle humour Hoba not only parodies the idea of 'the trek', but also criticises the government's handling of the land reform programme. Moreover, he also points to clearly visible deficits of the individual actors: 'Baba' Magudu is a work-shy, beer-drinking good-for-nothing, who maltreats his wife (and son) when he thinks fit, while 'Mama' Magudu tries to keep the family going, but cannot succeed when, after another attack from her husband, she cannot work on the land for months at a time.

Further reading

Lawrence Hoba developed this story into a collection of short stories, *The Trek and Other Stories* (2009). Read some more of these stories to expand your contextual knowledge of the land reform. There are two papers you may wish to consult: (1) Irikidzayi Manase, 'Lawrence Hoba's depiction of the post-2000 Zimbabwean land invasions in *The Trek and Other Stories*', *Tydskrif vir Letterkunde* 51,1 (2014), 5-17; (2) Terrence Musanga, 'Zimbabwe's land reform programme, migration and identity in Lawrence Hoba's *The Trek and Other Stories*', *African Identities* 15, 1 (2017), 3-13.

It might be worthwhile to find out more about the economic, social and political results of the land reform of 2000 (cf. Rachel L. Swarns, 'After Zimbabwe's Land Revolution, New Farmers Struggle and Starve', *The New York Times*, December 26, 2002; Lydia Polgreen, 'In Zimbabwe Land Takeover, a Golden Lining', *The New York Times*, July 20, 2012).

Study Tasks

- Reflect on how the land question and the gender problematic overlap and intensify each other.
- Examine the small carefully observed details in the story for its illumination of the larger picture. Give examples.
- What does Hoba's story tell us about the concept of 'farming'. How many meanings does the word contain from the mealie patch to the large diverse commercial project?
- When people occupied the lands, what kind of farming do you think they had in mind?

07: *The Sins of the Fathers* – Charles Mungoshi

Notes

Borrowdale: a wealthy northern suburb of Harare where rich and influential people live.

Mutukudzi: Oliver 'Tuku' Mutukudzi, Zimbabwe's most renowned musician and cultural icon.

Annotations: Comments, Study Tasks & Further Reading

Old Canaan, Highfield: an area within the high density area of Highfield, Harare.

Zezuru-Karanga: two different cultural groups each with a specific Shona dialect. The Zezuru are from central Zimbabwe, the Karanga live in the south.

Ruwa: a small town and an area south-east of Harare (on the road to Mutare).

Mabvuku turn-off: Mabvuku: a high-density area just outside Harare.

Chimurenga: In the Zimbabwean context, the Shona and Ndebele rebellions of 1896-97 are understood as the (First) *Chimurenga* (Shona for 'uprising'). The struggle for independence, which began in April 1966 and ended in December 1979, is called the (Second) *Chimurenga*. The carrying into effect of the 'Fast Track land reform' (2000) and the reorganisation of the state structures along authoritarian-nationalist lines running in parallel to it were ideologically presented by the government as the (Third) *Chimurenga*.

Manhize Mountains: if these 'mountains' exist, and they may, and they may be what we would call 'hills', they are in Chivhu, which bears little or no relation to the plot of the story except that it is Charles Mungoshi's home area. In other words they may be part of an imaginary or local myth.

Pazho people: see Manhize Mountains (above).

Comment

The first sentence catapults us into the story: 'Everyone had gone and they were now alone, Rondo Rwafa and his father, the ex-minister. Unknown to the father, the son – who'd never handled a gun before – had one in the inside pocket of his jacket. By the end of the day, he would shoot – or not shoot – his father.' Mr Rwafa, former Minister of Security, lays down *and* executes the law – *his* law – in his family and wherever else he can. And while he does not hesitate to employ thugs and murder to achieve his aims, he breaks up and eventually destroys his family (and himself).

On the one hand, this story is about the redistribution of land (as in 'The Trek'). Mr Rwafa has his eyes on a particular farm which he wants to snaffle before others can get their hands on it. In this respect, he stands in stark contrast to Basil Msamane, an MP and the father of his son's wife, who pleads for an orderly procedure. On the other, Mr Rwafa's hostility to Mr Msamane, has an earlier basis in that he regards Mr Msamane's Ndebele family as inferior to his own Shona clan – which is why he was against his son's marriage to Selina in the first place. When he is put to shame by Mr Msamane, he plots his (and his granddaughters') death …

Like 'That Special Place', this story is about the range of what people can do to each other, about the wounds and trauma that they can inflict on their bodies and souls. While there is no idea of 'healing' in 'That Special Place', there are moments in 'The Sins of the Fathers', for example, in Rondo's and Selina's relationship, which allow the reader hoping for their future.

Study Tasks

- Describe how the familial fissures represented in the text reflect on the national state of affairs and its associated discourse.
- How do you read the ending of the story, when Selina is prepared to shoot her father-in-law with a gun given to her by her mother-in-law?
- The stories in this collection often complement each other and in so doing help us to appreciation the complexities of history and society within Zimbabwe. Are there characters or attitudes in other stories that remind you of Mr Rwafa? Why? What do they have in common?
- To look at the wider context, you may want to consult the following paper: Jairos Gonye, Thamsanqa Moyo and Wellington Wasosa, 'Representations of the land reform programme in selected Zimbabwean short stories and Mutasa's *Sekai, Minda Tave Nayo* (*Sekai, We Now Have the Land*): A fait accompli?', *Journal of African Studies and Development* 4/9, December 2012, 207-217.

08: *Trespassers* – Chiedza Musengezi

Notes

chop chop: quick! quick!

Mutoko: village north-east of Harare.

Chikwaka Communal Lands: described as bordering 'the eastern side of Chapisa Farm'.

Mazowe: area north of Harare (near Mazowe dam).

Chichewa: a language spoken in Malawi.

Jumbo: village in the Mazowe valley about 10 km north-east of Mazowe.

ZBC: Zimbabwe Broadcasting Corporation.

Comment

Generally speaking, there are three parties concerned if land is to be redistributed: those who legally or illegally order the redistribution, those who receive the land and those who have to give it up. In this story the focus is on the latter, albeit in a complex way. The white farmer's family, after 'a century of work and investment', is told in no uncertain terms to leave the land. But so is Chembe, his foreman, born in Zimbabwe, but with a Malawian father. His pain is amplified by the facts that, on the one hand, he owes the white farmer his and his family's modestly comfortable existence and, on the other, one of his sons has joined the land occupiers.

The story successfully illustrates how easily people who want to do what they think is right can come into conflict. The white farmer's family has been on the land for about a century. We do not learn how his ancestors acquired the land. However, they and he have invested in the farm – not only economically, but also by establishing a small school for the children and building a clinic. Chembe is hardworking and reliable; he has worked on the farm for thirty-five years and the farmer trusts him. However, the hostility toward Chembe signifies a much larger problem.

After the Second World War, Southern Rhodesia industrialised and successfully developed commercial agriculture. They also benefitted economically from the brief period of Federation. Malawi and Mozambique by contrast remained relatively poor countries. Thus, just as Zimbabweans to South Africa today in search of work and 'greener pastures', so Malawians and Mozambicans had always come south and east in search of work in Rhodesia and then Zimbabwe. They were often welcomed as they were prepared to do work that many perhaps more educated Zimbabweans saw as demeaning. They settled in the country, often intermarried and had children here.

However, as has so often happened throughout history, when a ruling party or government feels threatened, they turn on people they suddenly decide to see as foreigners, with a different culture or religion or language. So, farm labourers were suddenly attacked as aliens, as it was assumed they were the white farmer's lackeys.[3] So, when the people of Mbare, the oldest high-density suburb in Harare, voted against the ruling party, they were attacked as 'totemless people'.[4]

Study Tasks

- Find out more about the conditions of labour migrants from Malawi in Zimbabwe.

- If you had to mediate between the three groups in the story, how would you proceed?

- If you want to learn more about the author, here is an interview with her: http://nai.uu.se/research/finalized_projects/cultural_images_in_and_of/zimbabwe/literature/musengezi/.

- Compare the three stories about the land invasions – 'The Sins of the Fathers', 'The Trek' and 'Tresspassers' – and consider how they problematise the concept of a single absolute narrative about the reasons for and the outcome of farm invasions.

---

3 See also *If Something is Wrong: the invisible suffering of farm workers* due to 'Land Reform'. GAPWUZ, Harare. 2010.

4 https://bulawayo24.com/index-id-opinion-sc-columnist-byo-152229.html

09: *Mainini Grace's Promise* – Valerie Tagwira

Comment

At the heart of this story is a mystery, an illness which is not named. While the reader quickly realises that this story is about AIDS and its repercussions[5], the story is told from the perspective of a fifteen-year old girl who has no knowledge of the disease. As a consequence, she remains in the dark – only to intuit the wretched circumstances she finds herself in at the last possible moment. More generally speaking, the story reflects circumstances very prevalent in Zimbabwe (but also other developing countries), where women, who either have no access to, or cannot afford, let alone persuade their menfolk to use condoms, are infected with HIV. In a socio-cultural context which easily permits men to have more sexual partners than women, women (who cannot protect themselves in the sexual act) are affected – literally: infected – by men who do not use suitable protection. Moreover, they have to bear the burdens of caring for the sick, looking after the orphans and, if they are infected, bearing name and shame.

Further reading

- Anna Chitando's dissertation 'Narrating Gender and Danger in Selected Zimbabwe Women's Writings on HIV and AIDS' (2011) discusses works by Virginia Phiri, Sharai Mukonoweshuro, Valerie Tagwira, Tendayi Westerhof and Lutanga Shaba (http://uir.ac.za/handle/10500/4707).

- *One Day This Will All Be Over: Growing up with HIV in an Eastern Zimbabwean Town* by Ross Parsons.

- Find out more about Valerie Tagwira and her views in an interview with her on the homepage of Weaver Press (http://weaverpresszimbabwe.com/authors/interviews/203-interview-valerie-tagwira-by-lizzy-attree).

---

5   In 2016, 1.3m Zimbabweans (an estimated 720,000 women) were living with HIV, the adult HIV prevalence being 13.5 per cent, the sixth highest in sub-Saharan Africa. See also 'Exploring Feminization of HIV/AIDS in Zimbabwe: A Literature Review', *Journal of Human Ecology*, 47, 2 (2014), 139-145.

Study Tasks

- Although economists may debate the point at which Zimbabwe's economy fell into recession, there is no doubt that the country has experienced decades of economic tribulation with the consequences mainly born by the poor and the middle classes. And many, perhaps most, families have splintered as people desperately search for a livelihood or education anywhere but home. In addition to this, families fell apart as a result of the AIDs, and the extended family, so often traditionally revered as providing a consistent support structure, also fell apart. Consider why Sarai is left so alone and unaided.

- During periods of desperation, Zimbabweans have fallen back on religion, the number of fundamentalist churches with charismatic preachers has grown exponentially; hope, and humour. How does Valerie Tagwira work the concept of 'hope' into her story, and what effect does this have on the reader?

- Valerie Tagwira is a gynaecologist, who has good reason to understand the multiple travails that women face. Her novel *The Uncertainty of Hope* (2006) explores the complex lives of two strong women under the shadow of the government's urban clearance programme (Operation *Murambatsvina*).

- With the exception of the doctor, all characters in the story are female. What does that signify?

10: *Message in a Bottle* – Isabelle Matambanadzo

Notes

Cobra: wax polish.

Talavera tiles: tiles of Spanish-Mexican origin.

UHT milk: long-life milk.

shweshwe skirts: cotton skirts printed with traditionally vibrant African patterns.

Bloomingdale: fictitious high-density suburb of Harare.

MFI: International Monetary Fund (IMF); the girl has transposed the letters.

Krango: very cheap, illegally brewed spirits (imported most probably from Mozambique).

Comment

Once more this is a story told from the perspective of a teenager, a fourteen-year-old girl. She describes her daily life with her mother in a densely populated suburb of Harare, their initially modest, but increasingly poor circumstances and the ways in which they try to support each other. Rare spots of light are the visits of Aunty Zina, who lives in Cape Town and apparently has enough money to treat them to good food and small items of luxury. But from the very beginning there also are allusions in the text which signal that the narrated events have been heading towards a catastrophe which, at the time of narration, makes it necessary for the nameless I-narrator to consult a psychiatrist. Step by step, we learn that one night, on her way home, her mother was brutally manhandled, abused and killed.

Tantalisingly, the narrative harbours several enigmas. First, the reader can only intuit that Aunty Zina has more money than the mother and daughter protagonists because she lives and works in South Africa. More importantly, there are only a few oblique references that help us to realise that Aunty Zina and the protagonist's mother were lovers – and this was the reason why she was killed. Finally, what was so 'special' in the way in which mother and daughter communicated?

It is possibly important to remember that single sex relationships are not welcomed in Zimbabwe. At best they are ignored, and a taboo subject remains taboo; at worst and usually for political, populist or religious reasons they are condemned as illegal, irreligious, and perfidious; and during such periods, gay people can feel very threatened. Robert Mugabe notoriously referred to gays and lesbians as worse than 'pigs and dogs'.[6] When a politician or a preacher mounts such an attack, it can act like a dog whistle implying that immunity

---

6 See https://www.ncbi.nlm.nih.gov/pubmed/20455134 and https://www.thepatriot.co.zw/old_posts/gays-worse-than-pigs-and-dogs/

will be afforded any perpetrators who decide to victimise the named group or individuals within it.

Study Tasks

- The intricate way, in which past events and present feeling are skilfully interlaced in the text, deserves special attention. The tone is set with the first paragraph: 'I felt the sinews of my mind stretch. And rip. This feeling took hold of me and wouldn't let me go. It came every time I thought about my mother and the things that happened to her that year. They'd tried to hide her from me, but we had our own special way of communicating. It had always been so.' What follows is a simple down-to-earth description of the girl coming home from school, which is brutally interrupted: 'My single bed pushed against the wall, was draped with a faded mint-green duvet. A teddy bear Mama had given me for my birthday rested its frayed head in the hollow of my pillow. She'd bought it from a lady who lugged sacks of second-hand toys from Mozambique. The psychiatrist had a similar bear, only new. He also had a mother, so how could he be sitting safely behind his big desk asking me how I felt?' It may be worthwhile following this dual perspective throughout the story and reflect on its construction as well as on its meaning.

- What are we supposed to make of the title? And of the message in the bottle given at the end of the text? Could it implicitly refer to the fact that, in Zimbabwe, being gay is illegal and also culturally taboo (cf. https://theconversation.com/zimbabwes-lgbt-community-why-civil-rights-and-health-issues-go-hand-in-hand-90546)?

- Listen to the author's statement (https://www.youtube.com/watch?v=hMEs3serWvg) on her self-understanding as an African feminist activist. Can it help to understand the story?

11: *Gold Digger* – Albert Gumbo

Notes

Mosi-O-Tunya: 'The Smoke which Thunders' (Kololo or Lozi language): the Victoria Falls on the Zambezi River.

D-grade O-levels: Secondary education in Zimbabwe is made up of two cycles, Ordinary Level (i.e. O-level), an exam taken at the end of form 4, and Advanced Level (A-level) at the end of form 6. Both exams are ranked by letter scale with 'A' as the best, 'D' as 'pass' and 'F' as 'fail'.

JC level: Junior Certificate level

Homelink money transfer: former agency of international money transfer.

Comment

This story pokes fun at two people, a young black Zimbabwean with limited means, and a young female Scandinavian tourist, each of whom sees the other as a stereotype of their race, gender and class. The former considers how he might woo the girl to take advantage of her comparative wealth and access to a foreign passport. The latter immediately feels pity for the man, who being black, must naturally be impoverished and exploited.

While we may be amused by the robust way in which the author explores these stereotyped figures and their behaviour, we are at the same time confronted by the serious questions he asks about the nature of humanity and the importance of being true to oneself.

Study Tasks

- Albert Gumbo is not only a writer, but also a political activist. Watch a recent statement of his: https://www.youtube.com/watch?v=7qWvqZynLak.
- Does Gumbo's statement enlighten the story?
- We have previously discussed the way in which in conflict or in war, the other side (whichever other side) is pilloried and reduced. These narrow bigoted definitions, rehearsed and repeated, allow

one to deny the other's humanity. In war this causes death, murder justified. How does a story like this, far removed from the context of conflict, allow us to explore and laugh at stereotype?

- How much of these stereotypes might be said to be partially true?

12: *A Land of Starving Millionaires* – Erasmus R. Chinyani

Notes

Usury: a revealing name, used here for comic effect.

'Mommy, Tadha-a! Mai, chaja-a, AMAI TIRIKUDA SADZA-A-A!!!' : Mum, we want sadza [we are starving hungry].

tuckshop: small shop or vending platform.

Comment

The title presents an apparent paradox: a 'starving millionaire'. But as this story of a small-scale money lender unfolds, we learn that he is struggling not only to collect his debts, but also to make ends meet for his family of three wives and twenty-nine children amidst family rows, evasive or absconding debtors and, most importantly, within an economy that is suffering from hyper-inflation with prices rising several times a day – and a dollar so worthless that it costs several hundred thousand of them to buy a loaf of bread.

Study Tasks

- Study closely how the author succeeds in mixing farcical, comic and tragic elements. Focus on the ending of the story.
- We have discussed how humour can offer salvation, restore dignity, diminish that which threatens to overcome. Zimbabweans have always been able to make the best of or to survive the most challenging situations through laughter. Discuss this idea in relation to this story.
- The topic of poverty is dealt with in many literary texts. To explore this field, you may want to consult Phenyo Butale, *Discourses of Poverty in Literature: Assessing representations of indigence in post-colonial texts from Botswana, Namibia and Zimbabwe*, PhD

Annotations: Comments, Study Tasks & Further Reading

Stellenbosch University 2015 (https://scholar.sun.ac.za).
- How does a re-reading of 'Queues' help you to contextualise this story?

Source: Arbeitskreis Harare-München-Partnerschaft, ed., *Simbabwe mit spitzer Feder. Politische Karikaturen seit der Unabhängigkeit/A Cartoonist's View of Zimbabwe. Political Cartoons since Independence*, München 2006, p. 40
- Consider the caricature above: can you find at least one other joke about hyper-inflation joke in Zimbabwe on the web. Put them together as a class. What does this tell us about what ordinary people have experienced? And how they are dealing/have dealt with the resultant hardships?

13: *The Donor's Visit* – Sekai Nzenza

Notes

Chiziviso ku chembere, shirikadzi ne nherera!: A message to old ladies, widows and orphans.

chi-one-day beer: a home-brew made in a 24-hour period, i.e. quite raw and strong.

sugar daddy: a man who has a sexual relationship with a markedly younger woman, who is usually materially rewarded, sometimes with a flat or 'small-house' or school/college fees.

Mugabe, Sithole, Muzorewa: Robert Mugabe is a politician who fought for Zimbabwe's independence and served as Prime Minister from 1980 to 1987 and then as President from 1987 to 2017. Ndabaningi Sithole founded Zimbabwe African National Union (ZANU) in August 1963 together with Herbert Chitepo, Robert Mugabe and Edgar Tekere. Abel Muzorewa served as Prime Minister of Zimbabwe Rhodesia 1979-80 in a transitional government before independence.

ZANU-PF: the ruling party in Zimbabwe since independence.

MDC: Movement of Democratic Change, the opposition.

pungwe: a meeting, usually held at night, and called by the freedom fighters during the struggle to exhort the villagers to support them. So-called traitors or 'sell-outs' could be and were judged and could be beaten or killed at the *pungwes*.

from Hwedza to Mazowe: villages north and south of Harare; the distance is roughly 200 km.

bira: ancestor worship ceremony.

Salisbury: Rhodesian capital, after independence: Harare.

Morgan Tsvangirai: a Zimbabwean politician (1952-2018), Prime Minister in the 'government of unity' (2009-2013). He was President of the Movement for Democratic Change – Tsvangirai (MDC-T) and a key figure in the opposition to former President Robert Mugabe.

Chembere one line! *Shirikadzi* one line! *Nherera* one line!: Old Women, Widows, Orphans.

muchakata tree: indigenous tree.

Blair toilet: a pit toilet of the 1970s.

bulgur: a cereal food made from the parboiled groats of several different wheat species.

Comment

'Today the donor's visit has given me food. But it has also taken Chiyevo away from me. I cannot tell Chiyevo what to do anymore.' This time, the narrator is an old woman, an *mbuya*, a grandmother, who is accompanied on her way to the food distribution by her seventeen-year-old granddaughter. As a grandmother, the narrator has a certain role in the education of her grandchildren. While they walk towards the centre, where the food is distributed, she reflects on the differences between things past and present, the changed roles of people and customs. Eventually, she will have to accept (more than grudgingly) that for example with regard to sex she cannot tell her granddaughter how to behave because she made her own decision to use condoms. She considers this to be a bad thing, but the reader will also have to think of the way in which her granddaughter is enabled to protect herself and claim greater autonomy in her relations with men.

It might be worthwhile reflecting on how the problematic of sexual relations is expanded in the story. At one time, the grandmother thinks: 'We are hungry, we are poor, but we still have a culture to follow.' What other cultural elements are described as being in the process of transformation?

Study Tasks

- What do you make of the following reflection: 'Truth. How much truth and how many times should we tell them what happened? How much truth should we leave out?'
- 'Right pocket for the ZANU-PF card and left Morgan Tsvangirai pocket for the MDC card.' Would you say the narrator is a pragmatist? Or is she a cynic? Or both?
- Can you think of comparable discussions with your grandparents?
- Examine the power relations between the donor and the villagers. Who else has power over them?

14: *The Rainbow Cardigan* – John Eppel

Comment

Siduduziwe (Dudu) and her brother Benson live, together with their grandmother, in Bulawayo. Strange as it may appear, their home is neither a house nor a shed: it is an empty swimming pool. Poverty has brought them so low. The children's parents died of AIDS many years ago. Their grandmother Ugogo enables them survive by means of her little knitting business. One of her knitting highlights is worn by Benson, a unique and colourful wool cardigan. When he fails to pass his O-Levels, Benson has to leave school for financial reasons. He follows the 'call' of newly discovered diamonds near Mutare. Surprisingly, he returns with about a dozen precious stones, which he swallows to carry out of the country to Botswana to sell them there. Wearing his shiny cardigan, he leaves with the promise to fetch Ugogo und Dudu as soon as he has turned the stones into money. But he never does.

Dudu finishes school; she is a curious student and a clever woman. But while being trained as a teacher, Ugogo has a stroke. As an invalid she cannot continue financing Dudu's education, but because Dudu is highly liked by her teacher, she is allowed to take part in one last field trip and some research. Outside of Bulawayo, Dudu observes and admires the Matopos area, its geological formation and bird-life. Following a weaver bird to a cliff and watching its nesting activities, she discovers the dead remains of Benson shrouded in his rainbow cardigan. Dudu is shocked, but when she wants to strew some sand on Benson's remains, she discovers the diamonds somewhere there where his bowels must have been. Back in the bus on the way home, those diamonds allow her to dream of a better life – just as Benson had promised.

Further reading

You can find further information on the political context of this story under (1) https://aidc.org.za/operation-hakudzokwi-happened-chiadzwa/ and (2) https://www.dailymail.co.uk/home/moslive/article-1213894/The-return-bloody-diamonds-Miners-gunpoint-

Zimbabwe.html. In the latter source, there is a map which marks the area.

There also is a good summary of what happened with regard to the blood diamonds under (3) https://www.theguardian.com/world/2010/jul/23/zimbabwe-blood-diamonds. Source (4) informs about Chinese-Zimbabwean relations: https://thediplomat.com/2017/11/diamonds-and-the-crocodile-chinas-role-in-the-zimbabwe-coup/.

Read other of John Eppel's novels. *Absent: The English Teacher* seriously considers the consequences of hyper-inflation using farce, upending stereotypic roles, making us laugh at the absurd while reflecting on how close it is to reality. It is a novel which begins with laughter and then a becomes very drawn to a character, turns serious.

Study tasks

- John Eppel, a poet,[7] is also a writer known for his use of irony and satire, and when the story begins we think it is likely to be a farce, why? However, it moves all too quickly from farce to a struggle for survival. Tease out these themes.

- Hope and humanity play their part in this story, how?

- Try to find out more about the Marange Diamond Fields, their discovery and history (Sources 1-3, above). Focus on the lives and working conditions of the 'illegal' panners and their lot following Mugabe's intervention 'Operation Hakudzokwi' in 2008.

- If you want to do some research into Chinese-Zimbabwean relations (Source 4, above), it might be worthwhile to focus on the continuous co-operation of the two countries since the Independence Bush War. The Chinese invested highly into Zimbabwean rebuilding of roads, electricity, agriculture and military infrastructure (National Defence Forces Camp). They were paid with stakes in diamond mines.

---

7   https://www.poetryinternationalweb.net/pi/site/poet/item/5757/John-Eppel

15: *The Mupandawana Dance Champion* – Petina Gappah

Notes

Kongonya: particular dance style. See https://www.youtube.com/watch?v=cP2tZTOrMVw

Comment

This story takes place in rural Zimbabwe, in a small town called Mupandawa in the southern district of Masvingo. We are introduced to three friends, two of them working together as teachers. Their lives and daily routines are described as monotonous and poor until a dancing competition is held in a nearby hotel. Here we meet the old coffin maker M'dhara Vita or Vitalis – a very simple man, with no school education but a striking dancing talent. After his winning the championship a daily routine of Friday-drinking and dancing develops in the local pub until one day Vitalis dies right on the dance floor.

The narration is very detailed and beautifully modulated, but full of compassion for the old man who despite his very simple living circumstances has found and lived for his passion – and died while pursuing it. The story displays a humour and lightness we find very often in Zimbabwean literature. At first, they seem misplaced in the obscure political context: the championship, for example, has to be cancelled because its title 'MDC' can be read as a promotion of the main opposition party. But the humour is simply a coping mechanism. And yet, the social relations depicted by Gappah are so powerfully authentic that we can learn through them what politically stirs up the country.

Further reading

If you want to find out more about the 'necessity' of humour, go to (1) https://www.theguardian.com/books/2016/nov/13/petina-gappah-zimbabwe-writer-interview and (2) https://www.theguardian.com/world/2015/may/27/zimbabwe-comedians-laughing-in-the-face-of-hardship.

For more information on comedy and satire in Zimbabwe consult Carl Joshua Ncube, Zambezi News (https://www.youtube.

com/watch?v=bWUCtgKXQxA) and Shoko Festival (http://www.shokofestival.co.zw).

Study tasks

- Why does the dancing champion seem to be such a positive and light-hearted persona – or why is he described as such? How is it possible that he appears not to be influenced in his actions by his living in a country with rampant inflation and poverty?
- How does the following quote fit into the picture? 'We laugh at ourselves. We laugh at funerals. We laugh even when things are not going well for us and we should be moaning and groaning.' (Chirikure Chirikure, award-winning Zimbabwean poet and dramatist).
- Zimbabweans are often thought of as being very resilient. Life goes on. And often life at its fullest. Which other story in the book might represent such an idea, why?

16: *Maria's Interview* – Julius Chingono

Comment

Maria is just eighteen and looking for a job as a maid. She has not been paid in her former job, is in dire need of money, food and accommodation. With a reference letter she is looking for something new. When she is invited in by her potential new employer, she is treated with disrespect, even contempt, during the interview. Trying to impress her new-to-be employer, she agrees to even open her bags when her new to-be-employer wants to take a look at her possessions. This act of mistrust and a check-up-call to her former employer about an expensive perfume she has in her bag, make her forget about her dismal situation and decline the job. For Maria, her dignity is more important than her physical existence.

Further reading

As a contrast to Maria's life see Instagram pages of young rich Zimbabweans: https://www.businessinsider.de/rich-kids-of-zimbabwe-flaunt-wealth-instagram-2017-11?op=1.

Not Another Day by Julius Chingono (a collection of stories and poetry). Also see his poetry here <https://www.poetryinternationalweb.net/pi/site/poet/item/5758/Julius-Chingono>

Study tasks

- The differences in living standards between the rich and the poor in Zimbabwe are huge. People like Maria have to accept many forms of humiliation and mistrust before they are given a job. Their word counts less than that from a richer person. What does it say about a society if some are richer than the rich and some are infinitely poor?

- Would you say that Mugabe's policy of segregation – those who were politically in favour of him and supported his politics versus those who were in the opposition or of no political value – has led to an economically and socially divided nation beyond the questions of skin colour and colonisation? If so, how do these different 'factors' interact?

- Julius Chingono was a mine-worker for most of his life. He wrote beautiful poetry of distilled simplicity which often featured the life of the poor, their humanity, dignity and sometime sense of caustic irony. Why is this apparently straightforward story of exploitation, so charged?

17: *Dinner Time* – Bongani Sibanda

Comment

The male protagonist of this story lives together with his relatives in the rural areas of Zimbabwe. His parents abandoned him; his father is unknown and his mother works in South Africa. The story focuses on the procedure of the family eating one meal of sadza, the exact amount each person gets and, at the same time, the arbitrariness of the portions: the elders get a lot and the children too little. And while we can almost hear the sounds that are made while the family eat the feeling of hunger is always present in the thoughts of the protagonist and makes him fantasise about possible ways to steal the last extra portion of sadza one day.

Further reading

You can find further information on Zimbabwean food poverty under (1) World Food Programme Zimbabwe: https://www1.wfp.org/countries/Zimbabwe and (2) Commercial Farmers Union Zimbabwe: http://www.cfuzim.org/~cfuzimb/index.php.

Study tasks

- This is a 'quiet' story with very little action, but the thoughts about hunger, starvation and repression are 'loud'. How does this compare with the hunger described in 'A Land of Starving Millionaires' or 'The Donor's Visit'?
- Does humour play a role in all of them? And if so how?
- Why does a small child suffer from hunger in a country formerly known as the 'breadbasket' of Africa?
- Exile and displacement also play their part. Which other stories speak of broken homes or families? Are there any parallels beyond this?

18: The Letter – Farai Mpofu

Notes

Ranah: ancient place in Israel, refers to a place of refugees.

Comment

This story tells us in great detail about the physical and mental torture the protagonist Juba has to suffer from being a Zimbabwean immigrant / refugee in Botswana. The I-narrator tells the reader in an imaginary letter to his mother from prison in Francistown that he remembers that, in Zimbabwe's Matabeleland, his family was accused of being part of the opposition party and that, as a result of that, he had to bury his mother and unborn sister. In Botswana (where he fled) he was not only prevented from marrying his girlfriend because he was a foreigner, but also mistreated and punished by her family, the clan and the state. Brought back to Zimbabwe we expect his long trail of suffering to end, only to hear him dreaming about his next attempt to cross the border to Botswana.

Further reading

Further information on migration can be found under (1) 'Women on the border of South Africa and Zimbabwe (report)', http://www.unhcr.org/news/latest/2008/12/4933e4444/16-days-activism-south-african-border-shelter-helps-young-zimbabwean-women.html and (2) Bill Derman & Randi Kaarhus, eds., *In the Shadow of Conflict: Crisis in Zimbabwe and its effects in Mozambique, South Africa and Zambia* (Harare.Weaver Press, 2013).

The Suitcase Stories: Refugee Children Reclaim their Identities with Glynis Clacherty and Diane Waverling.

Our Broken Dreams: Child Migration in Southern Africa – Save the Children

Study tasks

- Why does the protagonist use the medium of a letter to a dead person to describe his situation and feelings?
- What do you make of the last sentence ('It is always better to be treated like a dog in a foreign country than to be treated like a dog in your own.')?
- What gives this story its intensity? Consider this question in terms of the language and style, and the portrayal of character.
- Critics might argue that the story is a sentimental, self-indulgent melodrama. What might lead them to this conclusion?

19: *Shamisos* – No Violet Bulawayo

Comment

Method has fled from the political unrest in Zimbabwe in 2008 and become one out of many illegal migrant workers in South Africa. Here he finds himself living under rather poor circumstances in a shed in the suburbs of Johannesburg, working for two urban middle-class women as their gardener. His tale is predominantly about the contrast he experiences between home and exile. He has taken on a new name and assiduously tries to fit into the role of a rather simple worker who wants to make a living and send money home to his family. Through flashbacks and memories he mirrors his former life and characterises himself as a strong personality. In his migrant life, he is withdrawn and almost speechless. At the very end, an angry mob of South African workers invade the suburb of Eden Park, where he lives. They are determined to force the migrant workers to 'go back home'.

Further reading

Further information on the topic of migration can be found in (1) 'Migrant in Countries in Crisis (MICIC) South Africa Case Study: The Double Crisis – Mass Migration From Zimbabwe and Xenophobic Violence in South Africa' (https://reliefweb.int/sites/reliefweb.int/files/resources/SA_Case_Study_FINAL.pdf), (2) 'Migration in Zimbabwe, A country profile 2010-2016' (https://publications.iom.int/system/files/pdf/mp_zimbabwe_2018.pdf). You can also consult (3) *Zimbabwe's New Diaspora: Displacement and the Cultural Politics of Survival* edited by JoAnn McGregor and Ranka Primorac.

Study tasks

- Since 2000 and, as a consequence of the economic melt-down, many Zimbabweans have fled or chosen to go into exile – predominantly to South Africa and Britain. Read the information given by the *reliefweb – report* and on the 2008 elections in Zimbabwe. What were their reasons and hopes?
- The protagonist experiences and dies because of an act of xenophobic violence. What were the consequences of illegal migration in those countries affected?
- *Shamiso* is Shona for *miracle*: is migration in general an attempt to find a miracle? Or rather a necessity to survive?
- Which other stories allude to exile? What are the similarities (and differences)?
- There are subtle layers in the detail of this story, how would you define them and what do they reveal?

20: *A Secret Sin* – Daniel Mandishona

Comment

The protagonist's self-chosen exile is the UK. Jerry left Zimbabwe in the 1970s for study purposes. In London he tried hard to succeed but an eventually failing relationship with a white woman let him lose track of his studies and turn towards alcoholism. The great hopes and expectations of his whole family and, above all, his father were too much of a burden for him. He returns home after he has been called to his father's death-bed. When he is asked about his life in England he is too ashamed to tell the truth. Only in his thoughts he reveals that he has achieved nothing in thirty years of exile.

Further reading

On the problematic of exile cf. the novels and essays by Dambudzo Marechera. You could also read Brian Chikwawa's novel *Harare North* (London: Random House, 2011), which provides an excellent picture of the Zimbabwean community in London's Brixton. Cf. also Christopher Roy Zembe, *Zimbabwean Communities in Britain: Imperial and Post-Colonial Identities and Legacies*, London: Palgrave, 2018.

Study tasks

- What effect does it have that the narrator's voice is addressing the protagonist directly? This is a very unusual perspective; what kind of atmosphere does this mode of narration create?

- How would you define the tone of this story?

- 'Time is longer than rope, Jerry'. What do you make of this phrase at the beginning and at the end of story? Why does the narrator choose this frame for his narrative?

- Britain, in particular, but also South Africa, and the United States form part of an imaginary. Can you explain this?

- Why does the narrator find himself unable to tell the truth about his experiences?

21: *Seventh Street Alchemy* – Brian Chikwava

Comment

In his Caine Prize winning story, we meet two women, with very different professions – Fiso and Anna Shava. Apparently, an administrative officer in Harare and an old sex worker living at the beginning of the 21st century have nothing in common in the first place, but Chikwawa weaves their life goals and depending power relations cleverly together. At first the reader only inhales the city, its inhabitants, longings and desperation: in great detail we are guided through the centre around Samora Machel Ave., where poor vendors and day-to-day-professionals only just survive. On the corner of Seventh Street, Anna drives a child to death while Fiso passes by doing her daily routine. They don't meet but the reader knows that they both have been there. The title lets us hope that something magical might happen here on the corner of Seventh Street, 'some chemistry, some turning lead into gold'. But while we follow Fiso going through the administrative stages of acquiring an official ID, which would allow her to get a more promising job, nothing magical happens.

Further reading

On 'post-apartheid cities' cf. AbdouMaliq Simone, ed., *For the City Yet to Come: Remaking Urban Life in Africa*.

Study tasks

- Why does Chikawava choose the symbol of the alchemist? What is turned into gold?
- Or which different elements are merged into one?
- This story predominantly takes place outside, in the streets. What is the influence of the city (and the outside generally) on its characters and actions?
- Account for the humour in the story. Would it be the same story without it?
- Is it possible to read the story straight, as an account of struggle, poverty and tribulation? If not, why not?

- How would you position the narrator and describe his tone? What filter does this provide?

22: *The General's Gun* – Jonathon Brakarsh

Notes

Kombi: a small bus for public transport.

Youth Brigade: ZANU PF programme for young unemployed citizens.

Indigenisation and Economic Empowerment Act (2008): an act of the Zimbabwean government which decrees that at least 51 per cent of every company should be owned by black Zimbabweans.

Comment

During the land invasions which took place from 2000, also called *Hondo yeMinda* or war for the land, and the 'land reform programme', farms were seized from their white owners, often with all their property and their livestock. Some of the invasions were brutal. Contemporary commercial farmers were blamed for land that was seized by the BSAP and white settlers in the late nineteenth century, and by the Rhodesian governments during both the Land Apportionment Act (1930) and Land Husbandry Act (1969) when villagers were forcibly removed from their land. Reclamation in the early 2000s was made in a similarly broad-ranging way, some land was distributed to peasant farmers, though little to families that had actually been displaced by the previous regime, while the elite also contrived to secure the best and most highly developed farms and often the race to secure rich pickings was fierce, and highly competitive. During this period, there was no effective rule of law, the farmers, who were not infrequently humiliated by militia, could not turn to the police. Subsequently, when the Indigenisation and Economic Empowerment Act of 2008 was introduced, it was assumed that whites could lose their businesses at the stroke of a pen. It was a populist move during a time of economic crisis, and race was a hand always played at times of crisis.

This story, a farce, is set against this background. The action is set in a small city in the midst of Zimbabwe, in Gweru. Members of the Youth Brigade raid the shop of a white car dealer. Knowing he is powerless, he becomes abject before their demands. But before they are able to co-opt the property or purloin the vehicles, an army General appears with a unit of soldiers and has some the invaders killed, others beaten up and eventually arrested. His main (and only) reason for doing so is that by law (the Indigenisation and Economic Empowerment Act of 2008) he already owns 51% of the car dealer's company as well as of the profit it produces. Much of the action the reader gets to see through the eyes of a kombi driver who is close to the scenery. She is mesmerised by the General's gun which appears to be the absolute power-centre in the suppression of the raid. With the help of cleverness and her beloved trans-gender outfit, the kombi driver succeeds in stealing the gun and taking it to a party. There, the almost magic attraction of the gun lets the kombi driver and her friends feel as if they were all-powerful …

Further reading

You can gather further information on Southern African homosexualities from the following sources: Marc Epprecht, 'The "Unsaying" of Indigenous Homosexualities in Zimbabwe: Mapping a Blindspot in an African Masculinity', *Journal of Southern African Studies*, Vol. 24, No. 4, Special Issue on Masculinities in Southern Africa (Dec., 1998), pp. 631-651, and C. Riley Snorton, *Black on Both Sides: A Racial History of Trans Identity*.

Study tasks

- If the gun represents absolute power, there are other seeming absolutes, what are they?
- The kombi driver, a trans- or cross-dresser, is apparently the only one, who can disrupt the general's show of force by stealing his gun. Why is this so?
- The kombi driver can be understood as a trickster figure. Find out more about trickster figures (https://www.britannica.com/art/trickster-tale) and, if possible, apply your findings to the story.
- Describe the elements of this farce and how they create the desired effect.

- Research with the help of the given resources about homosexual behaviour (and its socio-cultural context) in Zimbabwe and Southern Africa.
- Cross-dressers are often larger than life, can you think of any other fictional characters of whom this could be said?
- Beyond the farce, outside the laughter, there are moments when we feel pity, whom for?

23: *The Grim Reaper's Car* – Nevanji Madanhire

Notes:

Okapi: brand name for a knife.

Tafara: township west of Harare.

Cafenol: a medication similar to Asprin or Paracetamol.

lupper: combination of 'lunch' and 'supper'.

Chimoyo [Chimoio]: small town in Mozambique.

Kapenta: a small fish, often dried.

Comment

The story is told by a nameless fifth-grader, who is ill and has to stay home in bed with a fever. She very distinctly describes the living circumstances of herself, her parents and a small sibling, Tati. They live in a high-density area called Tafara (on the outskirts of Harare), in a very small brick house. The protagonist describes their poverty with the detail of a sick child whose eye roves round the room and who has little else to distract her. The sickness, the fever and the smell of the paraffin (which the mother uses for cooking) make the protagonist feel dizzy and let her descriptions blur and fade into a dream where she meets a creepily smiling president in a big car who says, 'Let the children come to me.' Next day, the protagonist is still ill, the dream is repeated – but this time the president's face resembles a skull. The protagonist wonders what will happen if she enters 'that big black car'.

Further reading

This story was published in 2004. The Zimbabwean economy has not improved since then, and much can be found on the internet about its upheavals and decline from the collapse of businesses, the loss of agricultural earnings, the hyper-inflation of 2007-08, the high and escalating unemployment, its external debt, rampant corruption and the loss of its currency.

You can find information on the current situation in Zimbabwe in the following sources:

- https://mg.co.za/article/2017-11-24-00-gukurahundi-ghosts-haunt-mnangagwa
- https://the_guardian.com/world/2019/jan/23/zimbabwe-clampdown-continues-despite-mnangagwa-pledgee
- https://www.nytimes.com/2019/01/28/opinion/zimbabwe-mnangagwa-mugabe.html

Study tasks

- This story brings us down to the reality of ordinary people trying to live in such circumstances. Try to describe what makes the text so poignant.

- What do you make of the title? Is the president – at the time of the story's first publication (2004) still Robert Mugabe – to be seen as the protagonist's saviour or as the 'grim reaper' coming for her?

- What do you make of the fact that the president's words 'Let the children come to me.' echo almost literally the words of Jesus Christ as reported in Matthew 19: 14 (https://biblehub.com/matthew/19-14.htm)?

- Is it possible to read the text metaphorically? If so, what does the protagonist (and her family) stand for? For a sick nation, a failing/failed or 'fading' nation?

- The family represents most aspects of Zimbabwe's miserable situation: men with war-trauma, jobless men who are not able to provide for their families, mothers as the only surviving force, bad infrastructure and medical aid, political blindness and the illusion that the president is still the nation's savior.

- In November 2017, E.mmerson Manangagwa succeeded Robert Mugabe. Study the sources given above and try to find out if he brought any change to the country. Make a statement about what is meant by 'the long shadow of Mugabe'.

To Conclude

Through the texts we have had interleaving and overlapping stories that complement each other and help us to appreciate both the humanity and the complexity of this country, Zimbabwe, as seen through the eyes of some of its writers. We introduced the stories around eight themes, would you have chosen any others?

- Select one theme and introduce two or three different stories within it, explaining why you have chosen them.
- Having read this book, what would make you want to visit Zimbabwe?
- Why do you think we chose to begin this collection with 'Queues' and conclude it with 'The Grim Reaper'?
- Choose one story and write a review for a blog site, or a newsletter of your choosing.
- Choose one story and prepare interview questions for the author. These may be sent to Weaver Press, who will forward them to the writer and post the answers on their Facebook page.